The Goddess Particle
Brandy Gaye

Cover art by Daniel Govar
www.danielgovar.com

Thank you to my parents and husband of course, Siân for Welsh translations, Doug, my Buddhist expert, you, my fantabulous readers, my birth mom (wherever you are), and to singers, songwriters, authors and artists everywhere: keep making magic.

"The Higgs boson, the subatomic particle that has brought a Nobel Prize to Francois Englert and Peter Higgs, is so small that its discovery took 40 years. It is so big for physics, though, that it took on the nickname the "God Particle." Higgs, Englert, and their colleagues theorized in 1964 that there must be something that explains why other particles have mass, why things hold together, why you and I are able to exist. That something is the Higgs boson."

Ned Potter,
Forbes, The Higgs Boson and the Nobel: Why We Call it the 'God Particle'

Chapter 1
"First Time Ever I Saw Your Face" by Roberta Flack

2002

Swithin and his large father, Patrick, had seen a lot of blood in their line of work, but little could have prepared them for this.

Mandy stood smugly, arms folded across her Monkees sweatshirt while Tex Ritter's "Blood in the Saddle" twanged in the background. "I told you."

Something fell into Swithin's messy blonde pompadour, and he batted it from his head before realizing with disgust what it was.

"Is that an eye?"

Several hours earlier...

Tying her long dark hair back, 14 year old Amanda Heart had another rare opportunity to run away and she took it, along with her two favorite *Best of the 60's* CD's, her two favorite shirts, her bow and the money she knew was hidden in her "foster" mother's underwear drawer.

Forty five hundred miles away from their home in Wales, Swithin Hook and his father were in the States on monster hunting business and had finished up in record time. On the way to their next destination, Swithin nearly crashed his father's Bentley trying to get him to pull over into the lot of a small diner.

"What the devil, son!"

Usually well behaved to a fault, 14 year old Swithin had no explanation for his rash behavior other than to say that he really wanted waffles.

Mandy passed the same diner not too long after them, and the sweet smell of syrup made her mouth water. She knew she should keep going, but she hadn't eaten since this morning.

Midway through her Belgian waffle, two yokels decided they needed to rob the place.

"Everyone! Empty your pockets! Hands up!"

Swithin and his father stood along with everyone else. The thinner gunman foolishly had his barrel in Swithin's face, but neither he nor his father dared move for their concealed weapons yet.

"Is it empty our pockets or put our hands up?" Mandy asked sarcastically, wishing a bow and arrow wasn't so inconvenient a weapon.

"Hands up!" the second, portly gunman yelled, unamused. "We will empty your pockets!"

Swithin put his head down to conceal a smile at the American girl's sass, and then risked looking over at her.

The boy three booths over caught Mandy's eye as well, and he used his eyes to direct her to his cargo pants.

Mandy followed his eyes and saw a glimmer of silver. He had a weapon! If she could distract the goons again, maybe he could get the upper hand. Just as the first gun-laden robber was about to pick Swithin's pockets, Mandy spoke up. "I wouldn't rob them if I were you."

Both hoodlums looked her way. The nervous, smaller one let off a shot and grazed Mandy's arm.

"Ow!" she yelled, "You shot me!"

"Shut up!" the fatter one barked. "Shut! Up!"

"Fine. But I still think you're stupid for robbing them."

"Why!"

"Because the big one's about to rip your head off."

To say Swithin's father was big didn't exactly give an apt picture. He was large, but in an inhuman bear sort of way, proportionate in girth and height. Even clean shaven, his thick head of red wavy hair exemplified the bear aspect. Patrick grabbed the older thief while Swithin reached for his dagger and tossed it, taking out the younger one's gun. The young one charged out the door now that he was unarmed and facing down more than he could handle. Swithin poised to go after him, but Mandy stopped him.

"I got this."

She grabbed her bow and and arrow from her bag and headed outside. The little thug was halfway across the street and on the other side by the time Mandy took aim. At 3:00 a.m. there was little traffic.

He went down with an arrow to the knee.

If anyone had asked Swithin Hook what love was right now, he would have said that this was it.

"Who said archery isn't practical?" Mandy asked when she came back in.

Cops were called, and Patrick asked Mandy what she was doing out at this hour by herself.

Mandy stuttered for an answer, but Patrick was onto her. "A runaway," he deciphered after eyeing up her bag.

"Well? It's not what you think. I'm an..."

"You're going home," he blustered. "Problems cannot be solved by running away!"

The cops entered the diner and Mandy knew fighting would be worse than giving in right now. At least if she had Patrick take her home, she might not end up somewhere worse than where she came from. Although, that would be tough.

"Fine." She gave him the address and he agreed to deliver her.

The three of them packed into Patrick's Bentley and headed back to Mandy's apartment. "Pack it Up" by the Pretenders was playing. Patrick turned it off.

"He doesn't like my music, much. I'm Swithin," the young Brit offered with a smile to try and keep the mood up. "This is my father, Patrick. May I?"

He pointed to her gunshot wound and she nodded, prompting him into the first aid kit.

"I'm Mandy," she admitted quietly, pulling back her long, dark hair. Mandy hadn't spent much time around boys. She hadn't spent much time around anyone, really, especially anyone her own age. Swithin seemed completely flawless save for the slightly deformed right side of his bottom lip. She realized why when he turned back to face her and he was thoughtlessly gnawing on it.

While he dabbed some ointment on her arm gash, she eyed the inside of the luxury vehicle so as not to stare at her new acquaintance. Rips and stains covered nearly every surface but it was clean of trash and dust otherwise. A small gold cross dangled from the rear view mirror. The car bumped and Swithin's hand landed on Mandy's. Mandy caught Patrick's severely concerned eyes in the rearview mirror. Bothered by his concern, Mandy turned her attention back to the boy who was making her heart pound. "Where are you from?" she asked of their accents.

"Wales, mostly," Swithin smiled, letting go of her hand. The sweat left behind was cool on her skin. "Dad's from Ireland; Mom's from Wales. Which is where I grew up. We're in the States to help out with an eenopiht infestation. They're these little black rat things that spread disease. You know, like the black plague? I think we got them all, but only takes one to…"

"We're monster hunters," Patrick interrupted his young teenage son's babble.

"Seriously?" Mandy asked, more in awe than disbelief. "Then, maybe prayers do get answered."

"What's that supposed to mean?" Patrick questioned.

"Oh, you'll see."

Always wary, the two gents kept quiet the rest of the short way back to Mandy's apartment and were not disappointed with her warning...

What used to be a man and woman lay strewn to bits across the apartment walls and floor while old country tunes still played on a radio knocked to the floor.

Swithin and his father shared a concerned thought. "Did you do this?" Swithin gestured to the mess.

"I hoped for it," Mandy answered honestly. "I always hope for it and eventually they come."

"Who, girl?" Patrick had come to stand over his son protectively.

"The angels."

"Angels did this?" Patrick mused.

The girl's eyes darted to Swithin's tee which read, *I heart (insert classic rock band here),* and then to the small, silver crucifix hanging from his neck. "I don't know who did it. But it's happened three times before. And I'm grateful. These people are evil. They've kept me a prisoner."

"Who?" Patrick pressed.

"The Agency."

Before any more questions could be asked, sirens screamed and Patrick demanded they leave. Though his red flags were waving, he could not, in good conscience, leave the girl there.

After pulling away, Patrick checked his rearview for red and blue lights, but saw none. "Tell us more about these angels of yours, lass."

She looked to Swithin, who nodded his head reassuringly. She intuitively trusted him; his energy was pure and good. "They seem like real people. My foster parents, I mean. But they're not. All I do is study, and sometimes they would take me for ice cream or a movie. I tried running away, but they always find me and bring me back. They take my blood and my spit and everything in between, but I don't know what for. Headmistress Gwen won't allow any visitors or friends. So, I pray to escape and the angels come. It's a flurry of twinkly white lights and screaming--then blood. And now, you."

"We'll help you," Swithin offered.

"Maybe," Patrick added, warningly toward his overly altruistic son. "I'll need to know more. Someone else may be better suited for the job."

Mandy's stomach fluttered at the possibility of help. These two seemed her best shot yet, but she wasn't going to get comfortable. "They think we're stupid," she offered.

"We?" Patrick queried.

"There are others like me," she admitted. "There were, anyway. I haven't talked to any of them in a year or more. One of them told me about hunters, but none of us had ever met any."

"Well, you're in for the social event of your life," Swithin told her. "We're on our way to a sort of hunter party."

"Tell us what you know," Patrick demanded from the driver's seat.

Over the next four hours of driving, Mandy divulged what little she knew and learned quite a bit about the monster hunting.

The Agency moved her from place to place since she could remember. She'd had four sets of guardians, who'd all met the same fate. She'd met Headmistress Gwen only once and barely remembered the encounter, save for the fact that the woman wore all green. She'd been schooled in every subject imaginable and was allowed chaperoned outings to ballgames or malls, or movies and theatre. She rarely was able to hang around kids her own age.

"We were prisoners," she admitted. "It took me a while to figure it out and I don't know what they wanted with us."

"How do you know these kids?" Patrick inquired.

Mandy hesitated, but Swithin's honest face eased her considerably. "We kind of met inside our heads."

Patrick said nothing and Swithin picked up the slack. "Like a psychic link?"

"Kind of. I guess. But I can't control it. There have been seven of us, but some of them disappeared a while ago, and I haven't talked to Georgia in a year. She was the last one left besides me and she was 18. I think they could be dead. Or worse. We always seemed to converge in the same dream after bedtime."

There wasn't much more Mandy could say because she didn't know much.

"Well, you're safe now," Swithin tried to comfort, but Patrick shook his head.

"Don't make promises you can't keep, son."

Mandy understood all too well that she would never be safe, but appreciated the sentiment. Swithin sighed at his father's negativity. "Well, we'll do our best anyway."

"He's right," Mandy agreed with Patrick. "But thank you all the same."

Swithin and Patrick came from a long line of monsterers; people responsible for corralling, killing, protecting--or in any other way, dealing with things like gryphons, banshees, dragons, manticores and the like. Other types of hunters included ghosters, demonologists, deity specialists and so on. Although all hunters were familiar with the various mythologies and races, everyone eventually found a niche, and they all worked together on an open network to keep the world safe.

"The tabloids aren't always so far off," Swithin jested about moon monkeys and cat creatures. "When cracks from other realms open into this one, things can spill out. So, we clean it up, and usually no one is the wiser."

Fascinated at this new world she was being introduced to, it was all made better by this boy next to her who seemed to have a lot in common with her. They liked the same fantasy books, B movies and all types of music. They both had a thirst for knowledge, though Mandy admitted, she hadn't much of a choice.

"I had to study about ten hours a day or more," she explained. "But I actually liked it. Did you learn any other languages?"

"I'm fluent in German, Latin and, of course I know Welsh. Mae'r merched wrth eu bodd Welsh," he grinned.

"I have no idea what you said, but you look smarmy," Mandy laughed but she felt her cheeks redden. "I was learning Egyptian hieroglyphics, Sanskrit and Arabic."

"Whoa there, overachiever," Swithin put his hands up in surrender. "You win."

Mandy laughed. "It actually comes pretty easy to me." She practiced archery on Sundays since it was her "free" day, and Swithin complimented her shot at the diner.

"I'm a fencer, myself. Since I was..."

"Church is the best place for someone with your affliction," Patrick advocated, cutting his son's obvious interest in this touched girl.

Noting the gold cross on the rear view, Mandy sighed. She'd grown to loathe religion since it seemed to cause wars and because it hadn't provided any answer thus far. She'd prayed for help, guidance or answers, and for nearly 14 years she'd lived in constant fear. "It is a good place to reflect, I find," Swithin added, noticing her discomfort regarding the subject. "Kind of clears my mind. Like fencing. Maybe like archery?"

She nodded, understanding that at least.

"We've seen a lot of bad stuff. I guess it helps to have faith that something, somewhere out there is on our side." He grinned, lopsided.

"I'll, uh, keep that in mind," Mandy promised, suddenly wondering if prayers took fourteen years to answer. She wouldn't have been surprised, as there must have been a massive waiting list.

"God," Patrick inserted, "God is on our side. You'll have to excuse his blasphemy, Amanda. His mother is a pagan, and the Lord has surely tested me over and over when it comes to that woman! It does prove that He has a sense of humor!"

Swithin bit his lip to hide amusement. Mandy thought better than to go into her distaste for the church but was curious still. "Do you think there are angels? I mean, I call the things that killed my guardians, angels but I wouldn't think an angel would do that. I just can't bear to think of anything else."

The car became loudly silent.

"Course there are," Patrick finally campaigned for the side of good. "They just aren't as showy as those demon siblings of theirs."

"So, you've never seen one then. Has anyone?"

"Sure, sure," Patrick assured with conviction. "But I'm not one to question their practices, and neither should you be. And let's not assume your champions are, in fact, angels at all. There's many a beast out there!"

"We fought with a banshee just last month," Swithin piped up to break the tension.

They spent the rest of the car ride speaking on other creatures and of Swithin's adventures, of which his father proudly boasted.

At long last, they pulled into a large lot in front of a dilapidated warehouse. A dozen or so cars were already there. Lights and Elvis's "Hound Dog" blared from inside.

"It's a clambake," Swithin explained. "Hunters have them every so often to check in, brag and share news. Those who can make it do, or if not, they just hit the next one. We hold them all over the world and never in the same place twice."

"Someone in here should be able to help you, Amanda," Patrick repeated with more softness than he'd shown thus far. A tiny bit of dread rippled through her at the prospect of Swithin's departure back to Britain. For the first time in her life, she had found someone who had something resembling the answers she'd yearned for.

Once inside, Mandy felt even less alone. Thirty or so people lounged around, laughing, drinking and telling tales amidst a musical backdrop of 60's hits--Mandy's favorite era for music. Various games had been set up; darts, ping pong, and the like, along with a wooden table overflowing with alcohol.

"Patrick! You old fiend!" A dark skinned man nearly half Mandy's height approached, and it seemed almost comical to watch him next to Patrick's hulking form. "I recognize Swithy here, but who's the newb? Not one of yours, I don't think. But you have eight, don't you?"

"Aye, and they're all trouble!" Patrick and his friend laughed. "Dodson, this is Amanda. Amanda, Dodson Fer. Dodson specializes in lycanthropy."

"Charmed," Dodson took her hand and kissed it.

"Werewolves?" Mandy asked, more intrigued every minute.

"Dodson *is* a wolf," Swithin interjected.

"Now, don't go scarin' the young thing," Dodson admonished playfully.

"That would be hard," Patrick offered knowing what Mandy had already seen in her lifetime. "Where's the wife?" Patrick asked.

"Ah, you know Eleanor. Hates coming to these things. Can't say I blame her."

"No. I suppose not," Patrick agreed.

Swithin explained to Mandy. "Eleanor's one of the strongest psychics anyone's seen in a while, and people tend to bog her down with requests, so she never comes out. Come on, Mands," Swithin took her hand, "May I call you Mands? Let's get some food. I'm starving."

"Swithin..." Patrick began, hoping to pull his son away from an obviously portentous situation.

"See ya, da!" Swithin pulled Mandy away after catching his father's intent, and Patrick grumbled, but eyed a possible solution to his 'newb' problem.

"Erickson!" Patrick excused himself from Dodson and approached his fellow entrepreneur. "I was hoping one of you yokes would be here."

"Demon got you down?" the lanky Erickson smiled. He was the best demonologist around and a world class scholar. Erickson did most of the heavy lifting for all of the hunters when it came to research, but he was also called out on especially difficult cases involving demons. He preferred the desk job, but had his fair share of physical and mental scars from 30 years of fieldwork.

"I'm not sure. The young beour I brought in with me. She's got a problem."

"You think it's a demon?"

Patrick gave Erickson the details he knew thus far.

"Oh my," Erickson fretted after listening. He glanced toward Mandy and Swithin who were talking to a couple of other young hunters. "How has no one brought her into the fold yet?"

"We took her from some group calling themselves The Agency. I've never heard of them and I don't like it. All I can tell you is there was something dark in that room today. I'm still chilly from it."

"A demon for sure is capable, but so would a Class A wraith or a specter. I only live four states over and I'd like to think if it were a demon, it would have registered, but I'll look into it for certain. She'll be in your charge, I presume?"

Patrick looked over his shoulder at the youth in question, whose hand was girlishly mingling with his son's, and then at the goofy grin on Swithin's face.

"No. I can't take on a mark at the moment with Swithin in tow. He's really coming along. He's going to be one of the best."

"If you say that, it must be true," Erickson looked to Swithin with a new admiration. "But I can't take her either. I already have two apprentices, I've got four cases I'm working and I obviously can't turn this one away. Plus Bezeeble found my newest lodge so I have to move again."

"Didn't you just exorcise that clem?"

"Twice. Look, I don't know what to tell you, Pat. Everyone here is up to their eyeballs in work and wannabes. And you know the rule. Finders, keepers."

Patrick cringed inwardly at the boisterous laugher of his youngest son. He'd already deemed Mandy too dangerous to keep around. For one thing, this Agency would be looking for her, and he had no desire to bring them into his life. For another, Swithin was at that age where a pretty girl would ruin good sensibilities for certain. Patrick would know better than most. He'd been married to one since he was 17.

"Right, right," Patrick lamented. "Well, let me know if anything comes up in your research."

"I'm moving it to the top of the pile. Can't say I'm not intrigued."

Barring the murder of her third set of guardians, Mandy was having the best day of her life thus far. Finally, after years, she was in a room full of people who she knew could help her, and Swithin was the icing on the cake. Not only had she never had someone she could consider a friend, his accent had warmed her in places she didn't know existed and his charisma drew everyone to him. She'd never felt truly safe until today.

"'Ello, old friend!" a feminine Brit sounded behind them. Both Swithin and Mandy turned.

"Missers!" Swithin hugged her and kissed her ebony cheek. "I didn't know you were coming!"

'Missers' kissed his cheek too, lingering a little too long for Mandy's comfort. Mandy already hated her dark skinned peer and she couldn't quite place why. Maybe it was the extra short shorts, or the perfect braids or simple old-fashioned jealousy that Swithin just had his lips on her cheek. "Mother and I were here visiting cousins. You remember Callum and Rys?"

Swithin laughed. "What did they do this time?"

'Missers' rolled her big brown eyes. "Released a bunch of ant-lions at a political rally. The Prime Minister's here on business, you know."

"I didn't actually. But ant-lions? I thought they went extinct centuries ago."

"So did everyone else, so you can imagine the shock."

Swithin shook his head chuckling and seemed to finally remember Mandy was next to him. "Oh! Missers, this is Mandy. She's new."

"I gathered," Missy smiled out of social obligation and not out of kindness. "Kind of a plague or something are you?"

"Missy!" Swithin scolded.

"Well, I'm sorry but one does hear what one hears. Rumors are already swirling. Eight violent deaths in your presence," Missy eyed up Mandy with a mixture of curiosity and disdain, then she quickly turned back on her bubbles and grabbed Swithin's hand. "Oh! You must come see mother. She'll want to talk to you!"

Missy tugged on Swithin, but he planted himself firmly. "Well, I will. Of course. Um, wow. Is it hot in here? I need a drink. Fizzy drink anyone?"

"Yeah," Mandy nodded. "Coke. No ice."

"You know what I like," Missy grinned toothily.

"Ginger beer and a Coke coming up!" He hurried away from the girls, and Mandy giggled internally at his fluster, but her personal mirth was cut off by Missy.

"Our parents want us to get married."

Mandy's eyebrow went up. "Really?"

Missy nodded and feigned exasperation. "I mean, like, we're 14. I'm not exactly thinking about getting married, right?"

"Right." Mandy hadn't had many social interactions, but she didn't miss the subtext of the conversation. Swithin returned quickly, and Mandy took her Coke and the opportunity to jab her new enemy Missy. "I hear you two are getting hitched."

Swithin spit out his water as Missy gasped. "That's not what I said!"

Mandy took another sip of Coke. "No, it's what you said without saying it. I've known the guy a day. You don't have to get all territorial."

"A bit warm in here, don't you think?" Swithin reiterated. He nervously bit his bottom lip again which Mandy couldn't help but smile at.

"Not particularly," Missy frowned and took Swithin's hand. "Are you going to come say hullo to mum?"

Swithin pulled his hand from hers and grabbed Mandy's. "Of course! But I promised Mandy I'd introduce her to a few more people. I think Damien went out back. Come on then, Mands. He's quite a card, that one. I'll see you later, Missy."

Swithin pulled Mandy out the back door and didn't stop until they were outside and several yards away from the warehouse.

"Friend of yours?" Mandy chuckled.

"Yes," Swithin answered. "We grew up together. Went on our first hunt together, our birthdays are two days apart so we celebrated those. A lot. We were best friends for a long time, but lately, she's just gotten kind of, um..."

"Amorous?" Mandy smiled wickedly.

He turned his head to hide a blush.

"Well, she's pretty at least," Mandy observed.

"No denying that," he admitted much to Mandy's chagrin. "And a strong hunter. She's decided to specialize in deities, a faction that not many choose. Gods and goddesses are finicky and powerful. And then there are demigods and demon gods and, well, she's got her work cut out for her. She won't have time for anything else."

"Something tells me she'd make time for you." Mandy playfully poked him.

"Are you jealous?" He meant it as a jest.

"Yes," Mandy answered truthfully.

Swithin's mirth disappeared as he hadn't expected her to answer so seriously.

"Oh," Mandy backtracked. "I mean, um, well, of course I'm jealous. You grew up with all of this. You had a best friend at least, and were surrounded by something you love. I lived in fear every day. My guardians weren't all exactly nice."

"Oh! Well," the red in his cheeks started to subside slightly. "You're in now and once you're in the community, you're in for life. Though, sometimes, that's not all that long. It's kind of hot out here, too, isn't it? Wow."

Amused that she'd made him uncomfortable, Mandy took a seat on an old abandoned crate.

"So," he went on, "there's a code hunters go by. Finders Keepers. So, since we found you, we have to keep you," he grinned. "Have you ever been out of the country?"

She nodded. "Studied in Hong Kong and in Mexico City. And Headmistress Gwen was pretty adamant that I know about all sorts of faiths," she added, noting Swithin's crucifix. "Well, about everything, but she said that I could not be one with the Universe unless I understood all of the factions."

Swithin was not in the trade of selling religion to people so he kept his mouth shut and moved to something a bit less controversial. "Have you watched a lot of films, then?"

"Yeah. Pretty much anything I wanted actually, but I always liked the soundtracks best."

"Me too!"

"*Reservoir Dog's* my favorite right now, I think. I had to do extra homework for two weeks so Jack would buy me the CD."

"I think I love you."

After a second of awkward silence, they both broke out into giggles.

Their mirth was brought to an abrupt halt at the sudden sounds of war back inside.

"Oh! Guess the party crashers finally showed," Swithin mused.

Horrified at the sounds of screaming and gunshots, Mandy jumped from the crate, but Swithin reassured her.

"Clambakes are always attacked by something. You don't plop a bunch of hunters in one place and not attract attention. Sounds like a demon. Come on."

He pulled her back to the door and they peered inside. Sure enough, a ten foot tall pitch black creature with bubbly skin and broken horns charged a trio of drunk, mirthful hunters.

"Aren't they scared?" Mandy asked.

"Nah. Watch."

The demon charged, but then hit a sort of wall and roared. The hunters all jeered at it, taunting it with Latin phrases.

"Wards," Swithin noted. "You want to get a closer look?"

Mandy gave him an "Are you serious?" look and he laughed at her, but halted abruptly at the look of terror in her eyes.

"Mands? It's okay, I promise..."

"No, no...There's something else here."

While the rest of the hunters taunted the black aggressor, Swithin attentively scanned the room and both he and Mandy nearly jumped from their skin as a voice, indiscernible as male or female, sounded behind them.

"What are you looking for, young Hook?"

Mandy and Swithin tilted their chins all the way up until they both came face to face with a looming devil who grinned wickedly.

It batted Swithin away and Mandy yelped, turning to face the lithe beast. Colors of marigold shimmered from scales, but neither dragon or man, its tall, thin body curved like a snake and its long arms ended with stubby fingers and sharp talons.

"Mandy Heart," it greeted.

"Da!" Swithin called from the ground. "Patrick!"

Swithin was silenced with a lash of the devil's whip like scaly tail and Mandy yelped again. Dozens of shadows rose from the ground and took shape around him. Swithin scrambled to his feet and armed himself with the daggers he had hidden.

"What do you want?" Mandy trembled.

The creature moved fluidly, shrugging. "Not what I want, what I need. And to get what I need, I need to get what they want."

They, Mandy thought. The Agency.

Patrick appeared at the back door a second later, but it closed in his face with a whisper from the devil. Swithin was already up to his neck in quilled beasties and Mandy jerked to help him, but the devil grabbed her arm. It burned cold. Mandy winced.

The devil didn't take its milky green orbs from Mandy. "They said dead or alive," it continued softly to Mandy, gracefully writhing as if it would lose balance if it stopped. "And I find dead prey so much easier to carry."

Mandy hadn't been untrained in combat, having been taught archery and basic self-defense, but this thing was too much and she had no weapon to speak of save for her hands. She punched out and tried grabbing it, but it slipped through her fingers like liquid coiling around her. She could hear Swithin yelling and battling the lesser demons and she could hear Patrick trying to knock down the door, but the constriction quickly cut off her senses and jagged teeth were cutting into her shoulder.

She shrieked, and the next thing she knew, they were standing in a vast field filled with doors of every kind. Confused, the devil loosened its grip and hissed. "What trickery is this?"

Mandy was too busy catching her breath to answer, but it was a place all too familiar to her.

"This is where I kick your ass," she told it and suddenly she was far enough away from it and poised with a nocked bow. She let the arrow fly, but before it hit its target, the hellbeast stood rigid and then Mandy was back behind the warehouse on the ground. Swithin was tapping her cheek trying to get her to wake up. When she opened her eyes, the first thing she saw was his smiling face.

"Are you all right?" he asked.

"Why are you smiling?"

"Because you're all right. Come on then." He helped her up and she realized she was covered in brown devil blood and the devil was headless next to her. "These kinds of things are normal at a clambake," he reassured.

"Good to know." She shook wet chunks from her hands and noticed dozens of sizzling black spots on the pavement. "How long was I out?"

"Twenty minutes, give or take."

Patrick towered over the scene with a bloodied axe. "Swithin, go get the first aid kit."

His son nodded and jumped at Patrick's command. Patrick eyed the deep bite on Mandy's shoulder when Swithin was out of earshot.

"I should have put this axe through you instead of that devil. And one day, you may wish I had."

Chilled, Mandy's attention was stolen by Scholar Erickson's protégés, Bryson and Henry. The young men approached tentatively and Mandy nodded, indicating it was okay. Bryson was maybe 16, with a lanky frame and unshaven face while bulky Henry resembled an overgrown baby with soft skin and nervous eyes.

They sketched out the bite mark and took measurements for their records.

"A skyngahl," Erickson noted, stepping closer. "Rare and dangerous. Intelligent and ancient. My, my, you are fascinating, aren't you?" he asked rhetorically of Mandy. Swithin appeared another minute later with salves and bandages and was left alone with her to tend her wounds.

"They sent it," she told him. "The Agency. They..."

Swithin waited patiently for her to find the courage to say her words.

"It came here to take me back."

"We won't let that happen." He knew he shouldn't have said it, but he wanted more than anything for her to feel safe.

"Did I go somewhere? Did you kill all of those monsters? Can that thing come back?"

"Whoa, um, well? Yes, I got most of them before da and the others broke through the door. That devil will be a long time crawling out of whatever hell it went back to and no, you didn't go anywhere. That's an odd question."

"I'm an odd girl," she smiled weakly and explained how the devil bit her and they ended up in her psyche. "I only know because that's how I talked to the other kids. Maybe I shouldn't have said anything. It must sound strange."

Swithin set his hand on her arm. He exuded calm and she wondered briefly if he was some sort of wizard.

"No. No, I don't want you to keep anything secret, all right? I want you to tell me everything. We're going to get you through this. Whatever this is."

The roars of the black demon inside died soon after and the party came to a lull for a moment as the story of Mandy's encounter was passed around. Then, songs were sung and pints were passed. Patrick churned his thoughts on how impossible it would be now to pawn

Mandy onto someone else. Mandy was shaken to say the least, but Swithin brought her from her doldrums quickly with talk of music. Others gave them a wide berth as they walked to the bar, and the bartender slid them a glass of ale to share.

Chapter 2
"Hoochie Coochie Man" by Muddy Waters

A raucous high suddenly waved through the crowd and brought the party to life again. The front doors opened, and a classically good looking man entered wearing a faint-worthy smolder. He glanced around at the scorched floor, scowling. "Damn. I missed the monster."

Mandy had always admired the way movie stars looked back in the days of black and white, and this man would have put Gregory Peck to shame. The whole place drunkenly cheered upon his arrival and at her questioning stare, Swithin explained.

"Thomas Regal is at the top of the chain. He's not scared of anything. He's the best, which coincidentally has given him an ego the size of your America."

"What does he do? I mean, his specialty?"

"Primarily he's a ghoster, but he does it all if it pays. We're all pretty much surprised he's still alive. No one expects a terribly long life in this line of work, but I think he's almost 40 and couldn't be more reckless. It's weirdly considered good luck when he shows up to these things."

As indicated, the inebriated crowd flocked to him, and he shook hands and hugged everyone who approached in turn before heading for the bar. It didn't escape Mandy's notice that a couple of women pushed their way up to him a little forcefully as he doted on each.

By the end of the evening, things had settled down. No more monsters showed, the alcohol had been exhausted--even after two more runs for more--and several people lay passed out in various spots. Mandy had been introduced to so many people her head swam.

Never had she been to such a carousal! Missy managed to pull Swithin away for twenty minutes or so and Mandy was jumped upon by a couple of other young hunters. They had been taking notes with Erickson after her ordeal.

Gangly Bryson Pierce introduced himself first with an egocentric grin, and brawny Henry Cannon followed suit. They both also specialized in demons and hellhounds and the like which Mandy found no end of questions to ask. Erickson had taken them both on as apprentices and they loudly bragged about their exploits, which Mandy found boorish, but she listened patiently. Bryson seemed as if he took a lot of pleasure in killing things and didn't seem too remorseful when he'd mentioned accidentally killing a possessed person. Though muscular, Henry seemed more timid than not; a scholar rather than a field agent, so to speak. Bryson didn't let him speak much. Swithin finally came back to her side and swept her away, apologizing for his absence.

Mandy glanced back. "I don't know why you're apologizing to me. You're the one that had to spend time with Missy."

Swithin bit back a smile. "She's not all that bad."

"Besides," Mandy went on about Bryson and Henry. "I wouldn't have minded, but they're not terribly nice, are they?"

Swithin shrugged. "Henry is a follower and Bryson is a born leader. He's a bit of a dark sort, though, I'll give you that. I wouldn't consider them friends, I don't think, but they're all right hunters."

Mandy watched Bryson crush a beer can on his pimpled forehead and cringed when Henry cut himself doing the same thing. Missy was dancing to Def Leppard's "Pour Some Sugar On Me" blatantly trying to get Swithin's attention. How Swithin managed to be so nice about everyone was beyond her.

Hours later, Thomas Regal still prattled on to the delight of several people and was the only person Mandy had not been introduced to. Patrick pulled her away several times to introduce her all around. It was obvious he was trying to pawn her off, but she remained polite and fascinated all the same.

As the night had gone on, more and more showed up. Mandy could hardly believe that so much supernatural activity existed to warrant so many soldiers. Swithin explained that many were like her-- new. He expressed that most of them would not be around for the next clambake. "It's not a life everyone can handle. Some die, but most quit. As for the amount of activity, well, bridges and walls between realms break down all the time. Things are conjured. Ancient monsters escape. There's always something new or old on the loose."

Mandy always broke away from Patrick to find Swithin, and they continued their conversations about life and learnings. Though Mandy hadn't much practical experience in the world, she'd studied nonstop under her guardians, scholars and acclaimed professors. She'd attended a few schools short term, but for the most part was home tutored. Swithin had also been well taught, and they were keeping mental tabs of music to exchange later.

"I always felt as if I were some sort of experiment," she finally admitted to Swithin after a lull in conversation about 80's rock.

He shrugged. "Maybe you were. But I promise you're safe now."

"Your dad's right. You shouldn't make promises you can't keep."

He sighed, exasperated. "Fine. How about, I promise I will always do my best to make sure you're safe."

How could she not believe him when he so earnestly did? "All right. I suppose I can believe that."

While Swithin and Mandy found endless topics to speak on that leaned more toward things like museums and politics rather than blood or guts, Patrick had come to his end trying to find someone to take her. Erickson had been right. No one had the time or resources to take on another body. As if he did! Swithin was Patrick's youngest of eight and showed the most promise. Just tonight, he'd taken out a horde of deadly chitterbitters all by his lonesome! He wasn't about to let a troubled mark ruin Swithin's chances of being one of the greats.

A gaggle of girls tittered loudly at Thomas's punch lines. It hadn't even entered Patrick's mind to try and set Mandy and Thomas together. Years ago, Thomas had gotten three protégés killed due to his rambunctious manner of hunting, and everyone silently agreed that he would no longer be culpable for taking on extras, which suited Thomas just fine. Not everyone was happy with the way he conducted business and a few of them spread rumors that he had gotten his students killed on purpose specifically to avoid taking more on. Thomas never denied it.

"Thomas Regal! You old savage. How've you been?"

Thomas smiled warmly, as he seemingly couldn't help it, and took a drink of whisky without removing his cigarette. "I'm surprised to see you at one of these in the States."

"Well, we were here on other business not too far away, actually. Come to think of it, we came across a new case which I might be inclined to accept your help on."

"That's a relief. I was getting bored with all my own quarries piling up."

Patrick pulled Thomas away from the small crowd which had been listening to him and pointed out Mandy who still sat wide-eyed at the happenings around her. "See that young bure over yonder?"

"The one angling for your son? Hey, didn't you betroth him to Missy whats-her-face?"

"Don't be a gom."

Thomas snorted. "I just thought that's what you highborns do. Trade offspring to keep the lines pure or some bullshit."

"Now see here..."

"Look, Pat, word's already gotten around that you're looking to unload her and the answer is no. I sure as fuck don't owe you any favors."

He turned but Patrick grabbed his arm. "She can't stay with me. Did you hear her history? Eight dead caregivers in 14 years, brutally ripped limb from limb. I can attest. I saw it myself."

"Are you trying to entice me with a challenge?" He inhaled and blew it out in Patrick's face.

Patrick waved the smoke away. "Everyone else has done their parts with taking on protégés."

"And my three were killed. I can't teach my methods."

Patrick held his tongue about Thomas's 'method' of running into a situation blind and swinging. "Swithin is going to be one of the greats. Everyone in this room knows it. And she's, well, distracting among other things."

Thomas sighed and pondered over the idea after finishing off yet another large glass of Johnnie Walker. "Eight dead, hm? Demon? Ghost? Witch?"

"I've got Erickson on it."

More intrigued than anything, Thomas gazed over at Mandy and Swithin. Mandy was eating large forkfuls of someone's homemade lemon cake while Swithin was telling some story by flailing his arms. "And no one's going to come down on me when little sweets over there bites it?"

"Not me."

"And here I thought you gents from Europe were supposed to be so chivalrous."

"Will you take her on or not?"

Thomas hem-hawed with himself for a minute while Patrick sweated and Mandy went for another piece of cake. Thomas remained Patrick's last, albeit least-likely hope of finding a new place for Mandy. Their history wasn't what one would call good. "All right. Challenge accepted. We'll see who gets who killed first. You up for a wager?"

Patrick took a guilty breath full of relief. "You are a chancer."

"I'm going to assume that means something bad, but I don't care. By pawning her off on me, you've likely given her less than a year to live. What do you care, oh pious one?"

Patrick let the insult slide and had already planned on a hearty confession before flying back to Wales in the morning. Everything in his being told him to keep his family away from that girl, and if he had to chance a corruption to his soul to save his son, he would gladly do it.

"Uh oh," Swithin frowned. "Da's talking to Thomas."

"Is that bad?"

"They hate each other."

"Do tell."

"When Thomas was about our age, da took him on as a protégé, but Thomas proved too wild for dad to handle and they had a big fight. No one knows what it was about, but Thomas left and never looked back. Oop, they're coming this way. Looks like you'll get to meet the man of the times after all."

"Mandy," Patrick introduced, "I'd like you to meet Thomas Regal. He's graciously agreed to mentor you until this messy business of yours is solved."

"*WHAT*?" both Swithin and Mandy proclaimed at the same time.

"Da!" Swithin started in. "You can't! I mean, well, finders keepers. We found her! We have to keep her!"

"You mean I'm not going to get to see Wales?" Mandy griped. "Swithin said..."

"Well, he should never have promised the sort," Patrick stopped her whining. "Besides, Thomas does plenty of travelling."

Thomas nodded. "I'm all over the place. I just came from Prairie Village, Kansas." He immediately realized how ill exotic that sounded and shrugged it off. "Anyway, it'll be Peru or Antarctica tomorrow. You're in for adventure, if that's what you want, and I'm glad to hear it."

"But da," Swithin emphasized, "Thomas doesn't have the best...I mean all of his...you know!"

"Come on now," Thomas bantered gallantly. "I'm not as bad as all that. I was thinking of taking a well-deserved vacay anyway."

"How about Wales, since it's been talked up," Mandy suggested sourly.

"Now, you look here, bure," Patrick pointed his oversized finger at her. "It's a grand thing to be taken in as a protégé, especially by someone so accomplished. You'll go with him and you'll be grateful. Erickson is working on your situation, and I assure Thomas will conduct his own investigation. He loves a challenge, this one. Swithin, we have an early flight tomorrow so we best be taking our leave. Come on now." Patrick started for the door and Swithin hesitated, biting the corner of his bottom lip.

"Now, boy!" Patrick barked.

Combed to obey his parents, Swithin jumped, but set a nervous hand on Mandy's uninjured shoulder and patted it. "I'll, um, I'll call you."

"I don't have a phone," she reminded him.

Thomas already had one of his cards out and handed it over. "Call anytime, kid."

Swithin took it with a weak smile and turned to jog after his lumbering father while Mandy bleakly watched the first person she had ever felt close to make an exit. Worse still, Missy and her Amazon of a mother left with him.

Meanwhile, Thomas had been swooped upon by the gossip hungry crowd to which he announced his evening retirement much to their disappointment.

"Now, now, as you can see, I've taken on a new apprentice," he spoke to a suddenly alert crowd. Even those who were not near finally gave a long look toward Mandy, who shyly shrank. Thomas slapped his arm around her and continued. "And I'm going to need my rest if she and I are going to survive together. Sorry, people, so sorry."

Squeezed beneath Thomas's arm, Mandy couldn't help but see him pass a card to one of the bustier redheads. She winked at him as everyone else was turning away.

"You are really going to cramp my style, girl," he muttered to Mandy, still smiling.

"I didn't exactly ask for this," she muttered back.

"No. No, I suppose you didn't."

Mandy was unmoved by his rogue smile reminding herself to be grateful for the change of scenery.

Mandy opened the door to Thomas's black two-door Porsche, got in and was immediately startled by the translucent old lady sitting somewhere between the front seats and the back, staring straight ahead. Thomas took his seat as well, cigarette already dangling, and noticed Mandy staring.

"You can see her?" Thomas asked.

Mandy nodded.

"Hm. Thought I was the only one you showed yourself to, Edna. You're making me feel unloved." Thomas started the car and redirected to Mandy. "Don't mind her. She followed me home a year ago and no matter what car I'm driving, she won't leave. She just sits there, staring straight ahead. Never does anything remotely harmful, just…"

"Uh, Thomas?"

Thomas cranked his head over his shoulder to notice that Edna had turned her head to stare at Mandy, but before he could formulate a reaction, Edna simply smiled warmly and faded away.

Mandy and Thomas looked at each other then back to the spot where Edna had been.

"Edna?" Thomas called before laughing toward Mandy. "Well, well. Maybe you will be useful after all. Which is good. We've got a case in the morning."

"Like, a ghost?"

"We'll figure it out when we get there."

Swithin balked at the idea of sharing a flight home with Missy. Not that he didn't care for her, but she was not the girl he had suddenly become enamored with. Missy knew it as well and tried all the harder to coax his attention her way. Ever polite, he dodged each one of her suggestive plays.

Thomas did not mind talking. Or smoking. Or drinking. All at once. While driving. Mandy feared for her life as he raced down highways and blazed through red lights, blaring old jazz tunes. To Mandy's relief, they finally stopped and he purchased two motel rooms, one of which was already occupied by a certain redhead by the time they'd arrived. Thomas quickly pointed Mandy to her room and disappeared without another thought. She didn't even take off her clothes before falling onto the hard mattress. The clock said 12:34 a.m. and it began to sink in that only eight short hours ago, she'd been a prisoner and now she wasn't. But she was alone again so she turned the radio on.

"Red Rubber Ball" by The Cyrkle. One of her favorites and oddly appropriate. Even though he'd bid her farewell, she knew Swithin would call her soon. He had filled her with something she'd rarely felt in her life.

Hope.

With apparent friends and experts looking into her predicament, perhaps her roller coaster ride was nearing an end. She fell asleep listening to tunes from the past and dreamed happily of starfish and whales.

It took everything in Swithin's being not to call Thomas's number the second he found himself alone. They hadn't left America yet, as his father had received another case. It would be 1:00 a.m., however, and the likelihood that Thomas would even answer was slim to none. He'd never met anyone like Amanda. She'd been through so much and seemed too unscathed and normal. Maybe it should have been a red flag since most seasoned hunters still had trouble with some of their pasts. Swithin could easily understand his father's reasoning for wanting to unload Mandy, but he still didn't feel right about it and said a prayer for her to have pleasant dreams.

Mandy woke the next morning to a pounding on her motel door. It took her a few seconds to remember her situation and with stiff muscles, she stood from the same position she'd fallen asleep in and answered.

Thomas barged in holding a large pink striped shimmering tote and tossed it on the bed. "That should be everything you need for now. Come over to my room so we can get going."

Mandy nodded.

"Oh, and your boyfriend's already called. There's a phone in the bag."

"He's not my boyfriend," she pointed out.

"Said every teenager ever," he scoffed. "You can scare little old ladies away, but I wonder what else you're made of."

Mandy wondered that herself more often than not.

After he left, Mandy realized she hadn't said thank you, but she was still groggy from a deep but unrestful sleep. She wished she could remember what she'd dreamed about, but the lost memory made her uncomfortable, so she purposely dismissed it.

Inside the bag were sports bras, panties, socks and three rhinestone velour jogging suits in different colors, a pair of tennis shoes, hair ties, a hairbrush and sunglasses all with high price tags. She'd never owned anything so pretty. There were also toiletries. The little flip phone was nothing fancy, but she'd never had one of those either.

Her clock still read 12:34 a.m. and she could not help but wonder if it was stuck there or if the number meant something. It flipped to 12:25 p.m. and answered at least one of those questions.

Swithin's number had been programmed in and too nervous to call it back, she showered first and put on her blue outfit and new footwear. While brushing her hair, her phone rang and scared her.

Swithin.

She picked it up and answered.

"Hi," came the reply.

"Hi," she said again.

"So?"

"So."

"You sleep okay? Thomas treating you well?"

She couldn't deny that he was, with the bag of Victoria's Secret goodies on her bed. She didn't tell him that she hadn't slept so well.

"He's an okay guy," Swithin remarked, "I mean, he's a little full of himself, but he's the best at what he does. Can't deny that. We haven't left the States yet. Dad got wrapped up in a consultation so we're leaving in an hour." Swithin was more relieved than anyone that Missy and her mother had been on the original flight. "I guess we won't be back till next year, unless something comes up."

"Well, I hope it does," Mandy blurted, just realizing how much she already missed his company.

He laughed. "Me too. But you have a phone, now I see, so we can talk whenever. Just let me know when the number changes."

"Why will it change?"

"Hazard of the job. We kind of have run-ins with the law a lot so they like to chase us. As if we're doing something wrong!"

"Got it."

Several hours later, Thomas pulled into an upper middle class neighborhood where the streets were all named after trees and stopped in front of a large ranch at the end of a cul-de-sac.

"It tried to kill my Bernie!" the petite woman of the house said of her meek husband. "I jumped in after it and wrestled him to safety! That thing tried to drown us!"

Bernie nodded quietly and looked toward the in ground pool. Thomas followed the man's eye line and walked toward the water. A large deck had been built around a rectangular pool, complete with diving board.

The lady continued as they now all stood by the water, but Thomas cut her off. "You didn't kill anyone?"

She stopped abruptly and answered, affronted. "No!"

"How long have you been here?"

"We just bought the place. Short sale. Old owner left in a hurry. I wonder why," she snorted. "This was not in the listing!"

Thomas thought a second and everyone waited for his opinion. "Hey sweets," he addressed Mandy, "try to lure it out."

"But I don't..."

He shoved her in the water and continued to meticulously scan the area.

"It's okay!" Mandy yelled angrily after surfacing. "I can swim! Swithin was right! You're an--ahhh!"

"I get that a lot," Thomas responded, more to himself, as Mandy was pulled under by the specter. "Hey," he said to the homeowners, "don't let her drown. I'll be right back."

The couple raced around trying to find something to throw to Mandy while Thomas disappeared. They'd tossed her a life preserver and nearly gotten her to the edge when Thomas returned holding a hard briefcase. He opened it and handed a black disc down to Mandy.

"Help me out!" she gurgled, as the ghost held tightly onto her foot.

"Take it," he said. "Get it down to the drain. That's the point of entry."

"What!"

He threw the disc in the water and pried Mandy's fingers from the edge of the pool allowing the ghost to drag her under again. With no other option, she grabbed the disc and let the ghost pull her down into the deep end where she set the disc over the drain. Her foot was freed and she could not get out of the pool fast enough.

"What is that?" The woman of the house asked.

"A very powerful magnet," Thomas answered, lighting up a cigarette. "Should disrupt the energy pattern of your invisible little friend for a while. You need to drain the pool, break up the foundation and burn the body that's buried beneath it. Music helps, too. Anything electronic will weaken it, even if slightly."

The other three stared at him.

"What?" he shrugged.

"Well, we paid you to take care of this," the lady said.

Thomas laughed. "I draw a line at hard labor. You didn't pay me near enough. And I know you don't have any more cash to spare. Just get to the body and burn it. Easy peasy. But I mean burn it to ash. Don't leave so much as a pinky bone intact. Got it?"

The couple nodded and Mandy piped in, dripping wet. "So, it's not trying to kill anyone. It's just trying to tell someone that it's down there."

"They ain't all evil, sweets."

"Good to know." And she pushed him into the water.

During the drive home, Thomas passed the time boasting on and on about his best-selling books and his investments, his conquests over women and the men that hated him. Window rolled down to dissipate the cigarette smoke, Mandy listened quietly and let him go on, not really having anything to add anyway, and Thomas didn't ask.

Thomas had proven to have eclectic musical tastes and unknowingly endeared himself to Mandy. Jazz and early country, folk and old radio dramas, indie rock and old sci-fi movie soundtracks all graced her ears during the drive when he wasn't going on about himself.

He did spend some time going over the finer details of ghosting. Mandy listened intently as he spoke about salt, magnets, iron, fire, spells and detective tactics. "Most of the time, I just barge in like I own the place. When people are confused about what's going on, they'll take the lead from anyone who seems like they know what they're doing. Sometimes a little acting is required, but usually I can get what I want. I'm pretty persuasive that way."

"Of course you are," Mandy placated. Though she felt that this was the best chance she had of evading Headmistress Gwen, she couldn't help but feel like they were watching her. At night, she tried reaching out to her fellow inmates as she had done so many times before in her dreams, but could find nothing and no one. As much as she hated being apart from Swithin, Thomas provided adequate company at least and reassured her that she wasn't completely alone. He never did ask her about her past which suited her just fine.

Another two days, and two stays at fancy hotels, brought them to Thomas's home, which quite underwhelmed Mandy. With his fancy car and expensive tastes she was expecting a mansion, but he pulled into a two story suburban brick house in a middle class subdivision. He said nothing of it as they walked to the front door or as they entered, but Mandy soon found where the expense lay.

Modern high end furniture tastefully decorated the floor in crisp blacks and two walls were dedicated to a massive vinyl collection. The color motif changed from room to room, but everything was clean and modern. The bathroom had black walls with chrome fixtures and white accents. Nothing so far indicated hunting or travel. The small kitchen boasted white marble countertops, top of the line appliances and vintage pink metal cabinets complete with flaws from age; the first thing Mandy noticed to be dated.

He showed her the finished basement, where he told her she could reside. Here, the scene changed drastically. Deep golds and reds and browns gave an old world feel, while renaissance art hung in ornate frames. She had no doubt they were real. One wall was lined with books from top to bottom and she made a mental note to read all of them. Her large bedroom was white all around, waiting for personality, but included a spa, king size bed, plush carpeting and walk in closet. The walk-out basement indicated she was not a prisoner, as she had been used to in the past. Not a speck of dust was to be seen which Thomas attributed to a weekly maid visit. The only thing which stuck out was a dead plant atop a short wood bookcase. She reached out and poked the dry soil, assuming the maid had forgotten to water it.

"Don't touch that!" Thomas barked and jumped over to it.

Mandy backed away.

"It was my mother's," he said. "Her favorite thing and after she died, well, my brown thumb got the better of me. This was my childhood home. I mean, I'm barely home, so what's the use of a mansion, right? Not that I don't deserve it, of course, but with this lifestyle, you've got to have a base of operations."

The more Mandy hung around Thomas, the better she felt about being stuck with him. He may have been a bit full of himself, but buried deep, he hid something good. She also noticed he hadn't smoked yet inside the house. Mother must have forbid it.

When Swithin spoke of his abode, he simply referred to it as home. A home could be an apartment, a cottage or a mansion, but Swithin Hook lived in an authentic 800 year old castle. The Hook Estate rested on a cliff overlooking the Celtic Sea, boasted orchards, and a sizable family cemetery with chapel, his mother's pagan circle, gardens and guest houses with room surrounding to spare. Though the grounds had been named after Helen Hook's family for generations, Heliwr, she loved her new surname so much, she renamed the grounds when she took control of them after her parents willed it.

It was Tuesday and when Helen Hook wasn't hunting, she was baking. Her thick gray hair had been tied up into three braided buns atop her head and her face and knitted poncho were marred with flour. She'd had barely a second with her son since he'd returned from the States and now she and he shared a sweet meal while Swithin told the story of his American exploit.

"I knew I should have gone!" she lamented.

"Mum, who could have known any of this would have happened?"

"Auck, I should have never promised Elvin Hessinger I'd bake pies for his son's Bat Mitzvah. Who eats 200 pies? Two hundred! Auck! But what I really want to know is more about this girl you met."

She smiled coyly and Swithin's heart sped up. "She's special, mum. I really like her and I can't believe that dad pawned her off on Thomas Regal of all people!"

"Tommy isn't all bad, now, son."

"But finders keepers!"

Patrick entered the kitchen, humming an old Irish tune, and kissed his wife's cheek.

"Well, you're all bubbles," she observed suspiciously.

"And so will my boy be! Swithin! Son! I have good news!"

Swithin lit up immediately thinking it might have something to do with Mandy.

"You are going to meet his Holiness. The Pope has granted you an audience this very week!"

Swithin nearly choked on his tart. "Seriously?!" He was up hugging his father. "How! Why? What do I say?"

Patrick set a large arm around his son. "You can thank him for accepting you into Saint Bart's."

Swithin pulled away, aghast.

"Patrick Hook!" Helen chided. "What have you done?"

"What?" the big man defended. "How else will you get into The Ranks? Being a priest is the most honorable position in our line of work."

"And the most dangerous! How did you even..." Swithin stuttered. "I thought a priest had to recommend me."

"Please, son, I do carry some weight."

"You carry somethin' all right," Helen muttered. She'd never interfered in any beliefs her children had; she believed they were free to choose. But Swithin had always been his father's child and idolized him down to his faith. She knew it wouldn't last forever, but for Patrick to hurry it along was more than she could bare. "This is between you two. Don't eat all my tarts."

"What are you on about?" Patrick crossed his arms toward Swithin, ignoring his wife as she left. "You always wanted to be a priest."

"Well...when I was...I mean...I mentioned it...maybe...but..."

"Son," Patrick laid a heavy hand upon his son's shoulder. "Is this about wanting to have sex?"

Swithin's mouth flopped open and closed like a fish until he could sputter. "No! Da! God!"

"Boy!" Patrick chastised the cursing of God's name.

"Whatever! I'll do five Hail Marys later. And five more for you! How could you do this? You are going to call the Pope and tell him that I'm sorry I can't accept his acceptance."

"I will do no such thing!"

"I am not going to Saint Bart's!" Swithin stormed out of the kitchen and down the hall to his room.

It was still Tuesday and Thomas had decided he was going to teach Mandy to box. He'd been impressed by her archery skills, but pressed the fact that it was not practical. He'd won his fair share of underground matches over the years and after they'd spoken on it, Mandy had asked if he'd teach her.

It was cold out, however and she ran downstairs to get her jacket when Thin Lizzy blasted through her phone.

"Hey, Swith," she answered giddily.

"Do you have a minute? I'm so cheesed off, I don't know what to do."

"Whoa!" Mandy hadn't met angry Swithin yet. He was usually a definition of calm and she made a safe assumption. "What did your dad do?"

"He tried to send me off to Saint Bart's!"

"Isn't that a tropical paradise in the Caribbean?"

"Yes. And it's also the name of a seminary."

"A what?"

"You heard me. He tried to sell me into the priesthood!"

"Oh."

"He just wants to pull me away from you."

"Oh. Well, Swith, I don't share any love with your dad, but I can't really blame him. There's something wrong with me."

Swithin pshawed. "We've been over this. There is nothing wrong with you. You're just special."

"Nice way of putting it."

"Besides, you know what a priest is in the hunting world? The end of the line. They guard the most dangerous and evil secrets ever known."

"Sounds right up your alley."

He blew a sigh. "Yeah. I used to want to be one. I was kind of obsessed with church when I was young. Father Murphy at our local church? He came from St. Bart's. It's an exclusive seminary in the Vatican for any hunter who has the calling, or any priest who has been called to hunting. The stories he told me about things he saw and learned still haunt my nightmares."

"Jeez."

"But it should be my choice when or if I'm ever ready!"

"I agree," she placated honestly.

"He can't just....ship me off!"

Thomas had come to Mandy's room and grunted. "Teenagers. Ugh. Just came to get your jacket, huh?"

"Patrick tried to ship Swithin off to St. Bart's."

"I know."

"WHAT?" Swithin and Mandy asked in unison. Mandy set her phone on speaker and Thomas elaborated.

"The oaf just called me practically begging me to convince Mandy to convince you to go," he said to Swithin. "As if. I told him to sod off. That's right, right? Don't fret it, Little Brit. Come on, Mandy. Your lesson starts *now*."

Swithin grumbled, but thanked Thomas for his support.

"It's not so much supporting you as it is not supporting your father," Thomas corrected.

Mandy and Swithin said their goodbyes and hung up, but Thomas stood, pursing his lips in thought.

"What?" Mandy was afraid to ask, but did anyway.

"If Patrick thinks you're more dangerous than the priesthood, things just got a lot more interesting."

Chapter 3
"Moonchild" by Iron Maiden

And so it went for four considerably uneventful months.

While Mandy had to force herself not to get too comfortable in case Headmistress Gwen came after her, Thomas hosted all sorts of ladies. Mandy and Swithin were in near constant contact via phone, email, text and page. They would watch movies together over the phone, listen to new CD's, and sometimes they'd bake sweets simultaneously. Thomas could never disapprove of that, even though he rolled his eyes more than once at their wi-fi relationship.

Even though her 12 hour days of study were over, Thomas insisted Mandy read his best sellers which he loved to quiz her on. She caught up on films and music she'd missed out on, along with literary fictions which hadn't been on Headmistress Gwen's approved reading list. Thomas took her shopping and bought her anything she wanted, which consisted mainly of clothes, movies, music and books, but he made sure she had a high-end bow and arrow set complete with stunning handmade arrows. And that was what sealed her adoration for him.

Thomas explained. "Minky Pie makes all of our special equipment, and don't ask why we call her Minky Pie. I have no idea. Your arrows are blessed and forged with various herbs and spells. She makes the bullets for all of our guns, too."

Thomas owned a rather sizable gun collection. He spent hours with her over a period of time explaining each one and practicing with it. When she'd mastered guns, he moved on to alchemy. Thomas Regal was not a wizard by any stretch, but he told Mandy that every hunter had to know the basics. He had spells and homemade concoctions he favored and boastfully shared his knowledge.

Thomas had looked into a few cases, but each case turned out to be a hoax or a raccoon in the attic. Still, he loved to take the money, and though Mandy insisted she was ready for something dangerous, he told Mandy he wasn't in the mood for anything exciting at the moment.

Swithin mentioned more than once that cases of monster appearances had tripled since a few years ago. They were up in general since a few decades ago, which everyone found odd with the modern world swirling around. His family was on call 24/7 for a troupe of near unstoppable banshees which plagued the Irish countryside.

No matter how much she hinted or even outright asked, Thomas would not budge on taking her to Wales.

"I hate flying," was all he would say.

She never mentioned the fact she knew he was avoiding Patrick. "But you said you travel everywhere!" Mandy begged.

"When I have to. And your booty call is not a good enough reason."

It wasn't the first time he'd said something similar and not the first time Mandy blushed at the idea.

Though Swithin remained ever the gentleman, their flirting and innuendos intensified until one day Mandy mentioned something openly about kissing and when he didn't answer, she had to prod him for a response.

"I'm kind of in an abstinence club."

The statement rendered Mandy momentarily speechless, and so Swithin prattled on.

"Da signed me up when I was nine. You know, no drugs, alcohol, tattoos, violence." He laughed at the last one and corrected. "That's toward people, of course. Not monsters."

Mandy still had no idea what to say. She couldn't be surprised at the fact, given his and his dad's beliefs, but it seemed to have come out of nowhere.

"Mandy?"

"Oh. Um, well, sure. That's cool. And I mean, we're like, 3,000 miles apart so, not much chance of us doing the other thing," she blushed.

"Oh, sure, heh, heh," he laughed nervously. "I just, you know, thought I should tell you since you're kind of my girlfriend, I guess. Right?"

It had never been said aloud, but it warmed her insides almost unbearably. "Yeah. Yeah, I guess I am."

"Well, good. So, yeah."

"Yeah."

"All right then. So, yeah. I guess I'll, um, call you later."

"Yeah. Sounds good."

It would be Erickson to call the next day and break the sudden glee in Mandy's new life. Hoping he had information on the thing that had killed her caregivers, she practically snatched the phone from Thomas, who had already put it on speaker. Regardless, Mandy set the receiver down gently and asked the scholar to continue with what he'd found.

"Well, I have good news and bad news. The good news is that I found out who The Agency is. The bad news is that it's bad news."

"Go on," Thomas prodded.

"Primum Covina."

The Latin meant nothing to Mandy, though she knew it translated as first coven. The deep look on Thomas's face turned her blood cold. "Tom?" Mandy asked.

His face softened again into its natural nonchalant expression. "Erick, don't be ridiculous. Hunters killed them off thousands of years ago."

Erickson sighed. "Why does everyone always want me to do research and then not want to believe me when I find answers? Look. I took everything given to me; Mandy's descriptions, the drawing she sent of Headmistress Gwen's insignia, the significance of green, the psychic elements, and the experiments and, just so you know, I scoured each and every one of the places Mandy's been. Well, not the one that burned down. But my apprentices and I tore apart the apartments that Mandy said she'd stayed in. We ripped up floorboards of the ones where her guardians were murdered. And I found blood. Oh, it wasn't easy, but they missed a fleck behind a baseboard."

"And?" Thomas asked flatly.

"Nothing impresses you, does it?" Erickson complained.

"And?" Thomas repeated.

"My impervious resources linked the sample to the Mother."

When Thomas didn't speak, Mandy poked him and he jolted. She'd never seen him so much as flinch at anything and fear tickled her nose at the onset of tears. "Tom?"

Thomas looked at Mandy. His befuddlement hadn't waned. "Let's just say the secrets of things like Stonehenge are well known and well-guarded. Erickson, are you sure?" He turned back to the phone. "This is pretty farfetched even in this line of work."

"It's pretty exciting!"

"Not the word I would use."

"Tom!" Mandy insisted that he start talking. Thomas thanked Erickson, who said he'd stay on the trail, and they hung up so Thomas could explain.

"The Mother is a term used to describe the First Witch. Well, no one really knows if she was the First Witch, but she's the first one of note. And she was no Mother Theresa." He laughed. "In that respect, she was no Elizabeth Bathory. The chick nearly destroyed the world, but she was taken down by hunters and a happy ending ensued, blah, blah, blah."

"So, what does this have to do with me?"

"I dunno, sweets. But if her bloodline is alive and well, if it's gone undetected for all this time, it can't be good. I think, though, whatever killed your guardians must be on our side--so there's a plus."

"Yay."

As hard as he tried, Swithin could not finagle his way back to the States. His father still fought Swithin's relationship with Mandy and kept him busy with case after case, even if they were mundane cases of pest control, be them harpies or squirrels. Since Swithin was not allowed access to his inheritance until he was 21, he had little cash of his own. Even with the news of The Agency's true origins, his mother had stayed relatively quiet on the subject, though she seemed to bear

Mandy no ill will and often said nice--if not encouraging--things to Swithin about his budding relationship when Patrick was not around.

"Oh, sure, sure. She's mysterious and pretty," Helen Hook laughed. "Those are the girls that will get you into trouble for sure."

"Mother..."

"Oh, now, Swithin, I'm just teasing. I know there isn't a force on earth that can keep two kids from loving each other, and I'm not against her. You know that. Stop biting that lip!"

He did. "But da is."

"He wants what he thinks is best for you."

Swithin hugged her and helped her finish the pies she was working on to offer to her pagan gods. It never ceased to amaze him how his parents got on so well being so drastically different when it came to faith, but he admired them all the more for it.

The three of them attended a hunt together the next week. A small hoard of zombies had popped up in a local cemetery after some teens thought it would be fun to play around with an old book they found. It happened more often than one would think. His head still in the clouds about his new love interest, Swithin lost his footing and was nearly bitten, but rolled out of the way in time, and his mother came to his aid by slicing the monsters head off.

Patrick hadn't seen. "We won't tell him, dear," his mother smiled.

While his Walkman blasted Thin Lizzy's "The Rocker", Swithin dispatched the rest of them easily while his parents watched proudly, all the while wondering why anyone would ever think he could be some legendary hunter.

A bit more than a year after Mandy's introduction to the hunting world, she felt an itch to attend a clambake, and Thomas reluctantly agreed to take her. Kismet had reared her head, however, as Mandy got a call from Swithin two days prior telling her that he was coming to America! His mother had fronted him the money and though he had reservations about lying to his father, the lure of seeing his favorite girl trumped any sin which might have been occurring. Overly excited now, Mandy bounced around the house for two days, causing Thomas to vacate as often as possible.

The most recent clambake was to be held in a deserted cabin in Colorado. With summer, the mountain passes were clear and full of greenery and animals. Thomas threatened more than one reindeer and cursed several chipmunks who darted in front of his roadster. He pulled up in front of the oversized cabin and kept the car running.

"Aren't you coming?" Mandy puzzled.

"No. I rarely go to these things, and I'm looking at the reason why."

Mandy pshawed him and grabbed her pink travel tote out of the trunk before coming back to the window to say goodbye. Thomas chucked a little something at her, which she caught and then almost dropped again.

"Thomas!" she whispered loudly, embarrassed at the box of condoms in her hand.

"If you turn any redder, one of those hunters is going to mistake you for a devil and shoot you."

Mandy still fumbled through her mortification as Thomas explained further.

"I'm not your father. I'm your partner. And as your partner, I'm telling you that if you let Little Brit knock you up, this partnership is over."

Finding it hard to even shut her gaping mouth in order to say whatever it was she didn't know what to say, Mandy tossed the box back at him, and Thomas laughed at her. "Mandy, it's just sex. Seriously." He tossed the box back. "First of all, don't tell me you haven't thought about it. By the time I was your age, I knew more about sex than everyone in the local strip joint combined. And secondly, I know Little Brit's a bit churchy, but he's still a guy, and I can guarantee he's been thinking about it. Just get it over with. The first time won't be the best time anyway."

Mandy's mouth still gaped while her partner nonchalantly explained that he'd been gone for three weeks or so visiting a friend down south, which finally pulled Mandy back to some semblance of equanimity. "What?" she managed.

"You have the credit card, there're a few great hotels in the city and I'll come back this way to pick you up. Believe you me, when you're 16, you're getting a car."

"Thanks?"

"Don't mention it." He glanced behind her and noticed Swithin trying to unexcitedly approach. "Lover boy's coming. I'll call you when I'm on my way back. Remember! No babies!"

Before she could retort, he pulled away and Swithin had arrived. Mandy felt her red cheeks and hoped Swithin didn't notice. Someone was blasting Judas Priest in the background.

Swithin cocked his head, noting the song. "'Beyond the Realms of Death.' Seems hunters have a soundtrack sometimes, doesn't it?"

She agreed with a laugh. They'd talked every day for over a year, and somehow Mandy was as nervous as she'd ever been. And then Swithin noticed the Trojans, and she balked. "Oh my God-Oh! Um, Sorry!" She apologized about the use of God's name and about the condoms, because she was mortified, but she couldn't control anything coming out of her mouth. "These aren't mine. Thomas wanted me to use them. I mean, not Thomas. Obviously. Jesus. Oh! Sorry!"

Swithin chuckled and placed a calm hand over Mandy's. "It's okay. My mum gave me some too. Quite mortifying especially after the old man put the fear of God into me a couple of years ago. Adultery and all that. I mean seriously, you'd think that they think that's all we think about."

"I know, right?" *God, he's so cute.*

"Right." *Body, please behave yourself.* "Did you, uh, want to eat?"

Mandy jumped at the distraction, shoved the box of condoms in her shimmering pink tote and followed him to the party.

They mingled and gossiped for an hour; everyone wanting to know what Thomas was like in real life. Mandy had to tell them that he was exactly as they thought. "He's a promiscuous spendthrift."

She'd only told Swithin about mother's dead plant and didn't see any reason to ruin the reputation of shallow debauchery that Thomas had carefully carved out for himself.

Missy hadn't showed, and when Mandy brought it up, Swithin assured that Missy wouldn't be attending. "I'm kind of glad, actually. She rang me last week and asked me to go to the show. I think, like, a date."

"You didn't tell me that!"

He shrugged and nervously bit that slightly deformed bottom lip of his. "It's embarrassing, really. I miss when she and I were just, you know, friends. And I told her I kind of had a girlfriend. She lost the plot about it."

Mandy couldn't help but grin goofily. Her life had done a complete 180 and she could not have been happier. She leaned in to kiss his cheek, but he jerked at her movement and she ended up planting one on his lips.

"Oh! Sorry!"

Now he grinned goofily. "Don't think that warranted an apology."

"Oooh, better watch it, Saint Swithin," gangly Bryson Pierce approached with bulky Henry Cannon in tow. Mandy automatically looked for Erickson, as these were his two wards, but he was nowhere to be seen. Bryson was as thin as ever, and Henry had kept up on whatever gym regimen he had. Mandy doubted anyone messed with him. "You'll get kicked out of your little virgin club," Bryson chided. "Mandy, babe, you can do so much better."

Bryson'd meant to embarrass Swithin, but since Mandy already knew about his abstinence club, it mattered not. It wouldn't have anyway, as Swithin was above the two doofuses in every way.

"Bryson Pierce, how are you still alive?" Mandy retorted.

"What's that supposed to mean?"

"Um, Mandy," Swithin tried to interject.

"You're an idiot," Mandy went on. "I thought that was clear. Though, you're an idiot, so my bad for assuming."

Henry laughed and Bryson slugged him in the gut. "I'm ten times the hunter either of you will ever be! Last week, I..."

"Brag brag, brag," Mandy cut him off. "You're going to be a virgin for a long time. Come on, Swith."

Mandy pulled a smirking Swithin away to the bar for some sodas. "Ugh. What is with those guys? I mean why does Henry hang out with him?"

Swithin motioned the bartender for two Cokes and answered. "They were orphans. Mack Befids took them in when they were little and taught them to hunt. But he died. Well? I guess it was right before we met. Sad, really. Demon dragged him down to hell, but neither Bryson nor Henry know which one it was, so no one can really do anything about it. Henry's pretty book smart, so Erickson wanted him as an assistant. But he and Bryson are a pair."

"They sure are."

Swithin shook his head. "Now, now. Be nice."

"You're nice enough for everyone," she jested.

Sodas in hand, evening was almost upon them, and Swithin asked if Mandy would like to watch the sunset. With the conversations stale and the adults already drunk after an hour, the two teenagers snuck away to the lakeside and found a log bench.

Swithin sat second, leaving a modest foot of space between them.

"You know this is only my third visit to the States," he prattled as it grew darker.

"I know," Mandy smiled. "You've told me a hundred times. What you didn't say is how you got your dad to let you come. He's not exactly my biggest fan."

"It's just, you know."

"I'm cursed."

"We don't know that."

"How did you convince him to let you come?" Mandy pressed, sensing guile.

"He doesn't know. Not that he won't find out soon, but mum's actually the one that gave me the plane fare so if you have permission to lie to one of your parents given by the other, is it still wrong? I don't know. She was supposed to be able to raise me pagan, you know, but dad won a coin toss or something. And then I ended up really enjoying my faith, so I think she likes to jab at him when she gets the chance."

"Must be weird. Having different beliefs from your siblings. How many of them are pagan, then? I forget."

"Well, Me, Peter, Wendy and Mary are da's responsibility, and Michael, George, Peter and James Matthew are all heathens in da's eyes. Not that he doesn't love them," he laughed.

Mandy politely laughed. "And Mary is the one you don't get along with?"

"Well, she doesn't get along with me. She's ten years my senior, thinks she owns the family and I stole her spotlight when I was born."

"I'm sure you did. I'd love to meet them all."

"You will. They're just all older and out on their own. Wendy's over 40," he laughed. "When we are out together, people just assume I'm her kid."

Amused and blissful, Mandy turned her attention to the setting sun. "I've never actually watched a sunset before."

"Me neither, actually."

"Do you love it? Hunting?"

"Yeah," he didn't hesitate. "It's a rare life. Sure, it's bloomin' dangerous, but then I've held things that most people don't even believe in. I mean, I've ridden a unicorn."

"Yes, about that…you promised…"

"I know, I know. I've got to get you over to my neck of the world sometime."

"I'd like that."

A few seconds passed before Swithin spoke up again. "Mands?"

"Hm?"

"We're mates, right? Best mates?"

"I think so." Trembling slightly, Mandy skootched over, closing the gap between them. The evening light faded fast as Swithin nervously drummed his fingers on his lap and chewed his bottom lip.

"If you bite through your lip, it's going to make kissing pretty difficult," Mandy told him while she slid her hand over his to cease the drumming. The frogs in the lake had begun their nightly singing.

"Right, right."

And with the last bit of light, they closed their eyes and touched their lips together for several seconds before separating.

"Berffeithrwydd melys," Swithin sighed upon pulling away.

"That better mean something good," Mandy told him. "Not that it matters. Everything you say in Welsh sounds amazing."

"Well, then by all means, gadewch i mi cusanu chi eto," and he pressed his lips to hers again, only more confidently and locked hands in the dark.

After several more seconds of snogging, Swithin pulled away abruptly, and Mandy asked if something was wrong.

"No! No, not at all," he panted. "Just, um, oh. Oh, it's dark, isn't it?"

"Swith…"

He dug in his pocket for the small flashlight he had and flipped it on between them. The frogs in the lake were near deafening and Swithin had re-bitten his lip.

"Okay, what's wrong?" Mandy asked.

"Nothing. Well, nothing. Well, you know."

Mandy began giggling. "We're safe from temptation. The condoms are in my bag in the cabin."

"Naw, I got some in my pocket."

A beat passed and they both started laughing. Mandy eventually set her head on his shoulder and put his arm around her. "Best night ever?"

"I guess that remains to be seen."

"Stop it, you," he playfully shoved against her and they stared out into the darkness at the beam of light his little flashlight produced.

"I know. Your abstinence thingy. We can still kiss, though?"

"We're gonna," he stole another kiss.

The frogs were at an all-time high, but they could not drown out the twig cracking behind Mandy and Swithin.

Trained from birth to deal with such a situation, Swithin went from awkward teenager to skilled hunter in a matter of seconds, grabbing the silver blade he always kept at his side and leaping into position to face the woods behind him. Mandy was up next to him shining the comparably strong beam of light into the darkness. Monsters consistently appeared at clambakes, and as far and the young couple knew, nothing had reared up yet. "Think they're playing a trick on us?" Mandy asked of their fellow slayers.

Her answer came in the form of a rumbling growl to the left.

"I'm going to guess no," Swithin rejoined coolly.

If Mandy hadn't been scared out of her wits, she would have found Swithin's sudden unflappability reassuring--or even attractive. The growl came again, and she pressed up against him.

"Over there," he grabbed her hand holding the light and shined it back and to the left where a large cougar winced at the bright beam and growled again. "Well, it's better than a minotaur or something."

"What do we do?"

"I don't know. It's a big cat. Do you have a ball of yarn?"

"Swithin!"

"Well, I'm a monster hunter, not a cat wrangler. What? You want me to wrestle it?"

The lioness crouched forward, eyes on Swithin. Mandy screamed. Not a scared sort of scream, but a rowdy roar toward the big cat which made it shrink back slightly. Too flabbergasted to do anything, Swithin stepped back and let Mandy at the oversized kitten. The cougar flattened its ears and tried to look around Mandy at

Swithin, but Mandy instinctively stepped in front of him chastising the big cat loudly until it finally turned tail. Adrenaline pumping, Mandy still yelled after it was gone and Swithin set his hand on her shoulder to settle her.

"Well, that was inspiring," he complimented. "I'll have to remember that if I ever face down a nekomata."

"It wanted to kill you! Did you see that?"

"Kind of. Yes. The question is, why didn't it want to kill you?"

"I was scarier than it was," Mandy crowed proudly. "And you are delicious. I can officially attest."

"I love you," Swithin spouted.

That quelled Mandy's adrenaline, and she replied in kind. "I love you, too."

"No, I mean…"

"I know what you mean. I always know what you mean, silly. Except when you speak Welsh, but it doesn't really matter because everything sounds wonderful."

He kissed her again, hard and passionate, and she let him, wrapping her arms around him and enjoying the high. He groped for her hand and found it before guiding it down to feel over his pocket where the square outlines taunted her fingertips. She soon realized what he was implying and pulled away yet again. "Swith…we shouldn't. I mean, well, Thomas kind of encouraged it, but he's also kind of a whore, so I'm not sure he's the best influence."

"I'm nervous, too," he admitted.

"Isn't it against your…"

"Yeah. But I thought about it a lot. I wondered if you were, too."

"I'm a teenager. Hormones are kind of…yeah. Damned Welsh. Why does your accent have to be so sexy? They should write an 11th commandment that outlaws it if they don't want you having sex."

"A yw'n eich poeni pan rwy'n dweud geiriau brwnt fel mwd neu faw neu waed?"

"Stop it!" she laughed and jokingly shoved him away.

He came back at her and entwined their hands, playing around with them for a bit, and his mood dampened. "I had another sister," he admitted. "Bell."

"As in Tinker, I presume?"

He nodded. "I never knew her because I wouldn't be born for another five years. I was an oopsie baby, you know."

"I kind of guessed since there's a ten year age gap between you and Mary. How old was she when she died?"

"Ten."

"Did it happen on a hunt?"

He shook his head. "She apparently hated hunting. She tried to run away, and they found her body in the woods. She had tripped and hit her head on a sharp rock."

Mandy's face puckered involuntarily.

"I've thought about us a lot, Mands. Da would say you're a bad influence, but I'm not stupid. And wow, I just butchered the mood, didn't I?"

She grasped his hands and waited for him to look at her.

"What I meant to say was," he went on, "that so many hunters die young and they miss out on things."

"I know what you mean."

"Why don't we call that cab and find the most expensive hotel we can since Thomas is paying?"

Still holding his hand, Mandy started back up toward the cabin. "Room service and pay-per-view sound awesome."

"It's uncanny how you read my mind. Um, you can't actually, can you?"

"Not that I'm aware. But then, I wouldn't tell you if I could," she smirked.

Morning came. The clock radio came alive with "Do You Believe in Magic" by the Lovin' Spoonful, room service was ordered and clothes were put back on. Mandy chose a green tee with a ferret in a pumpkin on it, and Swithin donned one of his many band shirts. After mass at St. John's cathedral, a tour of the Molly Brown house, lunch at The Buckhorn Exchange and a movie, during most of which Swithin and Mandy made out, they headed back to the hotel, placed another order for breakfast to be delivered and ordered *Bruce Almighty* on pay-per-view.

The next day boasted the same kinds of fun, and the night came too quickly. Free from restraints, Mandy and Swithin enjoyed every second and nearly grossed themselves out with how cute they were. Swithin found no end of joy in taunting her with Welsh as it seemed to rev her up.

"You know," she kissed his cheek, "I'll tell you a secret. If you're ever trying to make me not be mad at you, I don't think I could ever resist that," she said of the language.

"Byddaf yn cadw hynny mewn cof," he grinned. "I'll keep that in mind," he translated.

She play-slapped him for the umpteenth time and he kissed her back, but then pulled away.

"Though, I wasn't planning on making you mad."

"Good plan."

The third day came and went as the one before. They visited the zoo and came back to the hotel for a swim in the afternoon. After a shower to rinse the chlorine off, there was an expected knock at the door. Mandy jumped up to get it.

"Ice cream's here!" she shouted merrily as she readied her tip money and pulled open the door.

Swithin jolted as his father came barging in yelling and swearing. Mandy let the door slam as she darted out of the large man's way.

"…and your mother isn't getting off so easy, either!" Patrick finished a sentiment. "The betrayal is nigh unforgivable!"

"Da!" Swithin tried.

"Grab your bag! We're leaving!"

"But--"

"Now!"

Biting his lip, Swithin averted his eyes and stepped toward his duffle. Mandy watched, horrified at everything. She knew the guilt of lying to his father had been eating away at him as was the shame of what they'd done. Still, none of it could be taken back and she regretted nothing. She hoped he didn't either.

"I'll call you," Swithin said, as he reached out for her while heading toward the door. His father swatted his hand away.

"You'll do nothing of the sort. This tryst is over. Do you hear me?"

"Mr. Hook…" Mandy began.

"Loving someone means hurting them even if it's for their own good," Patrick barked at her. "You're cursed. We all know it. Befriending my son has put him in mortal danger and his soul in immortal peril! He'll be praying penance for a week! Unless you've been drinking, too. Any body art I need to know about?"

"Da!" Swithin defended, affronted.

"Your opinion isn't the only one!" Mandy fought.

Patrick took Swithin roughly by the arm and swung him toward the door like a doll. Swithin winced while his father blustered on at Mandy. "You'll never live long enough to be a parent so you'll never understand."

Mandy slapped him. She didn't know quite why exactly. Being a parent hadn't even crossed her mind, but it seemed an appropriate response to an intentionally cruel statement and she didn't back down afterwards. It felt good to smack the oversized brute even if it did hurt her hand.

"Let go of me," Swithin demanded. "I'll come with you, but I need one minute. One more minute isn't going to affect anything."

Patrick pulled his eyes from Mandy and turned on his son. "You have 30 seconds. Make them count."

He stormed out, and after the door slammed, Swithin rushed to Mandy's side. "I'll call you as soon as I can. I promise. And I will do everything and anything to get back to you as soon as I can."

"Not if your father has anything to say about it." She didn't want to cry, but the tears came anyway.

"He can't hold me hostage forever."

"Just until you're 21."

"The inheritance doesn't mean anything to me, Mands, but I still have a lot to learn, and my father..."

"I know," she forced a smile. "You're going to be legendary."

Rolling his modest eyes at the vaunt statement, Swithin kissed her softly, lingering before pulling away. "I'll call you as soon as I can."

"You could stay. Tom's house has plenty of room and I know he wouldn't care."

"You are a temptress, aren't you?" Swithin swallowed a rather large lump. "I can't."

The pull of his faith held to strong, and Mandy surrendered. "You'd better call."

"I will. Caru chi." Patrick banged on the door and Swithin hurried to open it.

"Love you, too."

And he was gone leaving Mandy feeling as alone as she'd ever felt. Before she'd been taken into the hunting fold, she hadn't had many friends, but now she knew true happiness and kinship. Thomas wouldn't be back for at least two weeks and the loneliness would have crumpled her to the floor had another knock on the door not alerted her.

The ice cream.

She wheeled it in and lifted the silver lid. Bananas, cherries, and hot fudge covered nearly a gallon of ice cream. She looked at it for a minute, then picked it up and hurled it at the wall.

Chapter 4
"Premonition" by John Fogerty

After a bit, Mandy composed herself. She was truly madder than anything; about her unknown past, the dark niggling in her soul and her predicament with Patrick and Swithin. Swithin could have stayed if he really had wanted to, but he was so well behaved. Not that she hadn't been a bit of a bad influence, but any guilt about that flew out the window at Patrick's abrupt appearance today.

She called Thomas, but he didn't answer so she decided she'd go for a walk. The day was perfect weather-wise, and she desperately tried pushing Swithin from her mind. Church bells rang in the distance and did nothing for that cause, but Swithin always insisted that church was a good place to clear one's head. A gothic cathedral came into sight a few blocks away, and she tentatively entered through the brass doors finding the quiet disquieting. No one was home, at least, not at first glance. She padded down the white marble aisle toward the front, stained glass windows and tall arches looming overhead on all sides. Once at the front, when no one came, she took a seat in a hard wooden pew and inhaled the spicy incense. She closed her eyes and tried to clear her mind. She pictured a wall of white and took another deep breath concentrating on centering herself.

Whispering broke her concentration and she turned but saw no one. Still, the whispering slithered into her ears until finally, she could pinpoint it coming from the rack of vigil candles off to the side.

Looking around, she still saw no sign of life or unlife and slowly stood to warily investigate. The closer she came, the louder the whispers hissed and finally with a strong draft, all of them snuffed at once.

She gasped and turned, sensing several shades about her. The church nearly spun with them and they seemed to speak, but she could not decipher it.

Mandy ran. She ran down the side aisle and through the black blur of despair, pushed on the door and heaved herself out into the sun, but they would not cease.

As people walked the streets around her, glancing at her strangely, she noticed the darkened souls blurring reality. One by the street lamp, one wailing from the bottom of the stairs and one would have been blocking the street if anyone else could have seen it there. But no one seemed to notice them but her. A coldness found her and chilled her bones. Trembling, she ignored the spirits and hurried onward, back to the hotel, back anywhere familiar to her. The spirits followed, or perhaps were already whereever she went. They wailed and moaned in agony and pulled at her soul, but she would not give into them. Whatever they needed or wanted, she could not give it. Back at the hotel, she bypassed the elevator which hosted a blackened specter and bolted up the stairs, the wails echoing in the staircase nearly deafening.

At her room door, she dropped her key twice before getting the damned thing open, but she would not be safe here either. Her room was full of them, all gray and shapeless, moaning uncomprehendingly. The door slammed behind her and she began to cry out of fear, confusion and loneliness. She closed her eyes tight and put her hands over her ears. A loud knock at the door almost went unnoticed with the din all around.

"Miss?" a voice called. "Miss? Are you all right?"

Mandy opened her eyes and stared into those of a priest and a nun. She had never left the church. The choir was practicing their rendition of the Prayer of Saint Francis, and there were now about 15 or so people strewn about.

"Are you all right, dear?" Sister asked.

The din had stopped, the scenery had returned to normal; she was still sitting in her pew and with a quick glance, noticed the candles were all still lit.

"Have you seen a ghost?" Father queried again with some seriousness.

That snapped her to. "Why would you say that?"

"You look terrified. And you've been sitting here through two masses and confession," he told her.

"We had an incident a few years back," Sister elaborated. "But it is an old church and these things are to be expected when you're sitting over a hidden cache of yellow fever victims."

"Sister Cathy," the priest scolded.

"No, no. It's all right," Mandy said. "I'm okay. I think I just need to get home."

"Are you sure? We have a warm bed in back for people in distress," Sister Cathy offered.

Mandy stood. "I'm sure. Thank you all the same."

The sun had set as Mandy walked back to her hotel--alone and paranoid. She called Thomas again, but again he did not answer, so out of desperation, she dialed Swithin, only to be mortified when Patrick answered.

"I told you, girl, you won't be talking to him."

"Wait, Mr. Hook, please..." She desperately needed someone familiar even if it was her current mortal enemy.

"I said no!"

And the connection was cut.

Back at the hotel, she finally found a comedy on pay-per-view and fell asleep to the musings of Brendan Fraser in *George of the Jungle*.

When her phone woke her, light streamed into her room. The television blared a blue screen with pay-per-view ads running, and she quickly came to and jumped at her phone.

"Hey, sweets," Thomas greeted, "I saw you called twice. Something up?"

Where could she start?

"You and Little Brit doing okay?"

"Thomas..."

"Look, I can't give you advice in that department that nature won't provide."

"Thomas!" Mandy reddened for more than one reason. "I need you to come get me."

"I can't."

"Please, Tom, I need you. I need someone."

"Oh. Oh geez. Did you two break up? Already? Look, Mands, if it's about his performance, the first time's never that..."

"No!" Mandy moved away from the topic as quickly as possible. "But Patrick showed up. And I suppose Swithin's either home or nearing it by now."

"What?"

"And he's blocking any attempt for me to contact him. Please, Tom. I just want to go home. And…"

"That blustering idiot," Thomas muttered. "Look, sweets, I'm sorry. But I just got here and it would take me two days to get back if I sped so you'd be alone anyway. What's another three on top of that? Maybe there's a case nearby or something. That would keep your mind off of things."

Her mind was the case. "Tom, I really need to tell you som…"

"Hey, I gotta go. You'll be fine for a few more days. I promise. I'll call you when I'm leaving."

"Tom…"

"Bye, sweets."

And he was gone.

The next week and a half went by uneventfully. No more visions, but no Swithin either. She tried emailing him, but it was returned, and she couldn't believe that Swithin hadn't found a way around his father yet. With no one forcing her to study, she found her available time overwhelming. Her music was useless because every song reminded her of Swithin somehow, so she packed it away. She came across a local bookstore and purchased six books which her former tutors would have scoffed at. A sci-fi about a werewolf and a vampire, a lesbian romance, two young adult novels about Merlin's childhood, which she did reason to be somewhat classical anyway, something about a last unicorn and another about a mouse who had to join up with intelligent lab rats. She visited two more museums and hit several movies in the theatre. With her vision clouding her every thought, the last thing she wanted to find was a case. Thomas finally called, and it was another three days until he arrived.

On the way home, they discussed very little. She'd already distanced herself from the vision and didn't want to talk about it. Thomas offered nothing on wherever he'd been. The radio cranked out his favored jazz as they sped along the road, stopping only for food, shelter and gas.

They weren't home two days before Swithin finally called her.

"Sorry, love," he apologized. "Finally shook my babysitter. Da actually hired a guard. Can you believe it?"

"Yes," she tried not to smile.

They twiddled on at each other with goo and sap speaking of their time together and how they could possibly see each other again. Swithin had a couple of plans, but they would be hard to pull off with the sentry. And, in fact, he had to abruptly hang up when the aforementioned killjoy found him. Mandy didn't mind so much, knowing he was okay and being out of things to say. Though he had once told her he never wanted her to keep secrets, bravery eluded her when it came to telling him about the vision.

Thomas knocked on Mandy's bedroom door loudly the next day so she would hear it over her feel good 60's classics. Marvin Gaye and Tammi Terrell's "Ain't No Mountain High Enough" rang clearly through the walls. He opened the door after a delay in the okay. She was sitting in front of her laptop with an embarrassed blush to her cheeks.

Thomas calmly pointed out that her shirt was on inside out. And backwards.

"Tom!" she lashed out.

"Hello, Little Brit," he addressed the back of the laptop.

"'Ello, Thomas," Swithin's abashed voice answered.

"So, look," Thomas went on," I have to leave again. Probably for three weeks or so."

Mandy just stared at him slack jawed.

"What?" Thomas questioned, thinking she was still peeved about the shirt comment. "I am the master of all thing sex, except whatever this is," he waggled his hand toward the laptop and Mandy.

"No! Tom! What do you mean you're leaving for three weeks? We just got back."

"Hey, I have obligations that don't require you. I had a life before you came along, you know, and you were only supposed to live for a year, remember?"

"Sorry to disappoint."

"Apology accepted. But I'm not leaving you stranded this time, so I'll see you when I get back."

"You're going now?"

"Good a time as any. Anyway, just letting you know. See ya."

He shut the door and Mandy and Swithin waited as Mandy listened for the front door to open and shut.

"Well okay, then," she said.

"He's an odd one," Swithin pointed out. "Now, I believe we were regaling our night together," he mused.

Mandy flicked the screen playfully. "Don't you have an abstinence meeting to go to?"

He returned the screen flick.

Rain swelled the day Thomas finally returned. The first thing he noticed was dozens of yellow tulips blooming brightly in his front yard.

"When the fuck did she plant all of these?"

He would never admit it, but they did cheer him up a bit. Thomas hurried to the door and shook off once inside before calling for his partner. Mandy didn't answer. Not thinking much of her non response, he soon became aware of a hissing sound coming from the living room. Following it, he found that one of his favorite, and rarest, vinyls had been spinning long enough to place a permanent groove in the record. He pulled up the needle, while simultaneously reaching for his concealed firearm with his other hand.

"Mandy?" he called again, now alarmed and gun at the ready. If she wasn't dead or kidnapped, he would kill her for the ruined "Dial S for Sonny" LP. He noticed the voicemail button blinking and pushed play.

It was Swithin. *"Where are you? Seriously. It's hard for me to get away from the babysitter, you know."*

"Mands?" Message two.

Swithin was on message five by the time Thomas had checked downstairs and come back up. He looked in the garage, but Mandy was nowhere to be found. The only thing out of place was a cutting board on the kitchen counter with half sliced veggies on it and a pot of water on the stove. She was obviously making vegetable soup. "Disappearing is even worse than dying. Damnit," he cursed.

The rain battered the house and visibility was near zilch outside, but upon passing the kitchen window, he noticed a red blob out in the backyard amidst the downpour. After a few seconds of staring, he didn't see her move and hauled himself out in the storm to fetch her.

He carried Mandy inside, water and blood dripping everywhere, and knocked pretty much everything off the glass kitchen table while setting her on it. Her thumb had been sliced open and pulsed blood. After wrapping it, he checked vitals; her pulse was racing, her eyes were dilated, and her skin was paler than usual, but she remained completely unresponsive to stimuli. He pinched her, yelled, and finally slapped her hard enough that it would leave a definite mark, but nothing. Eyeing the phone warily, he knew he had no choice but to call an expert.

"Hello, Eleanor," he greeted when the woman picked up.

"Well, this must be an emergency," she guessed correctly. Then again, she was a psychic.

"I suppose you heard I took on a protégé."

"And she's still alive. Must be a tough nut."

"She is. But have you heard anything about her origins?"

"Lots of blood?"

"That's her."

"What is it you think I can do for you?"

Thomas purposefully hadn't spoken to Eleanor Fer for nearly two decades, though they remained aware of each other's escapades through the grapevine.

"I was out on a case for a few weeks and when I came home, she was out in the yard standing in a downpour. She's unresponsive to everything. Ellie, she needs your help. You're the only one I trust."

Silence sweated him for a few seconds, but she finally came back. "I'm actually in Japan at the moment, so I wouldn't be able to get there anytime soon. You have a doc nearby?"

"Yes."

"She may be lost in her mind somewhere, but her body is still alive. She needs fluids and sustenance. I'll be done here in three days. If she's not better, call me and I'll come."

They hung up with that, without saying goodbye, and Thomas turned his attention back to Mandy. After a huff, he carried her down to her room and grabbed scissors on the way. She would stay in any position, seemingly, so he set her on her bed facing away from him and gingerly cut the wet clothes from her back. It seemed less awkward then stripping her the right way, as he didn't care to see her bits, and though he couldn't help but see a few things while slipping her into a long shirt, he felt like he did rather well considering her helplessness.

He called Doctor Patil on the way to Saint Peters and had a nurse give her the message to expect him. Dr. Husna Patil did greet him soon after he'd arrived in the ER and led him to an empty room. The hospital was busy so he explained quickly and Husna hurried to get the IV started.

"She's completely dehydrated, Thomas," she scolded. "And her thumb!" she mentioned of the deep laceration. "You have no idea how long she's been like this?" Dr. Husna Patil hunted until she was in her mid-twenties. An orphan at birth, she'd been dropped on the doorstep of a fire station, and the firemen quickly found that she'd been dropped because of her interesting ability to attract ghosts. Mean ones. Word got out to the media, and a fellow hunter picked up on it, absconded with her and taught her the ropes. Hunting had never really set well with her, but she did like helping people and worked as a ghoster to put herself through med school, alleviating what had turned out to be a curse in the process. Now, she had little time to hunt, but gladly helped out where she could. She also had a great distaste for Thomas's lifestyle. "Running around with some innocent woman, no doubt, and you left this poor girl alone! You know she must be watched with her history!"

"I know no such thing," he argued. "She's been fine until today. Or whenever this happened. If she's not better in three days, Eleanor said she'd come."

"Three days! Ugh. Well? She's the psychic I suppose. I have rounds. Keep in touch."

While Thomas waited for Mandy to snap out of it, Mandy was also trying to find a way back. She already decided that it had taken her way too long to figure out she'd been transported to her psyche and made mental notes about how it felt so she would know, if there was a next time. Somehow, she feared there would be. She had visited with the other children in her mind on many occasions, and they had disappeared one by one. She could see ghosts and sometimes auras, but nothing had ever happened like this, or in the church.

She'd figured out she was in a vision when she cut herself chopping potatoes and it hadn't hurt. The day had also become sunny, whereas it had started with a thunderstorm. Wandering around, she didn't encounter anything ominous or out of the ordinary, but she wandered anyway, hoping to discover a way to wake up. Thomas would have to come home eventually, she thought. But he never did. Time stood still. The sun never went down and no one appeared. She walked up and down the street, but the houses were empty and the world was quiet. She had no idea how long she'd been like this, as time seemed to pass differently according to her last psychic jaunt. Upon heading back home, a young boy, about eight, was standing on Thomas's front lawn, staring up at the sky.

"Hello!" Mandy greeted enthusiastically, ecstatic to see someone. "Hi!"

The stranger gave no indication he'd seen or heard Mandy. Mandy approached him, lightly tapping the boy's shoulder. He wore a red sweater and olive khakis. His round face seemed confused and tired.

"Oh, hello there," the boy blinked and seemed to come to as if out of a daze. "Do I know you?"

"I don't think so," Mandy answered. She feared the worst. That this boy was someone like her.

The boy absently glanced around. "This is nice. Is this your home?"

"Yes," Mandy told him. "Do you know where you are? I mean, your body?"

"I'm right here," he said.

"No, I mean, are you asleep? This is a sort of dream, you know."

"Oh. Right. They said this would happen."

"Who?"

"The women in green. They scare me."

"They scare me, too," Mandy admitted, trying to keep on a brave face. "But we can beat them. Where are you?" Mandy pushed the boy for answers. Maybe she could get to him. "What do you remember before you came here just now?"

"I don't remember."

"Think!"

The boy turned from her and began walking. Mandy followed, but he stumbled. She helped him up, but he started blinking in and out. He began walking again. "It's been nice chatting with you, but I have to leave now."

"Back to where?"

"Home. It'll be time for my games."

Mandy shuddered. Her foster parents always referred to mind experiments as games. It suddenly dawned on her too late. They were using this boy to track her.

"Where are you?" Mandy pushed. If he could give her a location, maybe Thomas would help her take them down. "Where are they?"

The boy looked behind her, terrified. "They're here."

Mandy looked around and sure enough, the horizon had shifted from a pleasant sunset to a storm green.

"Don't let them find you," the boy said. "Stay away from them. They are evil. Evil. Evil. Evil. Evil. Evil. Evil. Evil. Evil. Evil. Evil. Evil. Evil. Evil. Evil. Evil. Evil. Evil. Evil....Aaaaahhhhhhh!"

The boy grasped his head and clawed at it. Mandy grabbed him and held him, but he screamed all the same until he exploded into ashes.

Tears filled Mandy's eyes and she began to shake.

"Mandy?"

A new woman's voice did not belong to anyone familiar and Mandy could not place a tone to it; friendly or otherwise. Mandy turned to find an attractive black woman around Tom's age. She stared at Mandy for a couple of blinks; long enough to put Mandy on guard. Then the woman smiled as if she'd lost a bet that she had wished to lose. "Mandy, my name is Eleanor and I've come to bring you back."

Eleanor. Mandy scoured her memory for the familiar name...the werewolf's wife. Dodson Fer's wife. The psychic. Green swelled all around. The air hazed over with it and Eleanor became agitated. "Take my hand, Mandy. We're going to wake you, now."

But the green stormy haze had come upon them all at once, making it near impossible to see and Eleanor dissipated into a million tiny pieces.

Thomas and Eleanor's awkward reunion did not go unnoticed by the Doctor, but she did not snoop. Nearly everyone in the hunting community knew the two had a past, but few knew details. Eleanor's mental abilities had yet to be matched, and no one alive could remember anyone's who had come close. She only assisted on the direst cases, and she'd heard enough about Mandy to know she was needed. Thomas or no.

Eleanor came to after the green swirl had ousted her from Mandy's conscious and nearly went into a seizure. Doctor Patil was in the room and jumped to Eleanor's aid while Thomas grabbed Mandy by the shoulders and shook her, yelling and ordering her to come back.

Mandy ran for cover to the nearby house, unable to see where she was going, but following instinct. She bolted through the door, closed it behind her and slammed her body up against it. Her breath caught in her throat as three women stood waiting in the living room. Mandy recognized them immediately from her time under The Agency's control; short Nharlthop, bedraggled Jalajae and unnaturally thin Agathon. Headmistress Gwen's top lackeys. They collected blood and did a variety of other tests as she was growing up. Sometimes, they even had to babysit.

They stood still, hands clasped loosely at their midsections and it was then that Mandy felt the cold tingle on her right ear. Mandy whipped her head to the side only to come face to face with a porcelain skinned woman in a green pillbox hat and high green collar.

"There you are," Headmistress Gwen grinned.

Screaming, Mandy awoke and Thomas tried holding her down, but she pulled away from the IV, bringing it crashing to the bed as she scrambled into Thomas's arms, clawing and clinging to him for dear life.

"Ow! Ow! Ow!" he exclaimed as she dug her nails into his back and neck.

Eleanor had come to stand on her own and so Doctor Patil coaxed Mandy down, assuring her that everything was all right.

"What was that?" Eleanor asked calmly.

Mandy caught her breath at long last. "Them."

"The Agency," Thomas figured. "Did they talk to you?"

"They found me," Mandy teared. "I'm the only one left. The rest are dead."

"The rest of who?" Thomas questioned calmly.

"The other kids. The ones like me. They were trying to warn me when I was in Colorado in the church. I didn't recognize them. I got so scared I pushed them away."

"Whoa, sweets, back up. Eleanor?"

Eleanor winced trying to recover from a massive migraine brought on by the ominous psychic cloud in Mandy's conscious, but gave her two cents. "Mandy needs to be trained to ward off psychic attacks. Unless she can push back, she'll be susceptible to their assaults again and again."

"Can you teach me that?" Mandy pleaded Eleanor.

Though Eleanor did assist on a case every once in a while, and she had seen some bloodcurdling scenes in her life, this case in particular instilled a chilling fear.

"You're the only one who could," Thomas pointed out.

Doctor Patil was paged and had to leave, but only after she was assured everything was fine did she go. Eleanor had been mulling over the idea of helping Mandy, and even though she had mixed feelings, she agreed at long last.

"You staying at my place, then?" Thomas queried, deadpan.

"It would be most convenient," she answered the same way.

"Dodson know where you're at?"

"He does."

With everything going on, Mandy was left insanely curious about their relationship.

Thomas and Eleanor left Mandy to rest, and Eleanor pulled Thomas aside out in the hall.

"Look, I know what you're going to say and you can save your words," he told her before she started.

"Can I now?" she asked.

"She's trouble. Duh."

Eleanor shook her head. "Oh, Tom, she's so much more than that."

He lifted an eyebrow but let her go on.

"Do you remember hearing stories about the Kanukin Coven?"

He laughed. "The stories that the veteran hunters tell the newbies to scare the shit out of them?"

"What do you think the Agency is, Tom?"

"Yeah, yeah. Erickson already told me. Primum Covina. The first evil coven. Blah, blah."

Eleanor finally became emotional and huffed. "You and Erickson knew about this and didn't tell anyone?"

"A baddie is a baddie. I've fought witches, demons, ghosts and everything in between."

"Not like them. You had no right to keep this from the community!"

"And why? No one stepped up to take Mandy when that oaf pawned her off. When word about this gets out, they'll be gunning for her, and Patrick will be leading the charge. He wants her head."

"That's a little..."

"And you're supposed to be a psychic," he mocked. "You don't know him like I do. You didn't see what I saw. When Bell died, he broke. The man doesn't have a soul any more, Eleanor."

Rattled, he took out his cigarettes and lit up while Eleanor accepted what she knew to be true. No one knew the reason Thomas had walked away from Patrick so long ago. They had never gotten along, but a lot of protégés and elders butted heads. Bell's death had changed Patrick for sure, and Patrick was brutal when it came to rules and regulations, and fierce when it came to his children. A nurse abruptly stopped and snatched the cigarette away from Thomas, scowling.

"Bah," Thomas waved Eleanor's concern off and reinstated his happy-go-luck -self. "Just another battle."

"No. It's war."

"Even better."

"Oh! You are incorrigible. There is something about Mandy they want. Something powerful inside her. I've never felt anything like it."

"If she's so bad why didn't you just kill her?"

Eleanor didn't answer and Thomas knew she'd thought about it.

"Really that bad, huh?" Thomas came back at her nonresponse.

"We need to know more. The only reason I didn't kill her right then and there is because we need to know what The Agency's up to. Mandy is our only link. I'll be at your place at eight." She turned on her heel and Thomas watched her curvy form go.

"You're getting soft, Ellie!" he called after her.

She flipped him off over her shoulder.

Desperate to know Mandy's condition, Swithin had finally gotten a hold of Thomas, and Thomas relayed the situation. Mandy was furious with Thomas for spilling her conundrum, but Thomas characteristically shrugged it off.

Eleanor wasted no time beginning Mandy's lessons.

She warned Mandy that she would jump into the deepest part and she didn't lie. The first night, Mandy closed her eyes as instructed and counted backwards from ten. By the time she'd reached six, she and Eleanor were standing in a vast sunny field surrounded by different types of doors.

"Didn't realize you were an outdoors type," Eleanor mused over the setup of Mandy's mind.

"I didn't really either."

"Well, it's more of a symbol of freedom, I think. You were a prisoner so long, the field and the outdoors represents liberty."

"What does yours look like?"

"I am an outdoors girl, so similar, just a lot more evergreens. But we're not here to talk about me. First things first," Eleanor began. "It was way too easy for me to get in here."

"I thought the idea was for you to come in and help me."

"You can't trust anyone, Amanda." Eleanor decided not to mention she'd already thought about executing her. "Not with your past and not with a hunter's lifestyle."

Mandy took note.

"It won't arise much, obviously, but even when you invite people into your mind, you need to come in first. You need to be in control. I see we're out in the open where you feel safe," Eleanor noted.

"But what about these doors?" Mandy asked, in awe of the lesson.

"They go to memories, ideas, plans and information. They are infinite."

"So, what are we doing here?"

"That woman wants something. I sensed it when we were all here."

Mandy gulped. "I know what it is. Follow me."

Of all her schooling, Mandy'd never learned anything like this and was both eager and nervous to learn to control her mind.

"We don't need to walk," Eleanor reminded. "None of this is real. Not in the physical sense. You need to realize when you are in a vision and when you are not."

Mandy understood what Eleanor wanted, but she didn't quite know how to do it.

"Just take us to wherever you are headed," Eleanor told her as if it were like breathing.

Mandy still wasn't sure what she meant, plus, Eleanor was distracting.

"Why don't you try going by yourself at first," Eleanor suggested, as if she'd read Mandy's mind. Mandy wondered if she had.

Eleanor disappeared to where, Mandy didn't know, but she no longer felt her presence. Mandy concentrated on where the anomaly draft was coming from and suddenly she was there. A dark grove of trees at the edge of the clearing knotted her stomach. She'd known this spot was here, but this is the first time she'd seen it. It had felt like a cold spot in her head.

"Mandy, this is your head," she told herself. "There's nothing to be scared of."

She wished she believed it.

Everything was eerily quiet as she headed into the grove. It became darker and darker until she ran into something squishy.

"Think about light," Eleanor's voice chimed in from somewhere in the dark.

Mandy felt stupid for not thinking that, but remedied it quickly.

Eleanor and Mandy soured their faces at a large, slimy black void which glistened.

"May I?" Eleanor gestured to the black tissue.

"Please," Mandy allowed.

Eleanor put a tentative hand out, but the slit pulsed and she jolted.

"What is it?" Mandy asked.

Eleanor could not get a reading on it. Whatever lay behind the doorway was too complex for Eleanor's mind to comprehend so she dare not touch it. "It's not good."

"Great. Do we go in?"

"No." Eleanor turned on Mandy and grabbed her by the shoulders. "That woman in green, that witch, she is evil, Amanda. And for whatever reason she raised you as she did can only mean she was grooming you for something. Probably this," Eleanor gestured to the dark crevasse. "You must guard this with your life. You mustn't ever, ever go in. Can you feel the power behind it?"

Mandy could. In fact, she felt it throughout her body. It was a heat that flooded her system and made her feel invincible.

"Ignore that," Eleanor said of the energy rush.

"You can feel that?"

Eleanor nodded. "You must ignore it. Power like that only comes with terrible consequences. Do you understand?"

Mandy wasn't sure how or why, but she did.

"You need to be vigilant. This is your head. You control what and who is in it, Amanda. Always remember that."

Two days later, Thomas's doorbell rang and Swithin appeared.

Mandy flung open the door. "How! When?" she exclaimed.

"Me?" he yawped. "Are you all right? Is Thomas here?"

"Hey, Little Brit."

Swithin finally stepped inside to greet Eleanor, Thomas and continue on with Mandy. "What happened? I know something did."

Mandy closed the door and sighed. "It's okay now. Does your dad know you're here?"

"Not exactly. Well, maybe by now. I knew something was wrong so I bypassed him and went straight to mum. I can only stay a week, though."

Smiling, Mandy finally hugged him, but knew he wouldn't let her off the hook, so to speak. "I still want to know what's going on."

Mandy let him go. "Swithin, this is Eleanor Fer. She's going to help me."

Swithin put his hand out in a hello, but Eleanor only smiled. "I'm sorry, but I don't touch people. Too many visions."

Swithin pulled his hand back. "Right. Well, it's nice to finally meet you."

"The last time I saw you, you were still a bun in the oven."

Thomas tapped Eleanor's shoulder. "Speaking of which, you hungry? Goldberg's has a hell of a rare filet."

"You're joking," she gestured to the young couple. "And leave them alone?"

Thomas rolled his eyes. "Look, Ellie,"

"Eleanor," she corrected sternly.

"She hasn't seen her boyfriend in over a month, and they have to play around his oafish father as it is."

"But they're…"

"Hunters."

"Young. What if…"

"Now, about dinner," he guided her out the door and she dropped the subject before it could get ugly.

Down in Mandy's room, Swithin dropped his bags and gazed around. "Looks smaller in person actually. But you actually did hang up the Thin Lizzy poster."

"Did you really just want to see my room to see if that poster was up?"

"Am I that obvious?"

"Yes," she took his hands and stepped into him, their faces pulled together like magnets while Bobby Vee crooned "Devil or Angel" over the radio.

Later, Mandy explained everything and Swithin listened in his patient manner until she'd finished. "Your father is right not to want you around me," she finished.

"Psh. I'll decide what's best for me, thank you. Eleanor is an amazing psychic. If she's willing to help you, I'd jump on it."

Mandy nodded, "Eleanor said when I'm strong enough, I should be able to block The Agency completely. I just wish I knew what that thing in my head was."

"If she said not to mess with it, then don't."

"I know, but..."

"Don't. She's right, love. If those witches want it, it can't be good. Wow. Prima Covina. Their stories inspired all sorts of scary stuff in ancient poetry, fairy tales and even the Bible. This is big. I mean, really big. "

Mandy sighed. "Well, maybe at least someday I can figure out where they are and we can try to fight. They're cowards."

"A true psychic. You just get sexier all the time, don't you? Wait. Can you read my mind now?"

Mandy playfully slapped him. "I don't have to!"

He took her hands while they sat quiet for a few seconds.

"I can't imagine how scared you must be," he admitted.

She twiddled his fingers in hers. "I always knew something was weird, obviously," she said. "And I did try to run away but they always found me. And now I feel like they know where I am and they're just waiting to pounce. Like they let you and your dad take me away and they're just watching."

"In case you haven't heard, I'm the up and coming great," he boasted with a smile. "And Thomas is the current reigning champion. Let them come."

"Yeah, it'll be when you're 3,000 miles away and he takes another four week vacation without me."

Swithin embraced her, holding her tight for a few minutes before Thomas and Eleanor came home.

For the hour before bed, Eleanor tried breaking into Mandy's mind and Mandy tried blocking her. Mandy felt she was slowly getting better until Eleanor told her she was barely trying to break through. "It's good he's here, actually," Eleanor spoke of Swithin. "The distraction will make you work even harder to concentrate."

Mandy agreed fully on that point.

"But as long as I'm staying in this house, you two will not be sleeping in the same room."

Neither Mandy nor Swithin appreciated her old fashioned values, but respectfully agreed. Thomas didn't speak up for them either. He didn't speak much around Eleanor, and Swithin and Mandy devised all sorts of reasons why.

Mandy and Swithin didn't have much alone time together for the next couple of days since Mandy practiced her mental strength with Eleanor all day. Swithin fully endorsed meditation, however, and sat in, eager to learn. Mandy and Swithin did study the normal things together; history, math, science, etcetera. And they worked on teaching each other archery and fencing in the backyard. Eleanor constantly pushed on Mandy's psyche throughout the day--pushing her to strengthen her mind.

The week flew by and though Mandy was thrilled with her progress thus far where her mind was concerned, her heart grieved for Swithin's upcoming departure. Her solace came the day before he was to leave.

Thomas had set up several fake accounts with numbers and emails in order for people to get a hold of him. He usually switched phone numbers on a weekly basis. He ignored a lot of the correspondence, but did find enough people to sucker out of money to supplement his book income. Besides, he needed stories for his next book, so the cases that weren't actually ghost cases could be embellished enough to seem real. No one, however, knew where he lived. Not even his agent; not even most hunters. So, when the doorbell rang on an early Friday morning, he figured it was his neighbor or the postman, but a distressed, twenty-something pregnant couple greeted him eagerly.

Thomas just stared at them until the young woman spoke.

"Um, hi. Are you Max Jaeger?"

"No," Thomas scowled at his pen name. Fans had found him once before and luckily it had turned out all right. He would actually consider them friends if he ever ran into them again, but he could not trust anyone at first.

"Yes you are," she insisted. "You look just like the guy in your book jacket."

"Then, why would you ask if I was him?"

Her mate butted in. "We're sorry to disturb you, Mr. Jaeger, but we have a ghost. A real ghost. Not a raccoon or a branch scratching the window." He lifted his shirt to show a fresh, stitched gash across his abdomen.

Thomas eyed it as Swithin, Mandy and even Eleanor crowded behind him to get a look at their company.

"I'm due in a month," the girl languished noticeably. "We've been trying to find you."

"How, exactly, *did* you find me?" Thomas growled.

"Locator spell we bought in Salem," the man answered. "Who would have known those things actually work?"

"Have you actually read any of my books?" Thomas sassed.

"Please. It's going to kill us," the man went on. "We've tried everything. Psychics, exorcisms and we even moved, but it followed us."

This perked Thomas up. "Followed you. And it did that to you?" He nodded toward the man's stomach gash. "All right. I'm intrigued."

The couple squealed with relief as the man handed over a notebook. "There's everything we can tell you that's happened. Our address and phone number. And witnesses."

Thomas took the book and opened it to see the address on the inside cover. He ripped it off and handed the rest back. "I'll also need ten grand up front. That's your consultation fee."

"But we..."

"Have already consulted, and so you owe me."

"We spent every last penny on the locator spell," the woman whined.

Thomas sighed. "Then, you got robbed. How exactly did you think you were going to pay for my services?"

"Oh," the woman frowned. "We thought you did it for free. I mean, your books must make you a lot of money..."

Thomas's laughter cut her short. The couple waited patiently while he chuckled his last snort and went on. "Look, honey, I'll give it to you straight. I'm a rather contemptible person."

His three housemates chortled behind him and he corrected himself.

"I'm an ass, to be quite frank. If that ghost wants to rip you up and serve you to Satan for breakfast, it's none of my concern. You tracked me down. You need my help. And it doesn't come cheap."

"Okay!" The man put his hands up in surrender like pose. "We have some things we can sell. Some stocks and some art."

Thomas sighed. "Fine. The fee is $75,000, and you pay for any expenses incurred during the hunt."

The couple slowly nodded and Thomas clapped his hands together triumphantly. "Then, we have a deal. I'll be there sometime soon," he told them and started to close the door, but Eleanor stepped in and took the rest of the notebook.

"Thank you. He'll look at this and be in touch."

The couple nodded and tried to speak up again, but Thomas closed the door in their faces.

"You haven't changed one bit, have you?" Eleanor chastised. "How are you still alive?"

Tom shrugged. "Lucky. What's the worst that will happen? I die?"

"You know full well there are worse things. And what about Mandy? Is this how you're teaching her to hunt?"

"She's still alive isn't she?"

"It's all about money with you, isn't it?" Eleanor went on. "They already said they spent every penny they had. $75,000? Are you insane?"

"They were wearing new Prada shoes. Anyone who has enough to hunt me down has more money than they know what to do with. Plus, Mandy needs a nest egg, right?" He looked to Mandy, and then at Swithin, and then back to Mandy. "Oh. Right. You're going to try and marry money. Smart move."

The two younglings blushed, and Mandy told Eleanor that she and Thomas hadn't taken any very dangerous cases.

Eleanor smiled coyly toward her old associate. "So, you are afraid of losing this one."

"I told you. Big Brit and I have a bet. The longer she stays alive, the more he owes me. She's his charge really anyway. Finders keepers my ass."

Mandy and Eleanor rolled their eyes while Swithin puffed up. "You and my dad are betting on how long she stays alive?"

"He didn't tell you that?" Thomas asked casually. "No. No I guess he wouldn't."

Swithin made some sort of disgusted sound. Mandy butted him with her hip. "At least you care about me."

He shook his head. "I can't believe him. But at least Thomas wants to keep you alive. I suppose that's more than my father can say, pawning you off on a lunatic."

"Hey, I'm right here," Thomas called out.

Swithin didn't apologize as Thomas piped up again. "I didn't deny it. I just wanted to remind you in case you were going to go on. I do have some feelings, you know."

"In any case," Eleanor spoke loudly, "you're taking this case, Tom?"

He pursed his lips and thoughtfully eyed Mandy who lit up.

"Yes we are!" she exclaimed.

Eleanor handed over the notebook to Mandy. "Then, you'll need this and more than Thomas's infamous luck."

"You're not coming?" Mandy asked Eleanor.

Ellie shook her head. "I've taught you the basics of how to protect yourself. It's up to you to find the will. You've got plenty of it."

Disheartened enough by Eleanor's departure, Mandy suddenly realized Swithin was supposed to leave in the morning, too. "Can you stay?" she wishfully asked.

"No. But I'm going to." He walked away and took out his phone while Mandy waited on pins and needles. Thomas disappeared into the bathroom with a magazine, and Eleanor approached Mandy.

"Tom is a natural," she admitted, "but do yourself a favor and do your research before you go, all right?"

Mandy nodded and squeezed the notebook.

"Has he showed you the community database at least?"

"Yeah."

Hunters from all specialties logged their current cases, pertinent information, pending cases, clambake dates, news of births, deaths and weddings--and even gossip. The internet was making things easier, but the database was also a good way for everyone to communicate via portal.

Eleanor went on. "I can't teach you everything, and you have a lot of natural ability. You're stronger than you know. I..."

The two women paused at Swithin's sudden rant in the other room. "You're betting on her life! How could you? No.... No! You listen...what?...Then, keep it. My inheritance is the only thing you've got to hold over me and I don't want it if it means catering to your barmy demands! Respect? Respect goes both ways, Father.... I'm staying for this case and then, and only then, will I come home....well, same to you!"

Swithin appeared in the kitchen a minute later, and the girls worried for him. He trembled ever so slightly. Mandy gently reached out and pulled his bottom lip from under his tooth.

"Please," he said, "tell me this case is going to last me the rest of my life."

Chapter 5
"A Career of Evil" by Blue Oyster Cult

With no time like the present, Thomas, Mandy and Swithin headed out that evening for the case. Mandy flipped through the notebook and noted the times, dates and incidents, but nothing really told her why the thing was haunting Kaylee and Bert Fiegling.

"That rag isn't going to tell you anything," Thomas insisted. "Hunting is about instinct and guts. Right, Little Brit?"

"Um, well, sure. But I had to learn what a basilisk did before I faced one."

"Well, that's just knowledge. Of course you need that. But hunting monsters ain't the same as hunting ghosts. They were people you know? They're all different. And unless you know who the ghost was, you just have to wing it. Most ghosters think too much with their head instead of their soul."

Swithin hadn't much experience hunting ghosts so he could not deny Tom's stance, or his record, or his reputation for being the best. Of course, there was also the fact three apprentices had died under his tutelage.

The sun was just rising as they arrived at the Feigling household the next morning. They knocked on the door with no response.

"You call them while I check the perimeter," Thomas told Mandy.

Mandy did so while Swithin nervously glanced around the ritzy street. The homes all had to be at least million dollar properties and had plenty of space between each. Like its neighbors, the Feigling home boasted copper gutters, river rock walkways and manicured topiaries, however, theirs were all trashed. The gutters hung from the broken Spanish roof, the walkways were stained with oils and paints and the topiaries had either been mauled or reshaped into lewd figures. The estate to the left had a FOR SALE sign on the front lawn and it looked as if no one lived in the mansion to the right.

No one answered Mandy's call. She and Swithin waited for Thomas to reappear and when he did, he shrugged off the non-response of his clients and had Mandy pick the lock of the massive oak door, which she did successfully on the first try.

"Best apprentice ever," Thomas smiled proudly as he walked into the house. He had taught Mandy a plethora of skills including lock picking and safe cracking, but not limited to shoplifting to learn stealth, hotwiring to always be able to get away, boxing to ward off jerks and piano, because Thomas was good at it and Mandy wanted to learn. Hunting added up to a lot of down time.

Swithin and Mandy looked around, sure they were being captured on someone's surveillance camera, and followed Thomas inside. The two kids followed as Thomas scoured over framed pictures, bookshelves and the pantry, where he helped himself to two Twinkies and a bag of Cheetoes. They headed up to the bedroom, but could find nothing there except an empty safe hidden behind an ugly modern painting.

"Call the fat cats again," Thomas told Mandy.

She did. This time, Kaylee answered, but it was almost too noisy to hear her. "Hello, Kaylee? This is Mandy. With T--, er, Max Jaeger. Where are you?"

"Hiding under a desk!" she screamed. "We're at the LiveLive Lodge downtown! That thing is trying to kill me again! Help! Ah!"

The line went dead again, and Mandy relayed the news. Thomas sighed. "Two locations? Their fee just went up," he said as he grabbed a Baccarat vase off a nearby vanity.

The posh LiveLive Lodge was indeed a shit show, as Thomas had so eloquently put it. The fire alarm was blaring, red and blue lights were flashing and the parking lot was full of ousted guests and their purse-sized dogs. The third floor, in particular, had broken windows, and two people standing out on the ledge; neither of which were the clients in question.

Mandy and Swithin followed Thomas beneath the yellow tape and, of course, were immediately stopped by a uniformed woman. "You'll have to step back," she said.

Thomas heaved another aggravated sigh, and when it seemed he would turn away, he bolted through the yellow tape toward the front door. Mandy and Swithin quickly followed after a blink, dodging officers and firepeople. No one dared follow them once they were all inside.

Electricity failed so the three had to rely on flashlights in the darker parts of the building. Still, eerily, "Possession" by Iron Butterfly played over the speakers. Swithin tugged on Mandy's sleeve.

"Remember when I said hunting has a soundtrack? You hear that, too, right?"

Mandy nodded.

"Good. It's usually only in my head."

They took the stairs to the third floor and, wielding holy water from various religious sanctums, opened the stairwell door.

Up here, lights flickered in the hallway, doors opened and shut by themselves, two people came screaming out of the far end and nearly took Thomas, Mandy and Swithin with them as they bolted down the stairs.

The room at the end of the hall found Kaylee and Bert cowered behind an overturned table while things hurled themselves at them. Mandy stopped cold at the sight of a Class B specter who turned and growled. She noticed first and foremost that even though he was ghostly transparent, his legs were even more so, as if they were ghosts themselves.

"Mandy!" Thomas yelled. "Can you see it? Douse it!"

Mandy did so with a special blend of water and Thomas called out a spell. The ghost wailed and fizzled away, leaving Kaylee shaken and Bert bloodied, but otherwise okay. The song also had ceased.

"Anything else you want to tell us that wasn't in your little notebook?" Thomas asked the rattled couple.

While Swithin helped the strangers in off the ledge, pregnant Kaylee divulged that the ghost in question was her husband. "Well, ex-husband," she corrected. "Only because he died."

"That wasn't in the notebook," Mandy noted.

"Well, I didn't know until now," Kaylee said. "He's never shown himself."

"You could see him, too?" Mandy asked.

"Just tonight. Right before he disappeared."

"They get stronger over time," Thomas told her. "So, you think he has a grudge against you getting together with this doof?" he nodded at Bert.

Green with sickness over the whole ordeal, Bert did not defend himself.

"I don't know," Kaylee whined. "I mourned and I moved on."

"When did your husband die?" Mandy asked.

Kaylee seemed to hesitate but finally answered. "Six months ago."

"Mourned and moved on, huh? Wow," Thomas whistled.

"Look, I loved my husband, but he was sick and I was with him when he died, but I saw it coming for three years. Bert was my rock," she defended.

"So, whose baby is it?" Swithin finally piped in.

"What?" Kaylee seemed caught off guard as if the answer should have been obvious. "It's Bert's, of course."

"But you're eight months in and your husband's only been dead six," Mandy told her. "Think that's why he's a little pissed?"

"Well, how should I know? He was delirious and sure, he had good days and bad days, but I fell in love with Bert. I want to move on with my life. Can you get rid of Jack or not? Oh! I hate to think that he's suffering."

"Right," Thomas said, unconvinced. "We just have to burn his body and that'll be the end of it. Where is he buried?"

Kaylee's eyes grew wide, and Bert finally threw up.

"He, um, well, I had him cremated," Kaylee disclosed.

Thomas sucked in his bottom lip and thought a minute while Swithin and Mandy waited on his expertise. "That's a problem," Tom finally informed.

Thomas made Kaylee and Bert meet them back at the house, which made Bert visibly nauseated again. Kaylee wobbled inside under the assurance, through Thomas, that Jack would be out of commission for a while.

"I think some tea is in order," Thomas headed to the kitchen. "Or something stronger."

Swithin and Mandy sat awkwardly with the two clients. Kaylee broke the silence. "Your accent is nice," she told Swithin.

"Thank you," Swithin continued the polite conversation. "Lovely home."

"Thank you," Kaylee smiled wanly. "Have you been doing this long?" Kaylee asked them.

"My whole life," Swithin answered.

"Oh, just a year or so," Mandy told her. "Long enough to smell out the rats."

Swithin coughed to cover up a chuckle, but before Kaylee could retort, Thomas returned.

"All right!" Thomas reentered the room holding two cups of tea which he gave to Kaylee and Bert. "I'll be right back with ours," he told his partners.

Bert and Kaylee took the warm cups and sipped from them, tired from their ordeal and not in the mood for any more 'polite' conversation.

Thomas returned a few seconds later and handed a cup each to Swithin and Mandy and kept a bottle of Everclear for himself.

"So," Thomas fell back in to the red leather Barcalounger and took a swig. "Is there anything in this house that belonged to your husband?"

"No," Kaylee assured. "When we moved, we only took the bare essentials. Everything else is new."

"No old love letters? A ring? A car? A comb?"

"I told you. We only brought the essentials."

"Yes. And you've been so forthright so far. Excuse me."

"We are paying you good money, Mr. Jaeger."

"You haven't paid me a dime."

After another moment of tense silence, sweat trickled down Bert's face. He sipped some more tea to try and hide his nervousness. Kaylee followed suit, also sweating, and Mandy asked the pregnant woman if she was okay.

Kaylee asked for some water, which Swithin stood to retrieve. Thomas downed his Everclear, waiting for Swithin to return. Mandy waited to follow Thomas's cues and so kept her mouth shut. She had nothing good to say to these people anyway; cheating on a veteran.

Swithin returned with water and Thomas spoke up again. "So, Kaylee, when did you kill your husband?"

"Excuse me?"

"Cut the act. He wasn't sick. He was handicapped. Mandy said his legs were deformed. I'm assuming he lost them in service?"

Kaylee tried standing, but fell back and Mandy went to help her, but Thomas held her back. Bert had turned a darker shade of green. Kaylee scowled at Thomas. "How dare you!"

"Oh! Kay! Cut it out!" Bert yelled. "Yes! We did it! We killed him!"

"Bert!"

"Kay!"

"OH! Fine." Kay slouched into the chair. "Yes. Jack lost his legs in service. And it changed him."

"He was my best friend," Bert cried. "I loved him. But when he came back, he was different. He lost his legs, and he became so depressed and needy. And I just couldn't stand it. Kaylee waited on him hand and foot and he just wanted more and more and the last time he called her a bitch was the last time."

Thomas heaved an eye roll. "Puh lease," he groaned. "You're horrible people. I should know one when I see one."

"He came back a monster," Kaylee whined. "I handed Bert the pillow and watched while he held it over Jack's face." Her face had turned red and a bit of drool seeped out of the corner of her mouth.

"Thomas!" Mandy lashed out. "Did you drug them?"

"Sweets, no amount of research in all the world would have gotten that information."

"She's pregnant!" Swithin concurred with Mandy's lashing.

"Bah. They'll be fine. Now, Kaylee," Thomas stood. "I'm an immoral asshole. I don't care what you did. All I care about is my money. And the price just went up to $100,000."

Kaylee tried to stand again, but couldn't and Bert just cried and cried. "We don't have it!" she told him.

"Bullshit. You have that alone in artwork and furniture. And I'm not doing a damned thing until I get cash."

"Not until the work is done!" Kaylee tried to fight but a supernatural rumbling echoed through the house.

"Sounds like you'd better hurry," Thomas taunted. "Your ex is a real fighter. They're usually down for days with that spell."

"Give the man whatever he wants," Bert yelled. "I can't take it! I can't take it!"

Kay huffed took off her massive engagement ring. "Here! It's worth ten."

"Kay!" Bert whined. "I bought that with every last cent I had!"

"You said give him anything!" she argued.

Thomas eyed the rock. "I'll only get three for it, but it's a start."

Thomas motioned Swithin and Mandy toward the door and they couldn't reach it fast enough. "Oh," Thomas added, "I'll be in touch after the kid is born. Seeing as it's Jack's and that's the reason he's haunting you, no need to do anything until the little beast is here. Good bait, you know."

He shut them in the house to argue and walked Swithin and Mandy to the car.

"Are all your cases like this? Seriously?" Swithin asked.

"In the juiciest ghost stories, the monsters, are in fact, the living people."

"I can't believe you drugged them!" Mandy chastised again.

"Look, I know Eleanor told you to do your research and you did. And did you find out anything pertinent?"

"Well, no, but..."

"There you go. We've been partnered long enough that you should know how I work for reals."

Exasperated, Swithin had to take a minute to soak all of this in while Mandy just shrugged it off and got into the car.

Patrick was less than thrilled about the case taking more than a month, but didn't want to hear the reasoning when Swithin tried to explain it. He disconnected in a bluster, and Swithin could only hope that the case would last indefinitely and then he'd have an excuse to stay in America indefinitely.

Now with Thomas as their only chaperone, Mandy and Swithin were left to their own devices, which meant, well, that Thomas warned Mandy more than once that he was not raising some bastard child. They kept up on their studies and Mandy remained disciplined in her meditation, as Eleanor had suggested. Swithin used the quiet time himself to reflect on his life and pray. He attended Sunday masses down the street. Mandy attended with him even though she wasn't Catholic. She kept out of the confessional, but did not dissuade

Swithin from his needs, and all in all, she left church feeling refreshed, at least, and closer to Swithin, so it was far from a bust.

Chapter 6
"Bela Lugosi's Dead" by Bauhaus

"You got a case, Little Brit."

Mandy and Swithin were playing with swords and bows outside when Thomas appeared on the patio. "Me?" Swithin questioned.

"Seems someone knows there's a Hook in the States. Word came down the line that some kids have gone missing in Illinois. They think it's vamps."

"Easy enough," Swithin told him.

"You up for a case, sweets?" Thomas asked Mandy.

"I think I was born for it," she smiled and swiped at Swithin with her foil, but he parried, blocking her attack and spun on his heel in a 180 in order to land a kiss on her cheek.

Thomas rolled his eyes. "We'll leave tonight."

"Two cases together," Mandy gushed to her boys.

"Yes," Thomas eyed Swithin, deadpan. "He's a case jackpot. When do you go home again?"

Their lead, Old Man Kinney was, indeed, old. He was bound to a wheelchair, blind from cataracts and hooked up to an oxygen tank. "You came! You did!"

Swithin took the man's hand gently and sat next to him on a nearby chair. "I'm here. My name is Swithin. I'm Patrick's youngest son."

"Your father helped me with a pixie infestation when I was a boy, he did. Didn't know the strength of sugar." He laughed loudly and the others could not help but chuckle. Old Man Kinney went from jovial to grave in a second flat, squeezing Swithin's hand. "They're eating our children."

"The vampires," Swithin confirmed.

Old Kinney nodded. "No one will listen to me. But I knew a Hook kin would, sure enough! Mm, hm, I did! Some others came by, but they said they'd send you. Hooks take care of monsters! Your father said so. Yes he did."

Swithin nodded. "We do."

"We have our own guardian angels, though. I'm not talkin' about them, no. They'll know how to find the baddies. They will. Mm, hm."

The trio shared a glance. "Angels?" Swithin questioned.

"Town used to be growing good until those baddies came. Talk to an angel. They'll tell you. Yes they will. Mm, hm."

"And how do we contact these angels?" Thomas asked incredulously.

Old Kinney smiled. "Break the law."

"All right. Mandy, scream."

They found a decaying alleyway full of trash so old, the flies had even given up. It was dusk, and Thomas took out his custom .44 Magnum.

"Why do I have to be the victim, just because I'm the girl?"

Thomas sighed and pointed his gun at Swithin. "Swithin, scream."

Swithin looked to Mandy. "The things I do for you." He let out a wail, screaming 'no' and 'help' and 'spare me'. They went on for a minute or so, attracting no one. Thomas waved his gun around menacingly.

About the time he was getting bored, something had him around the neck. Never one to be taken by surprise, Thomas maneuvered quick, bending over and pulling his assailant over his back.

The attacker hissed.

Swithin jumped in as the vamp got to his feet. "You're the guardian angel?"

The vampire did a double take. "Who told you that?"

"Angel?" Thomas rubbed his neck. "Where's my stake?"

"We're looking for whoever's taking the kids," Mandy piped up before Thomas could do more harm than good.

"I'm looking at the culprit right here!" Thomas took a step forward and the vamp shrank back. "Nasty bloodsuckers. Terrorizing this sweet little town."

"Terrorizing?" the vampire squawked. "We've saved this city!"

Thomas laughed.

"Let him talk," Swithin took command. After all, it was his case.

Thomas pshawed and took out a cigarette.

"We got here about 30 years ago. It's hard for us to blend into society, you know? This city was a disaster. Crime everywhere. We didn't want to draw negative attention, so we decided we'd only attack the hoodlums. Slowly, but surely, it's gotten better, you know? They call us angels. Us. It's crazy. But it works."

"Who's taking the kids?" Swithin queried.

"There's a rival clan. Our two mothers don't get on well. But there are so many of them. We'll be chased out soon. They're invading our home, taking the people. Their mother is expanding her turf all around and we're in her way. They've already started settling in downtown. They're living in Coconut Grove."

Swithin nodded confidently. "We'll take care of it."

"Well, this is a nice neighborhood," Swithin observed as he rolled up the car window.

"Yeah. I can see why there's a street named Hooker," Thomas stopped at a four way intersection's stop sign. Every building was boarded up and every street sign had been ripped down.

A seedy group lingered to the right, and Thomas rolled down his window. Swithin voiced a sense of reason from the back seat and Thomas turned on him. "Didn't you take down a kikiyaon last month?"

"Well, yes, but…"

"But, but, but!" Thomas mocked and turned back to the window where the kind townsfolk were upon them. "Good day, sir. We're looking for the Coconut Grove and, or, the proprietor of said Grove. Help a brother out?"

The 'brothers' exchanged smiles and glances. "It'll cost you."

"Well, duh," Thomas sassed. "I didn't think I was in Mister Roger's Neighborhood." He took out his wallet and handed over a wad of cash to the gang.

"Hey," a too skinny white dude with blonde dreadlocks down to his thighs pointed at Thomas. "I know you! You're that cracker that writes them books! My momma reads those! They're dope, yo!"

Thomas quizzically eyed up the young man. "You do realize that you are also of a saltine complexion?"

"He right?" the lead member asked. "You rich?"

"Poor people don't usually drive around in Beemers. Or carry around $600 in cash. Which I gave to you, which I think is a perfectly reasonable price for answering the simple question I posed."

The man nodded. "Two blocks make a right."

"Thank you," Thomas smiled toothily.

"Hey! Hey, man can I get your autograph?" Saltine asked.

Thomas sighed and took a pen from his pocket to sign the piece of trash that Saltine had found on the ground.

"Hey," Leader set his hand on Thomas's window before he could roll it up. "Coconut Grove isn't a good place."

"It's all right. I'm not a good man."

Thomas drove off, and Swithin finally started breathing again. Mandy laughed at him, and Swithin defended himself by saying he'd watched too many movies and also that people were the worst monsters, which Mandy could not argue.

Coconut Grove lay on yet another dead strip of street. It may have been a night club at some point, but the large neon sign had seen better days and the windows were all smashed in, but not boarded up.

"Interesting," Thomas noted of the unboarded windows when every other property seemed to have nothing but. Charged by Thomas's dangerous persona, Mandy headed in first, while her partner fought with a breeze to light a cigarette. Swithin tried to stop her, but she was through the revolving door already so he gallantly followed. The inside had been swanky at one time. In the lobby, velvet walls were now frayed and tagged while exposed wiring hung where once a dazzling chandelier might have. Mosaic flooring was chipped, covered in trash and caked with dirt. The doors to the back had been removed and Mandy disappeared through the opening.

A skylight lit up a dusty old ballroom, and Mandy was instantly swept away to another era. Jazz music filled her ears as flappers jived all around while men in tailored suits drank martinis and laughed about prohibition. Then, suddenly, it all changed, and now women were floating around in furs and flowing evening gowns. This place had been a hub for gang activity and illicit affairs for a long time. As Mandy spun, times changed again and pencil silhouettes adorned the women, while men were still sporting suits and ties. She was lost enjoying her trip into the past when the crowd parted to reveal a ravishing red head in a molded dress complete with an embroidered short tailored jacket.

An emerald molded dress and tailored jacket.

Mandy backed up a pace or two as the woman made her way toward her at a quick pace, but when she reached Mandy, she went right through her. Mandy turned to watch her pull a tassel on a wall tapestry and slip behind it like a ghost.

"Mands!"

Mandy came to and was back in the ratty old dive with both Thomas and Swithin yelling at her.

"I seriously hate when you do shit like that," Thomas grumbled.

Mandy ignored him and headed for the wall. The tapestry was long gone, but she searched for anything that might signal a secret door.

"Aha!"

She stepped on a tiny floor button and the seamless wall opened up.

"How did you do that?" Swithin asked.

She grabbed his hand and yanked him down the passage.

Flashlights were a must in the dark tunnel and since Thomas's was the brightest, Mandy and Swithin let him go ahead. When they hit the bottom, they found an unexpected lab of sorts which obviously hadn't been used in some time. Iron cages lined the far wall and were mercifully empty.

Swithin dug through some old files in a spider-filled cubby. "This one dates back to 1790."

"Tom…" Mandy's voice trembled and he swung his light toward her.

Even though the vision had prepared her, the sight of a musty emerald top hat adorned with ratty feathers and long dead flowers did nothing for her nerves.

"Coming into a vampire den at night? Brave or stupid?"

The trio spun at the feminine voice. Donned in a floor length ivory gown, her bronzed skin reflected the flashlight off of the fabric.

"Confident," Swithin answered.

"Stupid." She attacked, hissing and mouth open. Thomas wasted no time pulling holy water from his pocket and tossing it. Her skin sizzled and she turned to face him. But who was the stupid one to fight three hunters in a small space?

Mandy's custom wrist crossbows staked her as soon as she turned her back. The ivory dress quickly turned red.

"Burn her," Swithin ordered, glancing at Mandy and then eyeing up the old hat. "Burn all of it."

Thomas sprinkled kerosene from a flask and lit a match. He lit his cigarette first and nearly tossed the match when Mandy yelled for him to stop.

"Do you hear that?"

The boys perked their ears, and sure enough, a faint voice echoed from behind the wall of cages.

After a few minutes, they found a lever which opened a door to reveal another vast underground lab. More voices called out and Swithin lit up the room with a toggle flip.

No less than twenty children aged three to 15, were chained to the far wall. Lab equipment filled the space in between.

Cops were called and the firemen came to quell the blaze. Children were returned, and Swithin mentioned that it was all too easy. Thomas and Mandy agreed.

"Do you think The Agency has vampires working for them?" Swithin asked Mandy.

"There were other children. Maybe I was a kidnap victim. Which would mean my parents could still be out there."

Swithin took her hand.

"I don't like any of this," Thomas offered. "That cocky bitch we flambéed was no mother bloodsucker."

"I agree," Swithin added. "Let's wait it out another night."

They roomed at the Midnight Madness Motel and waited out the next day until dark. Mandy was the bait this time and wandered into the Coconut Grove area, seemingly alone and drunk.

Sure enough, a vampire attacked her from behind, but Swithin was quick to throw a paralytic dart made of blessed silver into its back. "Tell your mother that we're here and that she doesn't want us to have to come find her," he hissed in its ear.

The paralysis was short lived and this nightwalker scrambled to its feet, knowing better than to fight three hunters alone.

"That was really hot," Mandy complimented her boyfriend.

"It's what I do," he entwined his finger with hers.

"Jesus Christ! You have sex after a hunt. Not during it!" Thomas scolded.

In the meantime, Swithin coaxed out a few of the amiable vamps and asked them if they'd be willing to fight. They were unsure of dealing with hunters, let alone fighting alongside them against aggressive and numerous foes and disappeared back into the night.

"Cowards," Thomas muttered.

"They'll be back," Swithin told him with more confidence than he felt.

It was nearing 3:00 a.m. when a cold chill ran the hunters frigid. Quiet flapping all around signaled that the time was nigh. "You'd better hope you're right about the cowards coming back," Thomas whispered to Swithin.

"Well, well," yet another femme fatale began. "It's about time a few of your kind showed. We were getting bored."

"And hungry," another female, draped in red, added.

"You're going to be getting dead," Mandy sassed.

The vampire mother laughed, almond eyes twinkling in the street light. Thick black hair fell down to her waist and her kimono-inspired dress shimmered silkily. "You're not the first to cross my path, chickee. There are three of you and hundreds of us."

"Is this where I say something cliché like, 'those odds suck for you?'"

Thomas exhaled cigarette smoke. "Nice one, partner."

"Thanks."

"Cocky little desserts, aren't you?" Mother observed.

"Confident," Swithin corrected. "Don't you know who I am?"

"Should I care?" Mother asked.

Swithin gestured to himself. "Handsome...British..."

"You just described every man in the UK," the red clad vampire tittered.

"Touché, love. It'll be a shame to cut that pretty head off."

"He's a Hook," a voice from the shadows called out.

Whispers waved all around and gentle flapping made it obvious that some vampires left the scene.

If this perturbed Mother, she made no sign. "Well, well. Are we that big of a nuisance that it warrants a Hook?"

"He's just a baby one," red clad snickered.

"Even your father couldn't take us all on," she took a few steps toward them. "Even with two sidekicks."

"Whoa! Time out!" Thomas put his hand up. "I am *not* a sidekick. Don't any of you things read?"

More whispers fluttered and more vampires took leave. Apparently some did know who Max Jaeger was.

"Cowards!" Mother yelled. She eyed Thomas hungrily and was a second from pouncing when Thomas halted her again.

Affronted, she stood tall, hissing her displeasure at his lack of fear. Thomas lifted his key fab into the air and pressed a button to power on his car radio.

"Staying Alive" by the Bee Gee's jived into their ears.

"Disco," Swithin complimented. "An appropriate selection."

"Figured I'd change things up."

Mother attacked just then and Thomas threw himself in front of his youngsters and blocked Mother's assault. When the rest of her flock dove in, Swithin, Mandy and Thomas formed a circle.

"We're not getting out of this alive without help," Thomas slashed and gashed with weapon after weapon.

"They'll be here!" Swithin promised.

"They," *SLASH*, "Are," *CUT*, "Vampires! We are hunters!"

"Look!" Mandy ducked and Swithin took off the head of a male sucker, before noticing the small army headed their way. He stuck his tongue out at Thomas who, feeling more confident with the oncoming help, spun away to fight.

"Can't even admit I was right," Swithin complained.

With thirty vampires on their side, they stood a chance. Not a good chance. But a chance.

The turf war raged on. Mother disappeared, no doubt to watch from a rooftop. Not terribly long after the "angels" showed, a new wave of voices sounded. The people from the city flooded the street wielding anything they could use as a weapon.

Mandy was covered in blood and loving it. Never had she felt so free and able to take out the woes of her past. Her blessed and enchanted arrows found their marks, taking down vamp after vamp. Swithin, likewise, was in his element. He dodged and swung and sliced and diced like a pro ballerino.

When the vampire numbers dwindled, Mother showed her card by rushing Mandy from behind. Swithin was too far away to stop it, and he and Thomas looked back just in time to see the vampirella sink her teeth into Mandy's neck.

Mandy had been here before. Just like the demon at the clambake, they both ended up leaving their bodies and meeting in Mandy's mind.

"Your one of theirs," the vampiress spat blood.

The Agency.

"You steal children for them. For experiments," Mandy accused.

"And get paid quite handsomely for it, too. You don't build a vampire army easily in this day and age. Not without help and protection."

"Where is Gwen?" Mandy asked.

"I don't deal with anyone directly. I was to take children and leave them in that room you so callously burned down. They disappeared from there, and I don't care where, save for the fact they looked delicious."

With that, she screamed and they were back in the street. Inside Mandy's mind, their bodies had been vulnerable. The Mother had been raked by a rival vampire and they tussled for a bit before Red Clad staked her "angelic" enemy in the back through the heart.

A cry whistled through the remaining fighters as their leader slowly crumbled. Evil Mother bloodsucker made the mistake of taking a second to gloat, giving Mandy an opportunity to flask kerosene in her face. Swithin chopped off her head with an axe he'd pulled from a corpse and it rolled, shocked, to Mandy's feet.

Cigarette dangling, Thomas tossed a match at the wailing head, ending the reign of the clan.

The vampire from the alley was the only one brave enough to approach the trio when it was all said and done. "I think we'll be moving on. Too many whispers of 'vampire' and not enough 'angel.'"

"You taking over?" Mandy queried. Their Mother may not have actually saved her life, but it had been an effort.

"Naw. There are others better suited. I hope I don't run into you again." He scurried off, and Thomas, Swithin and Mandy followed suit before the worst monsters of all showed up.

The media.

Now, knowing that The Agency was employing other monsters to corral victims, Mandy, Swithin and Thomas searched out anywhere that had an unusual amount of missing children. The rest of the hunting community was also put on alert, and a couple of hunters had already reported successes in finding kids.

Mandy could not get through to Gwen, not that she really wanted to, but now she was angrier than ever. They found one other cache of kids in a vampire nest near Boulder, Colorado, but then the trails went cold all around. Gwen was surely onto them.

The call came three weeks later from Kaylee. The baby was here and they had Thomas's cash. Swithin, Thomas and Mandy met back at her house where a FOR SALE sign had a big SOLD banner across it. Swithin nearly asked if they should be conducting business here still, but held his tongue as Thomas waltzed inside.

Kaylee and Bert were there, baby girl in tow. Kaylee opened her mouth to speak but Thomas held out his hand, indicating his desire of payment up front. Bert handed over a briefcase. Only after Thomas took several minutes checking and counting and swiping a counterfeit marker over many bills, did he finally approve the continuation of business.

Mandy and Swithin were smiling and waving at the baby who was more fussy than not, though, who could blame the kid. Children were most susceptible to supernatural energies. There were stories about Thomas taking babies into certain situations to see if they would cry. Mandy never asked if they were true. She didn't have to.

"You sure you want to exorcise here?" Swithin finally asked. "Isn't the house sold?"

"How else were we supposed to get the money?" Kaylee snapped. "And I'm sure not doing it at our new place!"

Bert mewled next. "How do we do this?"

"Easy," Thomas announced as he stood and grabbed the baby carrier.

"Tom!" Mandy explained, worried about her partner's less than perfect morals.

"Relax, sweets. I've never hurt a child."

"On purpose," Swithin muttered.

If Thomas heard him, he ignored it and set the baby down in her carrier on the floor by the front door. "Exorcising a ghost from a living being is quite tricky," Thomas explained. "Things, you can burn. Even bones. But obviously, we don't want to hurt the little button here."

"No, we don't..." Kaylee reiterated, worried.

"Mandy? The chalk?"

Mandy threw Thomas the chalk, blessed by several different religious leaders, and drew a circle around the carrier. "Hm. Funny that he hasn't shown yet," Thomas noted, taking out his cassette player. He pressed play and "Blam Blam Fever" by the Valentines started playing. When Kaylee questioned him, he explained how electronics weakened energies of specters. Plus he just liked listening to music. Mandy was readying the electro magnets.

Swithin and Mandy then nervously glanced around which made Bert and Kaylee nervously glance around.

"Can we get on with this before he does show up?" Kaylee demanded.

"Oh, well, that would be impossible. We need him," Thomas assured. "Can't exorcise something which isn't here." He finished drawing a spell around the infant and explained that it would keep the ghost from absconding with her.

An unpleasant rumble vibrated the house and the doors all slammed at once. Bert panicked and made a run for the front door, but it wouldn't open. "Oh, sit down, you ninny!" Kaylee blasted. "If he were going to hurt us, he would have done it by now!"

"Not necessarily," Thomas warned. "Not while you were carrying his child."

"What!" Kaylee stood, affronted. "I already told you! It is Bert's child!"

"Then, why would your husband be attached to it? Huh?"

"I don't know! You're the expert!"

"Tom?" Mandy dipped her head to the back of the room where the ghost of Jack stood, glowering.

Thomas turned to Kaylee. "You swear that is not his kid? Your life depends on it, so answer truthfully. I'm not kidding around."

"It's Bert's! He didn't only lose his legs in the war. We couldn't have had sex if we tried!"

Thomas frowned placidly. "Damnit. I'm usually so spot on with these things."

"Tom!" Swithin pointed to the smoke billowing out from under the kitchen door and Bert pointed at smoke coming down the stairs.

"I knew the gas stove was a bad idea," Bert whined.

"So, that's what you were doing," Thomas mentioned abstractly of the ghost.

"Tom?" Mandy pleaded while she fanned smoke away from the baby and Swithin tried unsuccessfully to open a window.

"I'm thinking," Thomas furrowed, still unruffled.

"I hate ghosts!" Swithin uttered as he couldn't smash a window with a fire poker either.

They all looked up as the ceiling creaked and barely made it out of the way as the chandelier and half of the ceiling came crashing down.

Bert and Kaylee scrambled toward their baby who was unharmed. Debris and dust lay all around the protection chalk. Swithin helped Mandy up, and Thomas had jumped out of the way to land sideways on the briefcase of money.

"Ow," he gingerly touched what was surely a bruised rib. He stood and coughed, as did everyone else. Smoke had completely filled the room now and fire licked the bottom of the kitchen door.

"What the hell did you do to him!" Thomas yelled at Kaylee.

"We murdered him!" she yelled back.

"Well, I didn't! Why is he trying to kill me?"

"If he's not attached to the baby, what is he attached to?" Swithin coughed.

Thomas took a step to the side and nearly tripped on the briefcase. After a second of realization, he cursed. "The fucking money! The only thing in this room you didn't buy with his money was that baby and pudgy Bert here! Damnit! Damn you!"

Thomas wasted no time grabbing the briefcase and hurling it toward the kitchen door which was so brittle now that it cracked in two. Flames leapt out and consumed the briefcase almost purposefully. Mandy grabbed the baby carrier and tried the front door again which opened, and she ran outside with the baby. Swithin followed and Thomas dove after. Swithin pulled Bert, but before Kaylee could crawl over the mess inside, the door slammed again. Bert grasped and pulled and pushed, but it didn't budge and Kaylee screamed.

Someone had called 911 as the fire trucks were arriving that moment. Thomas, Swithin, Mandy and the baby girl were already on the street. Firemen pulled Bert from the porch, and he wailed as they tried fruitlessly to break into the house.

Thomas lit a cigarette and wandered over to Bert who sniveled, but after checking over to make sure his baby was okay, calmed.

"Your dead buddy in there a little possessive?"

"That's an understatement."

"He come from money?"

"He won the lottery before his last tour started."

"You buy your new place with his money?" Thomas puffed.

"A yacht," Bert whimpered. "We were going to sail the world."

"You're gonna have to sink it."

"Yeah. I get the idea."

"Sorry about Kaylee, but hey, congratulations on being a new dad!"

Mandy canoodled with the baby and Swithin sighed. "Okay, I changed my mind. I don't want you working with him anymore. He's a loose cannon!"

"The ghost is satiated and the baby is safe," Mandy defended.

"A woman is dead!"

"A murderer!"

"We almost died!"

"But we didn't!"

"Oh, never mind. Hey," he said after a beat. "You look pretty good holding that baby."

"Don't get any ideas," she growled.

Morning eventually came and Swithin had to face the dreadful occurrence of returning home.

"Can't put it off, I suppose," he lamented. "Though, I'm not sure what would be worse; facing da or hunting another ghost with Thomas!"

Mandy laughed. "He, ah, yeah. Kind of intense."

Swithin kissed her lingeringly.

"I love you," he said after reluctantly pulling away.

"I know," she grasped his hand. "I miss you already."

"I have no idea what he's going to do to me," Swithin worried. "But I probably won't be talking to you for a while."

"It's okay," she reassured. "In five years you'll get your inheritance and you'll be free."

"Five years seems like forever from now."

"You don't have to go back." She said it because it's what she wanted, but she knew Swithin's principles to be too strong and almost felt guilty for throwing out the temptation.

Almost.

He kissed her again. "I'll call you as soon as I'm able."

With a final smile, Swithin turned away from Mandy and headed home to face his father.

Chapter 7
"Dangerzone" by Kenny Loggins

The next two days were grueling as far as Mandy was concerned. Swithin hadn't called and Thomas embarrassingly tried cheering her up by offering up completely inappropriate activities.

"Tom, even with my fake ID, I don't want to go to a strip club. Men or women."

"Gambling?"

"Boring."

"Drinking."

"Tom, remember when you talked me into that the first and last time?"

He did and took back the offer. There was still vomit lodged between his front seats and it had stained his bathroom grout blue.

"Ah, I got it," he disappeared upstairs and came back with a little mahogany box filled with...

"Pot?" Mandy asked derisively. "All that shit makes me sick. The drinking and smoking. I can barely eat greasy food without my body throwing a fit."

"Not this, not this," he assured. "This is my special stuff. I get it once a year from a contact in Tonga."

"And you're going to share it with me?"

"If I thought you were going to throw it up or cough it out, I wouldn't offer, but hey, I hate seeing you all mopey. Of course, as long as you're dating Little Brit, you're going to be mopey because, you know, his dad's a pussing cock."

Mandy couldn't help but laugh as Thomas rolled two joints then headed toward the record where he set the needle upon one of his most prized vinyls; Roland Kirk's Triple Threat album. "Slow Groove" crackled to life.

"He hates me," she reiterated of Patrick, not for the first time.

"Join the club," Thomas handed her a Tonga blend and lit both of them.

He'd already introduced her to cigarettes and marijuana, so she knew the ins and outs of inhaling, but this was like sweet liquid smoke. Smooth and sweet like syrup. It filled her entire body with the first smooth inhale, and everything relaxed.

"Wow," she exhaled.

"Yeah, well don't get used to it," he exhaled as well and leaned back in his recliner. "I only have two more rolls to last three more months."

"We should go to Tonga," she exhaled dreamily.

"Sweetheart, I've tried. The guy does not want to be found."

They savored the meditative effects of the mysterious herbs and right before Mandy's last drag, she smiled. "I love you, Thomas."

"Yeah, you ain't so bad yourself, kid. I don't care what everybody says about you."

Joke or not, they both laughed, two unconventional peas in a pod.

"You know what?" Thomas sat up, epiphany inspired.

"Hm?" The herbs had lulled Mandy into a much appreciated mind-numbing daze.

"Going to Tonga is a stupid idea, but going to Wales, aha!"

Mandy sobered and joined Thomas in the upright position. "Seriously?"

"That bastard Brit can't tell me where I can and can't go, can he?" he dissed Patrick.

After a sober induced reality, Mandy deflated. "I dunno, Tom. Swith is going to be in enough trouble as it is."

"Bah!" He swung his hand lazily. "Little Brit won't stand up to his dad, but he's got something you and I don't have. Manners! Bwahaha!"

Mandy mulled over the idea. She'd wanted to see the UK ever since Swithin had talked it up their first night together and truly, anywhere else would be a welcomed change of scenery.

"Okay," she nodded and though she knew she should be excited and her heart should be pounding, she had never felt so relaxed. "Let's do it."

"That a girl! I will book tickets. Right after we sleep."

* * *

Swithin's most grueling task was to attend the month's abstinence club meeting. Hunting with Thomas was a breeze compared to facing everyone, but Missy was the club president, and he somehow found it too embarrassing to admit he'd faltered. Not that he regretted it. He saw the group differently now; more like a safe haven, an excuse that you could throw to someone until you were ready. He wondered how many of his peers were still virgins. They were not all hunters, but kids of the local churches, and no one knew what he and Missy did truly in their spare time. He knew at least two had tattoos they were hiding. Missy was one of them. She would do nearly anything to rebel against her devout folks. Her parents put his father to shame when it came to faith; threatening to disown her if they found out any discrepancies. They had the highest of standards for her and she met them, but not without some mutiny. Like his father, they would have loved to see Missy and Swithin together, but it wasn't in his cards.

"Hey, Swith. Welcome back. I heard you went back to America. Mandy's okay, I guess?" Missy asked.

He nodded. "For now."

"Well, good. I guess you two had a good time, then?"

"We actually went on a hunt together. With Thomas."

"Oh. Well then I'm glad you're alive!"

Swithin laughed. "He's not all that bad." Actually, he was, but Swithin found it difficult to say anything bad about anyone.

"Well, I've got some free time after group. You want to hit a film or something?"

Every time. Missy asked him out every time they saw one another. "Miss, I can't. I mean, well, we could go as friends, I mean."

She leaned into him and whispered in his ear. "You slept with her didn't you?"

He stepped away from her. "Look, she was sick and then we went on a hunt. Plus, Eleanor was chaperoning."

She crossed her arms defiantly and spoke a little louder so everyone could hear. "Look, if you don't belong here, then you can go."

He felt his cheeks redden. "Missy, don't do this."

"You had sex. You're out."

"I'm sorry I can't return your feelings. But when you act like this, it doesn't tempt me to change my mind." Knowing the others were staring, he couldn't bear to look around. He leaned into Missy's ear this time. "You're lucky I'm a gentleman and I'm not going to tell your mother about that butterfly tat on your posterior."

Missy gasped.

"Oh, stop acting like you didn't want me to notice." He stormed out without a goodbye, trying not to picture Missy blatantly bending over in short shorts, and wondering why dealing with monsters was easier than dealing with girls.

Soon after boarding a next-day flight, it occurred to both Thomas and Mandy that flying may not have been the best idea. Aside from the long term effects of the Tonga remedy, they both had a premonition that something was about to go very, very wrong.

Take off went smoothly and Thomas ignored the niggling, as he was apt to do, but sweat poured down Mandy's face and neck. The attendant brought her a cup of ice water, but Mandy reassured her that everything was fine. It was her first flight. When Headmistress Gwen's agency had taken her overseas, she'd travelled by boat.

Thomas managed to fall asleep beneath his black silk eye mask embroidered with a pink sheep, while Mandy could not shake the feeling of foreboding. A bit of turbulence nearly sent her into a full blown panic attack, and she clawed Thomas's hand. He calmly shook her off and returned to snoring.

A minute later when the airliner violently tipped to the left and the fasten seatbelt sign dinged, Thomas sat up.

"That's not normal," he stated and lifted his eye mask.

"This is your Captain," the Captain announced. "Please remain seated. We'll be upright in a ji..."

The plane flipped and everything and everyone who wasn't buckled in hit the ceiling. Screaming ensued and oxygen masks fell.

"THOMAS!" Mandy screamed.

He grunted and undid his seat belt, causing him to fall to the ceiling as well. He crawled to the overhead compartment three spaces down, opened it and dug for his bag which contained several hunting instruments which could not be detected by the TSA. Damn terrorists and their 911 scheme made travelling a hell of a lot worse for hunters, which had been part of their plan.

Mandy joined him a minute later, and as people screamed and magazines, cups and bags shifted, Thomas and Mandy went to work.

"It's not a ghost," Thomas told her, flipping through an old book. "Damnit!"

"What is it?"

"A demon. A pretty strong one, too."

"But why?"

"We'll ask later. I don't have the right book. Fuck!"

"Have you fought demons?"

"Sweets, I've fought everything. I have a death wish. Remember?" He dug through his bag as the plane flew on, surprisingly steady. 747's were not meant to fly upside down, but the demon's energy held it unnervingly steady. The Captain had not announced anything further and the screaming died down to mumbled prayers and uneasy acceptances of imminent death. As Thomas dug through his bag and grinded his mental gears, the corner of Mandy's eye caught an upside-down woman smiling. When she looked directly at Mandy, Mandy's heart froze.

The woman waved coyly with a green-gloved hand and Mandy's fear turned to rage. She knocked Thomas over crawling past him and when he noticed her path, he wanted to follow, but something grabbed him from behind.

More screaming ensued from the passengers as an ashen deformity dragged Thomas toward the cockpit, fighting and cussing.

Mandy looked back but Thomas could hold his own--she knew, or she hoped--and turned her attention back to the porcelain woman in the high collar green suit. Her pillbox beret had a neat little black ribbon tied around her chin as if she'd expected it might fall off.

"Call it off," Mandy pleaded, worried for the passengers. "Whatever you want, I'll do it, just call it off."

"Oh, darling, he's not with me. I mean, he may have heard it from a mutual friend of ours that Thomas Regal would be here, but I can neither confirm nor deny that. I'm just feeling so fortunate to have a front row seat to the infamous Thomas Regal's destruction."

Mandy's nerve about the plane crashing ebbed with the woman's composure, but she was not about to let Thomas die. Turning from the witch in green, Mandy charged back down the aisle over bags and debris as best she could. Screaming passengers nearly deafened her, but Thomas was putting up a good fight thus far. She knew he'd had several tattoos, and though he never elaborated on what any of them meant, the demon grabbed Thomas's arm but abruptly pulled back in pain, letting go a vociferous yowl. Thomas clamored back to his bag while the ashen monster licked its wound. Mandy met Thomas there and they said nothing; Mandy hoping Thomas had an answer, but fearing he didn't. The hellspawn thundered back down the aisle raking it's talons against the seats and drawing blood from those unlucky enough to be in the way. People started to unbuckle, though there was nowhere to go.

Mandy stood behind Thomas as he halted his bag search and sighed, defeated.

"Well?" he stated. "Didn't see this coming."

The hellion had reached them and grabbed for Thomas, but Mandy threw herself at it, yelling and commanding in some foreign tongue that she didn't even know she knew. The beast withdrew, cowering and smoking, as Mandy continued to purge it with some ancient incantation. A feeling drew Thomas's attention behind him to the smiling woman in green, and he turned toward her, but the plane began to flip again and he tumbled into an elderly couple who were still buckled in.

The demon had dissipated and the plane was upright once more, but the crowd didn't feel it safe to cheer under the queer circumstances. A tangible swoosh of relief eased everyone as they got to work helping clean up the mess and helping injured passengers.

Ever the ladies' man, Thomas removed his face from the 70-something woman's bosom and smiled his irresistible smolder.

"You're a very lucky man," he told her male companion.

"Thanks, but she's my sister."

"Well, then," Thomas turned back to her. "You doing anything later?"

Before she could answer, Mandy spun him around. "What the fuck, Thomas? What the fuck! Where is she?"

"Mandy, I am arranging a date. Do you mind?"

It took Mandy a few seconds and double take to realize that he actually wasn't kidding. The blue hair did have giant breasts, but...whatever. She let Tom to whatever it was that Tom did and scanned the plane for the woman in green--to no avail. When Thomas finally found Mandy toward the cockpit, he admitted to seeing the woman, but also noted that she seemed to have disappeared.

The Captain tapped on Mandy's shoulder, and she and Thomas spun around to be congratulated on defeating the apparition. Thomas waved him off, noticing Mandy's discomfort. "Luck, sir."

"Hey, I know you," Captain Gentile pointed at Thomas. "You're Max Jaeger. You write all those ghost books! Oh, my God! This was like, real! Are you going to write about this? Can I be in it?"

Mandy was glad for Thomas's ego as he wrapped himself up in a conversation with the plane's Captain and jumped yet again at a tap on her shoulder.

"Oh! I'm sorry, Miss," a young woman apologized to Mandy. "I wanted to tell you how brave it was to go up against that thing. I don't think anyone on this plane will sleep ever again. I thought stuff like this only happened in movies."

Mandy wished they did.

"Oh, here. A woman asked me to give this to you."

Mandy took the note. "Where is she?"

"You know, I don't know. She was wearing the cutest green suit, and I asked here where she got it but she..."

"Thanks," Mandy dismissed her, turned and opened the note.

We will always be watching. We will always be testing. You are stronger than we knew and I am so proud.

The ink faded away slowly as Mandy's heart pounded.

Thomas found Mandy a while later, sitting in the back most seat of the plane in the corner. The Captain had announced they were back on course and advised everyone to take their seats, so Thomas plopped down next to her. "You don't have to worry about media or anything. I've gallantly taken credit for everything."

"I think I just want to go home."

"Oh, come on, we're halfway there. Nothing will make you feel better like a little, what do they call it? Snogging, I think."

His suggestion did nothing for her and she handed over the piece of paper.

"What's this?"

"She gave it to me."

"There's nothing on it."

"It said that they'll always be watching and always be testing. That I'm strong."

"Bitches. But that last bit is good."

Mandy didn't acknowledge the obvious.

"Look," Thomas sobered. "You can run free or you can run scared. Erickson's on it. If they can be found, he'll find them."

The plane finally landed. Due to the unconventional nature of the issue, everyone was detained, but Thomas made a call to yet another connection Mandy didn't know and everyone was free to go within the hour.

"Thomas..." she breathed.

She pointed to the Captain who laughed and walked along with his uniformed copilot....a woman wearing a green scarf. She glanced over her shoulder and winked at Mandy and Thomas as she and the Captain travelled onward to their next destination.

Mandy moved as if to go after her, but Thomas held her back.

"It's cat and mouse, sweets. And right now, you're the mouse. She already admitted they'd always be close. You just have to bide your time."

Mandy took a page from Thomas's book and tried charging in again.

"Amanda!" He held her firm by the arm. "Right now they know a hell of a lot more than we do."

Defeated, Mandy yanked her arm from him and sulked, but Thomas always had something to say to bring her around, even if it was completely inappropriate.

"Now, let's go get you laid."

Mandy followed him to the luggage retrieval, shaking her head at her partner's complete lack of couth.

They'd decided not to ring ahead to the Hook Estate, lest Patrick pack up everyone and leave. Thomas complained endlessly about the compact car he was given in lieu of the luxury one he'd reserved, which the overly perky rental associate said had been put into the little car hospital. Swithin had always referred to his home as an estate, but as they neared the grounds, Mandy noticed what seemed to be a castle in the distance.

"Yeah," Thomas said. "I know. Pretentious, isn't it?"

"He never said...I didn't know...what the hell?" Mandy couldn't help it, having never seen a real castle and flooded with butterflies. How could he never have mentioned this?

As they pulled up the enduring drive, at least five groundskeepers waved and no less than four people hurried out to greet them. Mandy tried taking it all in; the staff, the enormity of the castle, the grounds and the feeling like she'd been thrust back in time. Every thought was lost upon seeing Swithin race out the oversized wooden doorway toward her. She readied for the biggest hug of her life and received it tenfold.

"What are you doing here?" he asked when he finally let go.

"Vacationing," Thomas answered. "From what I understand, you talked your little lean-to up the night you met her. Thought it was time she saw it."

"I thought you'd be happy," Mandy assumed.

"Well, of course I'm happy! It's just, well, da isn't and you're like, his two least favorite people and now, well, we've got kind of a thing going on."

"My favorite kind of time to show up," Thomas rubbed his hands enthusiastically.

"It's Heildonia," Swithin let on.

"Oh," Thomas drooped. "That old thing. Boring." Then he perked up. "Unless he actually finds her this time," he added thoughtfully. "Could be fun. You two do whatever it is you two are going to inevitably do and I'm going to go say hi to your mother."

Swithin watched him go and shook his head. "I love, you know, *that*, but does he have to keep encouraging it? It's weird. Isn't it?"

Mandy laughed. "I don't know. It's Thomas. I don't think he knew what to do with a teenage girl, so he treats me like another adult man."

"Oh. Well, equality and all that. I suppose that's tolerable enough. Wow. I can't believe you're here. Come on! Come on! I want to show you around!"

He didn't take her inside the castle, but far behind it, she thought to stay away from his father as long as possible. Instead, he gave a tour of the greenhouse, a guest house and the garage which was loaded with antique cars. The family cemetery was on the other side of a fragrant plum orchard, high on a cliff overlooking the Celtic Sea. The iron fence had been warped and broken in many spots and the writing had been worn away on the oldest tombstones, but there was undeniable magic in this space.

"Swith, this is so much more than I even imagined. You live in a kingdom. I thought, maybe a mansion or something, when you said you had staff, but this is over the top."

"And my ancestors have fought plenty of wars for it."

"I get it. I mean, why your family and everything mean so much. Do you think your dad would really ever disown you?"

"Honestly, I'm afraid to test it. I don't think mum would let him, but this is all just part of who I am. Where I come from."

"You have no idea how jealous that makes me." She forced a smile but felt her nose tingle at the onset of tears and, noticing, he redirected the topic post haste.

"I guess I owe Thomas pretty big, now don't I?" He referred to Mandy's appearance here.

"You have no idea," Mandy referred to the trip over.

"Oh! Oh, Mandy! The plane! That was you, wasn't it? How could I be so stupid not to have thought of that? I just was so happy to see you I completely forgot!"

"It's okay...."

"What happened? They're saying it was a demon. A pretty nasty one at that. Lucky Tom has some experience with the buggers."

"Thomas wasn't the one who stopped it."

At Swithin's inquisitive stare, Mandy explained everything about the demon, the woman in green, the note, the archaic language she involuntarily spouted and the fact that Thomas backed down from a fight with her.

"I'm actually glad you're with Thomas if you can't be here. He's not as bad as they say, is he?"

She shook her head. "He loves me. Even if he doesn't want to admit it."

Swithin pulled her close to him. "Well, I'm not afraid to admit it, am I?"

He kissed her fully and they took full advantage of their dwindling solitude.

At long last, Swithin dragged himself back to the main house. On the way, Mandy inquired about the Heildonia character he'd mentioned when she'd arrived.

"My family has been hunting her for several generations now. She saved one of my ancestors, but took a baby as payment. Apparently that hadn't been agreed upon."

"Yikes."

"Bad witches take babies for one reason, usually. To eat them or bathe in their blood in order to maintain youth. I'm pretty sure she's evil incarnate, but I've never met her, so as a good Christian, I withhold my judgment."

"Hey, I thought I was evil incarnate," Mandy play whined.

He laughed. "So, is it true what they say? Do bad girls have more fun?"

"Absolutely," she grinned wide. "Do bad boys?"

He kissed her. "My priest certainly thinks so."

They met Thomas outside the front entrance, smoking. He nudged Mandy with his elbow. "Feeling better?"

"Much," Mandy smirked. "People don't give you enough credit for your wisdom."

"Tell me about it."

"And you know that snogging only means kissing, right?"

"Really? Sounds so much dirtier."

Swithin cleared his throat uncomfortably. "Have you seen my father?"

"Oh, yes," Thomas grinned emphatically. "He brought out a bottle of Laphroaig 1899."

"Oh, dear," Swithin frowned. "He's being nice?"

"Flagrantly."

It didn't bode well.

Swithin took in a deep breath and headed toward the door, Mandy in hand. Thomas stayed put. "Good luck, kid."

Once inside, Mandy could once again hardly believe she hadn't floated into a fairy tale. Knights lined a grand hall, tapestries as big as Thomas's house hung over fireplaces and ancient furniture. One entire 20 foot wall was covered in Peter Pan posters and memorabilia, including a pair of Cathy Rigby's Broadway slippers. A 40-something woman with bright brown eyes approached quickly with arms outstretched. Swithin hugged her and then introduced her to Mandy.

"Mandy, this is Wendy. My wisest sibling."

"Flatterer. Even if it is true. No wonder you're mum and papa's favorite. Hello, Mandy. It is a pleasure to finally meet you."

Mandy smiled, instantly liking the storybook English woman. "Likewise." Swithin had spoken highly of his eldest sibling. She had forgone hunting to take up social work, where she met an American, married him and moved to the States--much to her father's displeasure.

"You here for the Heildonia hunt?" Swithin questioned, bemused. Wendy didn't usually come in for such a thing.

"No, it's been a year since I've been home. I missed mum and figured I'd catch up with some of you. The triplets just got here as well." She looked to Mandy. "Don't eat or drink anything that you've taken your eyes off of for one moment. Those rascals. I'll see you two later. I have to call Monty," she said of her husband and took her leave.

"There you are!" A weathered, yet comely woman who could only be Swithin's mother came charging down into the foyer next. Her gray hair was done up in two large buns on her head and she was draped in purples and greens with an excess of jingling jewelry. Swithin had only ever said the most wonderful things about his mother. Where his father, as Mandy knew, could be a brute, Swithin had never said a thing remotely against his matriarch. She seemed most distressed at the moment and that did not put Mandy at any sort of ease. "Ble ydych chi wedi bod?"

"We were, I...was showing Mandy around."

"Oh, Swithin, Swithin! Mae'n ddrwg gen i!"

"Steady on, mum. What's going on? What are you sorry for?"

Mum went on. "I didn't know, my darling. Doeddwn i ddim yn gwybod!" She finally looked to Mandy and her face crumpled more. "You must be her. Mandy. I'm Helen Hook, Swithin's mother. Oh, aren't you a beaut? Prettier than your pictures."

"Thank you," Mandy wanted to smile, but the tension prevented it, and Swithin grabbed his mother's attention back.

"What did he do?" Swithin asked of his father with trepidation.

"You're going to have to let him tell you. I can't. I just can't." She took Mandy's other hand. "You come with me. I'll show you around. You and Thomas must stay here, of course, no matter the brute's opinion," she said of her husband. "Go on, Swithin. He's in his study."

"Mum..."

"It's not as bad as all that, I suppose, but, oh, oh," she looked to Mandy again.

Swithin looked as if he were about to vomit.

"Go see what he wants," Mandy told him. "I'd like to talk with your mom anyway."

The sickened look upon Swithin's face did not dissipate as he nodded and turned.

"Mandy not with you?" Patrick greeted. "Thought you two were attached at the hip."

"Da..."

"No matter. You'd better get used to it is all."

"Da..."

"In fact, I am ecstatic that she and Tom decided today to drop in. Heaven could not have planned it better and who am I to argue with Heaven?"

"Da!"

"Son, you are truly a blessing and I knew it! And how could they resist you? Me? I'll go down as one of the greats for sure, but you? You'll be legendary."

Swithin refrained from saying 'Da' again and only offered a questioning stare to which his father babbled on.

"Drink?" Patrick had opened yet another bottle of rare scotch and offered Swithin a glass to which his son shook his head and awaited an explanation.

"Nepal, son. You're going to Nepal."

This meant absolutely nothing special to Swithin, and after a few seconds of trying to figure out if it should mean something, he gave up. "I am?"

"Yes, boy! There's a monastery there, heck, I don't even know where it is, but Lama Dorje has accepted you on as a student!"

Swithin did recognize the name. "You mean, Lama Dorje who saved the dragon of the Yandang mountains? Who slew the Mongolian Death worm? *The* Lama Dorje?"

"I've just received the letter in the post this morning saying he wants you as a student! Can you believe it?"

"No. I can't." Lama Dorje was *the* legend in hunting. He'd taken on very few students, taking decades with each. Ten years ago, he announced to the community that he would no longer take on any others, for age did not allow him time to train them sufficiently.

"I'm so proud!" Patrick hugged his son and took a drink.

The news was overwhelming for a number of reasons. Swithin felt the weight of the honor seeping in while still feeling somehow hurt. "How do they even know about me? I thought he wasn't taking on anymore pupils."

"Details aren't important, son."

"Yes. They are. How long is this training going to last?"

"Bah. You'll be his last student. So, however long it takes."

Swithin was beginning to get the picture. "There must be a list of people who want to see that temple. How did you get me in?"

"Er, well? I may have written. But they already knew about you. Of course they did! You're my son. I'm no lightweight in the world, son."

"And I suppose there's no phone or computer. I'll be completely cut off from everything and everyone."

"Of course there's a phone. It runs from the temple to the nearest village. For emergencies, of course."

"Mum didn't seem too thrilled."

"Your mother wants what's best for you just as I do."

"I think I'll take that drink now," Swithin took the news in and mulled over his father's ostentatious glee while his father hummed and poured.

"Now, be careful with that, son. That's 120 year old..."

Swithin hurled it against the wall of the study smashing the glass and sending whisky splattering against the 800 year old castle wall.

"This is bullshit." Swithin momentarily lost his composure upon his rarely used cussing, but regained his stance quick enough.

Momentarily stunned at his son's outburst and also wondering if Swithin's eyes had actually just reflected red, Patrick shook off his shock and waggled his oversized finger, blustering. "You never used to disrespect me before she came along!" Patrick said of Mandy.

"Yeah, well, the same could be said for you. You've treated me as a son, a student and on the rare occasion, a partner, but never an imbecile. You think I don't know that being around her is dangerous? That's the life, da. You think by sending me away, it'll separate us? And the worst part is you're using an opportunity you know I won't turn down. But it doesn't matter. Mandy will support my leave because she loves me. Which is more than I can say for you."

"Your love matters not to me. Just your wellbeing. And you'd better say your goodbyes. The taxi will be here within the hour."

Speechless, Swithin stormed out and found his mother and Mandy in the small servant's kitchen where his mother loved to bake when distressed.

Helen respectfully took her leave while the lemon muffins rose and Mandy forced a smile. "Helen told me everything. I'm so proud of you."

"There's nothing to be proud of. I haven't earned anything."

"You're too modest for your own good. Your mom said it's an incredible honor."

"No phone, no computer. I don't even know if I can write letters!" he continued fuming. "I don't have any idea the next time I'll see you or talk to you."

"Whoa, just chill, all right?" she spoke strong and calm. "Honestly, we never know when we'll see each other. It's not forever, Swith."

He heaved a huge sigh. "I can't not go. Turning down the Pope was one of the hardest things I've ever done, but this? I can't turn away from it."

"I know."

"But before I was only maybe a day away and now, I'll never be able to get to you if anything happens. I won't even know."

"Swithin, I'll be fine. I'm practicing what Eleanor taught me every day. Erickson is looking into it. You said he's the best, right?"

Swithin nodded and bit his lower lip. He'd made a promise to her that he would do his best to keep her safe. It was hard enough living in Britain. Now, it would be impossible.

"Time will fly by. You'll see." she strained to hold in tears. "Just think if we hadn't come until tomorrow?"

"I can't even comprehend any of this. I already miss you like 12 months out of the year and that's when I talk to you every day."

Mandy hugged him and held him tight. Her biggest betrayal at the moment was feeling that Patrick was right about putting distance between her and Swithin. After the demon on the plane, she had a whole new dimension of unknown to deal with, and those green women would no doubt hurt Swithin if they thought it would pull Mandy's strings.

Everything wrong in her life revolved around that damned darkness in her head. She had promised Eleanor, Swithin and even Thomas that she would not go poking around it, but the temptation grew more every day, if only to know what the fuss was about.

The young lovers found the rest of their party in the dining room where a sumptuous meal was being laid out and an argument swelled over a backdrop of John Field's piano piece "Nocturnes" by Mary Louise Boehm.

Several of Swithin's siblings sat around the table already. Wendy, Mandy already knew, and the bearded triplets were obvious. The younger woman with the sharp features must have been Mary. Mary had been born ten years before Swithin and had no love for his intrusion on her life. Her sour puss face reflected that she had little love of anything.

Swithin stood out as not only the youngest but he only blonde head in the room.

Thomas aimed a sharp comment at Patrick as Swithin and Mandy entered. "You should be grateful I took her on, and instead you act like you wish you'd thrown her into a river with concrete blocks tied to her feet. That's not actually what you wish, is it?"

Patrick blustered for a moment until his wife chimed in, disappointed.

Patrick cut her off before she got far. "Now, don't you start on me, Helen!" Patrick waggled his sausage finger at her. "Of course I would never wish the girl harm."

"Is that why you were betting on how long she'd live?" Swithin butted in pointedly.

"You hold your tongue, son!"

"Patrick Matthew Bartholomew Hook!" Helen shrieked. "A yw'n wir?"

Patrick could hardly deny it with Thomas's confession. "Don't you go speaking your tongues to me, woman! And anyway, well, why would she be any different than the others he stormed through hell's door?"

Thomas bit into his now generously honey buttered roll enjoying the show.

Patrick bellowed on. "And what is with all this food? Swithin's leaving any minute!"

"He most certainly is not," Helen argued. "Not until we share a last meal at least. I don't know when I'll get to see my baby again." She looked to Swithin with wistful adoration. "Fy melys, babi melys."

"I don't see why Swithin gets to go to Nepal," Mary Hook interjected. "The rest of us are ten times as practiced!"

The rest of Swithin's present siblings did not speak up for they all knew their little brother was special. He'd been an immaculate child. As always, Swithin combated Mary's loathing by being overly kind.

"I would take you if I could, Mary, dear. And that is a swell necklace."

"Shut it. You're nothing but an accident!"

"Mary!" Helen chastised.

"And you were a blissful plan," he rebutted as he pulled a chair out for Mandy. He took the seat next to her and everyone silenced as the whoopee cushion beneath the seat pillow flatulated. The triplets snorted and Helen rolled her eyes.

Mary would not let up toward her brother. "You and mother both marred this family and now you get to experience one of the greatest adventures ever! It's not fair!"

"ENOUGH!" Patrick yelled at his daughter, but she did not flinch along with the rest of them.

"Admit it, mum!" Mary screamed with ire. "Swithin's not even a Hook!"

No one breathed. Every family had its secrets and the Hooks were no different. A very old rumor flittered around that Helen had cheated on Patrick, producing Swithin. No one knew where it had started, but Patrick had quelled it long ago, maiming another hunter in the process who had chosen to mock, and now no one spoke about it, not even behind his back, for fear he'd hear about it.

Thomas bit into a crunchy piece of celery, breaking the silence. "Mary, I've wondered the same thing for years, but if your mother says nothing happened, then nothing happened. End of story."

Defending Helen was something Thomas could collaborate on with Patrick.

"Oh! What do you know? Reject!" Mary stormed off and left the table in awkward silence until the triplets burped in unison.

"Are we seriously chasing after Heildonia again?" Wendy piped up to break the tension.

Patrick obviously did want to deal with his youngest daughter's outburst, but showed the same passion for putting Heildonia down as he had for putting distance between Mandy and Swithin. Mandy began to feel a bit of a kinship with the wicked witch of Wales. Patrick swore that this time he'd found her hiding spot; a legendary cove off of Holy Island. Mandy noticed Helen's disinterest in the subject and, though she'd already taken a liking to the woman, liked her even more.

Swithin had hardly touched his food, and Mandy could only try and remain supportive. After the meal, Thomas defiantly held up the keys to the rental, glancing quickly at Patrick.

"Mandy, why don't you drive Little Brit to the airport."

Helen embraced her son to tell him how proud she was. "Rydw i mor falch ohonoch chi."

"Rwyf wrth fy modd i chi, mum," he told her he loved her.

Wendy hugged him tight and told him to take notes so they could share every detail later. His brothers noogied him roughly. Mary never reappeared.

Chapter 8
"Leaving On A Jet Plane" by John Denver

The tiny local airport had two runways and a small air traffic control tower. A jet was waiting, and Mandy and Swithin pulled up as the pilot was headed toward the aircraft. Unsure of what to say, Swithin sighed as Mandy kissed him. They kissed for what seemed like minutes until finally Mandy pulled away. "You have to go."

He agreed with a nod. "I'm so sorry."

"For being awesome? How could they not love you?" she asked. She wanted to tell him she'd be here when he got back, but somehow it felt like an unsure promise, and she didn't want to make a promise she might not be able to keep. He knew it as well and kissed her again before getting out of the car without another word.

The airport had exactly two gates, and Swithin double checked his ticket before heading over to Gate Four. Even having been to this airport many times in his life, he still had no idea why the gates were Four and Thirteen, but rolled along with it as it certainly wasn't the strangest thing he'd ever come across. The place was hopping today. A lot of local travel went to and from the small port as the proprietors were a well-established family name in Wales. Bus tours and transport also operated out of the airport so there was an abundance of people for six o' clock departures.

Swithin's lingering goodbye had melded into his flight time and by the time he got inside and through the mandatory, though laxed security, his jet was boarding. In line, he glanced around and the corner of his eye dragged his whole head around.

Sitting calm as could be in the worn old waiting chairs sat a near albino woman wearing a green pillbox beret. She didn't look up at him, but he knew who she was. Or, well, what she was. He jumped line and bee lined toward her, nostrils flaring.

"What are you doing here?" he demanded without introduction.

She was reading a *Glamour* magazine which seemed irrelevant since she could have written the damn thing herself. Seemingly out of the 60's, her pin curls and tidy green hat and skirt suit seemed out of place in 2004--and yet timeless. This could only be Headmistress Gwen.

"Dear, Swithin," she cooed without looking up, "there is nowhere on earth, or perhaps Heaven or Hell where you could go that we will not follow."

"Why?"

"You are the anomaly. We certainly didn't send you and your father to snatch Amanda from our observation. But after review, we concluded that field testing would be more informative."

"Field testing? Who are you?"

"Hunters. Like you. Only we hunt for the truth."

Swithin bored into her with his eyes.

"Scientists," she elaborated.

"And what of Mandy?"

"She is our greatest accomplishment to date."

"What did you do to her?"

"*Your gate is closing.*"

Her power of suggestion turned his head and made him call out, STOP. He took two steps toward the gate and then turned back to the green devil, but she'd disappeared. "Scientists my pale bum," he muttered to himself. "Witches. Ugh."

Though Mandy was heartbroken, it had been nice to mingle with some of Swithin's family since she'd never experienced real family time before. Between Wendy's shunning of the hunting lifestyle, the triplets' shenanigans and the eldest son Peter's nose buried in a law book his whole time there, Mandy realized how truly set apart he was from the rest of them. Swithin's father was right. He was a star, which only made her miss him more, and the realization hit her that she wouldn't be talking to him for a very long time.

* * *

Two years passed quickly and slowly at the same time.

Thomas had worn out his welcome quickly at the Hook estate after Patrick came back empty handed yet again. It wasn't the first time Patrick's vendetta against the old witch Heildonia has caused him grief, but he swore he would find her if it was the last thing he did. His family rolled their eyes and went on their ways. Since Wendy lived in Washington, she invited both Mandy and Thomas for a visit someday soon, which Mandy eagerly accepted.

Thomas asked Mandy how she felt about seeing the rest of the world. She jumped at his offer, of course. He found an Aka Manto in Japan, arias in New Zealand, zombies in Brazil and a troublesome Class B specter in Hawai'i, to name a few. Constant travel kept Mandy's mind busy for a lot of the time, and she never could gauge if Thomas had decided to travel for her benefit or if he'd been running from something himself. They were always still wary of missing children, but Mandy hadn't had anymore visions and she hadn't seen any sign of the green clad women, though she felt they were always there, watching, and it was slowly driving her mad.

Swithin's journey to Nepal had begun and continued with trouble. Prior to it happening, he was told he'd have to parachute from the plane through a rapidly thickening blizzard to a specific spot he could not see. Of all the knowledge in his head, Nepali was not a strong suit and he had trouble conversing with his pilot. He slipped into the chute, and the pilot slid open the door. Swithin tried to ask another question, but was shoved out backwards.

He was bundled head to toe, but the cold broke through. Snow turned to ice and tore through his protective gear. He had no idea how his parachute would survive the storm! As far as he could figure, the pilot had said count to 30, and so Swithin did, trying to remain calm, heading toward failure.

In the nick of time, however, the sun peered through the whiteout and in another five seconds, he was in a bubble of light.

He pulled the chord and after a jolt, was floating down peacefully toward a small nameless monastery carved into the side of a mountain. OM MANI PADME HUM stood out painted brightly larger than life on a flat cliff amid other intricate Indian gods and rituals. He knew he would never see anything like it again. A gust of wind carried him a bit far and he ended up in a young fir tree on the jagged side of a cliff, but friendly faces peeked over the edge and brought him safely to his indefinite home.

Swithin was taken to a large statue depicting Chenrezig, the embodiment of the compassion of all the Buddhas. His mantra, OM MANI PADME HUM was on nearly every surface in some form or another. Ancient temples towered and lush gardens full of flowers and fruit lay every which way. Most of the monks were overjoyed with the visit, but some stayed in the shadows working at their crafts. Swithin could not ingest all the positive energy, and tears came to him automatically at the beauty of it all. An elder monk approached him holding a small stack of items including four sets of red and yellow robes like the other monks wore, a red knit hat, a medium clay bowl and a small satchel which included medicines. Swithin was then taken through a stone gateway to a small courtyard where an old man in custom red robes stood waiting.

"Greetings, Swithin Hook," he said, bowing.

Swithin knew this could only be Lama Dorje and he bowed in kind. "This is the truest honor."

Lama Dorje dismissed Swithin's two guides and waved Swithin forward. "Come, young Hook, we have much to discuss and little time in which to discuss it."

Inside Lama Dorje's small dwelling, Swithin noticed the lack of possessions and pondered immediately on lightening his material load when he returned home. The plain room called to his sense of calm. Lama Dorje poured two cups of tea and took a seat on a large pillow.

"We have meditated for a long time about you, young Hook," Lama Dorje began. "Trouble is something we try to avoid here."

Swithin felt a pressure of guilt. "I don't mean to be trouble..."

Lama Dorje smiled. "You cannot hide from trouble, young Hook. It will find you wherever you go. But there is a difference between that and inviting it in."

The statement did not alleviate his guilt and somehow, he knew this ultimately had to do with Mandy. Wouldn't that put a bee in his dad's bonnet?

"There are those," Lama Dorje continued, "who would not have had you here, but we have all done much praying and there are skills you will need to hone for the coming war. You are already adept at patience and virtue and calm, but it will not be enough. I vowed never to take on another student, for I will not be around long enough to train them properly. I apologize for this, but I will give you what I have."

Mandy had Thomas take her to a linguist about the language she'd spouted on the plane and found out it was an ancient form of Egyptian, which the linguist had never heard, but deciphered based on certain vowels and pronunciations. Thomas and Mandy could only remember some of the words, and though Mandy had studied hieroglyphics, she had no recollection about how she would have known any spoken Egyptian, modern or ancient. In speaking with the linguist, she also found she knew dozens of languages, some of which she'd never heard of. Searching for answers only brought up more questions, but she had promised herself she would never give into the green witches and seek her psyche's crevasse for help. Thomas nonchalantly concluded for her that the magical hole in her head gave her access to the universe, past present and maybe even future; a thought that made her both satisfied and scared.

When Thomas stopped in a small tattoo clinic to touch up the skull and protection spell on his shoulder blade, Mandy made the decision to start her own tattoo collection and had a tiny Pac Man ghost inked onto her leg for each ghost she'd either helped or hindered.

She dyed her hair with purple streaks and boxed with Tom to keep in shape. Swithin was never far from her thoughts, but she had learned to keep him at bay and pondered often on the future of their relationship.

Night terrors plagued her sporadically and her appetite waned, but Thomas forced her to eat, acting as if nothing was wrong. Mandy took comfort in his coolness, false as it may be. The more she travelled the world, the more poverty, crime and injustice she witnessed, the more tempting the calling to enter the beyond became. She knew in her soul that *everything* lie just beyond that slimy slit in her psyche.

Swithin had taken to his time in Nepal like a fish to water. It had taken a bit of time to acclimate to the schedule, but once he had, he wanted every day to be just like it forever. Breakfast was served at

3:45 a.m. and lasted until 4:45 with meditation worked in before and after. Vegetable and Potato soup, roti--which was fried unleavened bread, fruit salad, milk tea and a variety of rice were served. Yoga and strict Dhyana, or meditation, for five hours followed, which Swithin found terribly difficult the first few weeks. Three hours of strength and agility came in after, which encompassed many of the martial arts he'd hoped he'd learn. Lunch came at 10:00 a.m., and studying followed for six hours or more, encompassing everything from learning to read and write Nepali and various hunting techniques to Swithin teaching his own country's rich culture to the monks. They seemed as eager to learn as they were to teach. More mediation was enforced before bed, and Lama Dorje pressed upon Swithin that this was the most important aspect of his journey here.

Lama Dorje had come to him after his first day and after Swithin greeted him with a customary bow, Lama Dorje threw him a pack of Oreos.

"You are truly the greatest man alive," Swithin complimented. He hadn't eaten since 10:00 a.m., as was custom and it was nearly 11:00 p.m.. In five hours, the day would repeat.

"I seldom allow frivolities. Those are our secret," Lama whispered with a wink.

"Duly noted," Swithin responded, trying not to rip into the package full force.

Mandy's internalization of her fear materialized itself more often and with stronger surges. Vomiting, migraines and debilitating muscles spasms tested Thomas's patience, but he carried on, holding her when he had to and mixing potions to help her sleep or stay awake.

Plus, after seeing Swithin in his element at home with his family and his heritage, Mandy wondered too hard about her own roots and where she'd come from. If she'd truly been kidnapped, her parents could still be out there somewhere. Thomas only rolled his eyes at her and told her it didn't matter, but she couldn't help but wonder anyway.

Unfortunately, it had put an unintentional rift between her and her Brit and without being able to talk to him, she instinctively dwelled on the negative without his positive light in her life. She loved him--she knew with every fiber in her being, but Patrick's glee at their separation had been warranted. The time apart had definitely forced her to reconsider her emotions and her life; such as it was. If she was thinking on things, surely Swithin had meditated on their predicament, seeing as that was about all he was doing in a Buddhist Temple. But while he was off finding peace, Mandy's soul only became more tormented. She could not contact Gwen no matter how she tried, as the witch hid well, and Mandy could only pray to whoever or whatever would listen to protect the world from Gwen's mania.

Swithin had been gifted a journal by his new friends and he meticulously scribed every detail of every day. Though he missed Mandy and wished more than anything that he could share this adventure with her, writing to her in the journal made him feel at least that she would be able to relive it with him. And even though he was not allowed contact to the outside world, Lama Dorje allowed him to write Mandy one letter, if only to help him concentrate on his studies.

As time went on, Swithin could not shake the feeling that the proverbial shite could hit the fan at any minute. Most all of the Lamas had been overly accommodating and friendly; sincerely glad for his presence. But there were a few who had not spoken to him at all. He had learned that they had taken a vow of silence to offset the oncoming evil which was believed to be coming.

Lama Ghan was one of these monks, however, he had also been elected to teach Swithin meditation. Luckily, it did not require speaking. Swithin had to work through the negative vibes each and every day to get to his Zen.

His meditation seemed most important to Lama Dorje, as the monk insisted that through mental strength is where physical ability came from. Swithin concentrated day after day, honing his chi and manipulating his energy; even Lama Ghan eventually complimented him with a nod, and Swithin noted it as one of the best moments of his life.

Thomas spared no expense on Mandy's well-being, even though he groused about it. Her first panic attack had come early in their travels and he found an off the radar acupuncturist with a specialty in anxiety. He took her to the best of the best in massage therapy, energy work and psychiatry. Herbs and spells helped her sleep at night, but night terrors still surfaced periodically as Mandy could feel her peers tortured under Gwen's experiments. Against Thomas's advice, she tried calling out to Gwen, tried to locate her, but the witch would not yield herself.

Swithin awoke in a fright himself, early one morning.

Someone or some*thing* was in his room and smelled of burnt turmeric.

It was still dark, and his candle was across the room. Lama Dorje did not allow him many modern conveniences in order to strengthen him and this included battery operated anything.

He was suddenly shoved from his mat and found himself being pressed upon by a man, though, it wasn't a man. Not really. The energy was wrong; angry. Swithin had never felt so much hatred and it nearly overwhelmed him, but he twisted away from the monster and headed outdoors to fight beneath the moonlight.

The aggressor followed, and Swithin recalled his teachings. Under the moon, he could see that this man was indeed a thing, so faintly a spirit of some sort. A furious one.

A bhut.

Bhuts were malicious spirits who died in violent ways and would haunt and attack the living. Even under the moonlight, it cast no shadow and groaned, ready to pounce. It was believed that lying on the ground could protect you, but Swithin knew better. This was a test of his will. His reason for being here.

Swithin could see no audience, but knew they watched. He dodged the ghoul a couple of times before being able to leap up top of a stone gateway where he closed his eyes and centered himself faster than he'd ever done. His mantra rang clear in his head and all else was gone from his mind. Suddenly, he was shoved from his perch and hit the ground hard. He rolled out of the way just in time to avoid being smothered by the anger of the beast. His body was a useless weapon against the monster, leaving only his mind as both defense and offense. No one would come to help him. The ghoul was in pain, and his test was to end it.

He dodged the bhut again and again, unable to rest long enough to find his center and he knew now that he would have to be able to call upon his chi while in movement. Lama Dorje had impressed upon him that he had the natural ability; a stronger one than he had ever seen. Swithin had wondered if the Lama knew something he wasn't telling, but had never been brazen enough to inquire.

He rolled away from the bhut again and as he did so, he took a breath and repeated his mantra. "Lord, make me an instrument of thy peace."

Getting to his feet, Swithin felt it before he saw it. A periwinkle haze around his being; a light of calm. If his heart was beating, he did not feel it. If he was scared at all, he could not sense it. He *was* peace.

The bhut rushed him as he effortlessly jumped from the stone gate, but Swithin merely smiled and touched a hand to the beast, rendering it helpless to resist moving onto the next world.

The monks appeared then and all congratulated him. Even Lama Ghan shook his hand. A feast was prepared and served, the day was taken to play games and drink and yet, Swithin still felt modestly unworthy among these men of wisdom.

After being gone nearly 14 months, Thomas and Mandy found their way to Thomas's home again. The mailman had been delivering mail everyday through the mail slot in the front door and it had piled up so much it nearly stuck when trying to swing it open. Thomas kicked it around when he got inside and headed straight for the shower, while Mandy carried in bags of clothes and trinkets she accumulated throughout her world travels. Most of what Thomas received was forwarded fan mail and junk. He had contacts at nearly every utility facility, so he rarely paid a bill. He'd gone up to shower and never came back down, probably glad for the solitude. The two of them got along well, but had been about 20 feet away from each other for most of a year and a half. Mandy had to admit she rather liked having the downstairs to herself.

Mandy had a definite soft spot for the cad, which she knew very few people had. The thought was reinforced by his little dead plant. She fondled the withered branches gently so as not to break them and smiled wishing she could help him find some sort of inner peace that he desperately needed. Funny, since she could not find her own.

She began to sort the mail, making piles of fan mail and throwing away the ads and the solicitations. When she neared the bottom, an unusual yellowed envelope stuck out and she grabbed it after a slight hesitation. It was addressed to her.

In Swithin's handwriting.

She gently if not quickly tore into it where she sat and noticed the date first; ten months ago.

Hey, Mands. I know I'm not supposed to have any contact with the outside world, but Lama Dorje realized that I was not going to be able to concentrate until I was able to at least write to you once and took pity on a lovesick teenager. Apparently, he was once one, too. So, since I have no idea when I'll be able to talk or write again, I had a couple of things I wanted to say. First of all, I saw one of those green women at the airport. I would have called, but my phone mysteriously, or not so mysteriously, stopped working and the reception isn't great here. She actually did talk to me and said they were scientists. I should have wrung her neck until she talked, but there was this weird energy like two opposing magnets between us. More questions than answers, I'm afraid. I'm assuming you didn't find Heildonia, since the world didn't crack in two or anything. I hope my sibs weren't too hard on you. The triplets can be kind of rough, and Wendy is sort of stuffy, but I like her. Did Peter talk about any interesting cases? He knows about a lot of them. Please tell dear Mary I said hi if you see her.

Nepal is simply perfect, and I wish you were here. You and my music! Play some Thin Lizzy in my honor, will you? I have a journal that I'm writing everything in so I can tell you everything, and I fully intend to bring you here one day. I am learning so much, my head might explode!

Please tell Thomas I said hello and I'll be thinking of you every day. I promise. I love you--caru chi-- Swith

Great. They were watching him too. It didn't put her at ease.

Pushing thoughts of the green devils away again, she headed down to her room with Swithin's letter and her bags, where she lacked the strength to put anything away. She lay on her bed and was asleep before she knew it.

The last seven months of Swithin and Mandy's separation dragged. They couldn't have known it would only be seven months until they'd see each other, but it dragged all the same. Thomas had his fill of cases overseas so he barely looked at his emails now that they were home. He did answer his fan mail, slowly but steadily, as he loved the ego boost each and every one of them provided. He even received several laughs at his coveted hate mail, which he adored even more because, more often than not, they called him out as a hoaxer and a fraud.

Mandy had backed herself into an emotional corner. As much as she missed her Brit, she dreaded the day he would come home. At least, she felt, in the temple, he was safe. And for her part, she'd checked with Erickson a couple of times, but he politely told her he would call her if he found anything else. She added that she would like to know if anything about her birth parents came up.

Thomas kept a steady supply of Xanax and Pepto-Bismol on hand, but rarely said a word about Mandy or her life; he just tried taking her mind off her troubles when an attack occurred by taking her out of the house; usually to his favorite strip joint, but sometimes the zoo or even for ice cream at 4:00 a.m.

The dark spot in her head beckoned her with curiosity, but she resolutely ignored it even though she felt it held every answer to every question.

Not completely dull to her woes, Thomas did finally make good on a promise he'd made earlier. He didn't go downstairs often; it was Mandy's sanctuary and he honored that, but the first thing he noticed was his mother's long dead plant.

It now had leaves.

Not one to be easily impressed, he characteristically shook off any feelings of foreboding or wonder and got back to the task at hand.

Mandy was in her room reading James Herriot's *All Creatures Great and Small*. She loved animals, but Thomas vehemently forbid any, claiming it would be rude of hunters since they were a people that tended to suddenly die. He wouldn't even let her have a fish. The book was most enjoyable, and it kept her mind from woes about Swithin. As of late, she'd considered seriously breaking up with him when he returned home. Something bad was inside her, something that could hurt him, and it terrified her. Thomas knocked and asked her to come out. She followed him upstairs and outside to see an old, purple hearse parked on the driveway.

She didn't want to jump to conclusions, but why else would a car be sitting on the driveway and, grinning, she turned to see him holding out a set of keys with a little ghost keychain attached.

She hugged him first and foremost, but he pulled away and snatched the keys.

"There is something you should know," he told her as she ran toward it. "I got kind of a deal on her. She's haunted."

"You bought me a haunted car?"

As if in response, the hearse came alive with a verse of The Doors, "Hello, I Love You."

Mandy couldn't have been more tickled and stroked the roof gently.

"I didn't really buy her," Thomas replied, lighting up one of his unfiltered cigarettes. "An old acquaintance said a band of gypsies traded her in and that he had no idea what to do with her, so he gave me a call. Junie here apparently is kind of temperamental, and he was glad to get rid of her. I didn't have any problems on the way home. She's got pretty much every song known to man on request so we're buddies."

Mandy was already in the driver's seat checking out the knobs and wheel. "I think I love you too, Junie. I'm Mandy," she replied to the song. "Tom! Can we take her out?"

"Knock yourself out. She pretty much drives herself, so that should make up for the fact I never actually taught you to drive."

Junie revved up and blasted "I Gotta New Car" by Big Boy Grooves as she peeled out of the driveway. Thomas exhaled a puff of smoke and waved jovially to his crotchety next door neighbor who clearly did not like the fact that a hearse would be parked on her street.

For Swithin, time had all but stopped. The only way he knew the date was because he kept his journal tediously up to date. The reward for coming through Lama Dorje's tutoring was the mythical ड्र्यागन, or dragon of Tilicho Lake. Swithin had always been fascinated by dragons, but they were so rare, or fierce, that few hunters bothered with them, even for the novelty. To meet one was of the highest honor any hunter could have bestowed.

Mandy had been right. The monks all adored him and he returned their love tenfold. If only everyone in the world could feel such peace, life would be perfect.

Twenty three months into Swithin's sabbatical, he awoke with a start from a peaceful sleep. Heart pounding, dizzy and sweaty, he took control of the panic attack quickly and scrambled from his kuti out into the open court. All was silent, but Swithin dashed toward Lama Dorje's dwelling, only to find everything still.

Too still.

Swithin padded into the small room and immediately flung himself down next to his Master. But Lama Dorje was dead.

Swithin called out loudly and the other monks hurried to his side, but there was nothing to be done. Lama Ghan snorted expectedly while the others prayed. Swithin could not bear to move from the spot next to man. He put his head down and prayed with the others, only to find a small green thread upon Lama Dorje's chest. Only his innate sense of calm kept him from breaking down into a tirade of anger.

In a will of sorts, Lama Dorje had made it clear that Swithin was worthy enough to be taken to इर्यागन, but he had already made the decision to turn down the offer if Mandy could not be with him. For something so great, he could not stand experiencing it without her, and the monks shared bemused, confused and understanding glances at young love.

With Lama Dorje's murder, it was time for Swithin Hook to return to the real world.

Chapter 9

"Tie a Ribbon Round the Ole Oak Tree" by Tony Orlando and Dawn

2005

"Remind me not to do that again." Mandy stood from her spot at the toilet, feeling the last of the bile had come up. Thomas handed her a warm, wet towel and she wiped her face. The previous night had been the roughest yet. Gwen had finally come to Mandy in a vision, demanding she come home. Her three lackeys were in tow; short, Nharlthop, bedraggled Jalajae and unnaturally thin Agathon. Mandy had not tried reaching out for Gwen this time. Feeling violated but stronger than she had in years past, Mandy fought them with her imagination using smoke and mirrors, bear traps and fire.

"Come on, Aggie," Mandy begged Agathon, the eldest sister, "we spent a whole summer together. Remember? It was actually one of the better times I had growing up."

Mandy almost thought she saw a glimmer of sympathy, but Gwen yanked Mandy around by the shoulder. "You are mine. Do you hear? I will find that portal and will gain my power. You have no idea the changes you could make, Amanda, if you just let me show you."

Terrified by the mere thought of being under Gwen's control again, Mandy pushed the witches from her mind with a sort of internal mushroom cloud, which made everything dark and blurred. A migraine ensued, and upon returning back to the real world, it took several minutes for Mandy to remember who she was and who Thomas was as her memories righted themselves.

A clambake was scheduled relatively close to home next weekend, and Thomas asked Mandy if she wanted to go. She shrugged it off, feeling weak and agitated, but Thomas told her he wouldn't mind attending. This did raise Mandy's red flag, but he laughed at her suspicion and, winking, merely said there was a new huntress he wouldn't mind getting a tour of. Mandy agreed to go with him for lack of anything better to do and logged into her email.

Nothing new.

Boring could indeed be a good thing. It meant no one was getting terrorized or killed, but it was dull to say the least. She should have known better than to tempt the universe because that very evening, a distressing call came from Erickson's protégé, Henry Canon.

"Erickson was tortured and shot execution style," Thomas told a numb Mandy.

"Do you think...?"

"It could have been anyone, Mandy," Thomas told her. "He was working a dozen cases at a time, at least. He probably had more enemies than any other hunter."

It didn't put Mandy's thoughts at ease, but then Thomas went on.

"Timid little Henry won't last a day without him."

Henry was not field material, but oafish Bryson was, and as far as Mandy knew, they were still close. Bryson had decided to pursue a career in stalking vampire nests while Henry became a scholar, but Hopefully Bryson would step up and help his old friend.

Thomas sighed and took a seat. "Erickson was completely paranoid with good reason, and he kept all of his research in a hidden location known only by one other person."

Mandy cocked her head quizzically. "You?"

He nodded. "He only ever told one person at a time, and if that person died, he told another. I'm apparently the reigning champ. And I'm telling you."

Mandy eagerly stood. "Well, let's go."

"Not so fast, sweets. What about the clambake?"

"Seriously? You need to get laid that bad?"

He shook his head. "Not for me."

"Uh...I'm not really..."

"Swithin's home."

"*What*?!"

"Look, it was my job to get you there so he could surprise you. Why else would I go to one of those stupid things?"

"How long has he been back? Oh my God! I'll kill him!"

"Not sure that's the response he was looking for."

Mandy paced around the room. "How could he keep this from me?"

"It's only been a week."

"And it's only been two years. What happened? Why is he home so soon?"

"I don't know and didn't ask. He called me and asked if I could get you to the bake, and I told him I would."

Mandy pondered her situation. "But what if the people who killed Erickson know about his hiding place?"

"Anything's possible."

"Then, we need to get to it."

"I can go get it. You go see your boy toy."

"No. Erickson was working on my case. If there's anything in there about The Agency, I need to know, and we owe it to him to make sure his life's work is safe."

Thomas raised an eyebrow.

"What?" Mandy blasted.

"You really that mad at Little Brit for not calling?"

"Yes. No. I mean, yes, but this is important. He'll understand if we have to wait another week or so."

"Mm, hm."

"What?"

"Well, I've already blown one secret and I know you're not going to back down from going, but there's something else you should know."

"What?"

"He's planning to propose."

Mandy's face drained of color and her jaw fell slightly.

Thomas chuckled and apologized again. "Apparently, he missed you."

Mandy tried formulating something, but no words came; just whines and grunts.

"Look, don't tell him I told you, but I think you should have all the facts before you go running off. Besides, it will make me look bad."

Mandy and Swithin had talked about marriage, about kids, about the day they would retire from hunting, and then they laughed. No one retired from hunting. And maybe two years ago, she did want to marry him, but now with so many unanswered questions in her life, she wasn't sure she was ready. Besides, his father would make them miserable. Did he have solutions or was he just eager to get on with life? Mandy had dreaded this day, and the upheaval in her stomach nearly sent her to the toilet. She wasn't even sure she wanted to see him at all.

"You don't look happy," Thomas observed.

"I'm not sure what I am," she admitted. "I want to know who killed Erickson and I want to see his research. That's what I want. Since I'm not allowed to know he's home, you call Swithin and tell him I won't be there."

"Mandy..."

"We're going after the research. Get ready."

Thomas had to make some arrangements which he said would take a day or two, but he did call Swithin, who in turn told him he would suck it up and call Mandy, who in turn didn't know if she wanted to yell, rejoice or cry.

"I'm sorry," Swithin repeated over the phone for the umpteenth time.

Mandy paced her bedroom floor. "I just thought that the first thing you would do would be to call me as soon as you could," Mandy chided over the receiver.

"Well, yeah. I mean, I wanted to, but, well, da..."

"Ugh. Seriously? When are you going to grow a pair and stand up to that bastard?"

"Pardon?"

"You're 18. You're a fucking adult."

"And you've been taking charm lessons from Thomas, I see," he commented on the crassness.

"Well, excuse him for being the only one who wants me. I haven't been living a cakewalk like you have." With a shock, Mandy realized she'd vented her frustration about something which Swithin could hardly do anything about.

He didn't say anything for a long minute, but Mandy had embarrassed herself into an etiquette corner and didn't know what to say either. It is kind of how she felt, though she had never intended it to come out.

Thomas called downstairs to her and she headed up, with silence at both ends of the phone, only to see Swithin in person with his mother, Helen, standing in the foyer.

"'Ello, love," Swithin said in stereo, holding a big bouquet of yellow tulips.

Mandy hung up the phone and stared at him. He'd grown leaner in muscle, but besides that hadn't changed a bit, and her heart pounded. Swithin clicked his phone closed and put it in his pocket.

"A allaf gynnig te i chi?" Thomas offered Helen tea in her native tongue.

"Oh!" Helen exclaimed. "You kept up on your Welsh."

"Helen, darling," he took her hand gently, "the only good thing that came out of living in your home was you."

"Byddwn wrth fy modd rhai," she accepted the offer of tea, and Thomas gestured her toward the kitchen. "I'll put these in some water," she took the tulips from her son and followed Thomas.

"I like the purple," Swithin said of Mandy's dye job after Thomas and his mother had gone.

"Thanks."

"So?"

"So."

"You're mad. I get it."

Mandy shook her head. "Disappointed," she said because she was mad. Mad enough to say something that she knew would hurt him more.

Swithin finally broke the invisible wall and stepped toward her. She let him embrace her, but didn't return the affection. "That's worse than mad," he said, knowing she said it because it was more hurtful. "Dywedasoch gyd bu'n rhaid i mi ei wneud oedd siarad yn Gymraeg i chi gadw rhag bod mad ar mi."

"I didn't understand that, but I think I know what you said and yes, it makes it very difficult to be mad at you when you talk like that. Brat."

Even though she had made up her mind about the future of their relationship before she'd known about his proposal, she prayed this wasn't a vision. After everything she'd been thinking, she knew first and foremost that she wanted him in her life. He made her better. And still, the proposal was hanging over them like a massive white elephant on a splitting string.

"Swithin..."

"I really did miss you," he said, still holding her. "And I may have gotten a little carried away. I know Thomas told you about my plan. That's why I didn't call. I've been planning and arranging since the moment I came home, and I've had to do it all behind da's back, so it hasn't been very cakewalky."

Mandy pulled away and slugged him semi-hard. "Don't go throwing things back at me."

"I guess, well, the other angle is, that, well, I guess I never thought you might say no."

Mandy didn't respond, which didn't lift Swithin's spirits any, but he quickly moved along and took out a journal with yellowed pages matching those of the letter he sent. "Well, here's my journal which accounts for every day we were apart. Even the last week. A lot of days are pretty dull, but a couple of the monks painted on some of the pages which didn't have much."

Mandy gently took the book and eyed it as if it were the most precious treasure in the universe. She loved him so much, but she just couldn't find it within herself to marry him. She didn't know if she ever would. He was so pious and such a force for good, while she had no idea what her true purpose was or where she even came from. How could she deserve anyone who was worth so much? "Why are you so damned perfect?"

"Well, that's a bit of a standard to live up to, isn't it?"

"Like you have to try. How do you think I feel? I can't be like you."

He pshawed, forcing lightheartedness into a thick conversation. "I love you just how you are."

"Swith, I don't even know if *I* love me. I don't know who I am or where I come from. How can you love me if I'm not even sure..."

In all seriousness, he put his hand up to stop her. "I do want to talk about it, okay? I just don't want to talk about it right now."

She nodded, not really wanting to discuss their future either. Two years ago, she would have jumped at a proposal, but now things were just, well, complicated. She realized things had always been complicated, but she just never had put so much thought in to them and, more than anything, missed the ignorance of youth. "Did Lama Dorje...?"

Swithin nodded. "They killed him," he said quietly.

The blood drained from Mandy's face.

Swithin murmured on. "The Agency. Planning this proposal kept me from going insane over it. We're so helpless against them."

"Why?" Mandy breathed.

Swithin shrugged. "I'm part of the experiment. And I guess they wanted me to come home."

Terror gripped Mandy's insides and twisted.

Her rejection had nearly buckled Swithin's knees, so he had to move on in order to keep standing.

"Hey, I'm really sorry. About everything. I should never have gone to the monastery. I should have held that green woman's head under a propeller until she talked," he babbled. "And I should never have planned an elaborate proposal without talking to you. And Erickson and Lama Dorje shouldn't have died."

"Swith, of course you had to go..."

"Yeah, but I left and I came back, and you're not in love with me anymore." He didn't want to say it because it's what he feared most of all. But it tumbled out anyway and he couldn't take it back.

Mandy shook her head vigorously. "No. No, that's not it. You're overreacting."

"Am I? Am I not allowed to overreact or be mad because I'm apparently so perfect? You know, I'm sorry I had a marvelous upbringing, and that I come for money and that I'm good at what I do. But what I'm most sorry for is that I'm so good and lucky that it's pushed away the one person who means more than anything to me."

Mandy sucked in tears. With everything else going on, the last thing she'd ever wanted to do was hurt him, and she was realizing her rejection of his proposal had affected him more than she could have imagined. "Swithin, it's not you..."

"Just stop. Stop right there with the ol' 'it's not you, it's me' bullshit. There. I cussed. Is that bad boy enough for you? I need to start bloody fucking cussing? Do I need to dye my hair blue and cover my whole body in tattoos?"

"Seriously, stop it," Mandy had gone from sad to mad in two seconds flat at his insults over her change of appearance.

"You want to know what's hard? Walking around with the expectation that you'll be a legend. It's a lot of weight to bear."

Mandy took in a breath when words failed her. She'd never thought about the fact that his reputation bothered him. He'd never let on.

Swithin hadn't really expected her to say "no", and so he hadn't anticipated any sort of rebuff. Even with his two years of intensive meditative training, he still could not calm his center. True, the focus had been on hunting and being one with the beasts, but the idea of centering was universal, and his mind was so far from centered, the idea of focusing wasn't even on the map.

The guilt he'd felt about leaving her, about letting that green femme fatale go, about not calling the second he got home had turned to apathy. As far as he was concerned, while he'd been off thinking of a thousand reasons why they should be together and turning down the opportunity to meet a dragon, she'd been figuring out why they should be apart. And of all the reasons? He was too good. Too good?!

"Bloody, fecking, cock, shit, shite, bullocks, fuuuuuck!"

Swithin belted out a string of expletives while Mandy stood wide eyed. Helen and Thomas came to see what the fuss was about. Mandy may have been the only one to notice, but a red tint gleamed in his eyes as Swithin then proceeded to pick up a nearby vase and smash it to floor before charging past Mandy, down the stairs and slamming the door to her room.

"You told him 'no', didn't you?" Thomas asked flippantly.

Helen put a consoling hand on Mandy's shoulder. "I should apologize. I rather encouraged him."

"It's not your fault, Helen."

Mandy took in a breath and headed down the stairs. Her radio was always on, as music usually gave her comfort, and she felt it helped keep intruders at bay in regards to her mind. The Association's "Never My Love", was appropriately playing.

She stood outside her bedroom door, listening to the lyrics and crying her tears. She would always love him. She loved him more than anything.

Loving someone means hurting them if it's for their own good.

Patrick's words came flooding back. He was right. The old bastard was right. The Agency had followed Swithin; had killed Lama Dorje, all to control him. All to get at her.

* * *

Mandy's bedroom door flew open the next morning and both Mandy and Swithin jolted straight up, Mandy struggling to keep the sheet over her chest.

"I thought you wanted to go!" Thomas boomed. "Get dressed and meet us outside."

He slammed the door closed again, and Mandy began laughing while Swithin finally pushed aside his inherent straight-lace, letting go a chuckle as well. "I, um..."

"Everything's kind of a messy blur."

"But a good one," he smiled.

She nodded. "Well, we should go. It's a long trip."

Thomas had packed everything they'd need, though he still hadn't said where they were going. "Those sexy bitches probably have our entire lives bugged with the way they just show up, and I'm not going to say anything out loud to give them a head start. I shouldn't have even told any of you that Erickson had a secret spot!"

Swithin told stories from his trip, as everyone was interested in Lama Dorje. Swithin said he was everything you would have expected him to be. Humble, talented and an amazing teacher. He didn't say anything about turning down a chance to meet the dragon because he knew they would all give him trouble for it. Though as far as he was concerned, he'd dishonored the Lamas, and maybe even the dragon, by turning down the opportunity. Perfect indeed.

"Erickson's cache. Is it in America?" Mandy asked after two days of driving and a particularly fetid motel stay.

Johnny Cash crooned Tom Paxton's "I Can't Help But Wonder Where I'm Bound" while Thomas zipped down the highway.

"Not saying."

Helen had plenty to talk about as well to pass the time, and they were all interested in the stories of her youth. She'd had to lie to

Patrick to get Swithin to the States--a fact which hadn't set well with her righteous son--but she assured him that the sin was on her head.

"Aren't you tired of being married to that buffoon?" Thomas asked her.

"Stop it, you," she chided playfully. "I'm still too old for you."

"Not possible."

"And too married."

"Hasn't stopped me yet."

"Thomas, seriously, stop hitting on my mum!" Swithin warned.

Thomas laughed. "Your mother..."

"Now!" Swithin barked, agitated, while the rest of the car smiled.

"Colorado?" Mandy said upon passing the state's welcome sign.

"You'll know when we get there," Thomas repeated, annoyed. "I seriously miss working alone."

Mandy stuck her tongue out at him from the backseat.

Another several hours later, night had fallen, and they were driving up some pretty steep and winding mountain slopes. No one in the car was afraid of dangerous situations, but the drop less than a foot from the car was rather unnerving with Thomas at the wheel. When Tom finally stopped the car, he got out and began unpacking the climbing gear.

Mandy stated the obvious--that it was near pitch black with only half a moon showing.

Thomas pushed a rope at her. "You know they're following us. You really want to stop for tea, crumpets and a nap?"

Mandy took the rope. She'd only been climbing once last summer in Japan with him.

"Just like the Kiso Mountains," Thomas reminded.

"When I nearly fell a thousand feet?"

"Just like that."

Swithin took her rope and modestly reassured her that he was an expert.

Of course he was.

No visions and no signs of anyone in green. Each of them was laden with flashlights wherever a flashlight could be worn or attached, and they all ascended a straight cliff, following Swithin's lead. Though Helen had been a champion climber in her day, Swithin was younger and more agile, making it easier for him to scale the rock. Mandy kept thinking if she made it through this alive, she'd marry him for sure.

Someday.

Thomas called out to Swithin about a cave several feet above him, and Swithin gave a thumbs up.

They all made it and crawled into the small space, Mandy wondering first and foremost how the hell she was going to get down. Thomas took out a piece of paper and glazed over it before heading off to the left.

"Hey," Mandy called out. "Wait for us!"

"I gotta take a leak," he called back.

Mandy would have guessed no one had seen the inside of this cave for centuries, but Thomas assured her that it was the one Erickson spoke about.

"Why on earth would you hide electronics in a damp cave?" Helen wondered aloud.

Her answer came in the form of a metal door, completely out of place around a corner.

"Don't tell me he's had some secret lair in here. How did he get everything in here?"

"I'm going to go with magic," Thomas suggested as he punched in the code on the keypad.

After a glance behind to make sure no one was following, Mandy entered the room last and shut the door until it clicked. Inside, book upon book was shelved in glass and metal containers. The room had been coated in some sort of green foam, perhaps to insulate or block signals. A massive computer took up the far wall of the large room-- all in all, maybe 1,000 square feet at first glance.

"So, this is where he got off to when no one could get a hold of him," Helen observed. "The cheeky little devil."

"There's no way he did all of this," Thomas noted, upon opening another door. "Look."

They all peered through another door which automatically promoted a lighting system to turn on and highlight a vast space, many times bigger than the entryway, all coated in the same green foam and filled to the brim with materials of all kinds.

"What is all this?" Swithin murmured.

Helen had picked up a bagged paper from a nearby shelf. "This is tagged with 3,700 BC."

Swithin came over for a closer look as Thomas swung around the flashlight, and pricked his ears for any signs of visitors.

"It's a letter of some sort. That's 500 years before anyone believed that written languages existed." Helen commented.

"I wonder what it says," Swithin pondered as he took it gently from her.

Mandy peered over his shoulder. "Roughly, uh, I have a handsome son; you have healthy crops, let's make a trade."

Swithin and Helen shared the same impressed, if not concerned expression.

"Hey," Mandy replied, "I don't like that I understand that any better than you do."

"Yeah, yeah," Thomas wanted to get the backup and get out. "You can come back later. Let's find this backup disc. It's supposed to be in Aisle Q."

They traveled down the rows and rows and artifacts which were mostly books, parchments, scrolls and tablets. An occasional statue or talisman would be displayed in a protected glass case, but the history of the world must have been in this cavern.

Each section was marked with a plaque depicting letters or numbers in several languages.

"I can see why he wanted it kept a secret, Helen mused over a section of rather amorous ancient photos.

"Here's Q," Swithin announced under a large, pewter plaque with multiple scripted Q's.

"This place gives me the creeps," Thomas said once again.

"I didn't think anything scared you," Mandy jested.

"So, you know this place must be bad," he didn't joke.

They wandered up and down Aisle Q with no luck of finding anything electronic.

"*Is* it something electronic?" Mandy finally asked. "Or are we looking for the wrong media?"

Thomas groused. "How else would you back something up remotely if it's not electronic?"

"Magic," Helen laughed in spite of it all. "You already said that yourself, Tommy."

"Didn't he tell you anything else?" Swithin asked.

"He gave me coordinates and the letter Q," Thomas began scouring book titles.

Another hour went by, and they'd pulled hundreds of scripts off the shelves to no avail.

Swithin played his music to alleviate some of the eeriness and rolled his eyes as U2's "Still Haven't Found What I'm Looking For" came on.

"Are you sure he said 'Q' and not 'U'?" Mandy spouted.

"I think I can be entrusted to remember a letter, sweets."

"Hey," Swithin had looked up from the tablet he was trying to decipher and noticed the empty shelving had a crease that resembled a door.

Mandy followed his eye line and saw it too. She was nearest, so after a go ahead look from her group, she pushed on the shelving and it opened.

"Bastard," Thomas muttered.

Inside, three books, two feet wide each, rested on golden pulpits.

"I hate magic," Thomas groused.

Helen, Mandy and Swithin all eagerly approached the tomes, but didn't dare touch them.

"We'll be in here for years trying to go through all of this!" Helen explained.

Thomas yanked the third book from its place to the gasps of his cohorts and sat on the floor with it. He flipped from the back and took out a camera to start taking pictures. "It will be some of the most recent stuff, Helen," Thomas pointed out. "Why don't you three go make sure we're still alone, huh?"

They left him to his devices and reentered the cavern. Mandy followed Swith and Helen, and before she knew it, a shot had echoed throughout the cave. Helen's lifeless body fell from behind a shelf as Mandy pushed Swithin out of the way to avoid them getting shot as well.

Thomas stuck his arm out and yanked them both back into the secret room, slamming the door and listening for the air seal to hiss.

"I knew it!" he yelled. "Did you see them? Is it those green sirens?"

"I don't know!" Mandy cried. "I don't know!"

"I didn't see anything," Swithin was rightly in shock over his mother, but was breathing deep and slow, biting his lip.

"We'll be taking that book, Mr. Regal," came a feminine voice from outside, penetrating crystal clear through the small ventilation grid above the door.

"I'll burn it first, you emerald hag!" he shouted back.

"Not if you value your son's life," she calmly replied.

Swithin and Mandy slowly swiveled their heads toward him, which he blatantly ignored. "If you're going to hurt innocent people, that's on you. You'll do far more damage with this book."

"And how, exactly are you planning to get out of here with it?"

Mandy broke free from the shock that Thomas had a son somewhere, and had been searching the floor and ceiling and walls. She quietly pointed to a hatch in the floor.

"I'm working on it," Thomas called back.

"Blow the door," Gwen commanded to her cohorts.

Chapter 10
"Harden My Heart" by Quarterflash

A deafening explosion woke Mandy from her premonition dream. She was on the living room couch beneath a furry purple blanket, but she didn't have time to think as Thomas's voice boomed from upstairs.

They all met in the kitchen and Helen began to make strong coffee while Thomas griped. "What the hell did we all just experience? A shared premonition?" he barked upon entrance. Few things rattled him and he didn't handle it well when they did.

"Glad you asked, because I have no clue," Mandy smirked back.

"We have a map of what not to do," Helen pointed out calmly while stirring honey into her tea. "We'll get in, get to the book and get down the hatch."

"Helen, you're obviously not going," Mandy directed.

"The hells I'm not," she smiled, then sipped.

"Mum," Swithin started.

"Don't you 'mum' me. I've lived through worse without a warning. Besides, if your premonitions are like those awful *Final Destination* movies, I'm dead anyway. Might as well face it like a warrior."

"Mum!" Swithin nearly pleaded.

"What? You're the one that made me watch them. Terrible things."

"No one is going," Thomas poured a cup of strong coffee and added extra shots of strong from a Grand Marnier bottle. "I'm sorry, Mandy. But the only way they are going to find out about that place is if they follow us there or somehow figure out a way to break into my mind."

"Or any of our minds, I suppose," she noted, seeing as they were all with him on the trip.

"Whatever. But I'm not going to willingly hand over a cave of treasure to those jaded lunatics. I'm sorry, Amanda. Your secrets are going to have to stay buried for now."

He exited the room and headed outside for a smoke. The others lingered uncomfortably for a short minute until Swithin brought up the obvious question on everyone's mind.

"So, Thomas has a son?"

Not even Helen had known, and so could offer nothing else. "We all have our secrets, dear."

Seeing as her strongest inner needs and desires were to remain unfulfilled, Mandy excused herself, and Helen grasped Swithin's hand so he wouldn't follow. "Give her time."

"We had two years apart, if you'll recall, and it seems to have ruined everything. Excuse me."

He rapped gently at the door not two minutes later, but Mandy didn't answer. He took a deep breath and opened the door anyway. She was sitting on the bed, facing away. Her music was on as always playing quietly in the background. "This Diamond Ring" by Gary Lewis and the Playboys didn't bode well.

He bit his bottom lip harder than usual.

She never looked at him. "Stop biting your lip."

He released the lip and tried wooing her. "Mandy..."

"Swithin, we've been together a long time, and maybe we just need some time apart to figure some things out."

"I..."

"I need some time. Okay?"

"I should have never gone to that monastery. I knew it."

"Yes. Yes you should have. Your dad is right about one thing. You are going to be a legend. We all know it. And I don't want you to ever, ever pass up any opportunity because of me. Do you promise?"

"No."

"Swithin, you can't wait for me to get my shit together, okay?" She didn't turn and face him. It was hard enough holding the tears back without seeing him.

He was trying not to cry, but the old song was right. Breaking up was hard to do. Especially when you were the one getting broken up with. He could not understand why she needed space or why where she came from mattered so much, but he'd never been in her situation either. He'd had the charmed life. And he had a feeling the harder he pushed her to stay with him, the further she'd drift. After the dream last night, or whatever it was, he did understand how hard it was to have your mind not be your own and to wake up knowing how things could have been, or feeling as if there were some other force meddling. As a young man of faith, he believed in a higher power, but never had he been so intimate with one. He hated leaving her to it alone, but he solaced she had Thomas, and maybe Tom would be able to lead her from her darkness. "Okay," was all he could finally manage to say.

He wanted to tell her he loved her and that everything would be okay. He wanted to apologize yet again for anything he did that made this all happen, but his mind was a jumble and he was about to break down so he took his leave.

Helen and Thomas glanced over as Swithin glumly reentered the living room.

"Oh, sweetie," Helen stood.

"So, that's it," Swithin swallowed. "She broke up with me."

"Bah," Thomas waved his hand in the air and took a swig of vodka with the other. "Give her a couple of days to realize she's being a jackass and then call her."

"Tom...." Helen chastised.

Swithin stepped into the room and took a seat on the couch. "Has she been having a lot of visions?"

Thomas took another swig. "Not really, no. I dunno. Maybe. She hadn't said."

"What happened while I was gone?"

Thomas shrugged. "We traveled the world, canned some ghosts and had a jolly time."

Swithin scowled at him, unbelieving. "No green devils?"

"Not that I'm aware," Thomas tried holding onto his nonchalance. "In fact, she actually tried contacting them, but they never answered."

"She's your partner. You were supposed to be watching out for her!"

Thomas's composure broke, his face twitched and he took a swig of vodka. "And where were you, lover boy?"

"That's not fair."

"Why? Because you got the chance of a lifetime? You honestly think I'm some heartless prick, don't you? You want to know what we were doing? We were travelling to over 40 countries and countless cities vanquishing ghosts and demons and voodoo lords. But you want know what I was really doing? I talked to nearly every person I've ever met trying to track down those green bitches while you were lapping up spring water in Dali-la-la land."

"Tom!" Helen tried, but Thomas spoke over her.

"You know, I know she puts you up on some pedestal, but the girl had just been attacked by a demon on an airplane. Is your head that far up your father's ass that you could completely ignore that and leave for two years?"

"Tom!" Helen scolded again.

"What?" Thomas went on. "You want to hear about her night terrors and her panic attacks? Her migraines? Her ulcers? Her anxiety got so bad in Zimbabwe, I had to take her to a witch doctor who may or may not have accidentally cursed me. You left her. That's what happened. And I've been cleaning up your mess."

Swithin had nearly bitten through his lip.

Helen huffed. "Thomas, you can't put this all on Swithin."

"I did not sign up for this, but your family made her my problem. Goddamnit! I need a cigarette." He stood and after two steps, back tracked and grabbed his vodka bottle before heading outside.

Two months flew by, and Mandy had not called Swithin. In return, Swithin had called her dozens of times and when she maintained radio silence, he went against his gut, took everyone's suggestion and gave her space.

Random tappings in Mandy's mind told her that the witches kept trying to break in, but she held them off as Eleanor had taught her. It took near constant attention. Mandy had become a guardian, and existence depended on her strength.

The tappings did not improve her mood, and in fact, had worsened it tenfold. Thomas had suggested several ways, and several boys, that would have relieved some of her tension but she buried herself in studying and meditating to prepare herself for her next battle with the bitches.

Likewise, Swithin became obsessed with keeping himself busy. Even Patrick had begun to worry when his son was found dusting the great attic, but only suggested a hunt, instead of anything having to do with the American girl he knew Swithin was so fond of. The hunt turned out to be a bust. A couple in Scotland thought their son had been lured in by a kelpie, but it turned out he had run away to get married to the eldest daughter of a clan they'd been feuding with for decades.

Swithin was not amused, and Patrick didn't offer any more hunts.

Helen tried telling Swithin that Mandy had a lot on her plate, but he already knew that. He just didn't know how to help her, and that's what was driving him insane. Meditation did not help, but he did spend several hours a day practicing Lama Dorje's custom, martial art which kept him focused. He went back to his Nepal routine of eating twice a day and working on his skills, biding his time until an answer came.

Worried about his son's mental health, Patrick threw a ball. The Hook estate hadn't had a gala in quite some time, and the "yes" RSVP's rolled in quickly.

Swithin helped his mother with the last minute preparations, and seven of his eight siblings were coming in for the occasion. His eldest brother, Peter, was a lawyer for the hunting cause and was stuck trying to get newbie Herbert Munsin out of the electric chair for murdering a doppelganger. Helen smiled as her son actually hummed while mixing cake batter. Sometimes her husband had a good idea after all.

The ball couldn't have been prettier. The Hook ballroom led out into a lush courtyard, and everyone was dressed to the nines. With encouragement from his father, Swithin downed his third shot of Irish Moonshine and was suddenly feeling better than he had in weeks when someone tapped him on the shoulder.

"You look lonely over here." It was Missy. Her long black braids fell to her waist.

"Wow." Swithin couldn't help but notice her low-cut powder blue gown, complete with bust enhancing corset. "You look smashing."

She tittered and clasped his arm. Perry Botkin's "Waltz of the Hunter" began playing. "Dance with me? I haven't seen you in so long, and we were best mates at one time, weren't we?"

"And what makes you think we're still not?"

Missy refrained from mentioning Mandy at all costs. "Nothing, I suppose. How sweet of you to hold me in such high regard."

"How could any man here not?" Chivalrously pulling his eyes from her ample assets, he set his empty shot glass down on the old wood bar and followed her out to the dance floor, where she made sure to hold on to him and whisper sweet things in his ear for the rest of the night.

Helen Hook was a woman who believed in letting people make mistakes. After all, being human was about making mistakes. And she'd had enough experience to know that no amount of unsolicited advice would change anyone's mind. She believed that the right thing to do was to stand as an understanding friend or mother or wife when certain decisions backfired.

But when she witnessed her youngest--her miracle baby--dancing cheek-to-cheek with Marta 'Missy' Breathnach, and her husband too gleefully enjoying it, she could not resist intervening.

"Patrick Hook!" she hissed into her husband's ear. "And here I thought you were trying cheer him up when all along you were setting him up. He's not ready!"

"Looks happy to me," Patrick grinned triumphantly. "Besides, no one is making him dance with her."

Helen could not argue that, but also knew that her son was in a vulnerable state. It was obvious to her that Swithin and Mandy were meant to be, no matter the road bumps they would traverse. Not that Helen didn't like Missy, but Missy had more going on in her life than Swithin's well-being, and Swithin's well-being was all that mattered to Helen at the moment.

Mrs. Hook sighed and watched Swithin twirl Missy around the dance floor in perfect elegance. He did seem happier than he'd been in a while, and he and Missy's history went back to childhood. She forced herself to mingle and let her son travel his own journey.

Swithin and Missy met again at a fundraiser the very next week where Swithin maintained a more sober appearance. Alcohol never made him feel right anyway, and he rather regretted canoodling with Missy the week before. She'd called a couple times and they chatted, catching up on lost time, but Swithin still felt she was giving off airs. Once again, she was dressed in a low cut number; purple satin highlighted her curves, and her thick braids were up. She sauntered up to Swithin, who had not had a drink yet. He smiled, making sure to keep his eyes above her chin.

"Missers," he greeted.

"I'm so glad you came tonight!" She hugged him and he gave her a little squeeze. "Mother is thrilled your family showed up. Good for the cause, you know? Nice shirt," she mentioned his tee donning The Clash, beneath his suit coat and red bow tie.

His family was generous at these types of things, which is why they seldom came to them.

"Thanks. You look nice, as well."

Missy overtly bent over to pluck a stray dog hair off her dress which gave Swithin an unobstructed view down the front of her cleavage. He realized he was staring and looked away, uncomfortable and agitated at her flaunt. Della Reese flooded everyone's ears with "Whatever Lola Wants".

"Missers," he said when she'd righted herself.

"Hm?"

"What ever happened to the girl who wore ripped jeans and band tees?"

"Um, I don't know. I grew up." She suddenly remembered he was wearing a band tee. "Well, not that band tees are bad. You pull them off nicely."

"I mean, not that you don't look, um, lovely, but um, maybe we could hang out sometime when you're not, er…hanging out."

Satisfied she'd finally gotten his attention, she laughed and he relaxed, having been nervous about bringing it up. But she pulled up the front of her dress a little, and they spent the rest of the night talking about music and movies like when they were younger. Even though Missy had chosen a difficult path to hunt, she retained her sense of humor, and they fell right back into their old friendship as if no time had passed at all.

Chapter 11
"Time After Time" by Cyndi Lauper

After another week, Thomas couldn't stand being around Mandy any more. Her violent mood swings had become less swings and more constant rage. Between her steady digestive issues, explosive PMS, being terrified that she'd wake up one morning and Thomas would be ripped to shreds and the looming fear of the green women, she never slept. She refused to hunt, practically refused to eat, and Thomas had no idea the last time she'd showered, but the flies were circling.

"I'm not a guy who pries into other people's business, you know that. But this has got to stop. You're going to Wales to make up with that kid and that's that."

"But…"

"That."

Mandy did wish things could just go back to how they were. Maybe Swithin would, too. Why were they fighting anyway? Because Mandy freaked out about the jade clan and had basically lost her mind. She'd thought that pushing him away would keep him safe, but it had only proved to make her miserable, and judging by the phone messages he'd left her a couple of weeks ago, he wasn't faring much better. He'd stopped calling all together, which both pleased her and irked her. She'd gotten her wish, but maybe it wasn't what she should have wished for. To top it off, she was too proud, or embarrassed or some other silly emotion to call and make up. Thomas was right. This called for a face-to-face talk.

Ugh.

Swith'd have to forgive her, though. He'd have to. After all, he was practically perfect.

The ride to Wales time went a lot smoother. Throughout the past few years she had constantly been reminded of Swithin's remark that hunters had soundtracks. Today was no different as the last song that played on her iPod was Air Supply's "All Out of Love." Though Mandy second-glanced anyone wearing green, she made it to the UK in one piece and so, thankfully, did everyone else. It was late by the time she got in and she still hadn't found the courage to call him. She still felt that whatever Gwen wanted was bad, and Gwen wanted Mandy and Swithin together. Still, Mandy was strongest with him so ultimately it was a risk she decided to take.

A cabbie was glad to take her up to the old castle after admitting he'd always wanted to know what was out this way up the long private drive. Mandy nervously babbled about the grounds and the fairytale essence of the place. With a thanks, she handed him a tip forgetting that tipping was mostly unnecessary in the UK. He still took it with a nod and left her at the front of the dark house. No less than three guards were always roaming, and Condel led them all.

Swithin said Condel had been with the estate since he was born, just like his father and his before him. Condel's family was as revered as anyone in matters of security and often gave advice to others about perimeter safety. Embarrassed about the breakup, Mandy nervously approached him, but he warmly greeted her without a hint of judgment, and Mandy remembered how much she felt at home here.

She admitted she wasn't expected, and he regretted to inform her that the family was out at a fundraiser of sorts for an old family friend whose old property needed much repair. He sent a maid for Florence, the head of house.

Florence cackled when she was happy and her cackle nearly deafened Condel and Mandy. Mandy had made friends with the woman on her last visit by sharing some of her American made candy corn, which, of course, she'd brought more of. Florence made sure Mandy had a bite to eat and a cup of tea after a hot shower. Feeling rather undeserving, as she knew they must all know she'd broken up with their favorite youngest son, she also desperately needed the tender loving care Florence was providing. She did let go that she intended to accept his proposal, and Florence cackled again.

"You can wait for him in his room, I daresay," she grinned. "He won't be long now, I wouldn't think."

Mandy thanked her for the umpteenth time as Florence disappeared down the torch lit hallway. Swithin's room was huge; nearly the size of Thomas's house. Mandy paced around a bit, resisting the urge to snoop, and finally laid on the bed. His hair gel had such a distinct sweet smell and she inhaled it. God, he smelled so good. A breeze came in through the open window and danced with the sheer curtains. The quiet and the breeze felt so good. Everything about being here felt good. She wished he'd hurry up so she could talk to him before she lost her mind again.

Agreeing to marry Swithin Hook would be the best thing she could possibly do for herself.

A knock on the door jolted her from the bed as if she was doing something wrong, but it was just Florence.

"I've set your things up in the guest suite down the hall, but thought you may want your purse. You left it in the kitchen."

"Thanks, Flo," Mandy took her satchel.

"Oh, you're so welcome, dear. I'm rooting for you, you know."

"I appreciate that, considering I'm the one that…mucked this up." She caught herself from cursing at the last second. Swithin's positive influence was already working.

"Oh now, dearie, we all have our youths to look back on and think we could have done something better or this or that. All you can do is move forward."

"Thanks, Flo."

The head of house smiled at her and took her leave.

Nerves propelled her up and into the bathroom which was the size of her own bedroom. Of course, Swithin had it decorated with rock music accessories. The AC/DC shower curtain was one of his pride and joys.

She was peeing when he came in, so she couldn't exactly run into his arms, but she finished in time to hear that he was not alone.

"You know if my da finds us, he'll kill us," Swithin's voice carried through the stone walls.

"Bah, your dad loves me."

Mandy cringed. Missy Breathnach. In his room.

"Yes, well, Father Murphy might not after confession on Sunday."

"You're going to tell him?"

"I tell him everything," Swithin confessed.

"Everything?"

And the quiet that followed could only mean one thing. Missy had her tongue down Swithin's throat. Mandy's insides clenched so hard, she vurped tea and biscuits. The bathroom had another door that led to the hallway and Mandy made quick use of the escape route.

It was late and she didn't see anyone else on her hurried way out of the castle. She'd even managed to evade the three guards on her way up to the old family cemetery. How could she be mad? She'd told him not to pass up any opportunities, hadn't she? She'd broken up with him, hadn't she? She'd ignored him viciously.

But Missy?

Ugh.

Out of breath and sobbing, Mandy reached the old family graves. It may not have been the best place where memories were concerned, but it was familiar in a mostly alien landscape. Her mind whirled with how to get home without him ever knowing she was here, but Florence and Condel would surely tell him. No, Mandy was stuck with no way out, but to face the fact that she'd blown it big time.

She had her phone in her pocket and considered calling him. That way, it would leave him an out where Missy was concerned. He could admit his relationship or not and Mandy could act like she never knew about it. She wished she didn't.

Gaining composure, she noticed the stone at which she sat was Swithin's deceased sister.

Tinkerbell Carys Hook.

She couldn't decipher the Irish and Welsh inscriptions, but they were beautiful whatever they were. She ran her fingers over the engravings. "I don't suppose I could get a little help?"

She suddenly felt a distinct presence and glanced up to notice a candle burning in the tiny cemetery chapel. The old stones seemed to barely hold up the wooden roof, and the whole thing was barely larger than a small shed. She warily stood, half expecting to meet this Bell, but balked as a woman in a short green a-line dress and matching pillbox hat stepped from the little stone structure.

"Hello, Amanda. We think it's time you come home."

A slight movement to her left caused Mandy to strike out and another lady clad in kelly green fell. Agathon, Nharlthop and Jalajae were among the small coven.

"Nharlthop," Mandy near pleaded, "remember when I was little and you used to bring my drawings to life?"

The witch's face flickered at the memory, but she did not move to help. Mandy's time away from these monsters had molded her into a fighter thanks to intense self-defense classes and Thomas's love of boxing. Three more witches came from the shadows. She was a fighter, not an imbecile, so Mandy yelled out for help.

"They'll never get here on time, dear," Gwen touted.

Encircled, Mandy weighed her options and none of them were good. She faked heading for the gal in front of her and instead round housed the woman to the left, which threw the other two off enough so that Mandy could take out the one in front with a left hook. She ducked and swept for a leg, but the woman was not behind her as expected, but standing with the Headmistress.

"Vulgar display, Amanda," the Headmistress scolded. "But informative nonetheless."

The last thing Mandy felt before falling was a small needle prick in her back, and the last thing she heard was the pretentious Headmistress Gwen. "We'll have to secure you tighter than I thought."

Swithin had given into Missy's advances, much to her elation, but try as he might, he could not shake a feeling of shame. He wasn't in love with Missy, but he was overwhelmed by his situation with Mandy, and Missy was an attractive, willing distraction. None of which made it right for him to be fondling Missy's bits. And still, here he was betwixt and between with her, not not enjoying it.

Being tangled up naked in silk sheets made it difficult for Swithin to not clumsily answer the gentle rapping in his bedroom door. Missy told him to ignore it, but a dark tingling told him he couldn't.

"Florence," he nervously cleared his throat upon cracking open the door. "What, ah, um, is there an emergency, love?"

Florence averted her eyes even if he was wrapped in a sheet and standing mostly behind a door. "Well, not exactly, I don't think, Master Swithin, but, oh, forgive me for prying, but I was just wondering and well, so I came by and I thought maybe things were going well, but…"

"You can't tell da, Florence. Please. Geez, Father Murphy's already going to have me doing penance for a month."

"Oh! Oh, mum's the word, dearie, but that voice with you, um, well?"

"Florence. Spit it out."

"Mandy's come to accept your proposal."

Swithin leaned in closer to the head of house. "Repeat that?"

"She arrived earlier, and we were in the kitchen and I got the more than distinct impression that she was only here for one reason."

Now it was Swithin's turn to swallow bile. "Where is she?"

"She was here. Waiting for you. That's the last I saw her. I didn't realize that you and Miss Breathnach were..."

Numb, Swithin didn't even realize he shut the door in Florence's face.

Missy bounced up from the bed across the room. "Come back, Swithers! You have no idea how long I've fantasized about this!" Her mirth disappeared when she saw Swithin's dire look. He didn't answer her questions, but began searching the room, including the bathroom, which he noticed had an unflushed toilet and an ajar second door.

"Swithin!" Missy whined as he threw on clothes. "Hey!" She grabbed his arm and spun him around. "What is going on?"

"Missy, I am so sorry. I know that doesn't begin to cover it, but I am so...Sorry."

Missy's tone flattened. "Amanda's here, isn't she?"

"Somewhere. Apparently. Excuse me."

He flew from the room amidst her cries of protest and began searching the castle. He ran into Florence in the kitchen and asked her to help him look for Mandy.

The three guards were called in as well to help search the massive grounds, and the castle wasn't so big that Patrick and Helen weren't soon alerted to the situation. Helen's priority became consoling Missy, as Missy wouldn't have it any other way, while Patrick berated Florence for not telling him of Mandy's arrival. Florence had lived with the family long enough to know how to handle Patrick and his temper. It wasn't the first time he'd fired her and it wouldn't be the last.

The grounds were grand and the castle was vast, so after ten minutes, Swithin wasn't so worried, but as minutes added up, he finally had a horrible, awful feeling along with a moment of clarity. The cemetery.

He raced past the gardens and through the woods, guards in tow at his command.

The cemetery yielded nothing.

"I know she was here," Swithin believed. "I know it."

"Son," Patrick had come with him lest there be danger, as he believed Mandy was incapable of being without it.

"Aneirin!" Swithin yelled for the graveyard's ghost. Aneirin had been the first of his mother's ancestors to be buried here and had stuck around to keep an eye on things. No one had ever seen him, but they all knew he was here. Sometimes he was nice to talk to when Swithin hadn't felt quite like confessing to Father Murphy. Aneirin had never seemed judgmental and he never talked back, but Swithin had to find a way to communicate with him.

"What makes you think she was here?" Patrick asked.

"I just know. Because I know her better than anyone. I know her better than she knows herself. I should have come here first. I should have never given up on her. God Damnit!"

"Boy!" Patrick sternly reprimanded the cuss.

Swithin would have to work hard on forgiving himself for his delusional indulgence in Missy. With any luck, both the girls could forgive him at some point as well. But that wasn't at the forefront of his mind. He scoured the ground, and the trees and the stones for any sign that she'd been here. Patrick sighed heavily, but said naught and waited for his son to do what he needed to do.

"Aneirin!" Swithin shouted again. "Please!"

Nearly another minute passed, and Patrick nearly opened his mouth to call Swithin away, but their eyes were drawn to the sudden candlelight in the small chapel.

Patrick warily accompanied Swithin to the tiny dwelling, and Swithin poked his head in, immediately noticing the green hat pin on the broken stone floor.

Swithin's knees gave out and he crumpled, sobbing until he threw up.

"Seal the grounds," Patrick ordered the guards nearby, knowing it was too late. He let Swithin go on until he had nothing left to heave and quietly helped him back to the house.

Swithin had regained some semblance of composure, but Missy greeted him in the kitchen, and it took everything he had to confront her. His mother was preparing her famous border tarts, and Swithin took a seat at the table. Surprisingly, one of the smaller rooms in the castle, the kitchen, was where the Hooks gathered in times of trouble, and Helen baked when she could do nothing else.

Missy must have heard the news already because she didn't speak; either that or she was just as mortified as Swithin that they'd been caught. If her parents found out, they would disown her. She lost the will to drink and pushed the tea away.

"Thank you for the tea, Mrs. H," Missy nodded to Helen and stood to leave. When it was obvious that she was not going to talk to him, Swithin grabbed her hand gently, and she turned to speak first. "I knew it was a long shot. Me and you. I hope she's okay."

She didn't give Swithin a chance to respond before she pulled away and took her leave. Not that he wanted to make a big scene in front of his mother, but Swithin wished Missy would have at least yelled at him.

Helen had already gotten onto the network to alert everyone of Mandy's kidnapping which meant Swithin had to call Thomas ASAP before he heard it from someone else.

"What do you mean *gone*?" Thomas inquired sharply.

Swithin was having trouble keeping his emotions in check. "They took her. Sometime in the last hour."

"Well, that's just all tickety boo and shit, isn't it? Why weren't you with her? Did you see her? Did she get to your place all right? Where did they pick her up?"

Swithin slammed his fist down on the table, startling his mother as he composed his answer. "I was out. And she was outside waiting in the family crypt."

Thomas held his tongue for a moment which prompted Swithin to ask if he was still there. Thomas answered by tsking. "I'd expect this from me. But you? You were shacking up with another girl already, weren't you?"

Mortified, Swithin handed the phone over to his mother. "I...can't talk to him anymore."

Helen took the phone and upbraided Thomas. "He's having a rough enough time as it is without you adding."

"Oh, it's not his fault. Those emerald devils were bound to catch up with her sooner or later."

"Any suggestions?"

Thomas had nothing. "We don't know a thing about them. Unless…"

"Yes?"

"Look, they don't want to kill her. They want to prick and prod her, but we'll see her again. Keep in touch."

"Aye. You do the same."

Helen clicked the phone off and set a consoling hand on her sulking son's shoulder. "He's going after Erickson's cave," she stated with a distinct nod to trouble.

Swithin perked up.

"Don't go getting any ideas!" she warned. "Dyna fy nghynnig, ac os ydych yn ceisio sleifio i ffwrdd, byddaf yn cwrdd â chi yno a byddaf yn spank chi! Nid ydych yn rhy hen i chi wybod!"

Swithin stepped away after the threat of a good old-fashioned spanking and tentatively knocked on the door of his father's study where he was called in. Patrick looked up from his papers and greeted his youngest offspring. "How you holding up?"

Swithin had no positive answer and closed the door behind him. "Am I being punished?"

Patrick stiffened slightly at the unexpected question. "Why would you say that?"

"Because I made a sort of agreement with God and I broke it. And now…" He could not verbally affirm that Mandy had been taken without breaking down again.

"God does not make accords. He set down a pile of rules and expects us to follow them and admit it when we've faltered."

"I thanked him nearly every day for her. I promised Him she was the one I was going to spend the rest of my life with, and when she broke up with me, I was so angry that I not only betrayed Mandy and my promise to Him, I mislead Missy, and now Mandy's gone which never happened until I…"

He had trouble admitting to himself that he'd been with Missy.

"Listen here, boy, we all falter. It's what makes us human after all, and if you think God is punishing you for your little indiscretions of the flesh, then you think much too highly of yourself. Those abominable women would have come for her sooner or later. We all knew it and there was going to be no stopping them. They trespassed on my land to do it! The monsters! Condel is in a fit over it, and I'll be lucky if he doesn't quit!"

Unable to shake his self-pity, Swithin stood, berating himself for his actions. Wherever Mandy was, the last memory she had of him was knowing he was with Missy. Even if God could forgive him, or not care, how could he ever forgive himself? Worse than his fling with Missy was the fact that he'd given up on his relationship with Mandy in the first place.

"Look, son," Patrick stood and grabbed a bottle of scotch from a glass cabinet. "Mandy's strong, and they're not going to kill her anyway." He poured two glasses and handed one to Swithin. "I'll admit, I'm not innocent in all this mess," he went on, "I should have been guiding you through this instead of praying the problem would go away. When Missy started courting you, I saw you were hurting and angry, but I thought that maybe Missy would win you over, and I let it happen. Even at its weakest, wrath is a powerful vice to carry. I should have been there for you, son. I'm sorry."

Swithin had to admit that he had been feeling a bit vengeful toward Mandy for breaking his heart, but Missy hadn't helped matters. "It was my decision," he took the blame, however, brushed past his dad and headed for the safest place he could think of.

"Tart?"

He huffed and took one, unable to turn down his mother's lemon tarts no matter his emotional state. "I can't just sit here and do nothing! There must be someone we can ask for help. There must be something we can do. I can't just spend my days praying that she'll come back."

"I pray Thomas will find something useful on the green whores."

Thinking on what he'd just said, Swithin suddenly sat up straight. "Pray. Mum!"

"Yes, dear?"

"The gods. You've been so loyal. Do you think they would help?"

"Oh. Oh, well, I don't know. You know they've been awfully quiet for a long time now. I mean, not that I've ever actually talked to one in person, of course. But the offerings used to vanish at least, and sometimes my prayers were answered. But, hm. Well, yes. Yes, it's been nearly a decade since I've felt them near. I don't know, Swithin."

"It's worth a shot. Can we ask?"

She poured a cup of tea and contemplated hard. "We'll need a pretty enticing offering."

"Like what?"

"Something you love. Something irreplaceable."

After a moment to ponder, he knew just the thing.

He met her out in her stone garden where she was setting down herbs and incense. "What did you bring, sweetheart?"

"Two years of my life." He handed over his journal from Nepal which he'd written primarily for Mandy.

She took the journal gingerly, nodded approvingly and set it gently down in the circle of prepared dried flowers and spices.

Patrick appeared not long after, but before Helen had started the summoning. "What's all this?" he asked, concerned.

"I'm going to try and summon help," Helen answered. "Now, step out of the circle."

Patrick blanched. "You're not going to try and bring one of those...those..."

"Careful," Helen warned. "They may be listening."

"I don't care if they are! You will cease this nonsense!"

Helen reddened, and Swithin stepped back a pace. His mother was a crown of calm under most circumstances, but when it came to her deities and her children, the mama bear came out. Patrick realized too late what he'd done in his ire at the entire situation, but not in time to escape the backlash of his words.

"Now, you see here!" Helen laid into him. "I gave you four of my children to raise as you pleased when it comes to faith and said not a word about the absence of your lord and god! My faith is mine to do with as I please, and if Swithin needs my help, or if he chooses to call to my gods, then that is his prerogative and his choice to deal with! I will not sit by and..."

"Helen!" Patrick yelled. "Okay! I'm sorry, my love. I'm sorry! I'm just flustered. You know that. If your..." he always fretted to use the word 'god' when it came to them, "Well, if they can help find the girl, then that is what must be done."

Helen calmed nearly instantly, which never ceased to amaze Swithin. His mother was the only one who could ever put Patrick in his place and the only one who Patrick ever apologized genuinely to. Helen turned back to her stone circle and began a long chant in ancient Gaelic. Patrick wrung his hands nervously, worrying that God was taking notes about his fraternizing with false gods while Swithin silently prayed to whoever he thought would listen about bringing Mandy home safely. Helen finished the incantation and stepped out of the circle, putting her finger to her lips in order to keep the boys quiet.

They all watched the journal and the circle of offerings for several minutes. Patrick finally tapped Helen on the shoulder, but she intently leaned forward, and a second later, the journal caught on fire. The three of them jolted. Swithin desperately hoped the burning journal was a good sign. He hadn't made any copies.

From behind them, a smooth feminine voice sang out.

"'S iomaí oíche fliuch is fuar

Thug mé cuairt is mé liom féin

Nó go ráinig mé san áit

Mar a raibh grá geal mó chléibh."

Swithin, Helen and Patrick turned to envision a sparkling, unworldly woman with thick red braids down to her feet woven with the light of fallen stars.

Swithin finished the song, Bheir mí ó.

"There's no music in my harp

My fingers knew naught but pain,

Then your kiss, that wondrous barb,

Brought song to my life again."

The goddess smiled and looked to Helen. "You have raised him well."

Helen bowed her head. "Much obliged, Goddess. Yes, he is a good child."

"I know," the goddess cooed. Her yellow robes flowed of their own accord. "I am Áine. And that is how I know."

Helen bowed her head further and gestured Patrick to do the same. When he hesitated, Helen explained that Áine was a goddess of fertility, and when he still debated on whether or not to bow to a god that was not his Almighty, Helen kicked his shin crumpling him over involuntarily.

Áine laughed a sweet tinkle of a laugh. "Helen, you have been loyal to the gods for so long, as has your family for many generations. I can forgive your husband's impertinence."

Patrick went to defend himself, but Helen kicked him again. Swithin and the goddess laughed.

"I know why you have summoned me, Helen Hook, but I am afraid I can be of little use."

As excited as Swithin was to see a real goddess, his heart sank.

Áine went on airily. "The modern age has been unkind to us, Helen Hook, but you have fairly raised your kin to appreciate our work and so I have come to you, but know this: I cannot help you find the girl you seek. The monster holding her--the monster who made her is impervious to our ways and we cannot ail him. They have warded themselves against us long ago and continue their ways of damaging existence."

"Him? Gwen is a woman," Swithin stated.

Helen glanced sharply at her son, but the goddess seemed not to mind the interrogation.

The goddess nodded. "He is the mastermind behind it all."

"Are they really Prima Covina?" Swithin questioned, pushing away the fact there was someone worse than Gwen.

"They have long sought out the truths of the universe and have unlocked enough to be ruinous. Gods from every realm have held together the fabrics they have frayed, and it may yet come to the time when we join you here to confront a great enemy."

"And Amanda?" Swithin pushed for answers, "What is her part?"

"That is yet to be known. Those who made her searched only for a doorway to knowledge, but know not what they have potentially unleashed."

"And what is that?" Patrick lifted his head and stood defiantly tall.

Áine pondered over her answer as if deciding the most appropriate way to answer Patrick and finally looked straight at him and said, "God."

Patrick blustered and sputtered much to the goddess's bemusement, but Helen and Swithin did not chuckle this time.

"God?" Swithin asked. "As in, like, God? I didn't know that gods and goddesses, you know, believed in God."

"We all answer to a higher power. The universe goes by many names. You and he call it God."

Swithin and Helen tried wrapping their minds around this, while Patrick still huffed to the side, but Swithin had to ask the question out loud that the other two were obviously thinking. "Are you trying to tell us that Mandy is....um...God?"

"Now, that is quite enough!" Patrick roared, but the goddess ignored him.

"She has great potential for power," she answered softly. "And there are those who protect her for that potential and those who wish her dead for it. All in the universe, be it stardust, or water, or goddess or ant has one thing in common. We all have come from the same energy. If it has been unlocked, things will become dire indeed." She floated to Swithin and grazed her radiant hand along his face. "She will need light."

Swithin immediately detected a hint of something he could only believe to be maple syrup, and he suddenly had another intense craving for waffles. He also did not miss the fact that she mentioned his glowing capabilities.

She stepped away from him. "Mandy's mortal being cannot comprehend her vast knowledge, but she has, at her fingertips, all that ever was and ever will be. The stronger she becomes, the more danger she will be in. And still, the more good she can do."

"The Agency," Swithin fretted.

"Cannot ever be allowed past the black barrier in Mandy's mind. I cannot stay longer. My mortal-like essence does not regenerate as it used to. Take care and know that there are those of us doing our parts even if you cannot see it. And Helen, I thank you again for your patronage. You keep us well. The tarts are much appreciated."

Áine faded away quickly leaving the three to ponder the predicament, but none had anything to say, save for Patrick. "Those aren't gods. They're monsters and should be treated as such!"

"Hold your tongue!" Helen reprimanded. "Or I'll hold it for you! Where is your God anyway?"

"Busy, I'm sure," he defended.

While his parents bickered, Swithin's mind whirled. "It's bad, then. So much worse than any of us could have thought."

Helen and Patrick halted their arguing.

"There were others like her, she said," Swithin went on. "But they're all gone now. None of them were old. Not even 19 yet, she guessed. We have to find her."

Even Patrick could not argue that point.

To his father's grave disapproval, Swithin put up the title to his inheritance to anyone who delivered Mandy to him, but no one could.

Thomas visited the mysterious cavern, but there was nothing to be found on Prima Covina.

Helen worked overtime baking.

Chapter 12
"Girlfight" by Brooke Valentine

Eleanor had been doing her part in trying to locate Mandy, though she did have to be somewhat secretive about the whole thing. Dodson hadn't exactly forbidden her to use her psychic reach to find Mandy, but he had strongly discouraged it for the safety of the pack.

But Dodson hadn't been inside Mandy's head. He could not understand what she was linked to and the damage that could be done if Gwen broke her.

Though Thomas worried inwardly for Mandy's well-being, he'd shrugged it off as a minor hiccup in life. He had no doubt she'd be returned, though in what condition, he would never have wagered. He found his home to be oddly disquieting without her antics. Who would have known? His appetite for greasy food, beer, gambling and adult sleepovers hadn't waned until he got an unexpected call from an old adversary.

"Hello, Regal."

"Dodson Fer. Well, well, well," Thomas tried keeping his air of nonchalance, but if the werewolf was calling him, it meant nothing good. "This can't be good."

"No," Dodson replied. "And the only reason I'm calling is because I'm desperate. Is Eleanor with you?"

Thomas sighed. "How long has she been missing?"

"Two days. She won't or can't answer her cell. It's the first time I've ever wished she was with you."

Thomas Regal was not a man to let emotions get the better of him. He'd been there, done that. He'd even pulled back where Mandy was concerned when he felt himself getting too close. Getting close to people never ended well. But Eleanor had wormed her way inside long before he'd learned to avoid relationships.

"Tom?" Dodson broke the silence.

Thomas didn't answer.

"Tom, do you think this has anything to do with Amanda's disappearance?"

Thomas knew it did. He didn't know how he knew, but he knew for certain that the green vipers had something to do with it.

"Tom?"

"Let's hope not," Thomas finally answered.

Dodson didn't say anything for a long while, and the two men sat pondering the situation.

"Things are bad," Dodson finally said.

"Things have always been bad."

"But even over the last hundred years, things have escalated. Do we really think those green she devils are behind it?"

Helen had filled Thomas in on what her goddess had said. He had no trouble believing it. The green bitches were trouble, and Mandy was undoubtedly troubled. They went hand in hand. "Unless you can find them, we won't know. I imagine that's why Eleanor is missing. She tried to find Mandy while you told her not to."

"Why you...!"

"If you had supported her, been with her, she wouldn't be missing. Mandy needs to be found."

"So, you're just going to sit around on your bare, pink ass and drink while they're out there?"

"I've already looked for them. I traveled the world doing so and came up with little less than nothing. That's right. I knew less by the time I was done, so please, lecture me some more on how much I don't love your wife."

Dodson grumbled something, and the men hung up without more words. If Swithin's inheritance hadn't been enough incentive to find the jade devils, maybe Eleanor's disappearance would light some fires. She had been a beloved legend in the community since a young age. He rarely felt helpless, but Thomas dealt with it by putting his fist through the drywall of his pristine living room.

Wiccans of Light were in short supply this day and age. Evil hunted them relentlessly, and so few witches, no matter how pure of heart, chose the path. Eleanor travelled to New York City to visit the only one she knew of.

"Namaste! Come in! Come in!" Cyndi greeted from inside her studio apartment.

Eleanor felt bad about disappearing, but she had no desire for her pack to be involved. She entered through neon peace beads into the spacious apartment and was handed a glass of fresh-squeezed organic orange juice by a bellbottomed woman with feathers in her straight hair.

"A wolf!" Cyndi observed wide eyed. "Far out."

"Thank you," Eleanor smiled. She hadn't expected a hippie. She hadn't known exactly what to expect, but the peace in this room could not be denied.

"What's up?" the wiccan asked, taking a meditative position on an overstuffed pillow.

"I need to find Amanda Heart," Eleanor admitted. "I'm strong, but she is well guarded."

The girl popped open one eye, but did not say what she was thinking. Eleanor knew that everyone had heard of Mandy by now, thanks to Swithin's inheritance offer. The Light Witch finally smiled and jumped up from her pillow. "You need more juice!" She banged around her kitchen grinding and pouring and shaking. A Wiccan of Light's primary job in the world was to produce positive energy and unleash it. They spent 90% of their time meditating and producing happy thoughts, 9% of their time rebuilding protection spells to hide them from the evils who wished them harm and 1% doing whatever else they did. They kept to themselves and moved often so it was difficult for even the good guys to find them. But they were the most powerful of the Light magic, and Eleanor only knew of Cyndi through an old contact of Thomas's. The good witch wasted no time handing over a potion with a smile, as if Eleanor had asked for a cup of sugar.

"Good luck, man. We'll all need it if those skags break her."

Eleanor didn't waste any more time, though she could have bathed in the positive light all day. "Thank you, Cyndi."

"Yeah, yeah," Cyndi shrugged.

"Can I pay you?"

"We're even-steven. Just kick some green butt. They're bruising my auras."

"Will do."

"Man, that Tomcat of yours was quite the gas way back when."

Eleanor smiled upon several conflicting memories of Thomas. "He's something all right."

Eleanor settled herself in a shack not terribly far from her pack's homestead in the Tongass National Forest. The Alaskan forest held the title of the largest in America at 16.9 million acres; a perfect place for a pack of werewolves, among others, to make their home. She set her precious herbs on black ceramic plates and lit them on fire in order to inhale the fumes. Her brain began tingling, and after a moment, her eyes glowed white with energy.

While Swithin nursed a stress-induced ulcer, Mandy caught up on reading. Once she'd awoken from the dart's tranquilizer, she found herself in a plush bedroom lined from floor to ceiling with books. She even found a small Siamese cat curled up at the foot of the king-sized bed. The door was closed, but not locked, and, cat in arm, she went exploring.

Candles automatically lit as she walked by, only to snuff once she'd gotten far enough away. Besides the cat, the manor was devoid of life. A thick mist surrounded the grounds, but when she chanced walking into it, she only reappeared in her bedroom.

Over time, she found that the kitchen restocked itself with her favorite foods so she sucked it up, biding her time reading by the fire, cat snoozing on her lap, waiting for the next kerfuffle.

She was not so engrossed in a copy of *Lots of Ways To Replace Cat Skin*, that she didn't notice the floor board creak behind her. "It's about time," she said to the noise without turning.

"I do apologize for my delay," Gwen responded. "You aren't my only experiment, you know."

"Charming." Mandy stood, rousting the cat from her lap.

"Ah!" Gwen noted of the feline. "You are getting on well with her?"

Mandy almost smiled. "She's cute."

"I was talking to the cat," Gwen corrected.

"Of course you were. So. What now?"

Gwen sighed. "This is new territory for me, which is exciting, but the end result must be me getting inside that portal. You can make it easy or difficult."

"It's not gonna happen."

"Amanda," Gwen took a few steps toward her, her green pumps clicking on the hardwood floor. "I will admit that it has been almost fun watching you grow and learn and fall in love. Once you were out of our controlled environment, you flourished. So much so, that we tried to replicate it, but it seems that only you have been strong enough to make it this far."

"Murderer," was all Mandy could manage. She was barely holding herself together in front of the witch, but she knew a physical attack would bear no results.

"Amanda, that portal in your head allows for endless power; enough to cure disease, war, famine and maybe even death."

"I'm not sure how the four horsemen are going to feel about that."

"I can't say I didn't expect you to choose the difficult path, but I'm warning you, no one knows you're here. No one is coming to save you."

"I'm not the one that needs saving. Existence does, and I plan to defend it to my death."

Gwen sighed. "Have it your way." She thrust her hand out, and Mandy went flying into the chair behind her.

Before Mandy could regain her senses, she found herself back inside her head in the familiar field. "Shit."

Gwen was there too, but she was not alone. Her three minion sisters were there, too. Sometimes, it had almost seemed if bedraggled Jalajae, short Nharlthop and unnaturally thin Agathon did not agree with Gwen's methods, but Mandy could never get them to admit it. Even now, they did not look as determined as she did, but Mandy did not let her guard down.

"Where is the portal, Amanda?" Gwen asked.

"At the corner of fuck you street and blow me lane."

"Now, who's charming?"

The group attacked at once. The field in her mind exploded into chants and strong winds and rumblings; all designed to push her toward the portal. Every ounce of Mandy's concentration was needed in order to keep from thinking about the portal; to do so would give away its whereabouts. She still had no idea what it was or where it lead, and she wasn't sure she wanted to. She envisioned a piece of paper slowly burning from the middle out to the edge. Not only did it keep her mind from giving away secrets, it made it too hot for the witches to stay long, and they were ousted.

The Agency was more powerful in their own lair and tougher to defeat. But Mandy never forgot what Eleanor had said about it being her mind and that she controlled what was in it. What Eleanor hadn't mentioned was the stamina needed to ward off attacks over a long period of time.

The assaults when Gwen or her crones tried to get inside her mind came often and with no pattern. Mandy would be reading or sleeping or bathing, or worse. Mandy would slip away to her field of doors and keep them at bay with illusions and willpower. Thinking of anything but keeping them out would give them an inch toward the dark portal they so desperately wanted.

She tired, but so did they. Distressing thing was, there were more of them. None were as powerful as Gwen, but the others took their turns wearing Mandy down. Exhausted, but unable to really sleep without fear of attack, time was growing short before Gwen and her green hags broke through Mandy's defenses and made their way through the portal. Mandy focused on an impenetrable wall of hot light surrounding her mind and could think of nothing and no one else lest they use the weakness to defeat her.

Mandy was surprised to be out of breath in her own mind, but it was time for a long overdue discussion. "I'm not giving up. I owe it to all those children you kidnapped and murdered."

Gwen chuckled. "My sweet thing, I didn't murder anyone. Now, if you are asking why you have survived, our calculations concluded that you had the one thing none of the others had. Something to live for."

It took a few seconds for Mandy to comprehend what Gwen was saying, but it twanged her gut hard. "They all committed suicide."

"I was going to bring you back. But as I watched you, I saw something new. You were falling in love. You found a family. A life. It has made you strong. I still haven't been able to replicate it, and even though I would like two of you to conduct proper research, I have accepted that just you will have to do."

"Well, Gwennie," Mandy had decided her plan already. "The thing about giving someone something to live for is that it also gives them something to die for."

Mandy took the risk and left Gwen alone in her psyche steps away from the portal she yearned for, and Gwen did take a short moment to consider it, but she needed Mandy alive.

Mandy shook off her return and glanced around her lush bedroom cell for anything to cause fatal damage. Books, no, a pillow? She couldn't suffocate herself. Not in time, anyway.

There was a picture on the far wall with a glass frame.

She ran to it and ripped it from the wall before smashing it on the floor. A large shard glistened, and she picked it up. The door to her room was unlocking and Gwen was screaming from the other side. Before Mandy did what she knew had to be done, she silently apologized to Swithin and Thomas, and plunged the glass into her heart.

The lack of pain surprised her, but the warm liquid told her it was done.

Still, she should have felt something. She looked down and her chest was wet, but not a drop of blood in sight. The glass has melted into water.

Gwen tsked from behind her. "Nice try, sweet pea. Restrain her," she ordered her multiplying minions.

Mandy would not be taken easily. She kicked and punched, taking down a couple of the witchy vermin, but they outnumbered her eight to one and tied her to the bed.

"Comfy?" Gwen asked.

Mandy huffed and closed her eyes. Exhaustion had overtaken her long ago and adrenaline had taken over, but it was waning. Mandy disappeared back inside her mind for what she knew would be her losing battle.

"Amanda!"

Mandy turned to see Eleanor and nearly fainted with joy.

"Are you real?"

Eleanor smiled and hugged her. "Yes. Yes, I'm here."

"Well, well," Gwen reappeared with reinforcements. "Just when I think I will get the upper hand, I'm surprised. How disappointing."

Eleanor growled, and everyone perked up.

"Do you really think your ability will help in here?" Gwen sneered. "We're not in your forests, young beastie."

"No. In here, I am so much more powerful." The next second, Eleanor had transformed into a towering monster; a much easier feat in the mental realm.

The battle for Mandy's mind ensued. With Eleanor's much needed help, Mandy was able to keep the green monsters at bay. Eleanor's lithe wolf shape gnashed and pounced upon the witches, calling out incantations and dissipating them into green dust. Once the nine of them were gone, Eleanor shrank back to her human self and assured Mandy that the women would not be back soon.

Mandy wanted to leave her mind and crawl into bed, but she knew she could only visit with Eleanor here. Still, she sank to the grass. It smelled so real and felt soft. "What is it?" she referred to the void on which the witches wanted so badly to enter. "What am I?"

Eleanor sighed and did not answer straightaway. But she did eventually answer. "Did you ever learn about physics?"

Mandy blew out a laugh. "Gwen was obsessed with it. Not that I ever saw her more than once back then, but physics were a large part of the mandatory curriculum."

"And you learned of Higgs bosun?"

"The God Particle? Yeah. I had to write a paper on it."

Eleanor looked to Mandy, expectantly waiting for Mandy to put two and two together. Tired as she was, it didn't take her long. "Are you saying that's what they were using me for? To discover the building blocks of the universe?"

Eleanor nodded. "But they did so much more. They manipulated your DNA to the point where they finally ripped a hole into matter itself. That dark spot in your psyche is a portal to an edge of time or the edge of the universe. I don't know. And I'm sure it holds more questions than answers, but they want it nonetheless. Mandy," Eleanor got down into the grass with her. "I seriously considered killing you the first time we met."

Mandy's stomach twisted. "Why didn't you?"

It seemed that Eleanor was trying to formulate a response, but she never answered and Mandy didn't pry. Eleanor's mind was melding with hers and she could feel that it had something to do with Thomas.

Mandy stood, wincing, as it felt like needles had been shoved into her skull. Ever curious about her anomaly, she blinked and she and Eleanor were standing by the black crevasse.

Eleanor let out a whine as the blackened wrinkle had dilated ever so slightly. It pulsed and oozed; a dark slimy entrance to worlds beyond.

"I'm so sorry, Amanda," Eleanor set a hand on Mandy's shoulder. "I should have told you what I suspected but..."

"It's okay," Mandy assured. "I know why you didn't. It terrifies me enough as it is, now that I know. I'm putting everything and everyone I know in danger just by being alive."

"I'm right here," Eleanor reassured. "We'll get through this. Close your eyes, Mandy. Envision a thick wall of impenetrable light pouring over your head. Picture it. Enforce it. Hold it. They must never ever get inside this passage. And Mandy," Eleanor took Mandy by the shoulders and looked her in the eye. "You must ignore your temptations to go through yourself. Do you understand? Too much power will warp you. You will lose yourself, Swithin and Thomas. You will become something else entirely."

Mandy eyed the door and cringed at the energy it leaked. If the answers to creation were indeed behind it, she wanted to keep it shut. She wanted nothing to do with it.

Eventually, the witches broke back into her head. If Eleanor hadn't been there to lend Mandy the strength she needed, Gwen and her lackeys would have won the battle. Hammer blows assaulted Mandy's head each and every time. Eleanor used her prowess to push them away and to remain strong to encourage Mandy, who slowly but surely learned to control what went on in her own psyche and protect the entrance to the edge of time at all costs.

At long last, Mandy awoke in her room with a start. Her real room in Thomas's house. Everything was quiet, and the small basement window indicated either dusk or dawn. She stepped out of bed, fully dressed and hurting everywhere. Gashes she'd received in her mind bled though her skin. Mind games took a toll on everything.

She limped to her door and opened it, calling for Thomas, but he didn't answer. Mandy made her way to the stairs and pulled herself up. In the kitchen, Headmistress Gwen sat, sipping tea.

"Welcome home, Amanda," she smiled. "If you want to stay here, all you have to do is give us what we want."

Mandy managed a laugh. "You mean, a trip to the edge of the universe where you can try and harness unfathomable power. Yah. No. In fact, I'm beginning to think it would be better for everyone if no one had access to it."

She grabbed a knife from the counter and before Gwen could stop her, she slid it across her neck, hard and deep.

As Mandy bled out onto the floor, Gwen came to stand over her, tsking. "It is becoming too much for you isn't it?"

She leaned down over Mandy's gurgling face and arched her eyebrows in a pleased way. "Good."

Mandy awoke with a start in her own bed again. "Awe, shit." Her neck was clean and she headed back up to the kitchen where Gwen sat again.

"Soon," Gwen announced," you won't be able to tell your mind from reality. With all of your strength protecting that black hole to the edge of existence, I will break you easily and still get what I want. Even with that she-bitch helping. I have learned much from the others. I will not fail with you."

"Then, round and round we go," Mandy grabbed the knife off the counter and threw it at the witch, but it went right through her.

Mandy concentrated on Eleanor and suddenly found herself next to her in the field.

They'd been inside Mandy's mind for an indeterminate amount of time. Time flowed different here, so it was impossible to tell.

Ellie sighed. "I've been away from my body for too long. I can feel it."

"Then you need to go," Mandy urged.

"I have a plan," she cut Mandy off again. "I have no idea if it will work and it will probably be uncomfortable to say the least."

Two green ones broke back into Mandy's mind with a vengeance, and Mandy used her imagination to shove them into giant cheese graters. She and Eleanor protected the black abyss in the back of her psyche with everything they had, causing illusions, traps and powerful energy surges that forced the women out of Mandy's mind. Eleanor had taken her wolf form, as it seemed to give her more energy.

Gwen threatened Eleanor's kin more than once, but Eleanor did not back down. "If you get a hold of that power, they won't be safe anyway," she replied huskily in wolf form.

"And your son?" Gwen hissed. "Are you so sure he is so well protected?"

Mandy hadn't known Eleanor had any children, but admired Eleanor's strength and faith all the more. "I am," was all she said.

"Then, you are a fool!" Gwen disappeared with that, and Mandy worried for Eleanor's family.

"Don't worry," Ellie reassured. "Dodson will see them coming a mile off. No one sneaks up on a wolf pack. Not even those old hags."

"I'm tired," Mandy didn't like whining, but it was true. Her body was left unattended for hours or days or even weeks at a time. She was dehydrated, hungry and sleep deprived on top of all of the bruising and lacerations she received inside her head that also appeared on her physical body.

"I know, sweetie. Can you hold them off by yourself long enough for me to initiate my plan?"

Mandy nodded, even though she wasn't sure.

"I'll be back soon. I promise. Stronger than ever."

Eleanor whisked away, back to her body, and not a moment too soon. Weak from dehydration and lack of sustenance, she gained her senses and stood, only to sense intruders nearby. Transforming would be nearly impossible with no full moon and in her exhausted state. Her plan would have to wait.

Three witches approached the shack faster than Eleanor could sneak away. She would need to concentrate if her plan were to work. She would call for backup, but she had no idea where Mandy was physically being held, and was too far away for anyone to come to her aid in time.

"Come out, wolfie," one of the witches beckoned as she pulled on the old wooden door.

It was daytime and light flooded the small shack through loose boards and gaps. But when the door opened, it was nearly blinding.

"We do like to be discretionary," the hag said, "but you are too much of a bother."

It was true about the discretion. The Agency, as they were known now, had only ever been in stories. They conducted their experiments behind veils of magic and tried not to attract attention. Especially from hunters.

Eleanor was trapped between the haglet and the back wall. She twitched, trying to bring out her wolf, but her body was too weak still.

"You'll never transform before we can get to you," the witch warned. She tossed blue sparkling powder toward Eleanor who dove to the side, holding her breath and closing her eyes and mouth to avoid the effects of the spell. The shack was indeed, a shack, and old to boot. Eleanor pooled all of her strength and broke through the back wall. The witches were after her immediately, and as Eleanor ran, she forced the wolf's strength out. She promised Mandy she'd be back and she intended to keep that promise. Besides, if Eleanor couldn't help Mandy, the girl would surely fail on her own. The fact she still triumphed was a testament to her will.

Eleanor picked up speed, her claws and teeth automatically emerging with her anxiety to get away. And as she ran, she concentrated not on getting away, but getting back to Mandy-- stronger, as promised. Without the proper time she knew she needed, it would be harder than originally thought, but she had no choice but to try.

The witches gained, as they flew through the forest after her. Eleanor was losing momentum and needed to gain any time, any seconds. There was a tall cliff nearby which looked over the Pacific Ocean. A cliff which boasted a soft blanket of Kinnikinnick at the top. A cliff that she and Thomas had visited one night, long ago.

As the witches gained, she turned and headed for the overlook. They followed, but were not quick enough to catch her before she leapt over the edge and fell to the jagged rocks below, using her precious last seconds to center herself and murmur a very difficult spell.

Chapter 13
"I'm Gonna Live Until I Die" by Frank Sinatra

The news spread like wildfire. Thomas wasn't the first to hear, but wouldn't be the last. Swithin could only feel guilty and relieved that it was about Eleanor and not Mandy.

Eleanor was dead. Her broken body had been found at the base of a cliff near her pack's compound.

Thomas barely had a living room wall left when he was through with his initial grieving. Swithin couldn't even stomach his mother's tarts.

The question still remained, where was Mandy?

After a lot of consideration, Thomas made the trip to Eleanor's memorial. Swithin had come too, as had Patrick and Helen and five more of their brood, along with pretty much every hunter who was available.

Like every gathering, food and music and beer were plentiful. "Leader of the Pack" came on by the Shangri-Las, and Dodson tripped over himself to turn the depressing ballad off. "Dust in the Wind" by Kansas came on next and Dodson nearly threw the player through the roof of the old barn they were gathered in.

"Who's responsible for this horrible playlist?" he roared.

Henry Canon would be the one to put a peppier playlist on which started with The Bugles belting out "Video Killed the Radio Star" and moved onto other unemotionally slaughtering hits having nothing to do with love, wolves or death.

Dodson Fer and the rest of Eleanor's pack, including her 25 year old son, Dwayne, were beside themselves, but brave and grateful for the turnout. There was barely a hunter whom she hadn't done something for. Her mind reading capabilities and psychic knowhow had saved a lot of lives and solved a lot of cases.

Swithin had already answered dozens of inquiries about Mandy and noticed Thomas standing far out back. Bryson Pierce and Henry Canon were together again and found him before he could get away.

"Heard you're not a virg anymore," Bryson bullied.

"Is that supposed to be an insult?" Swithin questioned with all sincerity. "At a funeral? Really?"

Puzzlement washed over Bryson's face and Henry spoke up for once. "We heard you two broke up before she went missing."

Swithin sighed. "Yes. Yes we did. Hey, you were one of Erickson's assistants, right?"

Henry lowered his head submissively. "I was, yes. Excuse me."

"Well, I was wondering..." Swithin wanted to ask him a few questions, but Henry scuttled off quickly and Swithin was left in Bryson's boorish company.

"So, she's a free agent if she comes back," Bryson continued on about Mandy.

Swithin furrowed. "Bryson, if you can woo Mandy, by all means, she's all yours, mate."

With that, he walked away not having enough calm in all the universe to deal with the brute.

Swithin caught Thomas smoking out back, away from the old barn where the memorial was being held. When a lot of hunters gathered, it had to be somewhere secluded and warded. Clambakes rarely brought more than four dozen or so, but funerals and memorials were tough since so many wanted to attend. The dilapidated old barn sat five miles from anything in sight and had seen better days, but had been warded to the hilt and sat on ground which had been blessed by several different religious leaders.

"I've never seen so many hunters in one place," Swithin commented, handing Thomas a stiff drink.

"Yep." He exhaled, took another puff and then downed the whisky.

Swithin stood silently next to him, curious about Thomas's connection with Eleanor. It was an elephant in the room. When Thomas had walked into the service, late of course, the room had gone even more silent. No one spoke loudly about it, but everyone had an opinion on his presence. It definitely helped keep Swithin's mind from darker places involving Mandy and what she might be going through.

Thomas inhaled the last of his cigarette and threw it to the ground while retrieving another. "I'm not feeling particularly talkative if that's what you're after."

Swithin had distantly hoped Thomas might loosen up, but hadn't expected it. "Well, I am kind of tired about fielding questions and comments about Mandy."

Thomas lit up another smoke and shook out the match.

Swithin went on, trying to be positive. "And, well, even I was worried about her being with you but, well, I think you've been really good to her, and she loves you a lot."

"Don't you have someone else to pep talk?"

Swithin rolled his eyes, and then none other than Eleanor's son Dwayne came out the back of the barn and made a beeline for the two of them. His complexion was lighter than that of his mother, but there was no denying his smile was all hers.

"Hey guys," he greeted with a smile.

Thomas shifted uncomfortably, and Swithin shook Dwayne's hand. He instantly liked his positive energy. Swithin easily imagined them as friends. "'Ello, mate."

"Are you Swithin? They said you were."

Swithin nodded and Dwayne bear-hugged him.

"Thanks." Dwayne offered.

Swithin wriggled a bit trying to breathe and Dwayne let him go. "For what?"

"They said you offered money to help find my mom."

Swithin reddened. "Well, that's not exactly..."

But he never got to confess that the reward had originally been for Mandy.

Dwayne turned to Thomas, who tried ignoring the kid, but Dwayne would not have it. "You're Max Jaeger! I read all your books!"

That peaked Thomas's interest. "You did?"

He nodded enthusiastically. "Mom said you're one of the greatest hunters ever."

"She did?"

"Yeah! Can I get your autograph? I'll be right back," Dwayne hurried off to retrieve something for the befuddled Thomas to sign, and Swithin didn't say anything, but smiled wickedly.

Dodson appeared before Dwayne came back and shook Swithin's hand but did not engage Thomas physically. "I'm surprised you came," he said.

"Almost didn't," Thomas replied.

"Any word on Mandy?" Dodson asked Swithin.

Swithin shook his head.

"Real shame, that."

"I'm sure if she's alive, it's because Eleanor helped her," Swithin offered. "I owe her everything."

Dodson patted Swithin's shoulder and they all turned to see Dwayne running back toward them. "You tell him?" Dodson asked Thomas.

"No."

"Are you going to?"

"No."

Swithin listened, slowly putting two and two together.

Dwayne had a ratty copy of Thomas's first book. Pages were falling out, the cover had been...chewed on? He thrust it at Thomas with childlike glee, along with a pen, and Tom took it gently, so as not to shred it anymore. Swithin noticed Thomas nervously swallow and wondered if Dodson had, but Dodson wasn't looking at Thomas. He was looking out toward the distance, his face perked as a wolf's would be. Swithin followed his eye line and suddenly had a very bad feeling.

"Tom," Dodson murmured.

"Hm?" He was still trying to fumble out an appropriate inscription.

"I need to you take Dwayne."

Thomas looked up, startled, a look the rare person had seen, but Thomas had the meaning all wrong. He too looked out into the surrounding field to notice the army gathering. It was hard to tell from this distance, but zombies were definitely part of the hoard. Their shuffling was unmistakable. And finally, one of the hellhounds bayed, prompting the hunters to pour out from the barn.

"I think it's a little late for that, Dods," Thomas replied dryly. He went back to signing the book, still having no idea what to say, and so he just wrote a generic, *Thanks for being a fan. Max Jaeger.*

The oncoming supernatural army had taken some of the glee from Dwayne's eyes, but he cuddled the book and ran back toward the barn regardless, Dodson yelling and chasing after him.

"You don't look so concerned," Swithin observed.

"You really didn't see this coming? We're a smorgasbord out here." He threw his cigarette butt to the ground and walked back toward the barn. Swithin found it rather sweet that Thomas had been more nervous about interacting with Dwayne than he had about the oncoming onslaught.

Patrick was already commanding the scene. He and Helen were the oldest and most experienced of the entire group, and no one doubted their capability. Weapons were being pooled; as no respectable hunter went anywhere without several. Counts of the oncoming enemy were being taken as they moved closer, and wards were being strengthened and doubled.

The demons and hellhounds would not be able to cross in to the sacred territory, but the zombies could and they seemed to be fresh as they neared.

The army arrived, surrounding the complex right up to its invisible, consecrated border.

A horned cretin with burnt skin on a sinewy skeleton horse rode through the parted army. Patrick and Helen met him at the front line, backed up by their own army, though it failed in comparison at least six to one.

"I don't believe you were invited," Helen began.

The cretin did not give into banter. "I am Zaza'Arth and this is my army."

Patrick now furrowed his brow. "Oh...kay. And why have you assembled here?"

"You have something I want and I'm not leaving without it. One of your brethren has stolen something of mine and if I don't get it back, you will all die."

Swithin's brother Michael snickered. "That's what he thinks. We can take these bags of bones."

Swithin, however, focused in on the whimpering nearby and looked around to see Henry Canon crying. "Hey, Henry, it's all right." Swithin remembered Henry's fear of field work. "Stick with me."

"N...no," Henry stammered. "They're here for me."

A few others standing around all twisted their heads at the statement.

Henry hadn't been known as an aggressor. The exact opposite. But he had been on Erickson's team. No one had been able to find who, or what, had brutalized the scholar.

"What have you gotten into?" Swithin whispered severely.

Henry's lip trembled. "His stone. We...We got his stone."

Swithin puzzled. "What stone?"

Swithin's eldest brother Peter stepped in. "Are you daft? Do you have it? Did you use it?"

Henry was shaking. "Don't hand me over to him. Please!"

Patrick was still bellowing out toward the demon Zaza'Arth, when the demon halted the not so pleasantries. "Enough! I will have my stone or you will all die."

"Well, probably not all of us," Helen chattered.

"What's this stone you're blabbering on about anyway?" Patrick asked. "Why do you think someone here has it?"

"It is my immortal essence. I know the one who has it. I can smell him." He took a long drag of the air.

Swithin and his brother were still trying to work out details from Henry, who, they were pretty sure, had wet himself. "Were you chasing after immortality?" Peter asked, worried.

Those who were close enough to hear had turned their heads, and the distraction was enough that the attention was taken from Zaza'Arth and directed to the north side of the barn.

"What is going on?" Patrick called.

Zaza'Arth rode his sinewy horse around the perimeter to the other side of the barn. People made a path for Patrick as he barged through toward his sons and the crying hunter, Henry.

"Ah! There it is! The mewling meat!" Zaza'Arth grinned toward Henry, showing off his jagged green teeth.

"He doesn't have what you seek!" Swithin yelled out.

"Quiet, boy!" Patrick commanded. "Let me handle this. Henry," Patrick stepped up to Henry and was a full three feet taller than the brawny boy. "Were you dabbling with immortality?"

"Father," Swithin pleaded.

"I said quiet!" Patrick barked.

Helen made her way through and was biting her lower lip alongside her youngest son.

"Henry?" Patrick repeated, louder. "Are you chasing after immortality?"

It was clear as day that he had been and the mystery of why Erickson had been killed was unravelling at last. He could not speak, he trembled so hard.

"Are you immortal, now?" Patrick continued.

"No! N...no, sir! We...couldn't figure out how to activate the s-s-stone, s-s-sir."

"We?" Patrick asked calmly.

His father's cold demeanor chilled Swithin. "Da..."

"One more word, boy and I swear you'll be sorry."

"Don't you threaten him!" Helen spoke up.

"Woman! You know the rules," Patrick stated deadpan. "Is this why Erickson died?"

Henry broke down, sobbing and nodding. "Demons....they came for us, b-but Erickson hadn't told us yet. About the stone."

"Who else, Henry?" Patrick's demeanor chilled everyone nearby.

"Patrick..." Helen tried calming him again.

"Where's the stone, Henry?" Patrick queried, ignoring his wife.

Bryson Pierce finally made his way to his oldest friend and stood in front of him. "Get away from him, Mr. Hook."

"Out of the way, boy! Unless you had something to do with this!"

"He didn't!" Henry cried. It wasn't hard to believe. He and Bryson hadn't been on the same team in years. "But I...I don't have it!"

"LIES!" Zaza'Arth called out. "He is the last of the three who absconded with it! Throw him to me and I will leave this gathering in peace."

Patrick ignored the demon's rant and shoved Bryson out of the way into Swithin. "Did you try and use the stone to become immortal?" Patrick's words were slow and deliberate.

Henry had definitely wet himself at this point and was bawling like a baby.

"Da!" Swithin tried stepping in, foreseeing the future, but Patrick struck out an oversized fist and punched his son away. He toppled into Bryson, and Helen opened her mouth to scream at him, but Patrick boomed. "You know the rules, Helen. The cardinal rule of hunting. No hunter is allowed to chase immortality. It's a dangerous and slippery slope. The penalty is death."

"HE IS MINE!" Zaza'Arth bellowed from behind the line. "HIS SOUL IS MINE!"

But Patrick had already put a knife through the young man's heart. Bryson choked back a scream, and no one questioned Patrick's move. It was true. Many centuries ago, a hunter found immortality and he was corrupted by it, aligned himself with dark forces and had nearly wiped out every other hunter before he was stopped. Then, it happened again. And again. It was found that immortality could not be handled by those who were not naturally born of it and it became a hunter's cardinal rule that death was imminent and protecting the world was first and foremost, even at the cost of your life. Patrick held the unofficial position of seniority over everyone and took on the responsibility of the punishment. Tears filled his eyes, as the task did his heart no favors. He picked up Henry and handed his body to a demonic minion standing over the line.

"There is your quarry. I'll not have you torturing his soul for 1,000 years."

Zaza'Arth sat tall upon his skeletal stallion. "You have not delivered my stone. And you have deprived me of my vengeance."

"Your stone isn't here, demon. Begone!"

Zaza'Arth would not be taken so lightly. His demons could not enter, but his zombies could and they would flush out the living fleshies. If he could not have Henry dead a thousand times, he would kill 200 hunters. He lifted his bone saber to the sky and bellowed "ATTACK!"

Helen pulled Swithin from the ground and they joined the fight which had been thrust upon them. Carl Douglas's "Kung Fu Fighting" blared on the barn radio.

Swithin had no time to digest what his father had just done as they were outnumbered. And the demons and other beasties outside the safe zone made the odds even worse. The sounds of battle rang loud; screams of triumph, fear and death circled. The zombies were tough old bones and didn't go down easy. Swithin had never heard of this Zaza'Arth before, but he sure packed a mean punch.

Swithin ran into Thomas, who asked if Swithin had seen Dwayne. They were at the edge of the circle, demons and hellhounds chomping at the bit for any hunter to step over the invisible line. Zaza'Arth sat calmly atop his skeleton steed watching the chaos. "I haven't seen him," Swithin admitted as he cleaved a head off an undead. It rolled over the mystical line and two hellhounds fought over it.

"Regal!"

Thomas and Swithin looked over the line at the unworldly, growling voice. Swithin didn't recognize the demon, but Thomas did. It was the same one who had come after him on the plane.

"Well, well, not so scary when we're not cooped up in a flying deathtrap, are you?" Thomas sneered and pointed to the consecrated line. "Too bad you're out there." Swithin beheaded a shuffler which had snuck up on them.

"Come out here and fight like a warrior!" The demon growled.

"Nope. I'm good here," Thomas retorted.

"Should you be taunting it?" Swithin asked.

"Ah, me and Bajrach go way back, don't we buddy?"

Bajrach growled.

"I kind of sent him to hell," Thomas admitted. "How'd you crawl back up, anyway?"

"The Agency sends its regards," the monster sneered.

"Green bitches," Thomas mumbled.

A huge surge in the fight pushed the two men back, knocking them over. Swithin quickly got to his feet, as did Thomas, but Thomas was now outside the safe line.

"Shit."

Bajrach grabbed him, and Thomas unsheathed his blessed knives. The demon knocked him down again and grabbed his ankles. Swithin was busy fighting off another zombie, and when he glanced back, Thomas was being dragged away yelling, "Go! Help! Dwayne!"

Swithin hesitated, but hoped Thomas could hold his own. He fought through the crowd looking for any sign of Dwayne. He passed Dodson who had transformed into a six foot, furry beefcake of a wolf, and they fought back to back for a few seconds while Dodson also inquired about the boy. "Have you seen Dwayne?"

"That's who I'm looking for!"

They were pulled apart a few seconds later, and Swithin slashed and dashed his way to the other end of the barn where he saw Dwayne holding his own against two larger bone shufflers. Swithin battled his way over to Dwayne and beheaded two creeps behind Dwayne, while Dwayne did the same for Swithin. They couldn't help but share a smile over the event. It was hard for Swithin not to be enamored with the guy. He exuded positive energy and Swithin fed on that like Oreos after twelve hours of not eating. They were relatively alone and safe for the moment. The battle had pushed beyond the border of the safe zone and hellhounds and demons now joined the fray.

Zaza'Arth must have bewitched the walkers for sure. Zombies were usually dusty and shatterable; these were wet and sinewy. Most of them were newer corpses, too. Swithin remembered passing a cemetery on the way to the memorial and wondered how many people would be shocked to find their loved ones' graves upheaved.

Jackie DeShannon's voice sang out "What The World Needs Now Is Love" from the radio in the barn. The hunters were holding their own; it was what they did. Holy waters and spells and weapons went flying every which way. There were plenty of werewolves to fight the hellhounds and rip through anything else that they crossed paths with. Swithin didn't see his parents, siblings or Thomas. He had to stop himself from dwelling on what his father had done to poor Henry; rule or no rule.

Dwayne tossed a dagger at another approaching zombie, and Swithin was brought from his thoughts. Zaza'Arth still sat atop his ghastly horse and smiled at the carnage. If anyone had tried to attack him, they had failed. Swithin saw a young hunter, Mike Yor go down and he did not get back up. There were still more zombies than hunters, and now, with more hellions in the mix, things were getting dire.

Zaza'Arth wasn't a beast, necessarily, like the birds or the bhut, but he was a monster. One of the worst kind--a demon. If ever there would be a time for Swithin to test his training, now would be it.

"Dwayne," Swithin pulled him beneath a tree where they could be alone for a minute. "Can I ask a favor of you?"

"Anything. Wow. I've never been in a battle like this!"

"Me neither," Swithin confessed. "But we can stop it, I think."

"And be heroes?"

Swithin nodded.

"I'm listening."

The positive energy flowing off Dwayne would have been palpable to a lay person, never mind someone who could harness it. And Swithin asked if could do just that. Dwayne agreed and trustingly held out his hand. Behind the tree, they would be safe long enough, Swithin hoped, for him to concentrate enough--to get strong enough--to blast Zaza'Arth back to whatever hell he came out of. Swithin took Dwayne's hand and pushed all doubt from his mind. He could do this. Lama Dorje had said as much. The goddess Áine said he was the light. He had to live through this. He had to be alive when Mandy showed up.

Swithin closed his eyes and pulled Dwayne's positive force to him. He would need every ounce. He breathed in slow and exhaled slower, feeling the power flow throughout his body like warm light. He blocked out the sounds of screams, and growls and blood, and focused on Eleanor; how everyone loved her enough to be here, on Lama Dorje and his faith, and on Mandy and how much she meant to him. "Lord, make me an instrument of your peace."

Dwayne pulled back suddenly. "Wow."

Swithin opened his eyes and took in a sharp breath at the new feeling. He felt...warm. Really warm.

"You're glowing," Dwayne pointed out, in awe.

Swithin checked his hand. Sure enough, a blue glow emanated from him, brighter than ever. He'd never felt so pure and calm. He smiled at Dwayne and headed out into the fight, weapons down, and went right for Zaza'Arth.

Dwayne followed him, giddy with excitement. He wasn't one to frown anyway, or have a bad time anywhere. He merrily slashed at a zombie, and while Swithin walked on, he tussled with a hellhound before Dodson barreled over in his wolf form and put it down. It took a couple of minutes for people to realize Swithin's goal and as he walked through the battle, merely running his hands across the baddies to subdue them so that the opposing hunter could finish them off. One by one, as he touched them, they became tranquil, seemingly innocent. Slowly but surely, he made his way to the mighty Zaza'Arth and called him down.

Zaza'Arth hesitated at the glowing young hunter. True, it seemed that it would be no contest, but Zaza'Arth had been fooled before. He stayed atop his horse and called for his minions.

The evil hoard abandoned their current fights and swarmed Swithin, who merely turned and smiled, his glow brightening and forming a protective barrier around him. The minions hacked and spit at him but they were soon lulled by the positive force, allowing the remaining hunters to take them out easily. Dwayne caught up to Swithin just then and eyed up Zaza'Arth.

"What sorcery?" Zaza'Arth growled. He jumped from his steed and it reared up, knocking Dwayne to his butt.

Swithin turned again to face the demon. "No sorcery," he related calmly. "Just peace. Your worst enemy."

Zaza'Arth bellowed and raised his bone saber toward Swithin who merely bent to the side to evade it, and it ricocheted off of his aura. "You cannot defeat me." Swithin shook his head. But even peace has to fight sometimes, and Swithin raised his knife and charged at the fiend.

Meanwhile, the skeleton horse had allowed Dwayne to mount it. While Swithin busied taking down the demon, Dwayne rode through the crowd beheading and stabbing anything undead or evil he came across. Swithin's parents finally made it to the front of the crowd to witness their youngest taking on the demon lord by himself, and Patrick went to intervene, but Helen held him back.

"This is what you wanted. For him to be a legend, right?"

Patrick huffed and went back to putting down a nearby devil.

The hunters had pulled ahead in numbers at long last, and as the evils dwindled, more and more joined in cheering for Swithin. His attending siblings were the rowdiest of all yelling obscenity after obscenity toward the bulbous demon. Dodson and the rest of the wolves stood panting at the ready, but Swithin had it handled, ducking and gracefully evading a blow only to stab the bastard in a tender spot. Everyone was enjoying the show, confident that their side would win.

Suddenly, Zaza'Arth's head went flying. Thomas's head seemed to take its place from behind the demon's twitching body.

"Are you having fun?" Thomas asked Swithin, brandishing his cleaver as Zaza'Arth's headless corpse fell. With his defeat, the few minions that were left either ran or were taken down easily. Thomas was covered in blood and bits of entrails and it was hard to tell if it was his or the enemy's. He also had a severe burn covering his right arm and he was wincing as if his eye had been injured. "Jesus, this isn't a game," he chastised Swithin. "And drop the glow. You look like a nightlight."

A couple of ordained hunters walked around blessing the bodies of the fallen hellspawn to make their returns harder or impossible. Dwayne was strutting around on his new ride, and his pack shuddered at it, but knew they would have to live with the damned thing. Swithin's energy drained and dwindled until his glow disappeared and he could once again feel the cool breeze blowing through the barn. With it, his sense of discord returned. As people patted him on the back and shook his hand and generally praised him, he took it all in stride. Modesty had always come easy to him. But when his father approached him to congratulate him on his success, Swithin reached for any sense of calm he could get.

He spoke over his father's praises. "You murdered Henry Canon, and I will have to pray long and hard to forgive you."

Patrick hadn't been happy about it either and tried to set a large hand on his sons shoulder, but Swithin batted it away and Patrick went on. "It did me no joy, son. But for the protection of all hunters, the rule is in place and must be enforced. A hunter who gains immortality, one who seeks it, thinks they are a god among men--we are not meant to be worshiped as false idols."

"That's rich coming from a man who wants his son to be a legend; a hunter to be worshipped."

"People will look up to you. That isn't the same thing."

"Isn't it? I understand the rule. And I understand why. But Henry could have been saved. He could have at least had a trial or we could have had a vote. Not to mention he may have known something about The Agency."

"Ah," Patrick sighed. "Now I know why you wanted him safe. That vixen you think you're in love with is just as bad. She'll bring ruin to everyone around her. And you'll go first!"

"If you ever lay a hand on her," Swithin stepped up to his father as close as he could and started up into his dad's eyes, "I will kill you."

Patrick said naught, and Swithin turned from him. Those close enough to hear the encounter acted like they'd heard nothing when Patrick spun around and began helping with cleanup.

Pink Floyd's 'Wish You Were Here' carried on in the background.

All in all, ten hunters had died. Not a bad percentage, but one would have been too many. Especially at a funeral. Many were wounded, some scarred for life, but the casualty count could have been much higher. Swithin found Dwayne cleaning gunk out of the skeletal horse's sinew. The horse had whinnied nastily to several others, but practically purred at Dwayne's touch.

"Nice steed," Swithin greeted.

"He is," Dwayne smiled. "Dodson said I could keep him, too!"

Swithin laughed at the prospect of a bunch of werewolves taking care of a horse which resembled a butcher shop.

"Is Thomas my real dad?" Dwayne asked offhandedly.

"Uh, why would you say that?" An uncomfortable feeling washed over the young Welshman, and he looked around for Thomas or Dodson, but they were nowhere to be seen. It had been so obvious when Swithin had finally seen them together.

"I'm not stupid," Dwayne said pointedly.

"I didn't say you were."

"My mom told me stories about him that weren't in his books. And I think he loved her more than anyone."

"Why would you say that?"

"He's the saddest one here."

Swithin patted the intuitive Dwayne on the shoulder. "I don't think he wants you to know."

"I won't say anything. Yet." Dwayne smiled mischievously.

Swithin was about to go on in thanks and praise Dwayne for his help, when he noticed a gray stone amulet around Dwayne's neck that had come out from beneath his Frankenstein tee. "Dwayne, what's that?"

"Oh," he lowered his voice to a whisper, "Henry gave it to me."

Swithin suddenly realized that it was the immortality stone that Zaza'Arth had been seeking.

"Dwayne? D--so you know what that is?"

Dwayne slid the necklace off. "It's bad. You should take it."

He shoved it at Swithin and continued cleaning out his new pet's bony crevices.

Swithin looked around to make sure no one had witnessed the exchange and headed over to the tree which he and Thomas had conversed under earlier. Bajrach's head was laying in a bloody puddle nearby while his body was several yards away, cut up and burned. Thomas did know how to fight. Swithin gave him that.

There was an old wheelbarrow which hadn't been touched in decades, and Swithin heaved it up and buried the stone beneath it with a little extra concealment enchantment and headed back to the cleanup.

Chapter 14
"The One That You Love" by Air Supply

Thomas never stuck around for cleanup duty. He'd also avoided any more contact with Dwayne and headed straight home where he resumed his habits of eating, lounging and drinking.

And gambling. After betting a small fortune that Billy 'the Goat' Troll would win today's fight, Thomas nervously watched from the comfort of his own couch wearing his Ghostbusters boxers and chowing down on beer and Cheetoes. He wasn't so engrossed, however, that he didn't miss the movement behind him out of the corner of his eye.

Whoever or whatever was in his house had headed into the kitchen. Up and alert, unarmed and barely clothed, he grabbed a small bronze statue and headed after it.

"Mandy!"

All caution gone, he dove for the girl as she bled out on the floor. She'd slit both her wrists.

"Fuck!" He dug for the first towels he could find and called 911 while wrapping her forearms, pushing away the faux déjà vu. "Why the hell do you keep doing this to me?" Mandy sat quietly, seemingly waiting to die and didn't flinch at Thomas's cursing or nursing. She'd cut deep and vertical. "What the fuck?!" He repeated over and over as he compressed both wrists at once. "Talk to me, sweets! Say something! Mandy!"

She only closed her eyes and turned away.

"Goddamnit, Mandy!" He shook her. "This isn't a vision! I'm real! You're home!"

At that she did look at him and whimpered a small laugh. "Oh, I wish you were Thomas, you nasty old hag." She placed a hand on either side of Thomas's face and kissed him firm on the lips.

It shocked him long enough to let her go, and she twisted out of his reach so that she could throw herself down the basement stairs.

He nearly tumbled down them himself trying to get to her. Luckily, her relaxed state allowed her to fall without breaking her neck. Nothing he said seemed to get through to her. "Oh, honey, what did they do to you?"

Thomas never kept his door locked. Anyone who was stupid enough to break into his house would get what they deserved, so the paramedics easily made their way to him when he yelled from downstairs.

He still didn't want to let her go, but seeing as the paramedics were all men, and not a bit of green in sight, he backed off and let them do their job. First he called Dr. Husna Patil who assured him she'd meet him at the hospital.

He slammed down the phone and debated whether or not to call Swithin, but he decided he would make sure she lived first.

Swithin's mother had forced him to eat and shower and be sociable. He didn't want to do any of these things, but Helen had been insistent, and no one turned her down. He needed no prompting to sleep, as that was all he wanted to do these days, anyway.

He awoke with a start during a particularly stormy evening. Rain battered the castle exteriors and leaked in through the roof. The lightning wasn't what had startled him, though, but the vision he'd had amidst yet another bloody nightmare.

"Swithin, she needs you. Hurry."

Eleanor.

Whether she was a ghost, or the whole thing was some figment, he had to believe it. Especially since the message came with a place. He didn't even tell his parents he was leaving. Florence, of course, was roaming the halls, and he kissed her cheek, telling her that everything was finally going to be all right. She yanked on his arm demanding to know what he was on about.

"It's Mandy. Thomas has her. I have to go."

He left out the part that Eleanor had come to him, as he didn't need Florence telling him he was crazy. He hurried out into the storm and had Condel drive him to the airport, weather be damned.

Mandy sat in a private suite, courtesy of Dr. Husna. She wanted Mandy kept close and under guard so Thomas didn't argue, though he could not keep her under guard forever. Husna and the tending nurses had to keep pulling the nervous cigarettes from his mouth; the only clue he was under any duress. The good doctor ran every test she could, and Mandy sat still for all of them like a zombie. Except zombies made more noise. And ate. Everything came back normal, but Husna and Thomas kept Mandy strapped down just in case.

Dr. Husna had agreed to be discreet about Mandy's reappearance until Thomas decided what to do about it. With Eleanor out of the picture, he still needed someone who could get inside her mind and convince her that this was not a dream, but there was no one he trusted when it came to Mandy.

Word was out that she was Gwen's creation, and some hunters slathered at the idea of taking out a single entity in hopes of being a hero to the world. As if his sweets didn't have enough to worry about.

During the medical tests, he had thought about it, but Husna said everything was normal save for the fact that Mandy was trapped inside her head like before. The only person Thomas knew he could trust was just a plane ride away. He took out his phone and dialed up Little Brit.

When Thin Lizzy rang behind him, Thomas stood and didn't like how much he'd been surprised lately. "How the hell did you know?"

Swithin let the door close behind him. He was holding four red tulips which Thomas eyed severely. "They didn't have yellow," Swithin groused.

"Doesn't explain why you're here."

"You're probably not going to believe this, but Eleanor told me."

Swithin glanced past Thomas at Mandy, sitting up in the bed with the same blank expression she'd had since she'd been returned.

"You're right," Thomas chatted. "I don't. Though, it is Eleanor. Her great, great grandma was a Light Witch so there is some of that hoodoo in there."

Swithin ignored him while making his way to Mandy's side.

"We have got to convince her that this isn't a dream," Thomas told Swithin. "Did any of that Buddhist monkey training tell you how to delve into someone else's mind?"

Swithin shrugged. "I'm years away from any of that. I'm not a natural psychic, just a showy animal coddler."

"You're still our best shot," Thomas shot back. "Does anyone else know she's back?"

Swithin took Mandy's hand. "Just Florence. Prolly Condel."

"Then, she's still safe for now. There will be a price on her head."

Swithin knew. It wasn't something he'd worried about until now. Until she'd come back. But he knew that some would want her dead. His father was on the list.

He took Mandy's hand and asked Thomas to leave, which Thomas agreed to, if only to go smoke without someone telling him he couldn't. Swithin called upon his time in Nepal and drowned out the sounds of the hospital, the smell of the disinfectant and closed his eyes, focusing on Mandy, feeling for her pulse and slowly matching it with his. It wasn't so much different than trying to lull the animals, as it was all about concentrating personal energy. Her heartbeat thumped in his ears and he stretched out his energy to embrace her. There was nothing in the universe he wanted more than to talk to her and hold her.

He envisioned them wrapped inside a warm cocoon of light; safe and alone.

A minute later, he opened his eyes and was presumably inside Mandy's head outside a wet, blackened doorway of sorts which resembled a festering wound.

"Wow." He took a second to be amazed at himself. "I had absolutely no idea that would actually work."

"You're welcome," Eleanor appeared, and Swithin was rendered speechless.

Eleanor smiled. "I don't have a body anymore, do I?"

Swithin shook off his sinful pride that he'd actually been the one to transfer himself into Mandy's head. "We all thought you were dead."

"I was afraid of that. I've been keeping an eye on the perimeters, but they've let her go haven't they?"

"She's in the hospital...I'm sorry. How are you here?"

"It's true, you know. You can never quit hunting. It always drags you back in. Has there been word of my family? Have there been any more deaths?"

"Not that I know of. You didn't answer my question."

Eleanor sighed. "I kind of moved into Mandy's head. Like a second personality. She needed all of me to help protect it."

"Where is she?"

Eleanor eyed the oozing blackness.

"I was afraid you were going to say that," Swithin muttered.

"She thought guarding it from the inside was the best bet. She may have been right. I guess the ol' headmistress figured the battle was over for now."

"So, how do we get you out?"

"That's a bit tricky. She and I had an idea, but you need to wake her up first."

"Me?! If you can't do it, love, what makes you think I can?"

"Because you're her light. I need to keep an eye on things. Hopefully I'll see you soon when we're not standing in someone else's brain."

Eleanor faded, and Swithin tried not to think on any of this too hard. Life for a hunter was weird, but this was off the charts.

He was able to slide inside the darkness, wincing as he did. Brackish slime covered him when he emerged on the other side, but it didn't bother him, as his breath had been taken away at the sight.

The vastness boggled him and pained him. Mortal brains were not built to experience the size of existence. He'd emerged upon black space, neither standing, nor floating. Though it was pitch black all around, he could see everything. He just was. But upon walking, he could sense the life all around him. There were no stars and yet, he knew this could only be space and time at its crudest beginnings and oldest tales.

Mandy stood at the edge of the darkness facing out to the clear. It wasn't white or black, but clear. Swithin had a hard time wrapping his head around it and stopped for fear of insanity. He was not meant to be here and the pressure threatened to separate his insides from his outsides.

He set his hand on Mandy's shoulder, but she did not acknowledge him.

"Mands?" His voice seemed as they were in a soundproof booth and yet it echoed in the distance. "Mands? We need to go." He could feel his insides contracting and his skin loosen.

"They're right about me," she said.

"Who?"

"Everyone."

"Let's talk about it outside," he suggested.

"I'm tired of fighting them," she said of The Agency. "You know that if I stayed here, I could learn how to wipe it out? I could be everything."

Swithin did not like where this was going. "Mandy," he grabbed her hand. "You are not God. You are Amanda Heart. You are coming with me."

He pulled her, but she didn't budge, as if she weighed 1,000 pounds. The strain was more than he could bear and he fell over. Blood trickled out of his nose and he whimpered. "Mands? A little help?"

She squatted and touched his face, upon which his body relaxed and he felt better than he ever had.

"We could stay here forever," she told him. "We could be everything."

A man of any lesser faith would have been tempted for far longer than Swithin Hook had been. He had considered it for a second, but this was not right. This was not their place. "Let's talk about it over waffles. What is with waffles and godly occurrences?"

Mandy turned and ran her hand just over the edge of existence without touching it. On his backside now, Swithin could see the edge. It moved so slowly. Upon a closer look, and in this plane, he could actually see billions of specks being placed and honed at the same time by billions of tiny little multiple-legged weavers.

"Spiders," he croaked. "The universe is built by spiders. And that is why killing them is the worst karma ever."

Swithin grabbed for Mandy again and nudged her so slightly that her finger dipped into the edge sending trillions upon trillions of specks into the clear beyond.

"That was bad, wasn't it?" Swithin guessed.

Mandy stood, alert now, and then the chittering began.

"We need to go," she said, finally seeming sane again.

The chittering became deafening, and Swithin grabbed her hand. The space beneath them wavered and made it harder for them to get back to the door. Swithin could not see it, but Mandy felt around with her eyes closed and her hands out. Swithin glanced behind to see a bus-sized claw come up over the edge of the blackness, and was more than happy that he never saw what it was attached to, as Mandy pulled him back in to her mind.

His fight was not over once they'd come back to her field. He'd never been in anyone else's mind and couldn't help but look around. Eerie silence beckoned his attention back to his love. "Mands," he whispered as he reached over and took her hands. It did feel so real in here. How did she ever tell dreams from reality? "Amanda, look at me. Please, love."

She resembled her physical self now; bland and lifeless. "You can't get in."

At least she spoke. He forced her to look at him by bringing her chin up. "I only want you to wake up. You're safe now."

She didn't respond and her pale complexion was graying.

"Mandy, I don't know what you saw or heard, but I am so sorry. I was angry and hurt. Not that it's an excuse, but you did break up with me, right?" His guilt about Missy poured out involuntarily.

Mandy still did not reply, and he let her go. "Auch! Can't you say anything other than 'I can't go in?' You were fine a minute ago! How about this? What's your favorite animal? What's the harm in saying that, huh?"

A few seconds passed and she whispered, "Wouldn't you know?"

Swithin bit his lip nervously. "Remember when I was in France and I made that haunted restaurant free all of their snails in payment of services?"

She smiled faintly, but it disappeared quickly. "I wish you were real."

"I am. Mandy. Mands. Please."

"You can't get in."

Eleanor reappeared. "This isn't the first time you've shown up," she said. "Gwen and the witches used every illusion in the book."

"Great," Swithin huffed. "So, what? You're going to stay locked in here forever? That's not totally smart, love."

"No one can get in." In a sudden burst, she pushed him away, and he suddenly found himself back in the hospital room, in a bed hooked up to an IV.

"Hey, Little Brit. Any luck? You've been in there for three weeks," Thomas relayed, slurping on a blue slushy. The flowers Swithin had brought were wilted and brown in their vase.

"No." It took a minute for the intense vertigo to cease and he threw up in a bedpan. "I don't ever want to do that again."

Thomas handed him a tissue. "Your nose has been bleeding for days and your eyes are bloodshot. Husna was worried." He casually took a sip of slushie indicating that he hadn't been. "So? Where is she?"

"No one can get in. Nobody,' she says," he reported. "Oh. And Eleanor's in there."

Thomas choked on his slushy. "What?"

While Swithin explained, Mandy hem hawed inside her head. Eleanor appeared and set a hand on Mandy's shoulder. "It's safe to go now," Eleanor comforted.

"I can't stay in there," Mandy eyed the portal. "I know that." The now imaginable power tugged at her temptation. "But I don't want to go back."

"Pushing him away because you think it's best will still hurt him," Eleanor inferred. "So, you can stay here and guard yourself or get out there and live your life. Bad things are going to happen and you'll just have to deal with them as they do. At least you'll have Swithin."

"And Thomas," Mandy grinned slyly.

Eleanor didn't take the bait. "Besides, you can't find me a new body if you stay cooped up in here!"

Suddenly, Swithin's voice rang in Mandy's head...

Thomas calmed down after Swithin's explanation, trying to act nonchalant, though Swithin could practically feel the man's heart racing. Thomas sat back and took a drink of blue iciness. "If you can't wake her up, I've got nothing."

"She's mad at me. I know it."

"Like you're the first guy to boink another woman right after a break up. You two make daytime soaps look tame. Just apologize!"

"I..."

"What?"

Swithin had an idea. Their hospital beds were close enough that he took her hand and a deep breath.

"Allwch chi faddau i mi? Can you forgive me? I love you. Rwyf wrth fy modd i chi."

It took more than a few seconds for Mandy to come to, but slowly and surely, she brought her bandaged wrist up to her face and examined the wrappings and finally felt real again. "That would explain why this time hurt more than the other times." She'd killed herself in her head over and over to keep the witches at bay. "They kept throwing visions at me. But they never talked like that." She looked over at her relieved friends, Swithin being the closest--and with a straight face, she asked, "I don't suppose you brought Missy?"

Aghast, Swithin sat up straight, regretting it immediately as his head throbbed. "The first thing you say to me. Really? Really!"

She reached for his hand and squeezed it. "Thank you. I told you that language works miracles."

"Where's Eleanor?" Thomas interjected.

"Oh!" Mandy had an overly excited thought and it hurt her exhausted being, but she trudged on. "Eleanor."

Dr. Husna Patil checked back in at that moment and smiled upon Mandy's recovery. "Glad to see you up!"

But Thomas had a one-track mind. "Mandy. Can you talk to her?"

"Maybe. Now that I'm a bit more coherent. She told me not to let anyone in and so I was trying to stay strong." Her face puckered and her eyes filled with tears.

"Amanda!" Thomas went to question her, but Swithin spoke over him.

"She needs rest, Tom. We'll figure out what to do about Eleanor later."

"What about Eleanor?" Husna asked.

"Never mind it for now," Swithin took control.

"No, no," Mandy put her hand on Swithin's, but looked to Thomas. "She'll need a body. Someone in a coma, someone who's not going to be waking up. You'll need to get their family's permission of course," she added, knowing she had to where her unethical partner was concerned.

"I'm on it." And he was gone.

Husna took some vitals before taking her leave as well.

Swithin and Mandy's beds were close enough so they could link arms and hold hands. Swithin squeezed her fingers in his. "You did break up with me," he defended himself against her earlier dig about Missy.

"I know."

"I'm just making sure that it's clear. We were not together. I did not cheat on you."

"Who are you trying to convince?"

"Myself, mostly. I feel disgusting about the whole thing."

"I'm not happy about any of it. But we can't take anything back. And I have bigger problems than Missy. And the fact she saw you naked. And that you two..."

"I just want things to go back to how they were," he quickly cut her off. "Before Nepal."

Mandy did too. True, she'd gone to Wales to accept his proposal, but now, she felt more than ever that she could never be truly happy until the green witches were stopped. "Me too."

"Well then, that settles it. Best mates with benefits forever." He kissed her hand wishing he was closer, but also wanting to sleep for weeks.

"We have a lot to talk about," she said of the Agency's plot and near success to find the edge of the universe.

"I know," Swithin nodded, knowing what he knew from the goddess. "But first, a nap, I think."

"That's the most wonderful thing you could have ever said to me. Wait. Say it in Welsh."

Chapter 15
"Poison" by Alice Cooper

Three Years Later

When he'd finally been given his share of the inheritance, Swithin looked into houses near Thomas and found a steal of a deal on an old estate on 15 acres, an hour away. It had been sitting for years at this point, supposedly haunted.

It wasn't.

He worked with social services and donated most of the living space to people in need, while he lived quietly in the small guest house.

Mandy still lived with Thomas but she had her eye on buying an abandoned asylum. She still hunted with Thomas-or scammed-and would also go out with Swithin a lot. Thomas pushed her to move out with him, but Swithin said they could not live together until they were married. Mandy was not sure if it was really his faith talking or blackmail. Either way, she wouldn't bite. A wall had come up between them and she could not find a way to tear it down.

It didn't keep them from staying overnight more often than not, though.

Mandy's mind strengthened tenfold and Gwen was rarely a problem. Ever alert and concerned over her, Swithin wondered if Gwen was just biding her time, or if she was grooming another 'Mandy' somewhere. Mandy did not try too hard to find out, happy to ignore fringe dangers.

Other hunters poked and prodded occasionally, still wary of Mandy's existence at all, but with Thomas and Swithin as her knights, no threat ever stuck around too long.

Patrick tried to rekindle his relationship with his son, but Swithin held Patrick at a distance ever since he had killed Henry Canon and for his distaste for Mandy.

All in all, life was good, but hunters knew better than anyone how quickly that could change.

Local teens from the Anjedan village in Iran had rousted a bull manticore from a long slumber in a nearby cave, and it began roaming the Amanabad Rural District, which equaled about a dozen villages. A few had died trying to fight it, and a few others had died trying to befriend it. An ancient beast in a modern world could never be swayed easily.

Being the current expert on beasties, Swithin charged in for the save. He and two mates tracked it down to a nearby lake and managed to get it back to its cave deep in a mountain.

No one could deny Swithin's knack for lulling beasties, and he had already become the legend his father had predicted for him. The manticore had been scared like any beast would have been, and cranky. Swithin wasted no time taming it and leading it back to its nest. His mates had come along, mostly to witness the act, and were duly impressed.

No one knew the cub was there until Swithin started losing feeling in his leg.

Mandy and Thomas were trying to oust a mischievous ghost cat in Idaho when Mandy got the call. Her near instant bawling prompted Thomas to pull over and ask what had happened. Mandy couldn't get it out, and he took the phone from her.

Helen was on the other end sobbing incoherently herself. After a minute of Thomas's badgering, Patrick's voice came over the line and stoically explained that the experts deemed Swithin to have no more than two days to live.

Needless to say, the ghost cat Mandy had been paid to exorcise escaped.

It took 14 hours for Mandy to reach Swithin's bedside. The poison had taken its drastic toll by burning him from the inside out. Most of his skin showed the raised, weeping red blisters. And because the poison was so potent, Swithin had been confined to a room in a bed which would have to eventually be burned, along with his body, to destroy the venom. Touching him had been ill advised as well, but Mandy kissed his forehead anyway, which hadn't yet shown signs of ruin. Enchantments and potions had been administered, but there was no cure for manticore poison. Centuries of trial and error had proved this. The fact that he was still alive at all was considered a blatant miracle as death usually came within minutes.

Patrick had wanted to kill him at once to save his son misery, but Helen wouldn't have it and they argued until they could no longer stand the sight one another. Helen, as always, won the battle.

Helen sat outside in her stone circle praying, while Patrick remained in his study drinking. Swithin's siblings were either scattered about the castle or on their way from various corners of the world. No one could stomach being near the young Hook. Mandy could not stomach being without him. New blisters appeared randomly every minute. He had hours at best.

"Hey, sweets." Thomas entered carrying two steaming mugs. He handed one to Mandy, who didn't drink it.

"All the power in the universe at my fingertips and he's going to die anyway." Even though Mandy had promised Eleanor, Swithin and Thomas that she would never try and harness the power beyond, never had she considered it so hard. The only thing which stopped her was that she would never be able to travel to the beyond, learn what she needed and be back by the time he was dead. Time worked differently between this world and that one and she did not know how to control it.

"Well? Helen's outside praying. Maybe someone will decide to answer," Thomas answered incredulously. When Mandy didn't respond, he took a seat on the chair next to her. "Look, the fact that he's even still alive at all is, well, there's something to it."

"Thomas?"

"Yeah."

"I need you to promise me something."

He laughed. "You know I don't do promises."

"You need to do this one."

"Let's hear it and then we'll see."

She pulled away from Swithin and looked her mentor in the eye. "If you die, I need you to stick around."

His eyebrow raised.

"If anyone can do it, you can!" she insisted.

"I don't doubt my abilities in anything."

"I can't do this again. I can't lose anyone else." Tears started forming and Thomas actually swallowed a sudden lump.

"Tears ain't fair, sweets."

"Promise me."

Far be it for Thomas Regal to admit he could not do something, and so he had no choice but to tell her that when he died, he would stick around, if only to make sure he could give her a proper goodbye. It seemed to quell her oncoming waterworks, and she mercifully spared him a hug.

No one doubted that Swithin Hook was special. Rumors had flown since his birth, but were quelled quickly. The fact that he could glow only fueled the fire, but unlike Mandy--who was seen as a potent catastrophe waiting to happen--Swithin was beloved by all.

So no one was surprised when he pulled through; the only person ever known to have survived a manticore sting.

Mandy let Swithin heal for several weeks, all the while thinking on her predicament of death and dying, Gwen and the universe. Though their faith in the afterlife differed greatly, Mandy tried believing in Swithin's Heaven, but she knew where she was going, and the thought of living alone for eternity inside that fetid portal in her head scared her more than anything.

She could not bear the thought of losing Swithin. Ever. Even to her own death.

She decided right then and there that there could only be one solution.

"We need to take on immortality."

Swithin spit his Jell-O out. Even after three weeks, his body hadn't come close to healing all the way. Digestive and respiratory problems persevered, but slowly and surely, he got better. His hair had returned with a vengeance, and thick blond fuzz covered his scalp. The skin wounds had all scabbed over and had stopped oozing. All in all, he was finally feeling alive again, but this bit from Mandy sent him into a bloody coughing fit, and she held his hand while he choked through it.

"No!" he wheezed. "Are you barmy? No!"

"You almost died."

"But I didn't. And I've almost died a lot of times."

"But..."

"Mands," he took her hands gravely, "we aren't meant to live forever. Even Jesus died, love."

"His death served a purpose. Our lives could serve equally as good. You know we're special."

He could not deny that, though his innate modesty kept him from admitting as much out loud. "Death is a part of life. It's why I strive so hard to be good. So, that when I die, I can go to Heaven. I know you don't believe this, but you'll get there, too. We will never be parted. Not really."

"I've seen the other side. There was no trace of white wings or golden halos. All I saw was a spidery monster and vast endlessness. If we believe two different things, if we go two different places, we'll be apart forever."

He squeezed her hand and remained strong. "God brought us together, Mands. And I'm still here. We cannot be broken unless we allow it."

She pulled away from him. "God didn't do anything! Gwen made me. I'm a monster."

"No you're not."

"I could be."

"I'm not going to let that happen."

"What if this...ichor...running through my veins goes bad. What if Gwen breaks through? We don't know what I am. We don't know what I'm capable of. I've resisted the pull from the energy. I hate Gwen that much. I won't ever give into it. But if I die, I won't have a choice and you can't come with me."

"Strength and willpower to live and to do the right thing. That is what you're capable of. We don't need to damn our souls to prove that."

"How can you be so sure that immortality will damn us?"

"Shh!" He motioned for her to keep her voice down. "You do remember what my father did to Henry Canon? For just researching it?"

"Your father is his own kind of monster."

Swithin could scarcely deny it. Henry's murder had irreparably soiled his relationship with his dad.

"You and me," Mandy came back to his bedside. "Young and invulnerable forever could do so much good. We deserve this."

Her ego about the idea brought Swithin to his senses after almost being tempted. "It's that kind of thinking, my love, that proves it is a temptation to be fought. Given enough time, the power that you speak of will even warp us."

She didn't want him to accept living with her forever out of guilt or obligation. She wanted him to want her more than anything. More than his precious Heaven.

Mandy insisted that she and he were different; stronger.

He insisted that was exactly why they should not give into the temptation.

The fight ensued, and just like that, Mandy's blissful existence had come to another halt.

Chapter 16

"Does Anybody Really Know What Time It Is?" by Chicago

Four Years Later

"Psycho Killer" spun on vinyl as Mandy twirled her waist long, brunette waves, waiting for her "class" to finish arriving. At 27, she was an accomplished ghost hunter--respected, if not feared, by her peers and the recent owner of an antique asylum.

After years of pining, she'd finally been able to purchase it with the money she acquired via Thomas's death eight months ago.

The asylum wasn't hard to find and, in fact, was a landmark 30 miles out of town that she'd personally kept alive with the tuition her 'students' paid. Ghost hunting was less than fruitful, but people would pay a lot of money to hear about it.

The building opened in 1901 as a boarding school, but when the first World War began, the government seized it to be used as a military hospital. The Great Depression saw it fall into disrepair, until WWII when it was once again utilized for wounded soldiers. By the end of WWII, there were so many veterans in need of psychiatric care that it finally became an official asylum, and even those who had not served could be treated there. Private donations and some tax money kept the large estate afloat through the Korean War, and until 1957, when all government funding was pulled and private donations were not enough to support staff and utilities, it was closed. There it sat, occasionally being molested by gang activity and graffiti artists; the ghosts of its past just waiting for time to end.

Mandy petted the small Siamese cat that rubbed against her leg and then scratched at the itchy new tattoo on her hip. For every ghost she vanquished or helped, good or evil, she continued to add new ink. Her entire left foot, leg, thigh, and butt cheek were covered in Pac Man ghosts. The good ones, she had their name inked beneath them in tiny cursive letters. Her only other ink was a fist sized Ms. Pac Man on her right shoulder blade. Today, she wore Daisy Dukes and a green, backless tank, so most of her work could be seen. Only her long, dark hair covered Ms. Pac Man. One of her biggest decisions in life right now was whether to continue the tats up her back, across her stomach or start over at the bottom of her right leg. Life was tough.

Mandy could not be found in a phone book or online. Interested parties had to know someone who knew someone in order to get here. Most of her 'students' had supernatural problems and had tried everything from fake psychics to failed exorcisms. Some came because they wanted to become hunters.

That never worked out so well for any of them.

"So," she began, "I assume most of you are here because you have an infestation of sorts that you can't explain. Is there anyone here who can see apparitions already without the aid of a tool?"

Several cats milled around the "students", begging for attention. The asylum attracted lots of strays, so Mandy had 23 cats and three dogs that she tended to. The dogs were more sensitive to ghosts and never came into the asylum, but hung out at the guest house. One girl in back raised her hand. Native American, perhaps, 15-ish. Where would a 15 year old get tuition for this?

"All right. That's about the norm," Mandy lied. No one had ever raised their hand and she couldn't lie to herself by thinking she wasn't intrigued. "So, let's get to the learning part, shall we?" She flipped on the old projector and it flickered to life on the white screen she pulled down. With a click of the clunky, vintage remote, the lights were off and she smiled at the nervous looks people shared.

"This," she nodded to the fuzzy picture on the screen of a fuzzy apparition, "is a ghost. There are many types of ghosts and apparitions all ranging from benign to deadly." She flipped the picture to another screenshot of several glowing silhouettes in a dark room; a picture she had taken herself in the basement of the asylum. "I learned to put them into classes, and so that's what I'll be sharing with you today. These are Class E spirits. Completely harmless. They have no idea you are even here. They don't talk to you, they don't move things--they just mingle with each other in the afterlife. This room has six or so at any given time."

Everyone looked around.

"Put on your goggles," she instructed, and they slipped on the goggles provided by her on each desk. Gasps and murmurs followed as the remnants of past patients roamed the room. "These spirits are lost souls with nowhere else to go. Not even I'm sure what happens in the afterlife, but these guys fill their time with chess and ball and staring out the window. The asylum has 345 such spirits roaming the halls, some dating all the way back to when it was a boarding house for troubled youth from 1901-1914. Now, if you'll look back here," she clicked to the next picture.

"This is a Class D spirit. These are the guys you see glimpses of out of the corner of your eye or when you feel a 'presence'. They are never fully corporeal and usually have some sort of angle for sticking around. They need something done to move on. Could be as simple as a proper burial or to say goodbye to a loved one. Most of the time D's are benign, but all classes can be either benign or malignant so it's best never to assume. Class D's can turn into Class C's, and the Class C's are where it starts to get interesting."

She flicked the projector remote again to show a picture a spirit standing over a little girl, and a few people gasped. "You can call them up using various methods, like an Ouija board or a séance. Sometimes they're benign--most of time, they are not. Benign cases aren't reported as much, though, so the statistics are skewed."

Mandy continued, "Class C through A and beyond are the ones you read horror novels about. Class C's turn into Class B's and Class A's when they gather enough energy. Speaking of which, that's what a ghost is, really. They are energy. It's what's left behind when your body is gone. Like light or heat, energy is all around you all the time. Energy can be very strong indeed, like a lightning bolt, and we've all seen what kind of damage they can do. Ghost energy is the same, from a little static shock to a killing blow. When you have a Class C apparition, it's serious, but not life threatening, yet. The key is to find out what it is connected to and sever it; usually with fire. But make sure you get every splinter, hair or fiber."

She changed the picture again to reveal a close up shot of a rather nasty Class B specter coming at the camera; a picture she also took in the asylum. "Ghosts feed off energy. It's why lights go out, batteries get drained, and why they scare you so much before showing themselves. Well, that's a two-fold. They need the energy to show themselves, but they also like to feed off of your fear; another very potent form of energy. Once Class C's get enough fuel, you'll begin to hear them; they'll be able to write messages and move things. Poltergeists are a common Class B menace. Like I said, they aren't all bad, but if I've been called in, it's usually not because my clients have been having delightful noonsies with dead Aunt Clara."

She flicked the pictures again to reveal a grisly murder scene. Two bodies covered in blood, one with a belt around his neck and the other with a hammer nearby. "And now, for everyone's favorites, the Class A's. These baddies are in it for purely selfish reasons. They want something sinister, and to get it they need power. Fear, as I said, is a strong life force for these guys. They love revenge and menacing for the fun of it. They are protective and very strong. These are the ones that can throw you across a room, drag you down a hallway--and the strong ones can possess you and make you strangle yourself or kill yourself with a hammer. They are partially sentient. They know they are dead, but they're not generally happy about it and want to get back to the land of the living. These are the ones in the movies, folks. The dangerous ones. Once again, they are linked to something, so find it and burn it. Spells can work, and the right words are very powerful as are a potent mixture of herbs. Fight nature with nature and all that. In fact, in this very asylum, we used to have a Class A booger. He terrorized the Class E's, me--tore at walls, tossed around furniture. He's the meanest one I've come across. He even killed four other paranormalists across six decades. Being a ghost hunter isn't glamorous or kitschy. It's not even fruitful in the money department. You have to lie, cheat and steal to get funds for gas, food and equipment. People will laugh at you, doubt you and sneer."

"What happened to your Class A?" an old woman in front asked.

"Oh, him?" Mandy laughed. "Had to burn his straight jacket. Who would think something would get attached to one of those?"

A 20-something guy with a ponytail and a notebook spoke up. "I heard he was still here."

"Myth," Mandy assured. "Would you all be dumb enough to come to a place with Class A poltergeist?"

Some of them shifted in their seats uncomfortably.

She smiled reassuringly. "We wouldn't be able to be here if he was still around. Any other questions? You've paid for it."

She spent the next three hours listening to people's issues and problems. Most people didn't take the class to become a ghost hunter's apprentice, but because they had ghosts of their own. Mandy sold herbs and handed out incantations. She gave away business cards of colleagues who could get the job done.

"Always do your research, people," she reminded. "Before you buy a house, make sure they didn't build it on a cemetery, and before you get that awesome looking old wheelchair at the thrift store to use as a movie prop, find out where it came from before you cart it home. Paying for a storage locker is better than dying. Now, is anyone here for the apprenticeship?"

Six people raised their hands. Six! That was more than normal. One, of course, was the girl in the back who'd been pretty still thus far. "Did anyone else have any questions?"

The rest did not, and Mandy dismissed them. The seminar had originally been for an apprenticeship, as new hunters were always welcomed into the community, but people with ghost issues and nowhere else to turn were willing to fork over the money just to talk to her. She had nothing better going on. The people she'd helped shuffled out of the room and tentatively out of the building. Mandy made sure the hallways were well lit and signs blatantly pointed toward the exit. Not that she didn't have her fair share of kids who broke in and tried staying the night, but these people paid good money to rid themselves of ghosts, not cavort with them. Now to her prospective protégés.

"So," she started, "I'll begin by telling you that there is a 100% chance that most, if not all of you, will not make it through today. If you do, you should know that your life will be over. Being a paranormalist of any caliber will consume your life. Things will follow you home. They will attach themselves to your stuff and to your family members and friends."

"I've already faced down a C," Ponytail bragged. "Burned his britches," he laughed.

Mandy already hated him, and the cats avoided him, which confirmed his douchbaggery.

"Then, you're a contender, aren't you? You've all got to spend the night here, though. Think you can make it?"

"You said all the baddies were taken care of," another young man pointed out.

Mandy grimaced. "Well…Actually, we do have to get going. We'll finish class in the caretaker's house behind us. He'll be out soon."

That always made them sit up straight.

"I didn't quite get his entire straight jacket burned and he absconded with a few threads. He's weak, but he gets stronger all the time." She glanced at the clock. "He comes out at three and it's already 2:4…"

Mandy went rigid, her eyes fluttered and rolled back in her head before she fell to the floor. Everyone stared at her, wondering if they should help or wait for something to happen. After a minute, Ponytail approached, knelt down and poked her.

"She's fainted," he assumed.

Everyone looked around nervously as the lights flickered and a few ominous bangings echoed from adjacent rooms. Suddenly, the classmates all screamed and made a run for it, a bluish specter charging right after. He roared and chased them down the halls, screaming in…Welsh?

The girl from the back of the class hadn't moved and now she clapped slowly and deliberately. "Nice projection."

Mandy opened her eyes, stood and dusted herself off. "Thanks, but it's not mine." She looked out the window at the young men running for their lives out the gate to their cars in the parking lot. The "ghost" disappeared immediately. "What's your name?"

"Catori."

"Which," Mandy scrunched, "means ghost. Interesting."

"It's what they called me at the orphanage. It kind of stuck."

"Ah. So, you're the real deal, huh?" Mandy took a seat behind the old metal desk. "I've done this six times now and haven't had anyone with real skills."

"It took me a while to track you down. I actually, also have a bit of a ghost problem."

"Why didn't you speak up with the rest of the class?"

"It's what I guess you could call a class before A."

Though her face betrayed nothing, Mandy's insides froze. Thomas trained her well and not much scared her. That's why she was so good at what she did. Ghosts had trouble feeding off her. The class before A --otherwise known as a Class Zero--didn't need to feed. Class Zero's were self-propellant.

"If there were a Class Zero apparition nearby, I would know. Heck, everyone would know."

Before Catori could speak up again, the bluish apparition reappeared and stopped long enough to look shocked at Catori's presence. "Hello, love."

She nodded. "Nice trick."

"Old distraction technique. Been in the family for generations."

"Nice shirt," she nodded at his Def Leppard tee.

"Where the hell were you?" Mandy scolded.

"I know, I know," he apologized. "The pastor's homily went on a little long this morning. The sin of swearing. I'm sitting there thinking, well, if you're being faced down by a rabid hell hound, you'd swear too, you old--" He stopped abruptly at Mandy's disapproving glare and turned his attention to Catori. "Don't mind her. She's just afraid she'll burn into a little crisp if she walks into a church."

Catori giggled, and Mandy rolled her eyes.

"Oops! Only have another 30 seconds to get back to my body."

He floated off through a wall, and Catori cocked her head. "He your boyfriend?"

"No," Mandy answered severely.

"He's cute."

"He certainly thinks so."

For the past two months, Swithin forced himself into Mandy's bubble every day. They had not been so near in proximity for so long in years and Mandy was still trying to figure out how to deal with it.

Swithin reemerged a minute later with his hand on his head. "Balls, that gives my noggin a whompin'." He was an inch taller than Mandy--lean, scruffy, and dirty blonde. "I'm Swithin," he held his hand out to Catori. "And you are?"

"Catori," Catori took his hand. "Cat for short."

"Pleasure," he smiled and kissed her hand.

Catori grinned for the first time Mandy had seen. But most girls gaggingly swooned for Swithin's Britishness.

Swithin picked up the Siamese cat and snuggled it. She had a white lip and white toes and was Mandy's favorite; even if she was from Gwen. "Well, I'm starved," Swithin went on, setting the cat down. "Projecting does that to a bloke, you know."

"I didn't actually," Cat told him.

"Well, you have a lot to learn. Come on then. Mands?"

"If we're going to Cat's house to see this Class Zero, I need to grab…"

"A *what*?" Swithin interrupted.

"Supposed Class Zero," Mandy corrected. "I need to grab a few things. I'll meet you outside."

Seventy five years ago, a demon had tried escaping the netherworld during an opening from a séance and had gotten trapped in a ghost. It was still one of the strangest records to date, but a ghost with the power of a demon hadn't been easy to stop and was the only Class Zero story she knew to be on record. Burning the ghost's mortal remains didn't work since it was now attached to the demon, and the demon couldn't be easily caught due to its now translucent nature. It had been partly luck at all that hunters finally took it down. Luck played a big role in the lifestyle.

Mandy headed to the office attached to the lobby and unlocked a large metal storage cabinet filled with gizmos and doohickeys. She filled a duffel bag with a few of them along with some herbs, magnets and various ghost fighting paraphernalia.

Lastly, Mandy grabbed her ratty, but still sparkling, pink tote and met her companions in the parking lot where Junie, her custom plum '67 hearse, was parked two spaces away from Swithin's ice blue '85 Aston Martin V8 Vantage Coupe--his gluttonous pride and joy.

"Nice wheels," Cat pointed out of the Aston.

"Thanks, love. She is perfect, isn't she?"

"Can I drive it?" Cat wondered.

Mandy and Swithin laughed. "No," he said. "But I am driving myself," he leered at Mandy's hearse. "I hate that heap."

"She doesn't like you either," Mandy reminded.

"She never lets me forget."

Cat eyed them back and forth. "Cars have souls now, too?"

Mandy piped up before Swithin could. "Mine does!"

The car honked as if in response.

"Feck off, you!" Swithin reserved cursing for when he really meant it.

"Can I ride, at least?" Cat asked Swithin of his British import. "I've never ridden in the driver's seat as a passenger."

"It's not the....whatever. Absolutely!" He stuck his tongue out at Mandy since he thought his car was better anyway, and opened the left side door for Cat.

As soon as he was settled and on the road, Swithin waited for Thin Lizzy's "Dancing in the Moonlight" to end, turned down the radio and called Mandy over the hands-free speaker.

"Hey, love," he greeted.

"Took you long enough!" she barked.

Cat rolled her eyes at Mandy's obvious denial that she had a boyfriend.

"You know I can't turn Thin Lizzy off!" he defended.

"It's a CD. Pause it. So, Cat, how's the ride?"

"Smooth!" Cat smiled.

"Swith and Junie had an incident a few years back. She hasn't forgiven him, and he hates her for it," Mandy continued the conversation.

"Like owner, like car," Swithin muttered. "Junie," Swithin scoffed. "What kind of name is that for a car?"

"The kind she came with," Mandy argued.

"You really need to let me put that thing out of its misery."

"She is a benign and helpful part of our community."

"She...Argh! IT is not a part of anything! IT is a menace!"

Cat listened to them bicker about Junie and various other things for about 20 miles until Mandy finally hung up. Cat wondered what she'd gotten herself into while Swithin mumbled inaudibly under his breath.

"So," Cat piped up, "Swithin. That's kind of an unusual name."

"Yeah. There was a bishop of the same nomenclature back in the 800's who had a knack for weather and such. He saved one of my ancestors, and so my family line has an oath to upkeep. There shall be one Swithin for every generation. My mother fought it, but I was kind of a late accident and my father insisted. My sibs are Michael, John, Wendy, Mary, James, Peter and George, since my mother has a Peter Pan obsession. The dogs are Crocodile and Smee!"

Cat laughed. "No Tinkerbell?"

"Bell died when she was young."

"Oh. Sorry."

"It's okay," he smiled to break tension. "My da's still not sure if mum married him for love or because his last name is Hook. She's a bit of a Peter Pan fanatic."

Mandy was following, and as soon as she figured out where they we going, Swithin's speaker rang again. Cat listened to them bicker again all the way to Spud Butts and followed them inside, where they continued to bicker about coming to Spud Butts.

"Can you eat ANYTHING that isn't a starch? Try a vegetable," Mandy chastised.

"Doll, I could die at any minute on any given day. If a potato takes me out, I'd consider myself lucky."

"Just get me a bowl of the soup and a garden salad," Mandy sighed. "What do you want Cat?"

"An All-In with extra pickles and chili. And a side of maple bacon sounds good to me!"

Swithin grinned at his win, and Mandy headed over to a table where Cat joined her. Mandy wiped off the seat and table with a disinfectant wipe from her purse before sitting. "So," Mandy began. "You have a ghost problem and you think it's a Class Zero."

"If that's what you call something worse than a Class A, then yes."

"So, why is it worse?"

"It's smart, sentient and powerful. It can move anything, and it can leave the house. Salt with iron kind of keeps it away. And before you ask, yes. I did all the research. My house is brand new, well, my dads had it built only 16 years ago over in Raleigh Hills. It's not on a cemetery..."

"That you know of."

"Well, no. Wouldn't they know when they built it?"

"Not necessarily. Some of the nastier specters are old and buried pretty deep. A tomb or an unmarked grave. The Wild West saw a lot of random bodies buried here and there. The slightest shift in dirt or sediment around it can loosen them. But if it's a Class Zero--and I still doubt it--it would have had to have been stirring for quite a while to get that strong. Most people think Class B's are A's, but they're not. Class A's are nasty pieces of work."

"Talking sweet on me, are you?" Swithin asked upon arriving with food.

"You are the nastiest piece of work, I know," Mandy quipped.

Cat looked back and forth at them again. "You sure you two aren't a couple?"

"Who said we weren't?" Swithin asked.

"Yes." Mandy said at the same time.

"Right," Cat was sorry she'd asked. "Well, anyway, back to my problem."

"What are you?" Swithin said with a bite of fully extra loaded baked potato in his mouth. Bacon grease dripped down his chin, and Mandy rolled her eyes before wiping it off. "Fifteen? Where are your parents?"

"They're in Tokyo," she shrugged, casually. "It was their dream vacation," she went on. "And I was supposed to be there, but this opportunity with you popped up and they're pretty freaked out about the whole ghost thing. They forked over the money to let me handle it since I can see them and all, and here I am."

"Hm," Swithin nodded. "Nice."

"So, for $15,000," Cat emphasized, "I hope you can help me."

"My seminar helped lots of people today," Mandy crowed.

"You mean your scam?" Cat retorted.

"Hey, it's not free, doing what we do," Swithin defended. Though, the argument was null in both he and Mandy's cases. He had more pounds than he knew what to do with, and Mandy had more than enough to live on. "Speaking of doing what we do," he turned to Mandy. "You coming over tonight? I'm leaving for Ireland in the morning to deal with that wail of banshees outside Naas."

"Swith, I'm not sure this is appropriate conversation."

"Good, see you at eight. I have to run, though," he shoved the rest of his potato in his mouth and stood. "Promised my car a wax."

"And it doesn't even care," Mandy ridiculed.

"Just because she isn't possessed by a wicked demon doesn't mean she doesn't care. Oh, and Eleanor's been trying to get a hold of you. I think she just wants to make sure you're doing all right."

"I'll call her when I get a new phone."

"Who's Eleanor?" Cat asked, sipping her soda.

"An old friend," Mandy admitted. "Did she say anything about Dwayne?" Mandy directed at Swithin.

He shook his head. "No. But he'll turn up. It's not the first time he's gone on some crazy walkabout."

"Who's Dwayne?" Cat asked, still sipping her pop, intrigued.

"My dead partner's son," Mandy offered.

"I gotta go," Swithin reminded, and he kissed Mandy on the cheek and then tipped his head toward Catori. "It's been a pleasure, Cat."

"Likewise," she smiled. When he was gone, Cat leaned in. "So, what is the deal with you two?"

Mandy crunched into a bite of salad. "What do you mean?"

"Well, he likes you, and you obviously like him, so why aren't you two, like, a couple?"

Mandy rubbed her temple, annoyed with the return of the subject. "Because the only thing I'm afraid of is commitment."

Cat shrugged and took a bite of her potato and a forkful of pickle. After a minute of silence, she changed the subject.

"If you could go anywhere in the world, where would you go?"

"Hm," Mandy thought.

"I know. It's a dumb question. You've probably been everywhere."

"Actually, no. I've never seen the northern lights or the pyramids. How about you?"

"Australia. For sure. I love kangaroos."

A flicker of a memory disturbed Mandy's being, but her face remained frozen in pleasantry so as not to give anything away. She'd had plenty of practice over the years to perfect her poker face. "You know Australia has more deadly animals than anywhere else right?"

"But Kangaroos!"

"Ha, ha, yeah, yeah. I like kangaroos, too."

The flicker of a memory was gone, but it had distracted Mandy enough for her to want to move on. "So, you really think you have a Class Zero, huh?"

"If not something worse."

Mandy scoffed at the minute possibility.

"And you're supposed to be the best," Cat continued. "So, if anyone can help, I figured you were worth the money."

Mandy shook her head. "I'm consulted more than I fight. Ghost chasers are a dime a dozen these days."

"Well, yeah, but not just anyone could handle a Class B or A. Or even a C, I wouldn't think."

"There are enough tough veterans out here that eat this shit up. They love the hunt and the capture. I don't get off on it. But yeah, I've faced down a couple of A's. Nasty beasties."

Mandy swallowed her disbelief at Cat's Class Zero speculation immediately upon seeing her house. She'd already had a bad feeling when the police tape and warning signs were posted at the subdivision entrance. Lawns were overgrown with weeds, and the further they drove on, the browner it got. Dead grass, trees, flowers and FOR SALE signs dotted the landscapes, all apparently due to a toxic landfill beneath the subdivision.

Catori's large Tudor house obviously was at the center of it all. Dry dirt made up the front lawn, the tree in front had split into three sections and a gray aura hung about the entire structure. FOR SALE signs were posted for the once regal houses to the left and right, and the houses looked broken--chipped paint, broken windows, missing shingles. Cat's house wasn't as marked, save for the garage door, which had been bashed in, and a broken security unit. Damn looters.

"So?" Cat asked. "What do you see? You don't look concerned. Can you see the aura?"

"I see it. And no use being concerned. They like that, anyway, and I like to disappoint them. Come on."

Mandy took pictures and readings outside the house, all around. She had Cat take pictures of the surrounding houses while she used one of her doohickey to read the ground.

Cat returned, and Mandy was still taking readings of the air and tweezing samples into small vials. "So," Mandy asked Cat. "No old haunted house. Mm, no thrift store finds?"

Cat laughed. "My dads hate thrift stores. Everything has to be new. And I never go, so don't think so. How would we know if there was a tomb or something underground?"

"A spell. Or you rough up the contractors and builders. You'd be surprised how many of them hide that sort of thing to keep from stalling the construction."

"Do you need to call in some other kind of backup besides your boyfriend?"

"No, and he's not. But I do need to know what we're dealing with. I can't believe I didn't feel this or that no one else reported it."

"I tried," Cat shrugged. "No one believes in ghosts, you know."

"Primal fear of the unknown. If you don't believe in it, it doesn't exist. Cable's done wonders but there are still more nonbelievers than believers."

"Well, and it's only been a couple of months since it's started to get this bad. It was mainly our house for years, and we learned to deal with the noises and the moving picture frames. But then, Mr. Winn next door hanged himself and Mr. and Mrs. Chester on the other side started fighting all the time. I think they got a divorce. Behind us..."

"I get the picture," Mandy cut her off. "It's not uncommon for this type of expansion to occur, just that it goes unnoticed. I guess since people think it's the landfill, it makes a good cover for the spirit in question. Was that sinkhole always there?"

Cat nervously eyed the backyard and the dip in the middle. She shook her head. Mandy went on. "I want to get these samples and these readings back to my lab in the asylum and go from there."

"Didn't you want to go inside?"

Mandy eyed Cat warily. "Where are you staying?"

"Well, not here obviously!" Cat shouted, prompting a laugh from Mandy. "Dads and I moved out and are up in the Beaumont Inn in town. Even they'd had enough." She turned sad. "They loved this house. It was their love nest, you know?"

Mandy patted Cat's shoulder.

"You really should marry him," Cat said of Swithin. "He's crazy about you."

Mandy didn't like talking about it and would have told Cat to quit bringing it up, but that would be talking about it. "So, did you ever have any psychics over or anything?" Mandy asked.

"One. But she was a total fraud. People like you don't exactly advertise in the phone book. I overheard a couple of amateur ghosters talking about you when they were checking out the house. Had no idea I was here. Ha! You should have seen them run when it came out after them!"

Mandy shrugged. "I've got enemies, too, you know. Can't be too open about anything."

"Yeah. Poor Swithin."

"Look, some offense meant here…drop the Swithin comments."

"It's just that you guys are so cute together!"

Mandy knew she wasn't going to get the girl to shut up about her lack of romance, and she needed to nip it in the bud before Swithin and Cat ganged up on her. "I'm in love with him. Okay? Is that what you want to hear? And if anything ever happened to him, I'd be devastated. There."

"Oh...kay...."

"Look, I know it sounds weird, but Swith isn't in the same line of work as me. Banshees are common pests, for sure, but he deals with monsters. Monsters don't care if you're scared of them or not. They're beasts. His calling is ten times as dangerous as mine. My last..."

Mandy stopped, realizing she was about to unload a lot of personal angst on a girl she'd known for 4 hours.

"You can dump on me. It's okay. I think we'll be friends for a while," Cat put her hands in her pockets and smiled.

"We don't even work together all that often. He helps with the seminars to give the fakes a good scare, and then I see him intermittently at meetings and events and stuff a few times a year. He's pretty busy."

"Events? Like monster hunter events?"

"Kind of, yeah. The world changes all the time. New things pop up and old thing things come back. We're a pretty close-knit community all over the world. Swith's at the top of his field, so he's gone a lot."

"So, why don't you travel with him, then?"

"Because I don't want to. Okay? End of discussion."

"But..."

"End."

They stood staring at the dead landscape, and the awkward silence prodded Mandy to speak. "He almost died, and I'll never forgive him for it."

"That's, um, harsh."

"Do you want me to drop you off at the Beaumont?" Mandy changed the subject.

Cat didn't pry anymore. "Nah, I'll take my bike. I like the exercise."

"Sure thing. Meet you back here about 10:00 a.m.?"

"Sounds good."

"Um, hey, if your bike is here, how did you get to my place?"

"Cab."

"Oh. Right. Well, see you tomorrow. Your dads must trust you an awful lot."

Cat smiled, but it was laced with melancholy. "Yeah."

Mandy gladly headed back to Junie, got in and closed the door. Something didn't set right with her about Cat for a multitude for reasons, but for now, she'd go back to her lab and start analyzing the samples so she could get on to concentrating on more important things.

Chapter 17
"Tainted Love" Gloria Jones

At approximately 11:28, in Swithin's king sized bedroom, in his king sized bed, Mandy pulled the disheveled covers over both of them and rested her head on his bare chest.

The main house was full of healing battered women and their families, but Swithin rarely visited and let the nonprofits take care of the large house and its guests while he footed the bills. The small guest house worked well for him.

Mandy listened to Swithin's heartbeat and almost found the peaceful place which she had been missing for so long. Eight months ago, Thomas left her and did not keep his promise to stick around. He'd died and without her permission! As much as she wanted to reach into her psyche and try to bring him back, she knew it would only end badly. She would never give into Gwen. Never. She hoped that hole in her head would just dry up and disappear.

Swithin was unreachable at the time, having gone to the Amazon to work through his hostility at her. Mandy had pushed Swithin away so hard, she thought maybe she had broken them for good, but ever resilient, Swithin found his way back to her at long last and she reluctantly accepted his presence back in her life.

The past eight months had been an emotional whirlwind, but as she listened to his heart she thought maybe, just maybe, it would all turn out all right.

"How's the new apprentice coming along?" Swithin asked as he lit up a joint. Two months ago, he'd finally gotten his phone working and heard the news about Thomas. He rushed back to Mandy as soon as he could and had not given into her cold shoulder again. He found his persistence was paying off, as she seemed to be slightly thawing at long last. They were falling right back in where they belonged.

"She's not an apprentice. She's a ghost."

Swithin nearly choked on his inhale, and Mandy sat up.

"Seriously?" she questioned. "You didn't get that at all?"

"I touched the bugger!"

"Don't talk about her like that. You of all people."

He shivered. "I hate ghosties. When did you figure it out?"

Mandy inhaled a drag and blew it out before laying her head back on Swithin's chest. "I think this morning in the seminar. She could see the Class E's. I can't even see Class E's. They are the lowest energy output."

"But...she eats! And...!" he shivered. "Does she know you know?"

"I don't think so. Not yet. And get this. I went back to the lab without her, so I could look up all the juicy details about her. Where's your phone?"

"In the other room."

"Go get it."

"OoOOh," he whined.

"Just go!"

He stood, and she playfully slapped his pale behind. After a particularly rough patch a few years ago, he'd gotten the word FAITH tattooed across his shoulders in AC/DC's iconic font. The 'I', of course, was a lightning bolt. When he returned, he'd logged into Mandy's portal and handed it over so Mandy could pull up the correct file. "There."

Swithin squinted at the screen. "That's a lot of blood."

"She killed her dads when she was seven. Eight years ago. Over 50 stab wounds in each man. Then, she stabbed herself 22 times before dying."

"So, she was possessed?"

"Obviously. I've been in Canada at that wraith thing, so I had no idea things were so bad. I just got back yesterday for our seminar."

"Class A?"

"For sure. And get this. There is no cemetery or anything under the house, but the entire subdivision was built on a landfill."

"You seem to have this under control, Mands."

"She tried to get me to go into her house."

"That's never a good sign."

"She can't be causing it though. She can't. Unless…"

"Unless she's the 'A' posing as a sweet little girl in order to muck you up."

"But why not strike already?"

"You're a honey pot of energy, honey," he kissed her head. "It wants to savor you."

Mandy sighed yet again. "It's a Class Zero, all right, in any case. She is or it is. I mean, she was dead when she was seven. I've never met a ghost that aged. And only a Zero can break free from restraints. It clings onto an idea, and until its desire is met, it can't be stopped. It's massive. You need to see the house."

"I leave at 5:00 a.m., love."

Mandy drummed her fingers on his stomach. She knew he wanted her to ask him to stay and she did need help with this case, however badly she wanted to ignore any talk of a relationship. She waited for him to take another long drag and spoke up with as much sugar as she could muster. "Don't go to Ireland, pwwwease."

He didn't answer right away, but she could feel his smugness. "Well, since you asked so sweetly, you'll have to call mum and tell her why I'm not coming. I haven't seen her in two months with all my attention on you, and all."

"Yeah, yeah. Cuz I asked for that. I'll call her."

"She might go easier on you if you'd accept my proposal."

"Good night," she said and rolled over. "We have a hard day tomorrow. Get some sleep."

"Mands…"

"I *will* leave."

Sighing, he turned out the light, and sunk down into the bed quietly.

Four or five minutes passed and neither one of them slept. Mandy seriously considered leaving, but rigidly lay next to Swithin, hoping he wasn't about to start the conversation that she dreaded.

"We're going to die, Mands. You can't get out of it."

He started it.

Mandy tossed the covers off and stood up in the dark.

"Mandy…Amanda!"

She fumbled around for her clothes in the blackness. "Have you changed your mind?"

"No."

"And neither have I. So, I'm so glad we've had this conversation."

The bed stand light came back on and Mandy squinted while pulling her shorts up.

Swithin was sitting up, dangling her car keys. "And your shirt's inside out."

Mandy put her hand on her hip and eyed the keys. "My car runs on poltergeist. You think I need those?"

He depressed and tossed her the keys.

She grabbed them. "I knew you were going to start this bullshit tonight! I knew it!"

"Mands..."

She headed out the door shoeless, desperate to get away from him. The last thing she needed right now was to poke this wound when she was still reeling from Thomas's death and the giant mistake she may or may not have made.

"Mandy!" Swithin tried jumping after her, but got tangled in the covers and ended up on his face on the floor.

By the time he'd scrambled to his feet, slipped into his pants and arrived outside, Junie was pulling out of the circle drive, playing "Drive" by The Cars. He ran and grabbed onto the driver's side door and yelled for Mandy. Junie gassed, but Mandy stepped on the brake; her face trembling to hold in tears.

"Please come inside, Mands. It's an hour and half back to your place. Come on."

"I don't want to talk about it."

"It has been four years, Amanda. We need to have this out."

Mandy took in a deep breath and pursed her lips. Had it really been that long? "You said you haven't changed your mind."

"Yes, but...can we just..."

"No. We can't. I told you then that if I couldn't have you forever, I didn't want you at all. But you're so fucking tenacious."

"I think you mean addictively charming."

She revved Junie, and he backpedaled.

"Okay, okay! Look, I have thought about it. I've done research and asked questions, but there's just no way...I'm still not willing to pay the prices asked or face the unknowns. Immortality is risky for so many reasons."

"Then, I guess we know who loves who more."

"You act like I don't want to spend eternity with you! That would be better than an eternal fountain of Guinness!"

"That's not the best comparis--"

"We're human, Mands. We're not meant to live forever. And any force that would allow it isn't worth tapping into. It's no different than that door in your head."

Her face finally crumpled and tears fell. He reached into her, but she shied away. She composed herself and spoke, but the tears kept flowing. "That door in my head is my destiny. When I die, I go there. You can't come."

Sobs ensued, and Swithin hurried to the passenger's side. Junie let him in, in a rare act of cooperation, switching her track to Roy Orbison's "Crying." Swithin enveloped his lover and swallowed his own tears.

Though Swithin had deviated from total devoutness, he still attended mass and confession and tried to uphold what he believed to be good Christian and Catholic morals and ethics. He clung to his belief that he--and all hunters--did God's work, and that something better waited for him beyond death. God meant many things to many hunters and Swithin had come to a personal agreement within himself that there was indeed a higher power, God or not, which he found it prudent to be respectful toward.

Especially since the woman he loved may or may not have been carrying around an active God Particle.

Still, he could not find the strength to agree to her terms of becoming immortal. Every argument softened his conviction on the matter, but he wasn't about to tell her that.

Cynical, Thomas had raised Mandy to believe that life was short, death was shit and whatever was on the other side had nothing to do with how you acted in life. With Thomas's death eight months ago, Mandy's innate fear of death became even stronger. Ghosters had a different view on life than other hunters, seeing what they'd seen. The afterlife could, indeed, be a messy place. And Swithin and Mandy rounded each other out in this way, each taking on ideals of the other.

Swithin prodded Mandy into celebrating Christmas and Saint Patrick's Day, and she'd even come to enjoy the holidays even though, for most of them, Swithin had been halfway across the world. He'd been her savior in more ways than one; her rock.

Swithin had broken nearly every commandment due to Mandy's prominent influence over his life and faced down more than one cardinal sin, but his virtue was such that he could always find peace again.

They sat quietly, reminiscing, Junie vibrating beneath them.

Mandy kept a wide berth between them, but Swithin didn't care as long as he could be near her again. He was not to bring up marriage, or immortality, or death or coupley stuff. As far as Mandy was convinced, they were just friends with benefits.

He did bring up coupley stuff, though, more than she wanted, and it ended up in fight after fight. Two years ago, during a particularly nasty bout, Mandy let go every nasty thing she could conjure. Even Swithin had let go several choice words unbefitting his personality. He hung up on her and headed out on a hunt in the middle of the desert to deal with a novice witchdoctor who had bitten off a bit more than he could chew in regards to voodoo. Zombies ensued, and he took his frustration out on them tenfold.

Swithin was gone and coincidence or no, The Agency struck. Distraught by the argument, Mandy's defenses were low, and Headmistress Gwen had finally broken through.

Swithin came back to the States to make amends, but found Mandy in that familiar comatose state at Tom's house. Thomas was nowhere to be found, but Mandy was now residing at the asylum, so she and Thomas weren't in each other's daily lives anymore.

Swithin had no clue how long she'd been like this, save for the fact he hadn't heard from her in two weeks. He'd been deep in the jungle helping the locals protect a mapinguari--or ancient giant sloth-- from loggers, and hadn't had reception. Thomas was supposed to have been keeping an eye on her, but he'd become lazy in his duties since The Agency hadn't been heard from in so long.

Eleanor's psychic abilities had waned considerably after she'd moved into a new body, and try as he might, Swithin could not break into Mandy's head. All he and Thomas could do was wait. Eventually, Mandy vanquished Gwen and came out of it.

Swithin had to be pried from her tired body, but stubborn as ever, Mandy threatened him again, even shooting him with an arrow. Finally, he'd had enough and moved back to South America and the mapinguari to work through his frustration and wait for her to come to her senses.

A monkey absconded with his phone soon after and he become supernaturally lost in the jungle with no way to contact anyone. Even the local tribes seemed to have disappeared. But once he escaped, he found out about Tom, he headed straight for Mandy. Having decided enough was enough, he started proposing every day. Mandy hit him once or twice and cussed at him or hung up on him, but every day, at least once, he found way to squeeze a proposal into conversation. He would not let her go a day without seeing him or hearing him. And so it went. Mandy could not be without him, but she didn't want to be with him. After he'd nearly died four years ago, Mandy told him if she couldn't have him forever then she didn't want him at all, but now, he had sufficiently wormed his way back into her life, and they had quietly dealt with the tension between them for two months.

Sitting in Junie, in the present, Mandy had also had enough. She was so torn between what she wanted and what she needed, something had to give. She ran her fingers through her hair. "I am not giving up this life without a fight. And you're going to either be all in or not in at all. You want to have it out? Decide."

"Mandy…"

"That's it, then."

"Come back inside."

"I need you for this case. But when it's done, so are we."

Swithin held in his eye roll. "You'll never be able to hold that up. I'll stop proposing. I'll stop pushing. But there's nobody else for me, Mands, so I'll wait. And if I die waiting, well, then that's on you, isn't it?"

"Your faith makes everything so much easier. You believe everything will come up roses at the end, but I know better."

"Easy?" he asked, incredulously. "You know what would be easy? Acting on what I want instead of what I believe. I've foolishly chosen the harder path."

He twisted away, put one foot out on the drive and Junie peeled out sharply to the right, throwing Swithin onto the ground, blaring "You Give Love A Bad Name" all the way down the driveway, through the gate and out of sight. Swithin picked himself up and dusted himself off, Bon Jovi still wailing in the distance.

"Miserable heap."

Mandy fumed all the way home, more at herself than him, as always. How could she ever be mad at him? Well, easy. She knew more about the universe than he did, but he tried so hard to be good and faithful that it was impossible for her to truly be angry. He was her light.

But he still pissed her off.

Once home, she said goodnight to Junie and pulled the cover over her as she liked. The hearse purred before shutting down for the evening, and Mandy patted the hood lovingly. The three mutts and most of the cats rushed to greet her and she handed out love accordingly. They always cheered her up. She was never allowed pets while under the supervision of The Agency, and Thomas said that having pets was cruel when there was a good chance you'd die any minute. But since these were technically strays, Mandy didn't own them; though she did spay and neuter each one, and feed and shelter them and love them. It was more like they owned her! Suddenly, a burning pain caused her to yelp and she lifted her shirt to find a charcoal blister on the side of her left boob.

Resisting the urge to pop it, Mandy swallowed her fear of the expected health development and checked the fridge even though she wasn't hungry. She fed the furballs--the dogs had to be fed outside because of their unwillingness to enter the place--and she checked the fridge again, but nothing had changed. She wasn't tired. Pushing away the impending venom, she remembered the night she and Swithin first kissed. It had been the best day of her life, and she often revisited the memory when she was frustrated with their situation. She slammed the fridge door, and her Save a Stray magnet fell off and slid under the table. Though she'd seen some secrets of the universe, she had far from figured them out, but nights like this, she thought on it a little more. She knew that damned abyss was destined to be her final resting place like she knew she was in love. It was just something she knew. She and Swithin were not going to the same place no matter how much he believed it. She padded around the quiet, weathered asylum a bit before making her way back to the fridge. The contents still hadn't changed.

A creaking door brought her from her funk, and she instantly reached for her concealed firearm. In a haunted building, noises were to be expected, visions were regular, and sometimes, the fridge contents actually did change. But she'd faced down human intruders before.

And then there was always The Agency.

She flipped on the light in the hallway. They went on one by one, buzzing, down the long, tattered hall outside the kitchen. No ghosts that she could sense. There was always that voice that told her it was an old place and sometimes drafts got in, but she always ignored it immediately. Someone or something was afoot.

She checked each room in the hall one by one. She kept all the doors closed for this purpose; when one was open, it meant something. But none of them were open and she hadn't heard one close.

Once at the end of the hall, she checked the bathroom, which she hated because it was infested with spiders, but a very quick peek told her all was well…And furry, and with many eyes and legs.

It was then she got the spine tingle. And it wasn't from an arachnid.

She slowly turned, wondering why she was slowly doing it as she was doing it. The lights went off one by one to illuminate a hulking cloaked figure at the end of the hall.

"Shit."

It came at her full force screaming and wailing. This particular critter didn't seem familiar, but then, haunts popped up all the time in this place no matter how well she thought she'd exorcised it. She fired two rounds of special bullets into it, but it still came, and she grabbed her blessed dagger, ready for a collision that never happened. The apparition disappeared halfway down the hall. Curious, which could be dangerous in this line of work, she headed toward the door at which it had disappeared, and opened it.

She tried closing it quickly but it was too late.

They'd gotten through.

Grumbling at both himself and at Mandy, not for the first time, Swithin didn't sleep well, and in the morning, headed to Cat's to get the show on the road with this supposed Class Zero case.

Cat was there, waiting, but Mandy didn't show, and after an hour, Swithin sighed his bad feeling away and headed to the asylum.

"Hello?"

"This is where she lives?" Cat asked. Though Mandy had refurbished a lot of the main hall and the downstairs rooms that she lived in, most of the inside retained its peeling walls and ceiling to floor filth.

"Don't ask me why," he said. "Hello? Mands?"

The asylum creeped him out, and he hated visiting, but at least it was daytime.

"You want to split up?" Cat asked.

"Usually, no. But I think we need to find her quickly, so I'll make an exception. Yell if you find something."

She headed off to the left, the kitchen, and he made a line for the grand staircase to check her room upstairs, but he never made it to the top before Cat called him.

He raced back down and turned the corner into the kitchen to see Mandy staring into the fridge blankly. The little Siamese cat sat at her feet purring. "Oh, not again."

"This happens often?" Cat was waving her hand in front of Mandy's face.

Swithin shooed the cat away, picked Mandy up and carried her to the thick wooden table. Cat brushed everything aside and Swithin set Mandy down. She was covered in lacerations and suction cup shaped bruises. Last time, he could not make it inside her head, but since then, they'd been practicing, lest the occasion should arise. Swithin had doubled his training in the mental arts.

"I have to go in after her," Swithin explained severely after another cut appeared on Mandy's forehead. "You stand guard."

"Against what? Where are you going? What do I do?"

Swithin went through his cargo pants and unloaded his silver blade, pistol, silver and gold bullets, high pitched whistle, dart gun, darts and herb bags on the counter as Cat wondered where he'd been hiding all of it. He unstrapped two more blades from holsters around his calves. "This place has some unscrupulous characters and that's all I have on me, but I don't think there will be trouble. I have to go." He took Mandy's hand, but Cat stopped him.

"Where are you going? What's going on?"

"Hopefully nothing we can't handle."

Swithin took in a deep breath, centering himself and gathering the necessary chi to meld with Mandy.

Like last time this happened, it had happened right after they'd fought. He'd hear about that for sure.

He reached out to her body with his energy and enveloped her in light, picturing them as one, envisioning the inside of her mind; the open field with doors, the smell of fresh rain and the warm breeze.

When he opened his eyes, he was there amid the doors, but he did not sense her. Her mind was here, but her psyche must have been elsewhere and he needed to find her. If it were like last time, time was of the essence. He made his way through the doors of memories, dreams, ideas and information, trying to find his way back to the black abyss which must have opened. It was incredibly far beyond Swithin's scope to deal with universe battling leviathans, but Mandy needed him, and they would succeed or fail together.

The moist, black crevasse was oozing some sort of brackish slime and that, worriedly, had not been happening last time. "Here's goes nothing."

He headed in and came out covered in goo, but found himself in a 10 x 10 room which Mandy was desperately trying to hold together. The walls kept pulling away and cracks yielded tentacles, rays of changing light, flying insectoid thingies and a heap of other nightmarish crap.

"Swithin!" Mandy called from the center of the small room.

This was not like last time. Last time, there was a beyond. A great wide beyond, and Swithin had to pull Mandy from it. She had been so tempted to let go of her body and surrender her soul to it. He had to talk her down, but he knew there were things out there. He could sense them and he could hear them right before he dragged her back. But this was all out chaos. If these things got through her defenses, the world, the universe perhaps, would be in a deep, deep doo-doo.

"What can I do?" he called over the cacophony of hissing and shrieking.

"I have to keep this room together. If there is one crack, one pin hole, they will get through. You're the monsterer! Do something!"

"Right," he replied, having absolutely no clue what to do. But Mandy could not handle fighting them off and holding the room together at the same time.

"We're not on a real plane, so to speak, Swith! You can bring to light any weapon you need!"

He took in a deep breath and turned to face a missing wall and a larger than life black pupiled eye. "Mother of fuck! Mandy!"

The wall reappeared and Swithin put on his game face. Concentrating, he brought a shiny rapier to each hand. "Let's do this."

Cat sat alone in the quiet asylum watching the two toppled bodies. There wasn't a lot that frightened her. She was after all, a ghost. But something was very, very bad about wherever her two new friends had gone. She jumped when Swithin's face suddenly produced a gash.

"Ouch! Bugger!" Swithin parried around an acidic tentacle wielding razor hairs, and didn't escape a lashing across his face. A few fleches, flicks and flunges later, Swithin had been able to repel the beyond beasts enough so Mandy could pull the walls together. While Swithin waited nervously amidst the banging and shrieking outside the walls, Mandy pictured the entire gray box they were in covered in a thick, hard amber. It took longer than Swithin cared to think about, but at last, it was done and everything went silent.

He sighed with relief and looked to Mandy who was aiming an arrow at his head.

He ducked in time, but still felt the whisp from the arrow's flight. Behind him, a squawking skeletal bat like creature writhed on the floor. He stared at it, and then Mandy pushed by him and stomped it to death.

"Seriously, how are you still alive when you won't kill anything?"

"I'm still a little dazed by all this, love."

She shook some of the purple goo blood from her shoe.

"Mands? Uh...how do we get out?"

Mandy looked at the far wall. "We run."

"Right. Uh..."

"I open a wall and we run." She headed toward the wall.

"Okay. Sure. But, um, how do I know you're Mandy and not one of those things trying to get me to let you out?"

"Good question."

"Kiss me."

"Pardon?"

"Kiss me. And not one of your 'I'm distancing myself from you for whatever bullheaded reason' kisses. Like you mean it. Like you used to. And if I don't buy it, we're going to be spending a lot of time here. I hope we can get cable. *Downton Abbey*'s on tonight."

Mandy thought a minute, wondering if she could let go all of her insecurities and fear long enough to convince him that she was real. She had no other way to prove it, and though it was smart of him to double check, she wished he was stupider at the moment.

He stepped up to her and put his arms around her. "Well? Are you Mandy or are you monster?"

"I wasn't aware there was a difference," she jested morbidly.

He gently pressed his lips to hers and held them there waiting for her, desperately hoping she was Mandy and he wasn't about to get his face bitten off.

Mandy closed her eyes and forced herself to feel safe. She recalled with vivid clarity their first kiss; the lake, the frogs...the cougar. She melted into the memory, for it was her favorite of all of them, and her body followed.

Swithin finally pulled away and grinned. "There's my girl. Let's go home."

A sharp pain on her side yanked Mandy from her peace. She felt around beneath her shirt and it was another blister.

"You all right?" Swithin asked.

"Yeah," she lied. "Just, you should know that these cuts and bruises are going to be a lot more painful once we're in the real world."

"Goody."

Mandy opened the wall and Swithin ran.

In a twinkle of blinding flashes, Swithin awoke in a panic, but he was sitting at the kitchen table, Catori praising God he was back.

"I honestly don't think God had anything to do with it," he breathed. Then he looked to Mandy who had not come back. "Shit. Mandy! Mands!" He shook her, but she remained blank.

"What do we do?" Catori worried. Nearly all of the cats had gathered in the kitchen.

"I'm going back in."

"But you've been gone for hours! It's almost dark outside!"

"I know, but time's different in there." He took Mandy's hand again, but didn't have to travel, for she woke up, blinking and hoarse. They were both covered in bruises and scratches. Catori tried cleaning them up and bandaging them.

Mandy still didn't sit up or move besides talking. "How long was I out?"

"I don't know. When you didn't show at Cat's, we came looking for you."

"You were, like, just gone," Cat added.

Mandy finally sat up with a groan. Everything hurt. Even her hair.

Swithin chastised her. "You were supposed to tell me when these things happened. When was the last one? You promised me you'd tell me."

"And I did. The last time was the last time. Right after our last fight."

There it was. Swithin bit his lip as she went on.

"You have no idea how hard I have to concentrate to keep them out. Whatever those witches did to me, whatever they built inside of me, those things can get through with it. I have to concentrate. And you…distract me."

"I'm sorry, love. I just…"

"I know. I'm tired of fighting, too. But until I decide it's safe to die, or you decide it's a good idea to become immortal, we don't have a cure for what's wrong with us."

"Even Jesus had to die, Mandy," he repeated.

"Don't spout your religious bullshit to me. I have seen things, and heard things and know things that human beings just shouldn't know. And it would be so easy to give into it. To take that step into the borders of the universe and….play God."

"Yes, well, my religious bullshit is what gives me the strength to put up with you and your blasphemous arrogance."

Catori just stood and watched them face off. Eventually, Mandy slid off the table, tired of fighting. "I'm starving."

"Seriously? After the…slime and the…eyeballs? I think those were eyeballs. Hey, where are you going?"

Mandy bypassed the fridge, grabbed a bag of veggie chips off the counter and headed out of the kitchen toward the stairs. The little

Siamese followed. "To bed. We have a ghost to vanquish. You two can have your pick of the guest rooms."

Before bed she checked her side for the black blister, but it had healed. Her body was still fighting, but slowly, slowly losing its battle against the manticore venom she'd siphoned off her love so many years ago.

Chapter 18
"Two Divided By Love" by The Grass Roots

The next morning, Junie purred beneath Mandy and Cat, playing "Welcome to my Nightmare" as they pulled up to Cat's home and parked.

Swithin arrived five minutes later and gazed out into the haze. "At least you can see a monster," he muttered to himself. "Ghosts just sneak up on you and give you the habdabs."

"Hi, Swithin!"

Swithin nearly hit the roof of the car as Cat appeared at the window. "Bloody hells, girl! Don't DO that!"

While Swithin gathered a few things from the back of his Aston, Cat met Mandy on the front lawn.

"You two okay?" Cat pondered.

Mandy ignored talk of Swithin. "I'll be in back placing a few more wards. We'll need them." She stomped off when Swithin walked up to Cat, shaking a vial of potion.

Swithin began searching outside, under rocks and in broken lawn gnomes for hex bags or residues. Cat stared, fascinated as he meticulously set out various pouches and other objects certain distances from the house. The house moaned, and he jumped.

"I thought you two weren't scared of anything," Cat chuckled nervously.

"Mandy's got balls of steel, or ovaries. Or whatever. I'm a scaredy cat when it comes to ghosts." He regretted saying it the second it came out, but Cat didn't flinch.

"Are you going to go inside?"

He laughed. "Absolutely not. Can you go inside?"

"No. The house locks up and this awful stench, like, pushes me away."

"So, there you go."

"Last night not go so well?" Cat asked.

She was a nosy ghost. He'd give her that. "It's an ongoing struggle."

"So, she said she won't marry you because your work's too dangerous."

"Is that what she said?"

"Uh, huh. But I think she's lying."

"Perceptive." He set a hex pouch beneath the downspout and eyed her, but nothing happened. She was a strong spirit, indeed.

Cat watched as he said a few words over the window and sprayed it with something. The house creaked, and Cat stepped away from it.

So, she was scared of the house. That nixed her as the Class A inside. Swithin went on. "She's been a little extra rattled since her mentor died earlier this year. The wanker."

"What happened?"

Swithin knew he was probably not supposed to say any of this, but he was too nervous not to talk. "He was an idiot."

"Nice."

Swithin backpedaled. He didn't hate Thomas and didn't want to speak ill of him, but the man had broken Mandy's heart and that was nigh unforgivable. "Tom was one of the best and the luckiest, and it's a grim reminder." He stopped scrounging around and griped to Cat, "He actually promised Mandy that he would never leave her; that he would always be around even if it meant coming back as a ghost! Oh. Then, he dies right? Firstly, he never shows for Mandy, and we come to find out that the bastard had two wives!"

"Wow."

"Yeah. One on each American coast. As 'Max Jaeger', he had two best-selling books, you know. And a movie deal. He wasn't low where the pounds were concerned and the two biddies are fighting it in court but he'd left his fortune to his son--who hadn't come from either of them."

"Sounded like a winner."

Swithin shrugged and peeled back a split piece of dead sapling. "He had his problems. We all do. So," he went on wanting to get off the subject of Mandy and find out more about Cat. "What's your deal? Your popses really leave you here by yourself?"

"Yeah. We're a pretty liberal family."

Liberated, he thought cruelly. "You adopted, then?"

"When I was seven."

"Good for them. Sound like all right blokes, then, right?"

She nodded. "This thing has been eating at us though, for sure. Whatever it is."

They rounded the back of the house where Mandy was busy setting down salt rings and chanting. Swithin headed for the oversized shed, but Cat hesitated.

"Is there something in there?" he asked, following suit.

"No," she shook her head. "No. Just, well, that's where my bike was. I had to get it away from him."

"Got it." Creeped out by the shed, Swithin turned his attention back to the house. "You, uh, come from the orphanage in Brainstead?"

She nodded. "You know it?"

He shivered. "Mandy's had a few cases there. Ghost children are the worst! Oh..." *Wait! She hadn't told them she was a ghost yet!* Swithin thought, biting his lip. "Um, well, anyway, and that place has been around since 1836. Technology interferes with them, so you don't get as many strong ones as you used to. Same with the monsters. All the radio waves and cell phone towers and Wi-Fi kind of inebriate them, so monsters don't mate as readily, but they sure are angrier! Whew!"

Swithin hadn't ever been so glad to see Mandy come around a corner, even if she was playing mad at him. "Finished!" he called out, stepping away from Cat.

Mandy ignored him and turned to Cat, trying to gauge her on the good/evil scale. "So, tell us about your dads. Any baggage? I mean, Class Zero's are tough. They don't need an object to hold them here and sometimes just an idea is enough to fuel their will. Until their desires are met, you can't get rid of them. Do either one of your dads have a past?"

Cat sighed and thought about it. "Not that I can think of offhand. Dad Fred was married once, but she's still alive."

"Did it end well?" Swithin asked.

"Not really. She wasn't real happy that her husband left her for another guy."

"Well, I didn't see any hex bags..."

"Hey, I actually have a class I go to on Saturday afternoons. Since I didn't get to go to Japan. I guess I'll see you tomorrow. Feel free to stay as long as you dare. It gets pretty rough after four."

"Right," Mandy nodded.

"Toodles," Swithin waved.

Cat rode her bike down the street and disappeared around the bend.

"Must need to recharge. Did she tell you anything?" Mandy asked.

"Oh, are we talking, now? Or did you want to have Junie play a song?"

Mandy glared at him.

"Something about the Brainstead orphanage," he surrendered. "And she was scared of the house. So, I don't think she's our baddie."

"Let's get to the orphanage and see what Sister Tammy says. Junie will drive."

"I'm not leaving my car here! What if that thing comes out and dents it or something?"

"Fine. Drive separate. Or, don't go. I don't care."

"Well, I can just meet you out on the main road. It's not that big of a...Oh, whatever.'" He headed toward the hearse who cheekily began playing Chopin's classic Funeral March. "But I pick the playlist!"

Sister Tammy had always been a friend to paranormalists. The Brainstead orphanage was founded in 1836 and had a long history; some of which was not so nice, and old ghosts still popped up here and there. It was about a hundred miles south, and Mandy and Swithin spent the driving time reminiscing about old cases and colleagues, different monsters and ghosts.

Swithin graciously kept his word and didn't slip anything resembling a proposal into conversation. Closer to the orphanage, the topic of Cat came up.

"She seems familiar to me," Mandy said. "But I can't place it. I must know her from here. Thomas and I vanquished a few spirits here when I was first getting started."

"Wanker."

Mandy didn't disagree. In fact, she was sorry she'd said his name at all as it just brought back the fresh memory of his death...

On the way back from a rather dull case of a Class B, Thomas stopped at a diner to satiate his need for grease, and Mandy searched the menu for anything that wouldn't come right back up. A buxom, young waitress came over and asked for their orders. Thomas couldn't help but be dashing no matter the circumstance, and the girl blushed.

"Bacon wrapped waffles, extra cheese and chili on the hash and grits with lots of butter." To Mandy, "Sweets?"

"Fruit plate," Mandy smiled. "Please."

While waiting, Thomas eyed up the other, slightly older waitress and asked Mandy if she thought he could get a two for one deal with the wait staff. Mandy just sighed and shook it off.

Food came and they ate. The fruit plate was ginormous, and Mandy was surprised she finished it all. Thomas, of course, didn't leave a crumb, and the buxom waitress dropped their check on the table--only, it wasn't a check, but a business card.

Mandy picked it up and looked at it. "Emerald Industries."

As soon as she said it, a completely different, weathered waitress approached. "Can I take your order?" she asked.

Thomas and Mandy shared a befuddled glance, but Thomas reordered everything with two sides of smothered ham.

"What?" he told Mandy. "I didn't actually eat." To the waitress, "Thanks, doll." The unfamiliar woman walked away, and Thomas leaned into Mandy. "What the hell was that? That wasn't one of your visions."

Rattled, Mandy shrugged. "I have no idea what that was."

"Gimmie that," he snatched the little business card from her and glanced at the address. "Guess we're not going home after all."

Mandy's memory blissfully ended as The Brainstead Orphanage came into sight. Like the asylum, it rested on its own acreage. The orphanage, however, still received tax funding, along with private donations from families, churches and orphan "alums". Though old, the imposing stone structure was modern and well maintained through volunteers and the children. After surviving wars, depressions, politics, and, of course, ghosts--it boasted a school, a pool, a gym, several tree houses, an arcade and even a Go Kart track. Sister Tammy had been the proprietor since anyone could remember. Mandy sometimes wondered if the woman was an angel. She'd have to ask Swithin. Magical creatures were his department.

"Amanda!" Sister Tammy shuffled over to her. The woman must have been 110 years old, but looked no more than seventy. Mandy hugged her and introduced Swithin who also got a hug. He hadn't expected it to be a bear hug from such a withered thing and his eyes bulged slightly.

"What brings you by dear?" Sister Tammy asked, still holding Swithin's hand. "No one reported anything, did they? OH, he is handsome. And British! Oh, you lucky thing, you," Sister play slugged Mandy. "I'll be asking him some questions for sure, just to hear him talk."

Swithin couldn't help but blush. "You American ladies are too easily entertained."

"Sister," Mandy went on, "I'm here about an old ward of yours. Catori--well, her adoptive name was..."

"Oh, we only had one Catori, dear. Such a shame. Such a pity. She was a good one. And those nice gentlemen who adopted her. Oh, we live for happily ever afters around here, and I thought for sure she'd found it. She was possessed, wasn't she?"

"I think so."

"I knew it!"

"But that was nearly eight years ago, now. Has something else come up?"

"You could say that, love," Swithin offered. "She has."

Sister Tammy squeezed his hand "Oh, if I wasn't married to the Lord, you'd be in trouble!" She still did not let go of his hand, and Mandy stifled a laugh. "Well now, that is a shame about Cat. But I can't say I'm surprised. She had the gift, you know. She was always walking around, talking to the spirits. When her fathers came along, I warned them about it, but they didn't seem too concerned. They were nice men. Doctors, I think. But my memory isn't what it used to be."

"Do you think something could have followed her?" Mandy asked. "Did she take anything from the orphanage?"

"No, no. Oh, you must put her to peace, Amanda."

"Do you recall if I'd ever met her?"

Sister Tammy thought a minute. "I don't recall. Why?"

"She just seems familiar, and Thomas and I were here."

"Oh, yes! What a charmer he turned into. How is he?"

"Dead," Swithin said.

"Well, that is a shame."

"He had it coming," he shrugged.

Sister Tammy eyed Swithin and then Mandy and patted Swithin's hand.

Mandy shook her head at the absurd insinuation and walked past them into the Great Hall. Sister Tammy and Swithin followed, kids running to and fro. It was the weekend and they were rambunctious.

Mandy tried remembering Catori. She knew she knew the girl. Some force prompted her to turn her head toward a basket of toys near the sofa in front of a massive fireplace. As she neared it, a memory trickled back. The fire was warm and the kids were loud, but her mind had quieted, taking her back nine years ago...

Mandy was at the orphanage with Thomas. They were there to check on a potential Class B, which had turned out to be a prankster. There were so many children. Mandy didn't particularly like kids, but she couldn't help but feel sorry for them. They had a million questions, too, and Thomas, the egomaniac that he was, never passed up a chance to tell his tales. Mandy used to think it was charming.

The wanker.

Still, he'd only been dead eight months, and she'd already forgotten how handsome he'd been; like from an old movie. Rock Hudson would have been jealous. And Thomas had taken her in when none of the other hunters would. Sure, Swithin's dad had strong-armed him, but he'd done it anyway. She was cursed. They all knew it. No one would have survived what she had unless they'd been cursed. Thomas had a bit of the devil in him, too, which is why they got on so well.

She'd spent 13 years with Thomas hunting, surviving and learning. He'd taught her to box and live life to the fullest. He truly had been the best. The entire community wagered there was nothing that could take them down. Mandy should have never made him promise to stay behind, but he swore he could. He swore he could do damn near anything and he'd never failed her before.

Until he'd died.

She could forgive him for not being able to stick around afterwards, but she could never forgive him for dying in the first place.

Kids circled Thomas near the fireplace, and he recalled the tale of a Class B that had been terrorizing a movie theatre. Mandy didn't see Cat with the kids surrounding Thomas. Catori would have been about four. Then, she felt it…the presence. She looked down, and there was Catori in a pink nightgown hugging a little stuffed kangaroo.

Kangaroo.

"Will you adopt me?" Little Cat asked.

Mandy wanted to say yes. Well, she hadn't wanted to then. But she did now. Unfortunately, she, nor Swithin, had the power to go back in time--she didn't think--and they weren't connected with anyone who was. Besides, time travel was another cardinal sin and The Agency had already tried and failed at that when Mandy was in their clutches. And this was a memory in Mandy's mind, after all. Nothing could be done.

"I can't, little one. But someone will come along. I promise. Go over and listen to the story."

And that was it.

Having found what she needed, Mandy popped back to the present.

"Well?" Swithin asked.

"She knows me all right," Mandy panted, thinking back on her and Cat's lunch conversation. "She asked me to adopt her and I turned her down. You know, I was only 17."

"And you hate children."

"I don't hate them. They just creep me out. After seeing what I've seen, you'd be creeped out by them, too."

"No convincing needed. So, you think she's after you, then?"

"It's possible. I've never seen anything as strong as her. Tangible, sentient and able to wander."

"You think she's the culprit?"

Mandy sighed. "I don't know. I can't believe some little kid would latch onto me hard enough after two seconds of meeting to stay behind as a ghost."

"Ghosts are a strange lot."

Mandy took the information she knew and tried to formulate a story. She'd met Cat when Cat was young. Cat latched onto her. Cat ended up in a house above a landfill with the remains of a dangerous, possessing spirit who forced her to kill her parents and herself...And yet, Cat clung to life. Cat was a--Mandy hoped--benign being. How? Catori certainly wasn't like any other spirit Mandy had come across or even heard about. She was at least a Class Zero-sentient, opaque and tangible, free floating, attached to an idea. She aged, even! But what idea was she latched to? Mandy had to rid the world of the dangerous, possessing spirit in Cat's house for sure, but first she had to solve Catori.

"Sister Tammy?" Mandy approached the old nun and Tammy knew something was brewing.

"Oh, dear."

"Sister, I need to know whatever you know about Catori."

"Well? Really, there's no trail, I'm afraid."

It was obvious she was hiding something, and that's when Swithin stepped in.

"Amanda! Tsk! Can't you see the poor dear is overworked?" He took Sister Tammy's hand and led her to a chair. "Let's just relax, shall we?" He took off his denim jacket, revealing his lean biceps and fitted Led Zeppelin tee. "Can I get you a cup of tea or a biscuit?"

"Oh, I do like you. Mandy, he's a keeper for sure."

Mandy smiled sardonically at Swithin. For every woman who used sex as a motivator, Swithin made up for it ten times over for men everywhere.

Sister Tammy set her hand on Swithin's. "Tea is good but I have something better."

She stood and bent over her desk drawer to pull out a bottle of whisky and three glasses. Swithin lit up. "That a girl! You're one of those Irish lasses, aren't you?"

"Second generation to live in the States," she grinned.

"My pop is Irish. Mum is from Wales, so I grew up there, but I spent a lot of time in Balbriggan with my gran."

"Oh, my grandfather was from Balbriggan! What do you know?"

Mandy cleared her throat. "So, we can color family trees later. Sister? Catori. Spill it."

After two shots, Sister Tammy sighed, eyed her guests and knew she wasn't going to get out of this.

"Well?" She looked back to Swithin who smoldered charm and put her at ease. "Her mother dropped her off when she was two. Said she couldn't deal with it anymore."

"Deal with what?"

"She never really said, but, well, I've been around awhile and I can sense these things. I knew Catori was...special. So, of course I pressed her for more information before I agreed to take her daughter, and she agreed to give me details, but I could not write anything down and I had to promise never to tell Cat."

Mandy took a seat across from Tammy who took another shot of whisky.

Sister Tammy went on. "I asked about the father, of course, and, well, that was the rub. The big secret. She said that Cat's father was a deity."

Without changing expression. Mandy swiveled her head toward Swithin. "Deities count as monsters. That's more your territory."

Swithin nervously rubbed the back of his neck. "Well, uh, if you want more of an expert..."

"I'm not calling Missy."

"Right." He addressed Sister Tammy, "What was his name, love?"

"Oh, I knew you'd ask. The steel trap is a little rusty after all these years. Mm, Gluten? Glue stab? Glow stick? Go scab?"

"Glooscap?" Swithin asked.

"Sure, sure. That might be right."

"Who is that?" Mandy asked, not really knowing if she wanted to know.

Swithin shrugged. "Not the worst, but when it comes to gods, it's never the best. I'm not the expert, especially with North American history."

"I am not calling Missy," Mandy reiterated.

"Fair enough." He took out his phone, typed in the name and read the description. "The Native American tribe, the Abenaki, believe that after Tabaldak created humans, the dust from his body created Glooscap and his twin brother, Malsumis. He gave Glooscap the power to create a good world. Malsumis could be good, but chooses to be evil."

"Well, Glooscap is better than Malsumis, right?"

Still looking over the info, Swithin shrugged. "Meh. Deities are wishy-washy. True, Glooscap is the better of the two, but modern Abenaki believe Glooscap is very angry at the white people for not obeying the rules he set down."

"Great. Angry deity kid."

"Exactly."

Mandy deflated. "A ghost of a demigod. Yeah. Gotta say that's a new one on me. Tammy, did it seem like Cat's mother was trying to hide her from her father or what?"

Tammy raised her shoulders. "She just said she'd had enough. Couldn't get much more. I was afraid for Cat, so we took her in. I know we should never have adopted her out, oh, I know." She began to tear up regretfully, and Swithin put a reassuring hand on her shoulder. "Cat was a good girl, though. I do hope she'll be all right, whatever's going on."

"We'll try our best, Sister. Thank you. Oh! Wait. One more thing. Do you think you can draw up another set of adoption papers for me?"

"Oh, Mandy, I don't know, with your line of work? A child?"

"It's for Cat. I think it might help her move on, if--you know-- she's been adopted."

"Oh! Splendid idea. I'll be right back."

Sister Tammy left for a moment, and Mandy conversed with Swithin. "We need to get back to that house and hope Cat's as benevolent as Sister remembers."

"You still think she could be an evil sort?"

"She's been around that nasty presence long enough and soaking in negative energy, so I just don't know. But if we can get her to move on, all the better."

"Well, I can tell you something about Sister Tammy. She's no angel, but there is certainly something good looking after her and this place. Kind of reassuring, though, eh? Sad how little we know about Good's side of things, isn't it?"

"That's because Good doesn't need tending to."

After Swithin smugly signed the adoption papers, noting that he and Mandy were now pinned together via an adoption--ghost or not-- Mandy rolled her eyes, bid Sister farewell and headed out to the hearse. The drive back was pleasantly uneventful. Junie played Monkees tunes while Swithin and Mandy theorized about the good deities, ghosts, angels and other positive beings. Swithin had more experience with it since he'd had to save a few, and his family had been charged with protecting some of the rare species centuries ago, but Mandy's occupation had taken her to mostly dark roads with darker entities. Not that a good spirit didn't pop up every once in a while, but usually content people moved on without vengeance or evil to keep them here. As they neared the house, Mandy wavered on her conviction that Cat was all good. Mandy wanted to believe it. Especially since in life, Cat had had the energy of a positive deity running through her. Or mostly good. But negative energy was a force to be reckoned with. Its purpose was to destroy and maim, and both Mandy and Swithin had been witness to its power.

Swithin dozed off about two hours in, and Mandy's thoughts led her back to the day Thomas died...

"It says Emerald is a pharmaceutical company," Mandy informed Thomas after looking it up on her phone.

He shoved the last piece of ham into his mouth. "We both know where this is leading, sweets."

Mandy did. And it terrified her more than anything. "This is a bad idea, Tom."

"You have been running from those green whores your whole life. Don't you want to fight back?"

"Why today? You wouldn't even fight one at an airport, and now you want to charge into the hive when they know we're coming?"

"We don't know they know."

"I have an invite in my hand!" She held up the business card.

"Have I ever let you down?"

Mandy thought a second, but she could not come up with one time. "No. But that sets the bar exceedingly fucking high."

"And how much longer do you have to live with that manticore venom in your system anyway? A year or two? Tops?"

"You sure know how to pep talk a girl."

He burped and shrugged. "Your villains, your call. But we both know that it was gods who dropped that card on the table. If they're using their limited energy to tip us, it's a good bet to follow it. Probably the same ones that ripped apart your foster guards. Gods don't take kindly to people who mess around with the universe. If they say go now, we need to go now."

Mandy stood and set a more than generous tip on the table. "It's as good a day to die as any, I suppose."

"That's my girl."

About 4:00 p.m., Junie pulled up and stopped in front of Catori's house, cutting "Daydream Believer" off in the middle, which suited Swithin just fine, as she'd played it ten times already. He tried to be civil with Junie and say he liked the song, which he did, but she responded by playing it over and over, while Mandy just rocked out to it.

Everything still remained dead quiet. No birds, no rustling, no anything. No Cat. Mandy and Swithin got out of the hearse and stared down the house.

"You ready?" Mandy asked.

"No. I hate ghosts."

"Come on."

The front door creaked open invitingly and Mandy rolled her eyes. "Really?"

"I hope that was the wind," Swithin whined.

She looked at him. "Really?"

"Bah. If it were a beastly barghest or a grindylow, I'd know how to handle it. But this?" He shivered. "It's just creepy."

"Yes, well they feed on that, so reel it in."

"Hey, she said she'd been attached to her bike." Swithin nodded toward the large shed in the backyard.

The duo made it to the back, and Mandy reached to open the door, but a massive wind blew, knocking Swithin over, and it grabbed Mandy by the ankles.

"Mands!" Swithin fought the bluster, but the gray aura had swarmed around her and was pulling her inside.

Mandy kept her cool and got inside her jacket, grabbed a vial of custom ghost deterrent, bit off the lid and tossed it at the gray fuzz attached to her legs. Swithin was still screaming when the thing dropped her and sucked itself back inside.

Mandy stood and checked herself over while Swithin hyperventilated.

"You have done this with me before," she reminded him.

"And I hated it then!"

"Yeah. Catori? Hey! We're here and we know all about you."

Nothing.

"That's underwhelming," Swithin muttered.

Mandy just look annoyed. "Damnit."

"What?"

"She should be here is all."

Nothing appeared, but Mandy looked around expectantly, then she froze. "Feel that?"

"My heart beating through my chest? Hard to ignore. At least I could stake a vampire."

"You are not helping." She blew out a breath and could see it in the air. Swithin shivered as well, as the temperature dropped rapidly.

"Come back out and play, beast," Mandy called. "I'm not afraid of you, and I'm not here for you....yet."

"Frrrrrreeeeeeeeessssssssssshhhhhhh meeeeeeeeaaaaaaaaaat..."

"Yeah. Sure. Whatever. Come out and let's talk about it."

A familiar voice called out. "Swithysweet?"

"Gran?" he turned to see his gran at the fence holding a plate of fresh steam pudding. Problem was, Gran had been dead for decades.

"Swithin!" Mandy yelled.

"Oh, I know, I know! Bugger off bogey! Awe, Gran…"

A sudden gust of wind knocked both Mandy and Swithin to the backsides, and Gran's body morphed into an image of the entity's true form for a moment before rushing the two hunters. Mandy put her hand out, which contained a tranquilizing mixture of herbs, lavender, salt and other choice ingredients, and called out an incantation. Mandy tossed out the mixture, and upon making contact with it, Gran dispersed, and the air returned to normal.

"Bloody hell, Mands! It could have killed us!"

"It'll get another shot. Definitely a Class A. Still not so sure how to get to his body without digging up the whole house."

Cat's voice rang out at the back door. "Excuse me?"

Mandy and Swithin turned, expecting to see Cat, but instead saw Sister Tammy holding a scalpel to her own throat. It was obvious Cat was controlling the nun from the inside.

"Cat!" Mandy scolded. This girl had been possessed and forced to kill her family and herself. What was she thinking doing it to someone else?

"So, you can beat him!" Tammy/Cat said, "Good. Now, just one more thing I need you to do and, judging by our conversations, I'll have to get nasty about it."

"Let Tammy go, Cat."

"I will. As long as you cooperate."

"I already have," Mandy said, digging in her satchel. She pulled out the adoption papers. "See? Swithin and I officially adopted you. We're a family."

"Well, that does speed things along. You are a smart one, aren't you? But we aren't done yet."

"What?"

"A family unit is a committed unit, Mandy. Committed. Do you understand what I'm saying?"

Mandy was getting the picture, but she didn't like it. "I signed the papers. I'm sorry I didn't adopt you when I was, you know, 17. Which, by the way, you should understand is a bit ludicrous."

"But not anymore. I knew we were meant to be family. Fred and Frank were great, and I will never forgive myself for letting that thing inside me. I should have fought harder to save them. But in the end, I belong with you anyway. We're alike, you and I."

"If you say so."

"Signing papers is easy, Mandy. You can still walk away from it. Though, it does limit my movement for sure--binds me, as it were. But it's not enough to satisfy my needs, and it won't send me into the light."

"Cat..." Swithin started, but Cat cut him off.

"I'm doing this for all of us, and you should be grateful!" Cat spat at him. "She'll never give in to you!"

Mandy shook her head. "You're not going to hurt Sister Tammy, Cat. You're not malicious."

Mandy took a step toward them, and Cat drew blood from Sister Tammy's neck. Mandy stopped, fearing for Tammy's safety. "I thought you weren't scared of anything but commitment?" Cat mocked.

Mandy regained composure.

Tammy/Cat went on. "I've been a little tainted, lately, Mandy. I'm capable, oh yes. And willing. All I ever wanted is a family and if I don't get it, I'll go mad. I'm strong, but I can't be here with that thing anymore! It's winning!"

Mandy knew it to be true enough. The only reason Cat had probably held out as long as she had was the fact she'd been a demigod. Even Class A's who began benevolent could get cranky or even homicidal if they didn't fulfill their reason for sticking around.

A wife had once stuck around to take care of her husband. But he eventually died and by the time Mandy had gotten there, the wife had gone ballistic without him. She didn't know how to move on. The evil lurking below this house would have taken a toll on the strongest of wills. Cat was strong, but she needed more strength. And Mandy needed her to defeat the evil.

Swithin leaned into Mandy. "*Is* she bluffing?"

"Are you willing to bet Sister Tammy's life?" Mandy asked.

"Of course not. Hey!" Swithin pointed at Tammy/Cat. "There wasn't another car out there. How'd you get here?"

Tammy/Cat floated up off the ground.

Swithin nodded. "Right. I hate ghosts."

Tammy/Cat spoke up. "Go ahead and ask her, Swithin."

"Oh, I don't think that's..."

"ASK HER!"

"Mandywillyoumarryme?" he spit out while cowering slightly. "Sorry."

After a long squint at Tammy/Cat, Mandy conceded. "Fine."

Swithin swiveled his head toward her. "Mands..."

"I said fine, all right? Yes. Yes, I'll marry you."

Swithin couldn't be happy about it, not under the circumstances, but he took her hand in solidarity, understanding the reason. Cat'd been tainted by the evil presence here. And, of course, she was part temperamental demigod. Hard to say which overruled which. Either way, Sister Tammy's life came first.

Mandy broke free from Swithin's grip and charged back out front.

"Elvis over on 55th and Oris can do it. He's a justice of the peace," Tammy/Cat said.

"Uh, well?" Swithin interjected. "You do realize that I'm extremely...well, I'm Catholic anyway. Pretty darn Catholic. I, um, I really should be married by a priest. And then there's, you know, counseling and paperwork and I really did want to see Mandy in a dress..."

Cat drew more blood and Swithin sighed. "But who doesn't love Elvis?"

Mandy seated herself behind Junie's wheel and Tammy/Cat in the back seat.

"I am so retiring after this," Mandy muttered as Junie started up.

Even the car had nothing good to play.

In town, Mandy knocked on the proprietor's apartment door, marked, KING. No one answered.

"Well?" Mandy asked Tammy/Cat.

"He's here. I can sense it."

Sure enough, a rotund bald man with a seemingly permanent lip curl answered. "Hey, I'm not available 'til Monday," he said. "If you'd like to make an appointment--Hey!"

Mandy barged in with Swithin and Tammy/Cat behind her. Elvis still seemed affronted, until he saw Tammy/Cat with the scalpel against her throat.

"Don't ask. Just marry," Mandy barked. "The quicker the better."

Elvis stammered out something, but Swithin shoved a wad of giant bills at him. "There's a thousand quid there."

Elvis quieted. It was customary to carry a lot of cash with you in this job to get what you wanted, and Swithin had a surplus. Best superpower ever. "Sure thing," Elvis agreed. "Should I get my wig on?"

Mandy shook her head. "Just do this thing."

Elvis pressed play on his boom box, and "I Can't Help Falling in Love" floated out.

"Nice touch, mate," Swithin nodded.

"Thank you very much," Elvis took a stance at the head of his sofa, called Mandy and Swithin over and placed them facing each other. "Short and sweet, eh? Well, Sir," he faced Swithin, "do you?"

Swithin, downtrodden, but honest, looked Mandy in the eyes, but Mandy looked away. "She knows I do."

"And little miss, do you?"

Mandy swallowed her tears. She would not cry even though her face was on fire from holding them in. Was this technically legal? No. Mandy didn't even legally exist and Swithin's family flew under that radar as well. Still, vows of marriage were vows of marriage and after sour look toward Tammy/Cat, Mandy nodded. "Yeah. Sure."

"You have rings?"

"Not on me, bloke," Swithin admitted.

"Well, I have a nice set for $299."

Mandy growled and Elvis went on. "Right. Then, by the power vested in me, I now pronounce you husband and wife. You may, uh, kiss your bride."

Swithin hesitated, but Tammy/Cat cleared her throat warningly, and he tentatively pecked Mandy's lips.

Elvis grabbed an iPad and had Swithin, Mandy and Sister Tammy/Cat sign it.

Elvis checked it over, nodded and sent it off. "Congrats....I think. Can I do anything else?"

"You've done plenty. Thanks," Mandy stalked out of the room, and Swithin and Tammy/Cat followed, leaving Elvis scratching his head.

"Those nuns are tough old birds." Elvis shrugged, closed his door and counted the money Swithin passed him.

Outside, Mandy hopped angrily into Junie, and Tammy/Cat got into the back seat, with Swithin in the passenger's side. Junie blasted Sinead O' Connor's "No Man's Woman", and Swithin had to stop himself from punching her dashboard. "Heap!"

"Knock it off, you two!" Mandy screamed. Junie did not go quiet, but lowered the volume to a whisper.

"Now, to deal with the easy ghost," Mandy punched the gas and they headed back to Cat's. It wasn't far, just a few miles, and Mandy was feeling a kinship with the desolate landscape. She wanted to be alone and halfway considered telling Cat she could deal with her own ghost, but it couldn't happen that way. Mandy knew full well that the evil beneath her house would continue to grow and that was mess she did not want to deal with later or leave for someone else to clean up. Finders keepers and all that rubbish.

Once at Cat's, Mandy barged from the car, and Swithin followed suit. "You've got what you wanted," Mandy seethed toward Cat. A big happy fucking family. You can go now."

"It doesn't work like that," Cat said from the back seat, lowering the scalpel.

"Uh, I think I've been doing this longer than you," Mandy retorted.

"But now that I have a family, why would I want to leave?"

Mandy lowered her head to see Tammy/Cat in the backseat, except the Sister Tammy facade melted away leaving just the Cat part. Swithin thought Mandy might explode and set his hand on her shoulder, pressing into her as much calm as he could.

"Mands..."

"Get out!" she screamed at Cat.

Cat exited on the opposite side of Mandy, and Mandy was screaming at the top of her lungs.

"How could you?" she berated Cat. "I don't care what you are! You had no right!"

"It's the only way I could be free!" Cat defended. "You said it yourself. Class Zero's are tied to an idea and that was mine. It was set. Would you have married him and adopted me just to free me?"

"You didn't ask!"

That shut Cat up.

Mandy raged on, mad at Cat, mad at herself, furious at her life at the moment.

"I believed that you were good! I had to! Because there's so much shit! There's! So! Much! Shit! You had no right! You should have talked to me! I was trying to help you!"

Mandy furiously hopped back in Junie and pulled down the street before stopping. She just wanted to be alone and couldn't drive any further. She was angry past the point of tears. How had she not known it was a trick? "Ugh! GHOSTS!" Junie started playing "If You Want to Sing Out" by Cat Stevens, since it usually cheered Mandy up, but Mandy turned the radio knob, and all went silent. The only other time she'd been this upset, she'd gone to Swithin, but now he was part of the problem, wasn't he? Well, he wasn't a problem. Mandy was her own worst problem.

Swithin sighed, chewing on ever-deformed bottom lip.

Cat sidled up next to him. "Is it really that bad?"

He put his hands in his pockets, and, for a change, sucked in his top lip in thought.

Cat went on. "She said she loved you."

Swithin still didn't answer.

Cat went on, "Two uber amateur ghost hunters came by a few months back; obviously rejects from one of Mandy's previous classes, and were talking about her and the asylum. I knew she had to be the one I was looking for. The girl from the orphanage. I felt it. And if it hadn't been, I would have never been able to reach her or leave here. He killed them. I couldn't stop him."

Swithin didn't want to face down Mandy, but he knew he had to. If they hadn't been in the middle of a crisis, he would have left all together and let her come to him, like she always did after they'd fought. He stared down to the parked hearse for another moment, long enough for Cat to speak up again.

"I'm sorry," she said.

"I've dealt with a lot of monsters. You're not one of them."

"I was so desperate," she babbled on.

"I know, love."

"What are the worst kind of monsters?"

He stared at Mandy's car and he ached for her. "Personal demons."

With a deep breath, he walked down the street toward his old friend and leaned into her open car window. "Hey."

"I want a divorce."

"Aw, come on now. I've been asking every day for the past two months. You could at least give it an hour."

Mandy rolled her eyes, more in disbelief that she had lost control of her talent for seeing through ghost bullshit and ended up in this situation to begin with.

"Have you changed your mind?" she asked.

"Don't be daft."

Junie sensed Mandy's discomfort and rolled up the windows, cutting Swithin off from contact.

"Mandy?" He tapped on the glass. "Come on. We need to talk." He tapped harder and Junie started blasting Meatloaf's "I Would Do Anything For Love."

"Cute, Junie. Really cute. Bugger off. Mands?" He tapped harder. The music swelled and Mandy brooded.

"Mands! Oh, bollocks." He walked around to the passenger side and when Junie wouldn't let him in and Mandy didn't order her to do so, the next thing Mandy knew a landscaping rock came crashing through the passenger window and Swithin was getting in, cussing at the car the whole way. "Bloody rust bucket!"

The passenger visor whacked him in the head and the seat reclined, sending him backwards before quickly flipping forward again, causing him to bang his face on the dash.

"Stop it!" Mandy yelled. "Stop!"

Action and noise ceased and Swithin stuck his tongue out at the ceiling, since he had no idea where the car's face was.

"Are you possessed?" Mandy yelled at him.

"No, only this bloody heap is!" Swithin shook off his rivalry with the car and got back to his rift with Mandy. "And I've had it bloody well up to here, Amanda!" He pressed the back of his hand against the ceiling. "I'm sorry I almost died! For the thousandth time! But it was years ago! And if you're still that pissed off at me for almost dying, you're gonna be damn well n' gutted when I actually kick it, and you'd best prepare yourself for it, because it's going to happen!" He paused to take a breath, but she gave no indication she was even paying attention.

"And!" he blasted on. "I don't want to hear any more about this blasted immortality or everlasting life unless you're going to tell me what's really going on in that barmy noggin' of yours!"

Mandy's first thought was the fact that even now manticore venom was weakening her, but she wasn't about to say anything. It would be too much like blackmail and she did not want him giving in for that reason. She wanted him to be with her forever without guilting him into it. She stared out her window and glanced in the rearview mirror. Cat was nowhere to be seen.

"AMANDA!" Swithin clenched his fists in frustration. As much as he loved her, sometimes he couldn't stand her. "Talk to me! This fight has gone on past beyond too long."

"You know what I want."

"Damnit, Mandy."

Her only recourse to his refusal was to cut him from her life and she and he both knew that would never happen. "Fine. If it makes you happy to have some bald Elvis to say we're married, fine. But nothing is going to change between us. We're not moving in together, we're not getting matching bath towels and we're not telling anyone."

Swithin did like the fact that a bald Elvis had married them even if there wasn't any legit paperwork. How could there be? Neither one of them existed in any system but the Hunters and Hunter weddings were joyously boisterous events to cast off the darkness of their world. His mother would not be pleased she was cheated of it. "So, what do we do?"

"I dunno. You're the relationship guru."

He sighed. "Well, maybe I've been away too much. I've been trying to give you space, but maybe space isn't what we need. How about we go on a few cases together? Maybe out of the country? Maybe somewhere neither of us has been?"

Her mouth tugged into a smile. Damn his positive energy. "Okay."

"Kay?"

"Yes," she nodded.

"And…maybe...you could tell me you love me. I don't think I've heard it in three years."

Mandy suddenly found her fingernails distracting, and she nibbled on them as Swithin went on.

"Maybe, you know, once a decade or something wouldn't be too much to ask."

Mandy bit at a cuticle and started Junie. "Well, a decade isn't over yet."

"Wow. I not only set that up, I walked right into it. Good one, Swith."

"And you owe Junie a window."

Junie honked in agreement. As much as Mandy aggravated him, nothing got under his skin like that hearse. "Agreed. And if we're married, you owe me a honeymoon. A long one. I hear there's a swinging banshee wail in Naas this time of year."

Mandy rolled her eyes and stepped on the gas.

"Where are we going, wife?"

Mandy glared at him out of the corner of her eye. "The police station to rummage through some missing people reports. That bogey's going down."

Chapter 19
"Beyond the Grave" Saxon

Mandy walked through the police station like she owned the place. When an officer finally stopped her, she said she needed to speak with Chief Reichert.

The cop pointed over his shoulder to the left.

"Thanks," Mandy added politely.

Mandy knocked on the door and pushed it open. Chief Reichert was on the phone yelling at someone about frogs, and Mandy and Swithin waited patiently. Chief Reichert was a short, rosy woman with short white hair and twinkling eyes. Mandy almost thought she was cute...until she hung up the phone.

"Not you," Chief greeted.

"Pardon?"

"You run that scam at the asylum. You know how many calls we get from people saying you robbed them?"

"Hey, if they want to give me money, that's their fault."

"That's what I tell them. You really have ghosts there?"

"Come see for yourself. You can stay the night."

"No thanks. What do you want?"

"I'd like to see any missing person reports from '90 to '01."

"Would you, now?"

"Yup."

"And you have clearance for that?"

"I've solved over 20 cold cases worldwide. I assume you're familiar with the problem over in Raleigh Hills?"

"The landfill is leaking toxic waste and killing everything. Yeah?"

"What if I told you it wasn't the landfill?"

"You telling me there's a ghost?"

"I am."

Chief Reichert held Mandy's stare for what seemed like forever. Swithin finally cleared his throat to break it up. "Fine," the chief decided. "Hold on."

She returned with a thick file folder and tossed it on the desk.

"These are all in one file," Mandy noted.

"Yep," Chief Reichert grabbed a handful of M&M's out of a bowl on her desk. "We figured it was a serial killer. How many were you expecting? We're a small city, Miss, er..."

"Hook," Swithin intervened with a smile. "Mandy Hook. I'm Swithin, her..."

"Friend," Mandy interjected, flipping through the file.

"Husband," Swithin corrected.

Chief Reichert stared at them, exasperated. "Weirdos."

"What are all these sticky notes?" Mandy asked of photocopies of several post it notes that said, *he's dead.*

"We had no leads on the killer, and the case was looking pretty grim. Then, about 2002, every victim's family got one of those. We kind of stopped looking for the guy after that."

"Right."

"Whatever," The chief waved her hand dismissively. "It's a cold case. Have at it. But don't be spreading your malarkey around and scaring the children!"

Her phone rang and she answered it. "What?"

Mandy and Swithin took the cue, the folder and exited.

Mandy mumbled to him on the way out about his introduction. "Really?"

"I've been waiting years for that. Don't kill all my joy."

In the car, over shakes, burgers and a large salad, they looked through the file. Mandy separated the victims from their family members. "Whoever ran this investigation was thorough. I'll give them that. They have pictures, names addresses of every victim and family member."

"Who are we talking to first?"

She flipped through them again. "I don't know. Hey, look at this. Think these two are related?"

Two men were marked as deceased. "Frank Vater and Fred…weren't Cat's dads Frank and Fred?"

"But they are in the victims' families list."

Swithin plunked a few letters into his phone, and sure enough, Frank and Fred Vater popped up.

"Bloody hell, Mands, look."

She scrolled through the news blip from late 2000.

"Fred and Frank Vater's daughter, Eloise, is the latest victim of the local missing person epidemic. At only four years old, she is the youngest to have been abducted. Others range from ages ten to 35. This has been going on for almost a year now, and authorities have no leads to date. Eloise was at the park with her father Frank, who says he bent down to drink from the water fountain, and when he turned back around, she was gone. No one saw a thing, though there were only three people at the park, since it was about 40 degrees. Frank says he went to the park with his adopted daughter every day, rain, shine, 0 or 100 degrees. 'It was our thing,' he said. 'She loved the big slide.' His partner, Fred, has been cleared of any wrongdoing."

Mandy did the math quickly. "Fred, Frank and Cat died in 2007. But there was no abduction. And," she flipped through the packet. "None of the other family members have died, at least, not according to this."

"We need to show this to Cat," Swithin suggested. "Do you suppose she knew they had another daughter before her?"

"If she knew anything, she would have told us."

"Yeah, but still. What are you thinking? I can smell the rubber burning."

"Eloise disappeared in 2000. Frank and Fred built their house in 2001. Cat said there were always weird things going on, but her dads just lived with it. Even laughed it off."

Swithin looked down at the copies of post it notes and put it together. "They buried a serial killer in their basement."

Mandy sipped her strawberry milkshake. "Yep."

"Well, that'll save us from digging up the landfill."

Mandy and Swithin drove back to the asylum separately, since Swithin wanted his car out of the Class A's path. Unlike her predecessor, Mandy never ghost hunted at night, so taking down their ghost killer would have to wait until morning. Still, she and Swithin gathered up the necessary ingredients, spells and equipment to fight the bogey and loaded them into Junie. He would be a tough nut, but Mandy was confident they could take him down.

They chastely showered together; Swithin exhausted and Mandy worried a blister would pop up. Hot showers were a hunter's best friend. Mandy pulled down the sheets, and Swithin turned out the light and crawled into bed next to her. The Siamese cat always slept above Mandy's head, and her purr was the only sound in the dark. Four other cats were nestled in the covers as well, but Swithin had become used to sleeping with them. As customary, when they were together in bed, he kissed Mandy's ear and reached around to fondle her, but she remained frigid.

"Oh, come on, Mands. If things are going to be weird now, I'll give you a damn divorce."

She didn't answer right away and was glad the light was off so he couldn't see the tear rolling down her cheek. Cat had been right. Mandy would have never given into him. She would have never accepted a proposal, but now that she had, and it was official, her obstinacy melted ever so slightly. No one made her feel safer or more loved than Swithin Hook. Perhaps it had been the influence of the good deity Glooscap after all.

"Mands?"

She gripped his hand and squeezed it. "I love you."

He softened and cuddled in next to her. "I know, love."

The next morning, Mandy tossed Swithin's arm off of her face and hissed his name, but he grumbled something about unicorn poop, while she strained to hear the voice yelling from downstairs.

"HEEEEELLOOOOO!"

Mandy really hoped she didn't recognize who she thought she recognized, and headed downstairs, cursing her better half's ability to sleep through anything.

"It's about time!" her uninvited guest barked.

"I have a doorbell," Mandy told Missy, whose three year old daughter was in tow. "What the fuck are you doing here, besides breaking and entering?"

"Ah, the master is gone, but his language lives on," Missy snidely referred to Thomas.

"And he would be so proud, so I'm not going to punch you for trying to diss him."

"Here," Missy held out an envelope. "Swithin's father told me I am to put this in his hand, and since he didn't answer his phone, I could only assume he was here."

"Yeah. We saw you called. Ignored it since we were, you know, in the throes of passion and all."

"Whatever. Been there, done that," Missy crowed. "He'll have enough of you one of these days and come back to me. You won't even marry him."

Mandy bit her tongue on that bit for now.

Missy griped on. "He wants stability. He wants a family."

"He has a family. One that loves him enough not to disown him."

Three years ago, Missy had ended up pregnant and unwed, a sin which her parents deemed unforgivable, and as she had always feared, they disowned her. Missy raised her hand as if to slap Mandy, and Mandy stuck her chin out, welcoming the first punch, but Missy just huffed. "As if you're perfect."

Neither of the women had seen Swithin sleepily lumber down the stairs in his tight, gray boxer briefs, and he hadn't noticed them either, until he hit the wall instead of the doorway that headed into the kitchen. "Ow." Rubbing his head, he tuned and finally noticed the two women staring at him.

Missy's little girl, Penelope, smiled. "Within!" She had trouble with her "S"s.

Realizing Missy was there and he was wearing next to nothing, he awkwardly tried covering up and fidgeted until he figured out that there was nothing to be done for his attire, so he leaned up against the wall nonchalantly. "Sup?"

Exasperated, Missy charged toward him holding out the envelope. "Ugh! Here. I told your father I would put this directly in your hands. I was coming to the States anyway, but I did think he liked me more than to do this to me!"

Penelope hugged Swithin's leg. "Up!"

Swithin timidly took the envelope and bent over to pick the young girl up, who was a mite heavier than last time he'd seen her. "Thank you," he said of the envelope. "What is it?"

"How should I know? You really think I would look at it?"

"Ride!" Penelope begged.

Swithin gave in and hoisted the girl up onto his shoulders, then proceeded to prance around making horse noises while Penelope giggled.

Mandy could not hate the child, but she was done being in Missy's presence. "Well, you've delivered it. I know you can't wait to leave, now." Mandy opened the door and Swithin took the hint, setting Penelope back down.

Missy stood rigid until Swithin finally asked her if there was anything else she needed.

"Ride!" Penelope barked again.

"I need to use the loo," Missy reluctantly admitted, not wanting to be here any longer than she had to.

Sighing over exaggeratedly, Mandy closed the door. "Left hallway, second door on the right."

"Mandy!" Swithin admonished as he looked to Missy. "Right hallway, all the way back. The other one has a bit of a spider infestation."

Missy shook her head disgustedly at Mandy, who just shrugged. "Oh, right. Forgot."

"Watch her, please?" Missy asked Swithin of Penelope before hurrying toward the bathroom.

Swithin approached Mandy while Penelope petted an affectionate orange tabby. "Not nice."

"You were having sex with her while I was being kidnapped by a league of deranged witches. I'm not obligated to be nice."

"Thanks for reminding me that I still don't feel completely horrible about that. But, you know," he defended, "you don't hear me making digs at Roger Barlay, or Frank Werker or Bryson Pierce."

Mandy took pause before replying. "First of all, I never mention Frieda Comely or Trina Noel either. Just Missy since I hate her. And secondly, I never slept with Bryson. Who the fuck told you that?"

Swithin paled.

Mandy gasped. "Oh, my God! Oh. My. God. Is that why you pushed him down the elevator shaft?"

Swithin paled further.

Mandy grinned wickedly. "You have never been sexier than you are right now."

"Hey! I could have killed him!"

"Oh, whatever. You knew the car was right below the opening."

Before Swithin could explain, Missy's screams echoed down through the asylum and Swithin straightened, alert while Mandy nibbled extra smugly at one of her nails. "Oh, right. Tyrone is living in that bathroom now. He said the library was too drafty. Who ever thought ghosts could feel drafts anyway?"

Swithin rolled his eyes as Missy tore back into the lobby. "Her! Her I expect this from, but you?!" Missy berated Swithin as she swept her daughter up in her arms. "Ugh! If I never see either of you again, it will be too soon!"

"Within!" Penelope cried.

Swithin waved to the little munchkin, Missy slammed the door on her way out and Mandy pursed her lips. "She told you I slept with Bryson and you believed her. How did I not know this?"

"Can I make you some breakfast, darling?"

"No."

"Well, you and I weren't exactly talking at the time. What does it matter? It was years ago, and you and I are happily married now. You win."

Mandy stalked off toward the kitchen and Swithin followed. "Well," he said to himself, "at least we're married."

"What does the note say anyway?" Mandy asked him when he joined her in the cookery.

Swithin slipped his finger beneath the family wax seal, slid the gold monogrammed paper out and read it to himself.

"What?" Mandy pressed, opening cans of cat food.

"Pft. He's found Heildonia again. Seriously. So much pomp and circumstance. The witch does not want to be found and he will not find her."

"He wants you to come home, then."

"Of course he does. But I have a case right now, so I'll tend to his silly little goose chase when we've defeated an actual monster."

"Ghost."

"Ghosts are monsters. Technically."

"Then, how is it you can face down a snarling werbadook, but you cower at the sight of a sheet over a balloon?"

"Everyone's got to have a vice," he defended. "I just happen to have two. Ghosts and you."

After breakfast, Cat met Mandy out by Junie and pointed at Swithin's car.

"I knew it!" she exclaimed. "I knew you two were meant to be."

"Yeah. We're working on it." She was still miffed at Cat's deception from the day before. "How is it? Being a free spirit?"

Cat smiled and floated a foot off the ground. "Wonderful!"

Swithin arrived on scene with a bag of gear. He had to borrow one of Mandy's shirts since he'd spilled chili on his yesterday. The most masculine of which was a blue tee with a bloody circus bear and a dead ringmaster that said, "You can't tame this" on it. Cat nearly bowled him over with a hug, and he ruffled Cat's hair. "Morning, Catori. Wow, that's so weird, that you're all tangible and stuff."

"I'm a Class Zero. We're special like that."

"You're a class something," Mandy muttered. Her pink shirt had a picture of a princess eating frog legs.

"Oh, come off it, Mands," Swithin chastised. "You know you're not really mad at her."

"Let's just call it a sisterly grudge. Now that we're family and all. Oh, speaking of which, your dads killed a man."

"What!" Cat went translucent for a flicker.

"Yup. Buried him in your basement. Damnit! I need the pick axe from the shed. Swith?"

"I got it. Don't re-kill her while I'm gone."

"Papa Fred and Papa Frank were the gentlest people in the world!"

"Maybe so. But they had a daughter before you," Mandy explained the disappearances and the timing. "I'm sure they didn't believe in such evil spirits," Mandy added. "Or they would have never put you in harm's way. They wanted a family. Just like you did. But I imagine they didn't figure they could sell the house that they had built with a body in it, either."

"I can't believe it."

"Well, when I dig up his body, you will. We may never know how they did it, but they did. Serial killers make nasty entities."

Cat rode with them in Junie, who seemed to have perked up some. She was playing "Happy Together" by The Turtles and hadn't harassed Swithin yet.

"What is with the song? Is she okay?" Swithin asked of the hearse.

"Why? She hasn't harangued you yet?"

"Yes. And I'm on guard."

Mandy laughed. "As well you should be."

"You know, when I scratched her, it was an accident. And it was five years ago!"

Mandy shrugged. "She's possessed. Spirits hold grudges. What can I say? You probably shouldn't have broken her window yesterday, though."

"Oh, but it felt jolly good."

Swithin was a nervous wreck, wondering what the car was setting him up for, and Mandy finally divulged that Junie always played happy music on the way to a hunt.

"How droll," he admitted. "Of both of you."

Cat snickered in the back as Swithin finally relaxed, until Junie played Sheb Wooley's "Purple People Eater", and Swithin could not help but notice his seat sink ever so slightly downward toward the purple hearse's floor.

They drove past the toxic landfill signs and into the subdivision. Everyone who had been forced to move were still just waiting for bureaucracy to take care of the "toxic landfill" problem. They pulled up in front of Cat's house and all got out.

"You ready for this?" Mandy asked Swithin.

"Never. I wish it were an acheri or an afanc or a broxa or a chonchon..."

"Are you done reciting the alphabet of evil?" Mandy cut him off.

"...or a Dokkaebi."

"Can we skip to 'g' for ghost?"

"If we must."

"Cat? We'll need your help."

She nodded bravely, though Mandy could tell she was scared. And she had a right to be. Specters as powerful as the one in the house could potentially still send Cat to a great nothing by sucking her energy from her. And, as Swithin had pointed out, Cat would make a very nutritious and powerful snack.

"Swith and I need to get to his body. He won't like that. You'll need to distract him. I already used a sedation spell on him, so it won't work again, but take this salt and throw as much on him as you can. And we have some electromagnets as well that should slow him down."

Cat took the salt and nodded. "That's it?"

"Well, we have to burn his body completely, so it will take a little time, but I have some pretty tough fire enhancements. We've already set up spells and laid out ingredients to weaken him. Class A's are nasty, but can be taken down easy with the right prep work. I'm no amateur at this, you know."

The house groaned.

"I think he knows we're here," Swithin observed.

The gray aura around the house turned black, and the front door swung open.

"This is the first A I've taken down without Tom," Mandy lamented.

Swithin set his hand on her shoulder. "Then, let's make him proud."

Mandy nodded, hauled the pick axe and her satchel over her shoulder and headed in like it was another day at work. Swithin and Cat shared a nervous glance and followed.

Swithin pressed a button on a remote from his bag, and the doohickeys that Mandy had set up in the yard blasted energy waves throughout the area in an attempt to further weaken it. The phantom attacked as soon as Mandy walked through the door. Even with the sunlight outside, the inside of the house was completely black, save for what came through the door behind her. Ghosts did like fighting in the dark. Swithin pressed play on his phone and blasted "Ballroom Blitz" to distract it. He handed it to Cat, wished her luck and headed down after Mandy, whose phone was playing "Evil Walks" by AC/DC--her go-to ghost hunting anthem. The phones wouldn't interfere with a Class A's energy too much, but it couldn't hurt, and they made a great distraction.

Cat taunted the ghastly beast with it, moving around the house effortlessly. It wanted Cat's soul and the power within it. It did take the cretin nearly five minutes to take out the phone, during a refrain of

"Help!", by which time Mandy had already located the body and gotten the pick axe into the floor twice.

"Let me do that, love," Swithin took the axe and wailed at the floor while Mandy set out some charms against the monster. At this point, the monster in question decided against chasing Cat around and went after the real threats in the basement. It could eat Cat later. Cat yelled after him and even tried grabbing his veil, but he snapped at her, flinging her through the outside wall of the house and into the backyard.

She shook it off and tried to get back in, but found she could not. She banged on the walls, tried the front door, but it had closed and was warded against her.

"Your phone stopped playing!" Mandy yelled.

"I noticed!" He swung harder, but the concrete was only chipping. "What the bloody hell did they pour? Gray diamond?"

"He's protecting his body! He's stronger than I thought he was. Damn it!"

She flipped through a ratty spell book and began reciting something in Greek. But the master of the house had found them. Mandy's wards were holding, and he pounded against them, his smoky form held back as if behind a piece of glass, but it wouldn't take him long to adapt. Mandy sprinkled a mixture of holy water, salt and lavender on the floor, and when Swithin hit it next, it cracked wide open. He pounded it again, but their hunter had broken through Mandy's protection spell and grabbed Swithin before she could do anything.

"SWITH!"

"BURN THE BUGGER-R-R-R!" he shouted as he was pulled up the stairs.

Mandy hesitated; a lethal move in this game. But she'd never fought a Class A without Thomas. Sure he'd turned out to be a Class A ass, but he'd still been her partner and her friend. His death had nearly devastated her into psychiatric care. Swithin's death would kill her.

"Damn it!" She ran up after him only to find the house brightly lit with furniture and a television playing Sesame Street.

"Nice try, Ghostie. Swithin!" she called out, only to realize Cat wasn't around either.

The sink hole in the backyard.

She made a beeline for the back door, but it wouldn't budge. The faucet turned on and the stove beeped. A little girl appeared next to her suddenly and tugged on her jacket. Ignoring it all, she ran back to the front door, little girl in tow. She couldn't help but notice it was the spitting image of Eloise. Mandy knew it wasn't real. She'd been trained to ignore all stimuli, but she was off her game and almost fell for the little girl's sad face before coming to her senses. She yanked fruitlessly on the front door, and the little girl yanked on her.

"Stop it!" Mandy yelled. "Ugh, you're not even real! Focus, Amanda!" She pounded on the door and called for Cat, but no one came.

When the little girl bit her leg, that was real and it hurt. Mandy yelled and grabbed for the monster, but her hands swiped right through the apparition. As she battled this little beast, a loud honking prompted her to move away from the door right before Junie came crashing through with Cat behind the wheel. Mandy wasted no time. "The backyard! Hurry!"

Swithin was clinging to a dead tree while the dark void pulled him to his limit. The gray fuzz wrapped around him, squeezing. He screamed, and Mandy grabbed him to release some tension. Cat showed up a second later, and then Junie barreled through the wooden fence and into the dark force, which temporarily loosened its grip. Swithin fell to the ground, panting, but not a few seconds went by before the darkness grabbed him again. He reached for Junie's bumper, and Junie full reversed, trying to pull him away.

"We got this, Mandy! Go burn him!"

Mandy didn't hesitate again and hurried back inside the house. She used every ounce of adrenaline to break up the concrete and packed dirt until she hit bone. Every thread had to be demolished or it would do no good. She ignored the honking outside and made sure to uncover the entire skeleton, noticing an old Brainstead orphanage logo on the shirt. She sprinkled her salt mix on it, plus a liquid accelerator of her own blend and lit the specialized match. It unexpectedly and abruptly went out.

"Sorry, sweets."

There was little that surprised her, but Thomas's ghost knocked her for a loop.

"What the fuck, Tom? What? The? Fuck?"

"Whoa! Language little lady!" he laughed. "That rift is pretty big out there. There's all sorts of things coming through." He took a step closer. "I'm sorry I left you like I did. I wasn't strong enough to stay for you," he went on, his arms opened for her, and though she had no desire to jump into them, she was still in shock. "I know I promised," he said. "But I'm here now. That thing out there opened up a pretty big hole."

She'd already figured out it wasn't Thomas, chastised herself for falling for yet another ghost trick, even if only briefly, and scrambled to light another match, but he lunged at her, and she felt him sucking at her prana. She shouted every ward she knew, slowing the process, but she could not break free. Suddenly, a fire lit behind her, and Thomas's figure pixilated.

"You wanker!" Swithin had tossed salt on the cretin, and Cat had lit the fire. The evil screamed and wailed as his body burned, but he still had strength.

"Keep him away from the fire!" Mandy yelled.

Cat guarded the fire while the cretin circled it. "There are a lot of things that crawled out of the rift outside!" Swithin panted.

"Later, honey!"

"Sure, sure," he collapsed on the stairs after being nearly torn in two and dragging his British arse inside. Mandy's bear shirt was shredded beyond repair, and Swithin would have plenty of new scars to show off at the next hunter's clambake.

Mandy and Cat guarded the fire, and the cretin looked for a way at it, wailing. The flame was purple now. A good sign, but it took a long time to burn bones to ash. Even with the help of magic.

The dark void growled as a panther would do and then lunged with all the strength it had left. Mandy stood in front of Cat, but the monster never hit her. It was blindsided by a light.

Two lights.

They held it down while it writhed and wriggled, weakening quickly as the bones turned to soot. Cat cried and Mandy grasped her hand. When the bones were nothing more than black powder, the darkness dissipated and the lights slowly guttered out.

"Can we still reach them?" Cat asked stoically.

Mandy shook her head. "No, sweetie. Their purpose was to kill that man and keep him from harming others. They're finished now."

Tears began flowing and Cat sniffled. "But I'm here. That thing was here."

"Some people aren't strong enough to stay around, Honey. We aren't all made of part god!" She stroked her hair. "But that doesn't mean they don't love us with their entire being." Cat wrapped her arms around Mandy. "We just have to treasure the time we have."

Mandy made eye contact with Swithin and he smiled weakly, glad to hear her talking sense. For however long it would last. His eye was already black and blood dripped down his forehead. Cat tugged away from Mandy and bent over the hole. "Look." She pulled out a small notebook and blew off the dirt. Inside, a detailed account of what Frank and Fred had done; how they had figured out who the killer was and when and where they killed him.

Apparently, all of the victims had been adopted. Some from other countries and two from Brainstead orphanage. He had been abused by his social care worker when he was a child in foster care and later in life, got a job doing maintenance at the orphanage. He easily befriended adopted people, making conversation with what they had in common; his need to kill stemming from abuse and long hours at the asylum. He never sexually assaulted his victims, so he had told Fred and Frank, but he would not tell them where the bodies were, either. Even under torture.

Cat found it hard to believe her fathers had been capable of torturing another human being. Even if the man had deserved it. They'd figured out it was him by reviewing footage of their security camera. Gus had driven by the house several times when they hadn't been home and Fred had written that, "he took our little girl, and we will deliver justice."

Mandy put the journal in her satchel, intending on delivering it to Chief Reichert later that afternoon. She still had an idea of how to find the bodies, if Gus had put them all in one place.

"Or an edimmu," Swithin went on, "or a funayūrei, or a gulon…"

"Or the worst beastie of all," Mandy called out. "A husband!"

Swithin laughed, and coughed and moaned; several ribs were broken for sure. "Or a sister."

Cat nodded in agreement. "That's right!"

Mandy gathered all of the soot from the hole and put it in a blessed bag. The ashes would have to be further decimated and spread around. One could never destroy something completely, but she liked to call ashes Class Z's.

Junie had sustained considerable damage as well. Gus's ghost had thrown her clear across the yard and through the tall wooden fence with Swithin attached. He'd be picking splinters out of his backside for weeks. She was upside down against the house next door playing "Spirit in the Sky" by Norman Greenbaum.

Swithin gently patted the car on its undercarriage. "We'll get you upright in a jif, Ol' Girl. And I'll personally buff out every scratch."

After the tow truck came with a spare car and helped flip Junie, Mandy, Swithin and Cat promised the hearse they'd meet her at the shop later. Mandy picked through the files and a couple of the victims' families still lived nearby. She headed to the nearest one and knocked on the door.

The old man was skeptical to say the least, especially after so much time, but he handed over one of his son's baseball gloves, and Mandy asked if she could burn it. Mortified, Swithin put his hand on the old man's and it seemed to calm him, and he agreed.

The baseball glove led to a vision in the flames of…the asylum.

"Of course it did," Mandy grumbled.

Chief Reichert read through the journal and led a team out to the asylum's vast acreage and dug where Mandy had directed. The old playground rocks were hauled away bucketful by bucketful, until the first arm was found. Sixteen bodies followed, including Cat's would-have-been-sister, Eloise.

Chief Reichert only gave an appreciative nod Mandy's way as Mandy and Cat took their leave. Swithin had wanted to come, but Mandy insisted he take it easy until his ribs healed. And his wrist. And his ankle. And his knee. And his face. She promised to be a good nurse, and he only asked if that came with a slutty costume. She poked a broken rib, and he cringed.

"Did you ever call your dad about that note?" she asked, tucking him into his bed.

"Yeah. I've got to get home. No time to heal, I'm afraid, before the next thing."

"You don't actually think he found her do you?"

"She finds him. Not the other way around. Are you going to go with me?" he asked.

"Yeah. But I'm not ready to make any announcements, yet."

"I know. It's not really how I wanted it to happen either, love."

"Get some rest."

She kissed him and left him to sleep, dreading the fact they had to travel to Wales sooner rather than later.

Outside the asylum, Cat asked if she passed Mandy's class.

"You did all right," Mandy admitted, yawning as she did so.

"What's next?"

Mandy laughed. "A hot shower, some good drugs and a long nap."

"Aw, man. I was hoping we could still make the banshee hunt!"

Mandy playfully slugged her. "Feel free, spirit. Feel free."

Chapter 20
"Do You Want To Know a Secret" by The Beatles

With Thomas's death, Mandy's life had changed drastically, and she would mourn for years, if not forever. She could almost hear Thomas telling her he was worth the pain. She smiled at the ego and missed him all the more. "If You Could Read My Mind" by Gordon Lightfoot started playing on her iPod, and she deleted it.

The bastard...

Emerald Industries was an eight story brick building in the middle of downtown Detroit. Thomas and Mandy had stopped for supplies, but drove nonstop afterwards. It was Thursday afternoon by the time they arrived; the small parking lot was gated, so they parked down the street in front of a liquor store. Foot traffic was heavy, as there were restaurants and shopping nearby, so the two hunters blended in with the rest of the tourists.

"How can they have hidden in plain sight for so long?" Mandy asked.

"It's the best place to hide, sweets. You ready?"

"Not at all." She followed him through the parking lot and they walked through the front door to find a modern lobby with a large, glass secretary desk and an old fashioned elevator. The walls were green, and it gave Mandy chills. Thomas approached the desk and addressed the attractive pin curled brunette who was wearing a green sweater. "We're here to see Gwen."

The brunette did not look up from her computer, but pushed her rim horned glasses back up the bridge of her nose. "Do you have an appointment?"

"Trust me, she'll want to know I'm here."

The secretary finally looked up, annoyed, but upon recognizing Thomas, blanched and gasped. She wasn't quick enough to send out any type of warning, as Thomas reached over the desk and slammed her head into it, cracking the glass. Mandy came around the desk, grabbed the dazed witch by the neck and squeezed. The witch wriggled, but to no avail.

"This is too good for you," Mandy hissed and the witch went limp. They hid her body beneath the desk and pushed the elevator button.

"I told you they weren't expecting us. Ye of little faith."

Mandy made a mental note to pray a thanks to the gods for their help. She knew there were many who hated Gwen and her work, and she would be glad to be an instrument of war for them. The elevator opened and they stepped in. "What floor?"

"Pick one."

Mandy pressed 8. "Might as well go right to the top."

When the doors opened, Mandy lost her breath.

It was a nursery. Five children were hooked up to whirling, buzzing machines which looked like they were from 1979. "I want to go," Mandy breathed. "We should not have come here. Not like this. Not unprepared."

"Mandy..."

"This isn't like the other hunts, Tom. The gods think we can handle it, but we can't. I've tried. I..."

"Fine." He stepped back into the elevator, and Mandy followed.

"Thank you. I know..."

"Oops." He pushed the 7 button on purpose, and Mandy scowled.

"One more floor."

The doors opened and prepared for anything, Mandy and Thomas took stance. Nothing popped out immediately, so they cautiously exited into a large lab of sorts. Tables covered in vials, cages, computers and old spell books filled the right half of the room while the other half held six empty hospital beds, complete with restraints.

"Well," Thomas eyed a nearby empty cage. "They know we're here."

"What was your first clue, genius, besides the fact that no one is here? Look out!"

Thomas turned with a right hook, sending a "woman" in a green lab coat to the floor.

"You know," he told her, "I make it a point to never hit a lady. And I never have."

"Gah!" Mandy was set upon by two more, but wriggled free before they could finish muttering any spell. They were nimble, though, and Mandy and Thomas were now in hand to hand combat. Thomas pulled a tarnished blade from his side and waved it around. The witches were wary of it, as it was old and blessed. He'd given Mandy something similar and she wielded it fatally. These were not Gwen's top of the line fighters, and the two hunters easily took them down. When the two dispatched with their assailants, Mandy turned just in time to see the blood begin to pour from a thin line across Thomas's neck.

Facial expression of anger, he fell to his knees, revealing Gwen standing behind him with an ornate scalpel.

Please let this be a vision. Please let this be a vision, Mandy prayed.

"I'm afraid not, dear," Gwen answered, reading Mandy's obvious thought. "I do so hate gratuity. Come on, now. This was bound to happen to him sooner or later."

Mandy didn't move. She didn't know if she could.

Three more witches appeared behind Gwen; her closest consorts. "I'm not sure how you found us. I can only assume one of those nasty deities spilled the beans. We're warded tight against them, but every once in a while they find us. They don't much care for our practices. Too cowardly and too weak to face us themselves, though." Gwen walked toward Mandy. They were in an open space between the lab side and the bedside. "What is so special about you? None of the others could take the stress, even with real homes and real families. Still, the portals never matured, or they finally gave up."

Mandy finally found her voice. "Maybe I'm the Highlander of experiments."

"I thought of that. But, no. I even tried using your biological donors again," she smiled coyly.

"Where are my parents?" Mandy demanded, getting angrier by the second.

Gwen ignored the question. "I will breed another portal and the minute you cease to be unique, we will have no use for you. Until then, we will never quit trying to wheedle into your psyche. I did truly think that Swithin's near-death experience would have prodded you into harnessing the powers from beyond, but I was both proud and disappointed. Your strength never ceases to amaze me."

"You..."

"Pish posh. I didn't poison him, if that's what you're thinking."

She doesn't know, Mandy thought. *She doesn't know I'm going to die soon anyway. She doesn't know Heildonia helped.*

Gwen continued, as Mandy wasn't going to speak on the matter. "So, unless you'd like to acquiescence, go back to your life and we will meet again, soon."

The witch turned toward the elevators, but Mandy sucked in her courage and spoke, "Maybe you haven't heard, but Swithin's moving to Borneo. We're over. And since you just killed Thomas, well, I don't really have anything to live for, do I?"

Gwen's eyes widened as Mandy pulled a gun on herself, but Gwen was quicker with a wave of her hand, and the pistol shot water. Mandy threw the revolver down and reached for another, but Gwen smugly flicked her fingers and every weapon on Mandy's person ripped itself from its hiding place and flew out of reach.

"Well, that's drafty," Mandy noticed after her clothes had all been torn.

"Give it up, Amanda," Gwen touted. "You're not going to die today."

Determined, Mandy turned her head toward the windows. She was seven stories up.

Gwen noticed, too, as Mandy made a beeline for the glass, but Mandy hit it full on, and simply bounced to the floor with a massive headache.

"Do you know how many things try to break in here?" Gwen asked, bored.

The crones laughed as Mandy tried drills and scissors and even a pencil, but the witches were too able minded and thwarted her at every turn. Mandy managed to land a punch square in Gwen's face and tried throwing herself down the stairwell, but she only ended up hurting. Gwen's minions were right behind her, and the next floor housed more computers and shelves of research. Nothing remotely deadly and not enough time to papercut herself to death.

Gwen finally appeared again, blood dripping from her nose and shook her head. "Not today, Amanda."

Mandy eyed around the room for anything she could use and racked her brain for any bit of knowledge, but her thoughts and actions came to an abrupt halt as a familiar voice rang from the elevator.

"Mands!"

Swithin had a blade at the ready, but Mandy deflated. "What are you doing here?"

He noted Gwen warily, who wore a flat expression. "I had a sort of vision and came right home."

"You shouldn't have come." She eyed his blade. "I don't suppose you want to stab me in the heart with that, do you?"

"What? No!"

The witches all melted away in puffs of smoke satisfied that their quarry was safe from self-infliction, and Swithin approached Mandy. "What is going on? Where's Thomas?"

Mandy inhaled several deep breaths, trying to keep her emotion in check, but the sobs came anyway, and she wrapped herself around him losing herself. "I'm sorry. I'm so sorry. I should never have said those things to you."

"It's all right, love. Mandy, where is Thomas?"

She cried harder. "Dead. Dead! You're all I have left."

He kissed her head and whispered in her ear. "So much for having no reason to live."

Mandy was jolted back to her senses and pulled away to see that this "Swithin" was none other short Nharlthop with a glamour on. The four foot crone pecked Mandy's lips and laughed while Gwen's voice floated in from elsewhere.

"Which, I should remind you, is the only reason he's still alive. Think about that next time you want to stick a pencil in your eye. Now, if you'll excuse us, you've mussed up our base of operations, and we have to start anew. Count that as your victory for today."

Swithin nudged her awake when the plane landed in Wales and noticed she didn't seem rested. He set his hand on her leg. "I miss the old blighter too," he said of Thomas.

Mandy shook her head. "I should have dedicated my life to taking those bitches down instead of blocking them out. How many kids have they..." she couldn't bear to finish. The guilt had come down on her hard over the past several months.

Swithin squeezed her hand. "Whatever you want to do, I'm behind you 100 percent."

That's what she was afraid of, but she said, "Let's just deal with Heildonia first. One witch at a time."

A venom blister popped up on Mandy's back, and it took everything in her power not to squirm and gain Swithin's unwanted attention. She'd never been so grateful to stand when they got out of the car at the castle. She always forgot how striking the place was.

"We should have invited Cat," Swithin noted.

Mandy shook her head. "I think she and I needed some time apart. Too much family time can be hazardous."

Swithin laughed, agreeing. Being a free spirit, Catori had the power to travel the world, and she wasted no time heading down under to Australia, promising to send a "ghost" card, as she had put it.

Condel stood guard as always. The few times Mandy had been here, he had never left his post. The first time, he had been warm toward her, but it seemed after she'd been kidnapped, he became stoic, as if he only now saw her as a threat to his young Hook.

He greeted Swithin with a smile and a handshake, but eyed up Mandy nervously and let them both go on their way inside.

"Amanda," Condel called out before the big doors closed.

Mandy stuck her head back out, and Swithin opened the door all the way.

Condel did not make eye contact with her at first. "I've been meaning to ask you something."

Uh, oh, Mandy thought, expecting her long overdue warning from him. *Here it comes.*

"Can you ever forgive me?"

Both Mandy and Swithin's eyebrows went up as the guard continued.

"The night you were kidnapped," he explained. "It should have never happened. I lost so many nights of sleep, I was so ashamed. I nearly retired, but the old Hook wouldn't let me," he said of Patrick.

Mandy took a few seconds to comprehend what he was saying, and she started laughing.

"Is that a yes or a no, miss?" Condel was nearly sweating, but Mandy ran to him and wrapped her arms around the big man.

"I thought you hated me," she admitted.

He finally gave a relieved smile and hugged her back. She didn't even flinch when he pressed on her blister. "What those witches did to you isn't any of your fault, Miss."

Swithin watched the scene serenely. He knew that Mandy had been aching for a family and a home, and the picture in front of him--the energy around him--proved that she now felt as if she'd finally found it.

Mandy let go of Condel after a good long hug and leaned up to whisper in his ear. "And it's Mrs., now. Shh."

Condel's eyes went wide, and he looked to Swithin.

"What is she on about?" Swithin asked.

Condel kissed her cheek. "Welcome to the family."

"Oh, sure!" Swithin played. "I thought we weren't going to tell anybody."

Mandy joined him back at the threshold and batted him playfully. He closed the door and continued. "You remember when I told you there would come a day when you would regret all the time you wasted not being with me?"

"Don't make me ask you for a divorce," she answered flatly.

"Yeah, I don't remember that day either."

As she was wont to do, Florence popped out of seemingly nowhere and greeted Swithin and Mandy enthusiastically as always. "How was your trip, dears?" she smiled.

"Well, we didn't crash or face down any monsters so that's a plus," Swithin answered.

"Doesn't look that way," Florence said of Swithin's limp and yellowing bruises.

"Where is everyone?" Mandy had to ask, although she didn't think she'd like the answer.

"Gone. Off to find Heildonia. Every one of them. Your father, mother and siblings." Florence did not bother hiding her fret and wrung her hands nervously. "They left yesterday."

Mandy's intuition itched. "Florence, you don't have the coordinates do you?"

"Oh, Mands," Swithin took a slow lie down on the chaise in the entryway, still babying his injuries. "Let's just enjoy a Patrick-free time, shall we? They'll be back soon enough."

Florence knew better than to ignore Mandy's instinct.

"I'll get the location if you'll hold here. Your mother left it for you, Swithin, against your father's wishes. He is in a hot mood about your absence."

Swithin bahed again, and Florence scurried away. "We don't really have to go after him, do we?"

"Your father and I have no love loss, but I kind of like the rest of your family."

"Even Mary?"

"Look, I know you and your father have grown apart but..."

"He tried to kill you."

"He's still your father," she continued. "Besides, I forgave him for that. It was years ago. Why can't you?"

Unable to believe Mandy was not a monster to be destroyed, Patrick deemed the risk okay and tried to subtly poison Mandy with a drink two years ago. To Patrick's dismay, Helen had absently switched drinks with Mandy, and Patrick had to fess up before he killed his wife.

Swithin rolled his eyes. "I did. Well, I tried. I'm trying. But that coupled with the fact that he killed Henry Canon and well, he's not quite the Christian I thought he was."

Patrick's actions had rattled Swithin's faith more than anything, and that's what he'd had to come to terms with. Mandy and Helen tried telling Swithin that, in that regard, he wasn't like his father; he had a pure heart and was a good Catholic. Helen explained that Patrick's sense of loyalty to his religion conflicted with his loyalty to hunting and had been doing so for longer than Swithin had been alive. Helen had admitted, "When your sister Bell died, it broke your father's relationship with God in a way that could never be healed. We've both prayed that none of our children would ever face that kind of torment." Still, it had nearly fully driven the wedge between father and son, and only because of Mandy's interference did Swithin even maintain a civil and open relationship with his patriarch; something which Patrick had never even acknowledged Mandy. Mandy hadn't known her real father and so, tremulous as it was, she knew Swithin needed his dad.

Florence returned with the coordinates, and Mandy's heart began to pound. Florence noticed the physical change and tentatively handed over the stationary. "Mandy?" she fretted.

Even Swithin sat up, groaning as he did so. Mandy swallowed a nervous lump. "Swith, we're going to have to go after your family."

"Why?"

"Because this is where Heildonia lives."

Florence huffed out a breath of woe, and Swithin painfully righted himself, but still did not stand. "And how, just exactly, do you know that?"

At long last, her secret would have to be revealed. "Because I've been there."

"Repeat that," Swithin said flatly.

"Oh!" Florence threw her hands out. "Who cares why, right now? Your family is going to be annihilated by Heildonia!"

"She's right, Swith. We have to go."

"But..."

Florence cut him off. "You'll never catch them on time!"

The girls looked to Swithin for an answer, and after a long moment, he grumbled. "Yes we will. Come on. Florence, would you let the guards know what's going on? Make arrangements or whatever it is you do."

Florence nodded and hurried off with a mission, and Swithin hotly limped toward the door. Mandy expected a berating, but it never came, and she followed his ire silently through the castle. Swithin huffed and opened a door far at the end of a winding hallway which led to a spiraling staircase down into complete darkness. "Where does this go?" Mandy asked meekly to break the smothering silence.

"Heildonia is only like our family's arch nemesis!" Swithin's thoughts exploded in response as he led her down into the darkness.

"I'm sorry," she said. "Heildonia promised she'd kill you all, and I promised I wouldn't tell anyone."

"I'm not just anyone," he spat back.

He had her there. "Well, it's just that you and I were fighting for so long, it just never came up."

"Whatever. Are you going to tell me or not?"

"Well..."

"Hold on."

They'd apparently reached the bottom of the stone stairs, and Swithin had to light a torch. The large, musty space was cluttered with old knights and crumpled tapestries; broken and forgotten things from 800 years of castledom. Swithin made his way to a thick wooden door in the floor. He pressed his finger to the thick wood, spoke a spell, in what Mandy could only figure as some type of ancient Aborigine, and the door lit up, scanning him for nearly a minute before it creaked inwards. Mandy winced at the power which smacked her and followed her husband down the ladder.

"Swithin, you never told me all this was down here!" Mandy chastised.

"We apparently all have secrets, don't we?" He took pleasure in throwing the fact in her face, but moved on at her unamused expression.

"I'm technically not supposed to know. But Wendy found it when she was little via a passage from the guest suite, and since then everyone used it as a sort of Hook sibling initiation rite. Mum and da don't know we know."

The room went on into darkness past where Mandy could see, but when Swithin switched on the lights, it seemed to never end.

"It's not all magical, of course," Swithin told her, "but valuable nonetheless."

"Magical?" Mandy could barely wrap her head around what she was looking at without thinking all of it was magical. Mandy eyed emerald statues and mounds of gold and jewels amongst small pedestals with sheet-covered prizes of unidentifiable worth. Crystal, silver, bronze and gold sparkled everywhere; the Hook family treasury. Even Swithin had momentarily ceased his resentment and seemed bedazzled by it all.

"I haven't been down here since I was little," he confessed. "It's still just as amazing, isn't it?" Way in the back, through yet another door which was guarded by yet another spell, laid another room.

Mandy could feel the energy stronger than before. Evil lurked here. Swithin pulled her inside and closed the door. Carefully placed objects sat on pedestals, and many were covered in glass domes. "I can't believe you've never told me about this," she absently told Swithin while he sorted out a sheet covering a rather large object.

"Really? You're going to spank me for not telling *you* something?"

"It's complicated," Mandy turned to him about Heildonia. "I need time to explain, and you're not going to be happy about it."

"Well, I already knew that."

Mandy mustered up every ounce of sugary sweetness within her. "Well, just remember, Sweet Husband, you're stuck with me 'til death parts us." She soured quickly. "And that's your idea, not mine."

He cast a mocking scowl at her and pulled a sheet off of the object behind him. Mandy blanched. "Is that an honest-to-God magic mirror?" Mandy squealed.

"God had nothing to do with it," Swithin answered.

Mandy had stepped up to the golden glass and wanted to touch it so badly. "How does it work?"

"No. Not until you tell me what you know. If we're going to face that witch, I need details."

"What about your family?"

"They'll survive ten more minutes. Spill it."

"You may want to sit."

"That bad, eh?"

"Maybe bittersweet would be a better description."

"Stop stalling."

"Right. Well, it was right after you were stung by the manticore. Your mother called me and told me that you were in a coma, but you were going to die. Swithin, it was the worst day of my life and you know I've had some doozies."

His face finally softened, and he took a seat on a nearby golden bench while she regaled on.

"I mean losing Tom is, well, but I thought I was going to lose you. I don't think I would have survived it. Anyway, of course Thomas and I were on a case when your mom called. We were dealing with that ghost cat I told you about, but we left so he could drive me to the nearest airport. We never did go back to that cat... I wonder if..."

"Stay on track, love."

"Right, well..."

Far be it for Thomas Regal to admit he could not do something, and so he had no choice but to tell Mandy that when he died, he would stick around, if only to make sure he could give her a proper goodbye. It seemed to quell her oncoming waterworks, and she

mercifully spared him a hug. Mandy gave her attention back to
Swithin who seemed he would die any moment. Barely breathing and
wheezing at that, it was nearly unbearable. Blisters began to come
through on his cheeks and Mandy had to look away. The only two
who could stand to be in the room, Thomas lit up another cigarette
and was to alert Helen if it was time. He would finish this smoke and
fetch her; a task which he was not looking forward to.

The deathly silence was broken by an unfamiliar woman.

"I'm not surprised Patrick's not in here tending to his favorite
bairn."

Thomas and Mandy were up and about-faced.

The intruder gave off an evil vibe, wore boot cut jeans and a
fitted lavender tee with a ferret on it. Her untamed red curls flew
every which way, save for a braid adorned with a tiny skull.

"Heildonia, I presume," Thomas asked flatly.

"Oh, how lovely! My reputation precedes me."

"What do you want?" Mandy spat. "To gloat over a dying
Hook?"

"On the contrary, dearlie. You have something I want, and I have
a way to get it. Even if it means helping a Hook," she shuddered.

"I'll do anything!" Mandy yelled in desperation.

"Mandy," Thomas warned.

"Anything," Mandy emphasized, putting her palm out to Thomas
to quiet him.

Heildonia chuckled. "Mandy Heart, the Goddess Particle in
person."

Mandy stiffened, then relaxed. "So. You do know who I am."

"Daft little twit, of course I do. No witch worth her hexes
wouldn't know who you are. I'm no fool." Her nostrils flared as she
formed her next words. "The Agency's made an enemy out of you.
Not so smart. No one in their right minds piss off a goddess."

"Don't call me that."

She shrugged. "You want to see your boy toy live to fight another
day? Take me there."

Mandy knew she spoke of the portal; the edge of the Universe.

Thomas took out a cigarette. "Mandy, that's not a good..."

"Can it, Tom," Mandy never broke eye contact with the witch.
"You save him first."

"Well, that's a little unorthodox," she bantered, eyeing Swithin's withering body. "But seeing as his time is extremely limited, I'll make an exception. Do we have a deal?" She held out her hand, and Mandy took it without hesitation.

It burned, and she pulled away, now having a seal scarred into her flesh; a contract. The next thing Heildonia did was take out two small vials. She handed them to Mandy. "The rest is on you. You drink this one," she held out the small green glass first, "and get this one in his mouth."

Mandy took the small potions. Thomas tensely inhaled his cigarette in nearly one drag.

"Oh! And you'll need this," she brought out a small dagger from somewhere in her messy curls. "Cut yourself. I'd recommend your hand, but some like to be creative. You'll need to slice him up too, and hold your wounds together no matter what. His potion will push the poison from him, and yours will draw it into you."

Mandy swallowed a lump and Thomas sighed. "Fucking witches. She never said she could cure him, Mandy. You didn't listen."

"Pish posh, dearlie!" Heildonia defended. "He'll be fine! She just has to take it from him."

Mandy had no objections to dying for him, but it still wasn't exactly what she had pictured. "Fine. Let's get on with this." She downed her vial.

"Sweets..."

"Let it go, Thomas," Heildonia waved her arm thematically while Mandy carefully tilted the other container between her lover's lips.

Heildonia continued. "She's strong. If I thought she was going to die right away, would I have made this bargain? I need her alive."

Thomas and Mandy looked to her expectantly, and she complied with an answer. "Your DNA is special, Amanda. Everyone knows that. I figure it will be years until that poison finally overtakes you."

Thomas briefly remembered his mother's plant popping back to life with Mandy's presence, but shook off the incident. "You don't have to do this, sweets."

"Yes I do. He's better than me. The world needs him."

Thomas rolled his eyes and made a gag face while taking out another cigarette. He could not do anything but admire her for doing exactly what he would do.

"Tom," Mandy ordered. "Watch the door."

"Just come lock me out. It'll be easier to explain that way when someone comes along. Witch, you seal it when I'm gone. I seriously don't want to watch this anyway." He left, and Mandy walked over and locked the latch. Heildonia murmured some enchantment while Mandy approached Swithin's languishing form. She gently lifted his arm by unmarked places and sliced it with the dagger. Thick, dark blood slowly seeped.

"Here," Heildonia chirped. "You'll have a few seconds to tie yourself to him before the pain starts. If you break contact, you'll just spill venom all over the place and he'll end up dying anyway."

Mandy took a thick black band from the witch and wasted no more time cutting her own palm. She pressed it to him, feeling nothing, but Heildonia urged her to tie the band around their hands. Mandy did so and not a second too soon as the fire jolted her.

It was as if she set her hand on a hot stove, but could not pull away. The feeling never dissipated, and Mandy screamed and writhed, but the band held her to her Welshman.

On the other side of the door, Thomas winced at Mandy's scream, but it had been her choice. Her screeching would surely bring attention, and he patiently waited for spectators.

"Just keep holding, dearlie," Heildonia cheered. "May take an hour or so!"

Mandy screamed louder.

Sure enough, Patrick showed up first. "What's going on?"

Thomas slipped on his acting cap. "I don't know! The door is locked!"

Patrick pummeled it with his weight, not a light load, but Heildonia's spell held.

"What's happening?" Helen arrived with a plate of baked goods. "I can hear her screaming all the way in the kitchen! Is he…" She wondered about her little boy's condition.

Patrick lunged into the door again. "Get me a pickaxe, woman!" he called to Helen. "I'm getting into that room!"

Mandy's voice went hoarse, but the pain persevered. She had no idea how long it had been, but her eyes had dried up and she prayed to anyone to let her pass out. The banging on the other side of the door was of no consequence, as Heildonia sat knitting in the corner of the room. Swithin hadn't budged, whimpered or improved in anyway.

"If this doesn't work, witch, I'll have your head!" Mandy would have spit, but her mouth was dry. Her skin was flaking. Her eyes were cloudy.

"If this doesn't work, you won't be alive to do anything," Heildonia knitted and hummed "The Lilting Banshee."

At long last, Patrick, along with several others, beat down the door and rushed in. Thomas noticed immediately that Mandy and the witch were gone and saw no reason to say she'd been in here when the door locked. While Patrick and several younger Hooks searched the room, Helen approached her son tearfully and quivering. He was still, as he had been, but as she stood over his blistered body, his eyes swollen shut and his hair in clumps around his head, his lips moved ever so slightly and he whispered, "Mum."

Meanwhile, Mandy found herself in a cluttered cabin filled with books, skulls, bottles and hundreds of other eclectic items. Heildonia had given Mandy something to ease the fire beneath her skin and something else to make her sleep until the venom settled, and Mandy's blood found a way to fight it.

Mandy awoke with a start after dreaming of nothing at all and found she was still in the cluttered cabin. It was dark outside and a jar of fireflies served as a night light. She found a candle and some matches next to the bed and lit up the room. Archaic junk was everywhere. Piled up to the tall ceiling in some spots. Heildonia was a pack rat.

Mandy crawled out of the room over piles of books and scrolls, and headed down the hallway toward the firelight.

"Feeling better, dearlie?" Heildonia looked up from a book and waited for a response.

Mandy wasn't sure how she felt. "Is he better?"

"I'm sure he is. But I'm not going back to check."

"Then, we don't have a deal."

"Correction. I don't have to go back to check." Mandy's host waved her hand toward a painting on the wall, and it swirled and focused until Mandy could see Swithin's bedroom. He was sitting up at least, with fluid still attached via a needle, but he was alive, and her heart swam.

"There. See? Now, it's your turn."

"Now?" Mandy was still exhausted.

"You can hang around here as long as you like, but I figured you'll want to get back to your boy toy as soon as possible."

Mandy had to focus for a minute, and then she called the witch over. "Take my hand," Mandy said, and Heildonia did so.

"No tricks, now," the witch warned.

"I'm too tired to even think about that. Now, be quiet."

Mandy closed her eyes and centered herself. She'd never actually taken someone inside her head before. Usually people broke in and she had to keep them out. Or, Eleanor or Swithin were allowed, but they'd never actually wanted to come. Mandy wasn't at all sure she could do this. But she opened her mind, and Heildonia did the rest. Before Mandy knew it, she was standing in her familiar field of doors.

"Marvelous," Heildonia commented, once they were among the doors. "But you know this isn't what I want to see, right, dollop?"

Mandy sighed and headed toward the black fissure, and when they'd come upon it, she sensed Heildonia's apprehension.

"Sure you want to go in?" Mandy asked.

Heildonia nodded, trying to keep a brave face, but Mandy felt her fear and wondered why she wanted to see it so badly. Still, a deal was a deal, and she had no desire to see the consequences of denying a witch her contract.

They slipped through the black, slimy cleavage and were officially out of body.

The pitch quickly erupted into a light ahead, where universe had not yet formed. The quiet chittering of the weavers was the only sound and it echoed. The ground, if that's what you could call it, was like an unwavering waterbed; squishy, but unmoving.

While Mandy kept all senses peeled for any sign of trouble, Heildonia marveled at the sight. Her eyes teared and her chin quivered. She rolled her lips together and blinked to compose herself.

"Those flapping cunneys actually did it."

"Yep," Mandy absently agreed, hanging back by the door. It took everything in her reservoir of strength to ignore the powerful calling of the edge. Existence could easily be her plaything if she would only dare to meddle...

Swithin. She had to focus on getting back to him.

"Can we go now?" Mandy urged.

But Heildonia ignored the question and crept to the edge of the dark with some trouble. Mortals were not meant to be here and pressure in her head built. Still, she marveled.

"I wouldn't do that if I were you," Mandy warned. How easy would it be to push the witch over the edge? Then again, if it didn't kill her, Mandy shuddered to think what could occur. Unwritten existence realm existed beyond the web. Mandy felt its pull and forced herself to ignore it. This was not her. She was not a goddess, not a witch; just an experiment. Just a girl. A hunter. She had dedicated her life to stopping things like this from happening, and she would not give into Gwen's desires that she transcend. "Heildonia! You've seen it! Let's go!"

But the witch would not heed advice, too mesmerized by the workings of it all. She knelt down to observe the edge of creation, slowly but surely knitting itself together, readying itself for existence. She lowered her hand and hesitated, but then ran her fingers through the knitting, dissolving it and scattering miniscule bits of darkness into the light yonder.

Mandy's brain twinged as Heildonia laughed at the sheer fragility of the edge of time and space. Her laughter ceased as a bus sized gray claw appeared from somewhere beneath the blackness and hooked around to the pitch on which they stood.

"We can go," Heildonia quickly agreed as a deafening chittering made both the girls wince.

Mandy turned and tried to find the doorway back, but she'd only been here once; after which, she'd vowed never to return.

Another claw appeared and another.

"Amanda!" Heildonia urged.

Mandy closed her eyes and felt for the scent of her own mind through the sounds of thousands of others. Going through the wrong passageway back would prove disastrous on multiple levels that she could not begin to understand. She didn't even know how she knew there were thousands of passages, but she did. She couldn't comprehend how suddenly, the meaning of life was all too clear, but she had to concentrate on finding her body once again.

Six iridescent purple eyes rose up just then over the black horizon, each wet and hungry.

"AMANDA!" Heildonia yelled.

Amanda found her passage and slipped through; the witch right behind her. Though Mandy had thought of leaving her there, the unknown variables would have been too great a risk.

Back in Mandy's field, she crossed her arms and stared down the panting enchantress. "Well? Are you satisfied?"

"Just take us back," she groused.

Mandy did just that and found that she now knew exactly where she was. She knew Heildonia's secret location; the one Swithin's family had been searching for generations. Coming back from her mind had always been jarring, but this in particular was especially dizzying. She whirled around, knocking over a small mountain of paraphernalia and falling on top of it.

"Clutz!" Heildonia barked, trying to get her own two feet beneath her.

Mandy wished more than anything that she could spend just one day in this house going through the stacks of enchantments and crates of baubles. She took a second to get her bearings and placed her hands beneath her to push up, when a glint of sparkle caught her eye. She moved an old, faded map and grabbed the glitter beneath it.

An emerald green hairpin.

Mandy was up and facing Heildonia in two seconds. "You're one of them!"

Heildonia eyed the accessory and snorted. "That old thing?" She snatched it and blew on it, turning it to dust.

Mandy panicked and looked for the door.

Heildonia let her squirm for a moment before speaking out. "Oh, calm down, dearlie. Yes. Yes. I was once in The Agency. Though, it wasn't called that back then. What were we? Oh, damned if I know. It's changed names so many times."

Mandy settled, but did not let her guard down. "Why did you walk away?"

The witch laughed. "I didn't walk. I ran! And now I'm in hiding for as long as my long life will be. You couldn't possibly think I'm living in this fetid bubble to hide from that Hook clan vendetta."

"Why did you make me take you there?"

"I wanted to see it before she did. Simple. And she will see it Mandy. By Hook or by crook, hm, hm," she laughed at her play on words, "she will get what she wants."

"Why are you helping me?"

"Balls, I should have known you'd have a hundred questions!"

"Why!" Mandy demanded.

"The enemy of my enemy is my friend. Well, maybe friend is a bit much. It was more of an exchange after all."

"What happened? Between you and Gwen?"

Heildonia's shoulder raised into a carefree shrug. "I realized where I was on the food chain. She has not."

Tense, but interested, Mandy let her go on.

"Does she still try and contact you?" Heildonia asked coyly.

"Not for a while, no. But I never let my guard down."

"Smart girl. Could you....find her if you wanted?"

Mandy's face split into an understanding smile. "You never wanted to help Swithin. You needed a reason to get to me. And I will tell you right now that I will never let that woman inside my head. Never."

"You let me in."

"I didn't know what you were."

"And what am I? I am not a true witch, nor Wiccan. No, The Agency transcended the common definitions long ago, using science and magic together to achieve results. Some would call what they do evil, but it is truly just a hazardous quest for knowledge. Knowledge that I know now is not meant for anyone, save for the creators themselves. They have cloned people and dinosaurs and planets. They did it long ago. They can replicate existence, but can't find its origins and that is what you hold."

"How do I stop her?"

Heildonia laughed. "If indeed there is a way, you're the only one who could do it. Though, at what cost, I could not say."

Mandy remembered all too vividly the temptation to reach into the cosmos and grab the power. Surely, she could quit Gwen in her tracks, but she feared being able to handle it.

"You want me to kill her. That's what this is all about."

"I wanted to meet you. I may know my place, but my thirst for knowledge has not waned. Besides, even if you did find a way to destroy her, someone or something else would step up and take her place. Amanda, you must never let her in there."

"Thanks for the warning, Captain Obvious."

"I mean it. They should have never made you. But you're stronger than she anticipated, and apparently, one of a kind."

Mandy shuddered at the thought of all the children who had suffered under Gwen's tyranny. She cursed herself for being unable to locate the bitch to stop her. Wait. Maybe Heildonia could help in that department.

The witch had seemingly anticipated the question. "You need to go."

"But you..."

"Now." Heildonia shoved Mandy toward the door, and they both stumbled over stacks of old papers. "She can track you, and you've been here too long already."

"But..."

"And it goes without saying, darlie," Heildonia warned as she pushed Mandy out the door into her swampy abode, "that if you ever tell anyone where I am, I will destroy every. Last. Hook. Just for fun. And, then I'll go after your Thomas." She smiled toothily and slammed the door.

Mandy felt the sincerity like a fiery breeze and nodded to her promised silence.

Back in the present, Swithin took a few seconds to absorb the story and finally said, lightly, but with tears forming. "Your impression of me is abysmal. I thought my accent meant more to you than that."

Mandy didn't respond as she had nothing more to say.

"How long do you ha...ve?" he choked on the words. "How bad is it?"

Mandy lifted her shirt to reveal the black blister on her back. "She said I might get four or five years before the poison overtakes me."

"Bloody hell." It slowly dawned on him that it had already been nearly four years since the poisoning. "So, this is what that immortality bit was all about? This is why you barely spoke to me for four fucking years? And here I thought you were inconceivably mad at me for almost dying."

"I was. I am. Losing you would--"

"But I wasn't the reason at all. You just wanted immortality to save your own skin because you're so terrified of dying, because you don't think anything good is waiting for you."

Swithin's intensifying anger was contagious, and Mandy reddened. "Fuck off. Better yet, fuck you. Of all the people in the world, you should know me better than that."

"You weren't ever going to tell me, were you? You were just going to leave in the middle of the night someday and let me die wondering what the hell happened to you, weren't you?"

"Okay. Maybe you do know me better than I thought."

"Mandy!" His eyes reflected a flash of red. Mandy had once thought she imagined it, but now she was sure it had been there. Pure anger.

"But you're wrong about the immortality! Heildonia's potion was the only option given at the last possible minute, and I took it. And yes, I was going to leave you. I still am. There is no way I am going to let you see me like that," she referred to his pustuled dying form.

Swithin didn't speak for a long minute. Mandy called his name, but he had turned from her and held his thoughts inward.

"Swithin, please say something."

After another few beats, he said, "Yes."

"What?" His sudden calm was palpable and soothed her.

"Yes. The answer is yes. I've changed my mind."

Mandy took in a sharp breath, knowing he was talking about the immortality that had caused their rift years prior. "Swithin, that is not why I did this."

He finally turned back to her. "I know. In fact, I know lots of things. I know that a gribbleschnick's favorite food is Braunchweiger and jelly, and I know, I've always known, that I love you more than you love me."

Mandy went to speak up, but he spoke over her.

"It's okay," he went on. "I came from this perfect life, and you had baggage. I always understood that, and I knew I had to love you all the harder. I accepted that a long time ago. And sometimes, yeah, sometimes it was hard to deal with, and I faltered. I'm not as perfect as you think I am, but I told you I would not abandon us again. Not after the last time. I promised you. And I've kept that promise. I knew I loved you more and now, well, now I know I was wrong."

She shook her head, but he still did not let her speak. "I have lied for you, stolen for you; I have disrespected my father, given into lust, greed and wrath for you. I nearly murdered Bryson Pierce."

At that, Mandy finally let out a disbelieving snort. She had scoffed at his guilt over Bryson's fall many a time. "Swithin, you won't even step on bugs. You knew the elevator car was there when you *accidentally* bumped into him."

"No. I didn't."

The prospect chilled Mandy.

He went on. "When," he sighed, disgusted at himself, "Missy told me he'd slept with you, I lost it. I know I shouldn't have believed her, but I was so livid, I wanted him dead. Of course, I had no idea he'd already knocked Missy up, and she was just using me to hurt him."

"How did that little wench know you'd actually kill him?"

"Because she knows you bring out the worst in me."

This fact also gouged Mandy's insides.

"I knew he'd be at the next clambake, and so I went, waiting for a prime opportunity. When I saw his little clique standing by the open shaft, no one was the wiser when I tripped and fell into him. Whoever would believe that perfect Swithin Hook would murder anyone? Not even Bryson. He thought it was an accident. Everyone did, and I let them because I had no idea how to deal with murder in my heart. You still weren't really talking to me. I've never even told Father Murphy. Missy's kept her mouth shut surprisingly, but she had her own secrets she didn't want spilled. I've also given her a lot of money."

"Swith..."

"I have put off this idea of immortality," he spoke over her, "because by essentially becoming gods, by acting on the fact that I love you more than Him, it will decimate my faith."

Mandy teared. "This isn't what I wanted."

"Immortality is the only way to save you. Don't think I haven't thought on it in any case. But now, faced with losing you, I have to justify turning my back on Him again. And I can only pray that this is the path He wants me on."

Mandy went to him, wrapping her arms around his trembling body.

Swithin asked. "Why would He give me a test he knew I would fail?"

Mandy had no polite answer so she refrained from speaking. Their relationship had rollercoastered for far too long, and it was high time that the ride morph into a steadyish track. Still, Mandy had no idea how to respond to his revelation that she made him a worse person. She had no idea how to console him when it came to religion. He spoke up before she could think on it too long.

"But Mandy," Swithin's tone changed; lowered to a severe warning tone. "No one can know about this. You know that. My father killed Henry Canon for it without as much as a thought. If anyone finds out that we--and especially we--are hunting immortality, we will shoot to the top of every hunter's most wanted list."

She sniffled back a snort, ignoring the quandary. "I'm on half of them already anyway," she jested.

He held her a long time, quietly, and breathed, finally feeling not only relieved that the long standing fight was over, but that he actually felt satisfied with the decision. He'd prayed for an end to it, prayed long and hard for an answer, and none had ever come, save for Mandy's insistence that they should pursue everlasting life. And between their gifts, he reasoned, they could do so much good for the world.

The problem regarded the fact that with immortality came power, and power corrupted even the purest of souls. And Mandy's soul was not pure to begin with. "We need to go," Mandy said.

"Right." Swithin turned back to the mirror and the problem at hand. "A few words to turn the girl on and then just tell her where you want to go. Specchio specchio così splendida! Umilmente liberaci da questo posto!"

While the mirror seemingly warmed up with Swithin's verbal Italian switch, he explained the artifact's history to step away from their heavy conversation. "Some say the mirror was made for a pharaoh, though which one is lost to history, even if it's true. There are no markings to indicate where the thing originated. It was given to my family as a gift by a prince of Naples in the early 1700's for some rather tedious supernatural cleanup and get this...Giambattista Basile had been a courtier there 100 years before."

Mandy had to place the name, but it came to her quickly. "The author? Didn't he write down, like, 'Puss in Boots' and 'Cinderella'?"

"Lu cunto de li cunti," Swithin confirmed. "'The Tale of Tales'. A collection of fairy tales. History says he died in 1632. Legend says he disappeared into this mirror."

The mirror took on a golden glow, and Mandy suddenly lit up herself. This was the coolest thing she'd ever seen. She smacked her husband.

"How dare you keep this from me?!"

"Don't start that again."

Swithin plucked a saber from nearby, and Mandy followed suit, taking up a couple of sais. Swithin instructed her to think of Heildonia's lair and grasped her hand tightly. "And don't let go of me, or I'll be lost forever."

Mandy squeezed his hand tighter, took a deep breath and stepped through the mirror, melting into it like soft butter.

Appearing roughly on the other side, they fell to the soggy ground and breathed in the low lying fog. Mandy stood first and helped Swithin up. He quickly felt his head, chest, legs and crotch then sighed, relieved. "I think I'm all here."

Sure enough, Mandy recognized the marsh.

"A witch who lives in a swamp," Swithin observed. "How cliché."

Mandy then noticed that his black eye was healed. "How are your ribs?" she verbally followed up her thought.

Swithin felt them next and wonder crossed his face. "I think they're healed."

"Well, your face is better, too!"

"How is your back?" Swithin hopefully noted of the blister.

His sister, Mary, yelled out in response. "Like someone stabbed it, traitor!"

Swithin and Mandy turned at his sibling's screech.

"Mary!" Swithin exclaimed to his older sister. "Where is everyone else?"

"Inside!" she retorted. "I was told to keep a lookout. Where did you come from?" Mary did not sound happy about being left to guard.

"Da sent for me," Swithin answered plainly.

"That was well over a week ago," Mary complained. "Just like you to disrespect our father!"

"I was on a case," Swithin defended. "I came as soon as I could. Excuse me for not wanting to partake on one of these barmy goose chases."

"Don't you talk about our father like that!" Mary blurted out, wagging her finger at Swithin. "Show some respect!"

"Mary. Have you cut your hair? It's just ace."

Mary squinted disdainfully, and Mandy noticed a piece of paper on Mary's back. She went to take it off when Mary turned on her violently and grabbed her wrist hard. "Don't touch me."

Swithin took the opportunity to grab the sign.

"My aura kills puppies," he read aloud. "The triplets strike again," he noted of his elder brothers.

Mary yanked the sign from his hand and crumpled it.

"Mary," Swithin sighed, "stand aside and let us in. Heildonia's in there."

"Father told me no one goes in and no one goes out."

"You really hate me that much just for being born, that you're going to let your family die?" Swithin posed urgently.

"Da can handle himself," Mary quarreled.

"No!" Mandy bickered back. "He can't!"

"He told me to keep you out, and that is what a good child does. Respect."

"Keep us out, specifically?" Swithin nearly squeaked he was so affronted.

"You're a traitor," Mary went on. "For being with a monster," Mary sneered at Mandy. "He said if you help Mandy, then you'll probably help the witch, too!"

Mandy sputtered at the traitor comment. She knew Patrick had no love for her. But to pit his children against each other? That was a new low for even the old man.

Swithin exploded. "Is your head so far up our father's arse that you can completely ignore the fact that he's about to get slaughtered?" Thomas's words echoed out of Swithin's mouth and took a second to shake it off.

"Oh, enough of this," Mandy threw the first punch, but Mary blocked it and jabbed right back.

Mandy blocked a barrage of punches and dodged a stabbing. She'd already gotten to her own blade, but had no interest in killing

Mary. Too bad Mary didn't feel the same way. Swithin's sister fought to kill and was trained well enough to take on two opponents.

"I've got ten years training on both of you," Mary touted, spinning from Mandy's uppercut and then pouncing over Swithin's leg sweep.

"Did you ever think," Mandy shouted while ducking, "that Patrick left you out here because he was worried something might happen to you?"

Mary hesitated long enough for Swithin to land an elbow to her ribs. She retaliated thusly with a headlock, while Mandy went on.

"You're his baby girl! You worship him! You mean everything to him! Of course he left you out here!"

Swithin bent over and flipped Mary onto her back hard. By the time she'd caught her breath, Swithin slid into the wavering bit of air which led to Heildonia's lair, and Mandy followed. Mary managed to get up in time to cut Mandy's calf, but Mandy rolled back into Heildonia's lair once again. Swithin was standing at the ready, eyes closed, concentrating, and when Mary made an appearance, he merely unfurled his palm toward her chest and forced her back out with his chi.

"Luckily, I'm not strong enough to kill anyone with that move yet," he smiled.

Mandy stood, limping from the bleeding gash on her leg and took her husband's hand.

"Mandy, the blister," he reminded her hopefully. She could still feel it oozing and shook her head. Swithin grumbled about the worthless mirror.

Chapter 21
"Rhiannon" by Fleetwood Mac

They waded through the thick fog and all of the traps which had been released. Poison arrows had been unleashed, a pit had been uncovered and a troupe of Helacious frogs had been slaughtered. Their singing was used as a defense, but had the effect of making one suicidal. "Seriously, da?" Swithin lamented. "These are an endangered species."

They walked on, careful to stay on the path. It wasn't easy, as Heildonia had enchanted it to veer into various poisonous and man eating obstacles.

The pained moaning was the first clue they were near, and sure enough, Heildonia's little clearing appeared and she stood gloating over Swithin's family who were being squeezed by an oversized thorny vine.

"Ah, Patrick," Heildonia applauded gleefully, her wild red curls highlighted with gold strands today, and she wore a gray knitted poncho over jeans and red peasant top, "I should have let you find me years ago. This is fun! I may even go through the trouble of bringing your sweet Tinkerbell back to life just so I can kill her!"

Heildonia cackled as the vine tightened. The small thorns cut slowly into the gasping victims, but the witch was not enthralled enough not to notice her new visitors.

"Well, well, well," she greeted. "Welcome back, Amanda. I thought we had an agreement." Mandy choked back her offense, and Heildonia raised a brow. "Well, if you didn't tell him where I was, how did you find me?" she addressed Patrick, who could not answer due to the sharp vines in his neck.

"He's not completely inept, witch!" Swithin defended automatically, momentarily forgetting the rift between him and his father.

"Swithin, stop," Mandy chastised. "Heildonia, please let them go," Mandy pleaded.

The witch snorted. "Never. Unless you have something to offer."

"I already took you to the abyss. What else could you want?"

"Take my soul," Swithin offered immediately as if he'd seen it coming. His parents tried screaming out, but the vine tightened, and they squealed instead.

Heildonia's other eyebrow went up and betrayed her false disinterest. "Oh, pish posh, darlie. One soul for your entire family? Hardly seems a bargain, does it?"

Swithin knew he had her on a hook, so to speak. "Even if that one soul is Patrick Hook's legacy child?"

His brothers would have normally scoffed at that notion, even in jest, but none of them could breathe and were stuck full of thorns at the moment. Heildonia pursed her lips. The idea was delicious. With his soul in her possession, none of the Hooks would dare bother her...among other things.

"You sign it away first, darlie, then I'll release your family," she agreed.

"Swithin..." Mandy warned.

"We haven't got a choice," he repined. "She won't accept anything less."

"Take mine!" Patrick wheezed.

"And what good are you, you old fogey?" Heildonia prattled. "Besides, this will torture you more, and I do relish that idea above all else."

"Where do I sign?" Swithin asked, quickly noticing that two of his brothers had already passed out from either pain or asphyxiation.

"I'll need your blood," she told Swithin. "Just a drop will do."

She pulled a peacock quill from somewhere in her poncho, and he bravely held his hand out. Heildonia pricked it with the tip of the quill and then squeezed it into a small vial, which she also seemed to pull out of nowhere.

"I thought you said drop," Mandy complained.

"A drop, an ounce. Don't quibble," she sassed. "Wait here while I prepare this." While she disappeared into her shambling cottage,

Swithin worried for his family who were struggling to get free against the tight vines. Mandy took his hand and squeezed it nervously.

Heildonia returned quickly with a parchment full of words smaller than an ant's toe. "Swithin," she began, "I must stress the fact of the matter that you've offered yourself of your own free will, and I, in no way, lured you here or forced your hand in this decision."

"Well, that's not entirely..."

"Good! Sign here and here," she held the quill out, and it dripped with red ink.

"Well, though," Swithin did not take the pen, "you didn't give me much of choice, did you?"

Heildonia straightened and cleared her throat. "Did you or did you not offer your soul to me, unprovoked? Did I ask for it? Did I lure you here? Or did you follow your idjit father?"

"I told you it was a bad idea," Mandy muttered.

"Bad idea or not," Heildonia retorted, "it was his idea. If it wasn't, the contract won't work."

Swithin could not argue that fact...he didn't think...and took the quill and parchment. "But I do have a sub clause," he added.

"What?" the witch asked flatly.

"An end. This is a family feud, fanned by my father. Once Patrick Hook is dead, this war ends, and my soul will be mine again."

Perturbed, but not beaten, Heildonia drummed her fingers together. "That will require more paperwork, but if they agree, I see no reason why that can't be arranged. And seeing as your final family member has joined us, we can have her sign as well."

Swithin and Mandy glanced back to see Mary chopping at the vine, which only seemed to make it angry. Heildonia grabbed the parchment back from Swithin and marched toward the hostage Hook clan.

Mary took up stance toward the witch, who merely waved her hand, and Mary's dagger flew from her grasp. "Really?" Heildonia asked, bored.

Heildonia waved her hand again and the vine unwound, allowing Patrick and the triplets to fall to the ground, bloody and gasping for breath. Wendy crawled to them, checking vitals and Peter, his eldest brother, got to his feet.

"You all right, S-man?" Peter asked.

Swithin sighed. "Meh."

"Your dear Swithin and I have come to an agreement, Monster Hunters," Heildonia announced to the Hooks.

Patrick stood, pained and weak, but stood all the same. Even at 70, Patrick Hook remained a bulky man. Rarely did a hunter make it to 50, let alone seventy, and he and Helen were well respected for their strength and skill. Not only were they both still alive, but eight of their nine children had made it well into adulthood.

Heildonia crowed on. "His soul for your lives. Seems a waste if you ask me, but it was his idea, not mine," she grinned too triumphantly to make anyone think she hadn't seen this coming somehow.

"I'd rather die," Patrick wheezed.

"Well, I wouldn't!" Mary chimed in.

"And I don't blame, you, sweet sister." Swithin kept up his act of kindness, and Mary stuck her tongue out at him.

"Oh, Swithin," Wendy frowned.

Heildonia continued loudly, "I will need all of your signatures."

"I'm not signing anything," Mary defiantly stood forward.

"I need you all to sign it," Swithin answered. "The contract is binding only so long as father lives. And upon his death, this feud is over. My soul is a small price to pay for the family's sanity."

Helen looked to Heildonia. "Please, is there anything else?"

"This was all your son's idea. And I'm only happy to oblige, of course. This fight has gone on long enough, and let's face it, it's not really a fight. The only reason you're all not dead already is because I knew you'd come in handy. And I do love being right."

"This feud is over," Swithin reiterated. "Do you all understand?"

They all looked to one another--all but Mary--and hung their heads, nodding and defeated.

"You're all cowards!" Mary proclaimed. "Why don't you just die for da, Swithin! Blood for blood and all that!"

"My, my," Heildonia crossed her arms thoughtfully. "Your little heart is blackened. Do you want an apprenticeship?"

The insinuation from the witch to Mary--that Mary was like her--was enough to bring Mary to her senses, even if only momentarily, and she stepped forward to snatch the pen and the parchment.

"So, we are all agreed," Heildonia finalized. "This feud ends now. Any attempt to break this contract will result in your dear little Swithin's murdered soul. Are we clear?"

"I'm not signing it without reading it first," Peter told her. He was Swithin's eldest brother and a lawyer.

"Oh," Heildonia whined, "that'll take weeks."

Swithin set a reassuring hand on his brother's shoulder. "It's okay, Pete. Just sign it. Everything's going to be okay."

Peter cast a nasty glance at Heildonia and signed the scroll.

The rest of them signed in turn. Helen cried, and Patrick was the last to give it up. "If you hurt him," Patrick started, but Heildonia shook a finger at him.

"No, no, no! Threats are considered breach of contract in paragraph H, section 62. We wouldn't want you to smash his little soul so soon, would we, big guy?"

Patrick harrumphed and turned away to go sulk near her vegetable garden.

"Is that everyone?" She looked over the parchment. "Excellent. Swithin, darlie, there is one more thing. I do need a bit of your soul, just to seal this together. Not all of it, of course, but a dollop. You won't miss it."

He stepped up to her, and she never actually touched him, but swirled her finger an inch from his chest,, and he gasped sharply as she brought away a puff of sparkling energy, which she then pushed into the parchment. It crackled and smelled like clean cotton before quieting.

"What about Mandy?" Mary asked. "She didn't sign it."

Heildonia chuckled. "Oh, little me," she addressed Mary, much to Mary's distaste, "I now control Swithin Hook's soul. What more do I need to control Mandy Heart?"

No one liked that.

"I've already taken you to the edge of the Universe! What more could you want from me?" Mandy asked.

"You took her where?!" Patrick boomed.

"Mind your business," Heildonia hissed.

The others were content observing for the moment, trying to take everything in, but Patrick wasn't one to stand by silently. "I certainly will..."

Patrick's voice was cut off by a mere wave of Heildonia's hand as she tittered. "Oh, dearlie," she returned to Mandy, "that was hardly the edge. An edge, perhaps. But the tip of the iceberg, I think the saying goes. And I have no desire to go back!" She shivered thinking on the monsters there. "What I want," she growled, "is Gwenighinifal's head."

After a brief round of silence, Mandy laughed. "Headmistress Gwen? You think I wouldn't have killed her already? You wanted Swithin's soul to *make* me do that?"

"Gracious, Amanda," Heildonia straightened herself. "Of course that isn't why I wanted his soul. But first matters first."

"What changed your mind? I thought you said she could not be stopped."

"That was before you had an army behind you with something to lose."

"And do you know where Gwen is?" Swithin asked.

"No," came the reply. "But your wife can find her easily enough. Oops."

"Your what?!" Now Helen was up in arms.

"You're officially a bitch," Mandy spat at the magic-maker for spoiling the news.

Heildonia just smirked. "I just thrive on chaos. Keeps me healthy."

Helen blared on, while her husband still had no voice. "When did this happen? Where are your rings? Was it in a church? How could you keep this from your mum?" Helen was obviously heartbroken that she hadn't been informed.

"Mum..." Swithin began.

But Mandy redirected the conversation back to its root. "Why do you really want his soul?"

Heildonia only grinned, and the next thing anyone knew, thick, flashing smoke filled the air, and they all awoke back inside the Hook Estate. Slowly but surely, everyone got to their feet.

"Bastard witch!" James Matthew complained, picking a thorn out of his rear end. Florence was there already and started fussing over wounds inflicted by the thorny vines, but Patrick brushed her aside and reiterated, hoarsely.

"Why did you take her to the abyss? How is it that you've met with the witch before, girl?"

"She's a traitor!" Mary piped up.

The question quieted everyone's groans, and they listened intently as Mandy explained.

There were many questions afterwards, and she half expected Patrick to berate her for not divulging the secret of Heildonia's whereabouts sooner, but he held his tongue through the whole thing. When she was finished at last, she pulled her sweater back down over the blister, and Wendy stepped forward, grasping her hand gently.

"So, how long do you have?"

"I don't know," Mandy admitted. "Maybe another year. Heildonia said there're too many unknowns about my makeshift genetics to be sure."

"So, you could heal completely?" Peter asked optimistically.

Mandy shrugged. "Swithin's safe. That's all that matters to me."

Swithin grunted, but held his thought in on the matter.

Everyone stood around, nursing the much needed pints which Michael had dispersed mid story. Finally, Swithin did speak up. "I do actually have something for you," he said. "I'll be right back."

He took his leave, and Patrick slammed his mug on the table. Everyone looked to him, as he hadn't said a word.

"I owe you an apology, Amanda."

No one had expected that. Especially Mandy.

He forged on. "From the minute I saw you, I assumed you would damn my son's soul. And now I've caused it all the same."

Mandy shook her head. "That was his choice."

Patrick pursed his lips and his face trembled ever so slightly to hold back the tears. "Can you forgive me, girl?"

Everyone looked from their patriarch to Mandy. "There's nothing to forgive, Patrick. We both want what's best for him."

Patrick nodded. "Do you have a way to take down Gwen, then?"

Mandy thought a second. "I may. But I'm going to need all of you." She looked around at the compliant faces, save for Mary. "Mary?"

Mary didn't answer straightaway, until George nudged her harder than he had to and she nearly fell over. But she nodded.

Swithin returned just then and felt the confidence within the group. It gave him the courage to slip a white ring on Mandy's finger. Mandy smiled. "When did you have time to get this?"

"I carved it out of dragon bone that Lama Dorje gifted me. I did propose once before, if you'll recall, though it wasn't the best day of my life. But it's still your ring if you'll have it."

Mandy smiled and deflated. "Of course I'll wear it." Giving into this romantic couples thing was getting easier and easier by the second, once she'd let her guard down.

Helen squealed. "Oh!" The woman was grinning so hard, Mandy thought her face may split in two.

"She married me three days ago," Swithin explained. "It was under duress, but she hasn't filed for divorce yet, so I consider that a win."

"I haven't had time," Mandy defended weakly.

Helen screamed and wrapped Mandy in a bear hug. The rest of her new siblings followed suit, and more libations were passed around.

Patrick even hugged Mandy so hard Mandy had to cough a rib back into place.

Swithin hadn't been present for his father's humble apology, and confusion seemed to have melted his face. "I was gone for two minutes. Did a hell freeze over?"

"So, what's this plan of yours?" Mary asked when the celebrating died down.

"We're going back to Heildonia's, but we're not going alone. Everyone get some rest and we'll head back when you're healed. Swith?"

"Yes, love?"

"I need to go somewhere quiet."

While everyone tended to their wounds and theorized about Mandy's possible plan, Mandy and Swithin found solitude in his bedroom. Mandy had to bat his advances away a few times while she tried concentrating on the task at hand.

"What is with you?" she asked of the foreplay.

"Sorry, love. I, uh, think I know why Heildonia wanted my soul."

"And that warrants having sex during a crisis?"

He pulled her close and leaned in for a kiss. "She wants our baby."

Mandy pushed him away violently. "What?!"

Disgruntled to say the least, he turned from her. "Sorry! Auck! It's in the contract. It must be."

"What the hell...why...what?"

Swithin shrugged. "Witches like babies. Well, they like to bathe in their blood and suck out their essence for some of the darker spells."

"Okay. Sorry I asked."

"But *our* baby in particular might be rather sought after for whatever unique qualities it might possess."

Mandy's hand instinctually went to her lower abdomen. "Good to know. But, we'll deal with that later. Control yourself."

He huffed, aggravated by Heildonia's hold on him. "What is this plan of yours?"

She explained how Heildonia used to be in Gwen's coven. "Heildonia can't kill Gwen by herself, and now that she's got us under her thumb thanks to your..." Mandy didn't feel right insulting Swithin's father anymore. "Thanks to Patrick, she can make us do anything."

"Let's have a baby," he sounded almost drunk.

"Knock it off."

Swithin squelched. "I can't! I'm sorry!"

"Heildonia asked for Gwen's head. She didn't say it couldn't still be attached."

Swithin slowly put Mandy's plan together. "If they're enemies..."

"We pit them against each other. If we can lure Gwen to Heildonia, Heildonia will have no choice but to help us fight. Gwen has no idea that I know Heildonia, and that she's the one who helped me cure you. We'll have each other and your family to fight. We can call in other hunters."

"Nope. That's in the contract. We can't tell any other hunters where she is."

"Does Headmistress Gwen count as a hunter?"

"I guess we'll find out if I suddenly keel over."

"That's not funny."

"I'm not laughing."

Mandy sighed. Pitting the witches against each other was the only idea she had. Plus, she was now eager to come up with an offense against the green devil. Mandy didn't like it, but she had to open her mind to Gwen.

"Keep your baby maker to yourself," she warned her husband. After all, her body would be vulnerable.

He scratched his arm as if he were an addict. "Yeah, yeah. Be safe in there." He leaned in to kiss her, which turned deep and passionate within two seconds. Mandy pushed him away again.

"Swithin!"

"Maybe I'll just wait outside. Or, maybe I'll just send mum or Wendy in. And go take a cold shower."

"Just get out!"

Mandy closed her eyes and found herself once again amidst the doorways to her psyche. She took in a breath and readied to face her most formidable adversary.

Headmistress Gwen appeared with a mist around her feet; presumably some sort of protection spell.

"Well, well, this is a surprise," Gwen greeted.

The last time Mandy had seen her, she was drawing a blade across Thomas's neck.

"I'm calling in a favor."

Gwen laughed. "Do ask. This must be a doozy."

"After everything you've done to me, you owe me big."

"I said ask, sweet one."

"Swithin kind of contracted his soul to another witch, and we need it back."

Gwen primly straightened her green hat and took a long, slow breath in. "Heildonia."

"Why am I not surprised that you know that?"

"Call me what you will, but don't treat me like an imbecile. You want me to destroy her. Is that it?"

"Can you?"

Gwen gave off her Hollywood smile. "I would have taken her out of the picture a long time ago if I'd known where she was. And I suppose if I want that tidbit, it requires following you into whatever trap you've set. You do drive a hard bargain, Mandy Heart. I have wanted this chance for a very long time."

"I don't really give a shit about your fucking history. Will you come or not? And don't you dare ask me for anything after you took Thomas."

"My dear, sweet prize, your...partner...ran in guns blazing one too many times. I digress, however. I will help you, if only to try and mend our bond."

Mandy snorted. "Is that what we have?"

"I gave you everything. In time, you'll come to see."

"You made me a monster."

"I made you a god. That...boy...you've chosen to fall in love with is holding you back. For instance, you have at your disposal the abilities to do anything anyone could ever want. You could blink me from existence if you desired it so."

"I will not tap into the cosmos no matter how much you'd like to see your little experiment flourish."

Gwen sighed again. "You know, I was a bit disheartened that you didn't come to me for help when Swithin was dying."

"Are you trying to tell me there's a cure for manticore poison?"

"Of course there is. For you. You can have anything you..."

"Yeah, yeah, yeah. I just have to dip into creation itself. It's not going to happen, lady!"

"Well, I suppose I only have myself to blame for your obstinacy. After all, I handpicked your parents."

The statement punched her, but as tempted as Mandy was to bite at the subject, she refused. "If you're not going to help, we're done here."

"All right, all right. I do owe the little flower a good lashing. Heildonia's been hiding from us for far too long. I can get around her contract stipulations in regards to you telling me her whereabouts, but it will harm your more angelic half."

"Fine." Mandy let the information flow. "Just don't kill him. Or I will reach into the cosmos and pull out whatever I need to in order to see you ripped to shreds."

"There's my little monster."

Mandy suddenly regretted her last statement, but Gwen was gone, and Mandy cursed.

She reappeared in Swithin's room, but he was nowhere to be seen. Wendy, however, was sleeping on a sofa beneath the large stain glass window.

"How long was I out?" Mandy rasped sleepily.

Wendy's eyes shot open and she looked at her watch. "Almost a day. Swithy said you were going to contact The Agency. Did it work?"

"We will be less at least one evil witch by the end of this, and that can only benefit everyone."

Everyone took a week to heal. The thorn gouges were deep, and Helen had to pull out some powerful healing herbs to hasten the curing.

Everyone was overly sick of Swithin's involuntary, lusty advances toward Mandy to which he replied, "As long as she holds my soul, I'm kind of obligated to be her bitch. I'm not real happy about it!"

They slept in separate rooms, and Mandy avoided him at all costs. She wasn't sure who she wanted to die more, Heildonia or Gwen.

The contract pulled at Swithin hard, and as if baby making on the brain wasn't a big enough problem, he had slept through mass on Sunday. When his father approached him about it, he yawned, seeming completely confused.

"Why would I go worship some unseen deity who obviously doesn't give a bollock about me?"

Patrick nearly choked on his own ire, while Wendy simply pointed out, "Well, I guess we know which bit of his soul is wrapped in that contract."

After a week, Mandy pushed to head back to Heildonia's. She contacted Gwen and had The Agency meet them at an inn near the marsh.

Heildonia was visibly shaken by the appearance of Gwen and her crones in her yard, but snorted it off. "Oh, I suppose it was inevitable that I face you again, lover. Might as well be when I have a gaggle of hunters on my side." She looked over to Mandy. And tsked. "Semantics. I didn't specify that I wanted her head detached. Well played, dearlie. Ooh, the mistakes we make in haste!"

Gwen stood tall and regal in green and spoke to Heildonia of Mandy. "Don't feel too off, sister, dear. Our little Amanda here didn't tell me she was in cahoots with you, either."

"You both suck," Mandy retorted. "I suppose asking that you take each other out is too much, so I'll have to be happy with one for now."

Gwen redirected toward Heildonia. "I'm quite impressed that you've managed to amass no less than the entire Hook clan as an army."

"You always did underestimate me, lover," Heildonia purred.

Gwen's eight witches faced down the Hook children, but no one started the battle.

Heildonia produced the contract, and the nose on Headmistress Gwen's ever pleasant face flared; the only indication she was rattled.

"I have his soul," Heildonia bragged. "Which means I have her," she placed her hand atop Mandy's head, which Mandy shook off immediately, "and I've seen it, and it is glorious. I'm not too small a woman to admit when I'm wrong. You did it, sister," she referred to opening the God Particle to the Edge of the Universe.

The other witches growled much like cats, but Headmistress Gwen held them back with an arm out. Gwen smiled and opened her mouth to speak, but Heildonia cut her off. "Not a chance, you cunneybush. You will never see that place! Our wars end today."

Swithin found Mandy's hand and squeezed it. The tension had mounted to palpability as the fog had thickened around the edges of the clearing.

Gwen hissed, losing her cool. "You are a fool."

"Mandy," Heildonia cooed, "I was almost beginning to like you. And in fact, I arranged a bit of a gift for when you delivered Gwen's head, but now I think it may be more useful during this impending battle."

She snapped her fingers and everyone's eyes were drawn to her cottage where a familiar figure strode out.

"Hey, Pat," Thomas greeted Swithin's father. "Close your mouth, old man. Did you really think death was going to keep me down? Hey, Helen. Little Brit."

While everyone, including Gwen, managed their surprised faces, Thomas got in Gwen's face. "I'm not sure whether to kill you, or to thank you."

Mandy was the only one who personified furious instead of shock. "Asshole!"

"Hey, sweets," he grinned and looked to the Agency, grinning. "Bitches. Is that everyone?" He looked around.

"Impossible!" Gwen yelled. "That blade I slit your throat with should have sent you straight to hell! Forever!"

"And it was a lovely visit, but I decided not to live there." His smarmy attitude hadn't changed, and he looked more alive than ever.

"How!" Gwen demanded.

"Turns out I have friends on the other side. Who would have known? Plus the fact that I'm sort of bound to a promise I made." He winked at Mandy.

"Asshole!" she repeated. "Where the fuck have you been?"

"Hey! I also have lots of enemies on the other side. It took a while to crawl out, even with help. Donia here, of all people, expedited it."

"Waitaminute," Swithin finally interjected. "You are dead. And you're bound to a promise which is kind of like an idea, which means you're a..."

"Class Zero, kids. In other words, Thomas times awesome to the infinity power." He floated a foot off the ground for effect.

"Asshole," was all Mandy could manage to think toward him for making her go through emotional hell.

"Enough!" Headmistress Gwen commanded, her pillbox cap coming loose in her angst. She cleared her throat and regained composure. "Care to make a wager, sister dear?"

The air sparked with electricity, raising the hairs on everyone's necks.

Heildonia laughed. "If I win, you die. What more could I want, dearlie?"

Gwen gestured to her eight pretty crones. "Our daughters."

The eight witchy minions exchanged keen glances. Over time, they had realized that Heildonia had been right in leaving Gwen. Gwen's quest for power was too considerable, but they were too weak in mind to leave their mother sorceress. And even now, they would fight for her because she had a hold on them, and they resented Heildonia's abandonment.

Heildonia sucked in a deep thoughtful breath. "And I suppose you'll be wanting young Hook's soul for your victory, then?"

"Let's not be hasty," Swithin blurted.

"Speaking of wagers, Pat," Thomas interjected, "Mandy's still alive. You owe me, what? About 10,000 quid?"

Patrick scowled, and the rest of the Hooks all rolled their eyes at the fact that Patrick had bet on Mandy's life at all.

"Deal." Gwen finalized, ignoring Thomas.

"Are you insane?" Swithin pressed Heildonia about wagering his soul.

"It will make your family fight all the harder for me, won't it?" the witch grinned.

Swithin's family, who'd been quiet up until this point, charged the witches.

Thomas immediately possessed one of them and fooled another long enough to pull her heart out.

He tossed it to Wendy. "Burn this, will you?"

Wendy nodded and took out a lighter.

"Don't kill them!" Heildonia barked as she readied for Gwen's attack.

Wendy hesitated about burning the heart, and Thomas grunted from his host body. "Seriously?"

Thomas was then quickly exorcised from his host body by another witch and then had to contend with two, but it suited him just fine, especially since he had countless new attributes as a Class Zero.

Wendy knew that the heart she held could be used to bring back the crumpled woman at her feet. Heildonia would have to use dark magic to do it, but she did still hold Swithin's soul and Wendy didn't want to give her any excuse to spoil it. She quickly buried the heart in a nearby flowerpot and got back to the fight.

The Hooks were all armed for killing witches and were holding their own. Gwen made a line for Heildonia, and Heildonia whispered to Swithin and Mandy, "This is the part where you wish me luck."

Swithin nor Mandy responded, unsure of their feeling on the matter. Fury enveloped Gwen as she flew toward the trio. Swithin stood tall, but she bowled him over, and Mandy jumped out of the way. Gwen and Heildonia began an arduous battle of energy. Sparks flew between them as they tried to fend each other off and kill each other at the same time.

Mandy stood in time to knock a tooth from one of Gwen's companions, and Gwen spun out of the path of Heildonia's spitfire long enough to order her minions that Swithin and Mandy were not to be harmed. Hisses answered, and the battle between the Hooks and the Agency raged on. If the Hooks were holding back in order to keep from killing the biddies, it showed. They were getting their arses handed to them.

Patrick nearly beheaded one of the hags, but her sister knocked him from his feet, and he went down with a thud. Helen threw a pouch of wormwood at the two haglets to deter them long enough so her husband could get back to his feet, but Helen and Patrick, though skilled, were not as quick as they used to be, and did not evade sharp lashings from the sorceresses.

No one's deep wounds had completely healed from the thorns, and they were all covered in blood already.

The triplets had formed a triangle and fought on all sides, working together like a machine, while Peter was busy enchanting more ingredients. Mary defended him ruthlessly, but one of Gwen's covenettes slithered by Mary, knocked Peter from his task and scattered the few protection pouches the Hooks had left. Desperate for any foot up, Mary ran for Heildonia's house.

"This is not good, love," Swithin noted to Mandy, helplessly watching the fight. "We need to do something!"

Mandy also watched, not sure where they could jump in, but she used her bow to shoot a poisoned arrow into Gwen's back. Gwen screamed and reached back to pull the arrow out, but she was unmarred by it. It did give Heildonia an opening to char her adversary, but she was visibly weakened and took the short break to catch her breath. "We must be two of the most powerful hunters on the planet. These bitches should be child's play!"

"Seeing as one of them is holding my soul, witches aren't really my forté." Swithin muttered.

Just then, Heildonia broke loose from her battle with Gwen and was able to shout out a spell, bringing all witches great discomfort; even herself. As she said it, the magicians cowered and bled from their noses, and the Hooks and Thomas were able to dismember two more of them, but Gwen wouldn't lose so easily.

"Egredietur dominus meus, exaudi orationem meam, ad infernum, et mundo corde nefariis sororum! Me Magister quaerere scientia ita quantum desiderium!" Gwen was on the ground by the time she'd finished it, but she finished it, and her brethren regained their strength. Heildonia, however, anguished, and Swithin noticed, not too late, the ground beneath her begin to bubble and crack.

His soul at stake, Swithin pulled Heildonia from the deadly spell, and everyone ducked as a flurry of winged pony sized devils came up from the crevasse to play.

Dirty and bleeding, Gwen grinned at her flying saviors.

Mandy took out a couple of wings with rocks and arrows which grounded them, but they were fierce and wild with sharp hooves and gnashing teeth.

Heildonia was not out of the woods yet, either, as a larger demon arose from the ground from which she had just been saved. Swithin obediently took stance against it, and his sister Mary called out to him from Heildonia's doorstep. She'd rummaged through the house to find any sort of useful implement. "Catch!"

He put his arm out and caught a saber, lightweight and sharp.

Mary called out to the demon. "If anyone's going to kill him, it's going to me! Bugger off!"

Gwen and Heildonia were now weighted by Heildonia's spell, and with the winged demons, Gwen had gained the upper hand. Heildonia called out to the remaining witches and pleaded.

"Daughters! Hear me! I wronged you by leaving, but what choice did I have? You see her power! You know what she is capable of! Help me, daughters! Defeat her and we can go back to how things used to be! Do not let her win! Our world is at stake!"

Gwen gritted her teeth as she slithered toward Heildonia, but the younger witches did give pause. The Hooks let up as well, seeing that their adversaries were thinking of switching sides. With the flying monsters gnashing about and a ginormous demon charging, the Hook clan needed all the help they could get!

Jalajae, the bedraggled eldest of the haglets who had been facing down Peter decided for the rest of them. She turned and flung a spell at a large winged creature, and Peter joined her in the battle.

Heildonia laughed at her triumph. "I win either way, sister! They are mine again!"

"When I win this, you are all dead to me!" Gwen finally lost her ever-present cool at the loss of her daughters. Gwen and Heildonia continued crawling toward one another, chanting opposing curses.

Peter and Wendy had found Heildonia's garden and started plucking and sniffing and combining, while Mary and one of the witches continued the fight to guard them, now with an enchanted dagger and some useful vials of liquid deterrent. She tossed one at a flyer and it splattered over the thing's legs, causing them to lock up. It could still put up a fight, but was now stuck to its spot.

Mandy found herself out of sharp things to shoot and eyed Swithin's battle. He would be able to fend the bulbous devil off for a while, but things were dire even with the remaining witches on their side.

"Hey, sweets," Thomas floated over. "This is so cool," he smiled in reference to the floating.

"Don't be an ass," she continued her charade of anger. "I'm going to be mad at you for a long time."

"Yeah, yeah. I know that look. What are you thinking?"

"I'm going to give our old pal Headmistress exactly what she wants. Watch my body, will you?"

"Mandy! Don't!" Thomas warned, but it was too late. She had disappeared inside her head.

Swithin parried and dodged and found the sword to be most helpful, as it was enchanted with a cold spell. He jabbed and sliced, and everywhere he did, the demon's skin turned white and icy. He noticed that Mandy was standing blank eyed near Thomas and let his guard down long enough to cuss and get walloped by the demon.

While everyone fought for their lives, and some enjoyed it, Mandy wasted no time entering the black abyss of her mind once again. She'd never done so with such haste, as she knew time flew differently here, and for all she knew, the fight was already over weeks ago. She concentrated very hard on the current time and kept the seconds with her, demanding to the universe that she be sent back promptly.

The first time she'd come here alone, Swithin hadn't been far behind, and he kept her from falling into the clear. The second time Heildonia had been with her, and Mandy knew not to travel so close to the edge. But she needed the edge and needed it quickly. She felt the thick webbing beneath her feet wave as the countless weavers wove endlessly.

Try as she might, she could not ignore the clear beyond, and it whispered to her deepest parts. It would be so easy to give in and use it to wipe Gwen out of existence. Unimaginable power called to her from the clear beyond and nearly begged her to fall into it. She reasoned with herself that just using it once wouldn't hurt anything. In fact, by taking Gwen out, it would help a lot of people. Then again, that's exactly what Gwen wanted. If Mandy gave in, just once, Gwen would win.

The abyss held all of her desires and dreams, the answers she sought and the vengeance she yearned for.

Vengeance.

The ends, she decided, would not justify the means in this case. She may not have wanted to harness the abyss, but she did need the weavers. Keeping her thoughts on ending The Agency's reign, she bent over and scooped up a bit of edging which instantly drove the miniscule weavers mad.

"Come on guys. I need you."

She opened her eyes to find she'd actually come back before she'd left. The winged demons were just coming down from the sky and Swithin was jumping to save Heildonia from falling into a black abyss of her own. "I'll never understand that place," Mandy muttered of the abyss. "Nor do I want to." Nausea nearly overtook her.

Thomas noticed immediately she didn't look well and had rushed over.

"Hey, sweets?" he asked almost with concern.

But she ignored him and took a stumble toward Gwen, who was still struggling to get to her feet. "Hey, Gwennie! I've got what you want!"

Gwen halted her assault on Heildonia and looked toward Mandy. The three witches left their battles to the relief of the Hooks they were fighting, and even the winged devils halted what they were doing, as if response to Gwen's emotions. The gargantuan demon crawled from the crevasse and looked puzzled as to why he'd been called up.

Mandy trudged toward Gwen, bloated and nearing green in color. In her hand, she held the coveted black fabric of time and space, wavering of its own accord.

"Is that?" Gwen asked, reaching for it.

Mandy handed it over, and everyone gasped. Before Mandy let go, she squeezed it, breaking it into billions of tiny shreds and flicked them all over the Headmistress. Gwen was too mesmerized by the black swatch to notice Mandy fall to her knees.

"Mands!" Swithin rushed to her, warily eyeing the demon as he did so. He shook her, and her eyes opened, but rolled back in her head.

"You're up, honey," she managed before passing out.

"What the bloody hell does that mean? Mands? Mandy!"

Her mouth opened and thousands or millions of the near microscopic weavers poured out. Swithin jumped back and skittered to a safe distance. Gwen wasn't so lucky. Holding the fabric made her the prime target, as the tiny weavers desired their work back. They engulfed her and she screamed. Her three remaining daughters stood in horror, hissing and wailing. The flying devils watched with interest for only a few seconds before flying back to whichever hell they'd come from.

The tiny weavers picked and chewed at Gwen trying to reclaim every infinitesimal faction of their web. She screamed endlessly and swatted at them but could not remove their swarm.

Mandy passed out, but Thomas said she was still alive, and Swithin sighed relief. Still, what had she meant? His gift did land in the realm of calming beasties, but he would have no idea where to start with billions of edge of space and time critters.

Gwen fought hard, spewing spells and somehow managed to get to her feet. Heildonia had fallen, exhausted and spent, but still watched the show with an amused expression. Mandy's eyes fluttered open and witnessed Gwen's comeback. Now glowing red, she had driven nearly all of the weavers from her with a spell, though they still kept in a close circle around her.

"I will not be defeated so easily, Amanda!" Gwen floated off the ground began muttering a final spell. The weavers chittered and kept close, but could not break through her defense.

The Hook family all wailed suddenly and were dropped to their knees due to Gwen's spell. They then fell to the ground, moaning, as if being crushed.

Mandy's body did not respond to her pleas to move. Her insides were torn, her outside was beaten and yet, she had to get up. The weavers were not the only thing that had followed her here.

Thomas charged Gwen, but hit an invisible wall and landed in a pile of weavers, who ignored his presence. He was not what they wanted, and they chittered louder at their intended prey. Gwen eyed Thomas severely. "You have way outlived your usefulness! This time, you will stay in hell!"

She lashed out and a bolt of green electricity sizzled through the ghost Thomas, who screamed and evaporated.

Mandy watched, still weak, but seeing Gwen kill Thomas twice pulled motivation from deep within her.

Gwen laughed triumphantly at Swithin. "Your soul will be mine, young Hook and then Mandy will do my bidding! You are her greatest weakness! No god can save you now!"

Mandy pushed herself to her feet, aching and cracking. Every muscle pulled and every organ squished. "Swithin..." she rasped.

He turned to her, glad to see her up. "What can I do?"

Gwen shot a bolt of energy at Mandy, and Mandy flew back again, landing hard on her back. The rest of the Hooks squealed in agony as they were pressed against the ground, helpless to move. Heildonia had not a lick of power left, but began to crawl back to her cottage. Gwen was able to stop her as well with a flick of her hand, and Heildonia fell unconscious.

Swithin's thoughts went back to the weavers. Maybe he could control them somehow...he closed his eyes and centered himself, bringing to the forefront his serenity amidst chaos.

With his eyes closed, he was the only one that didn't see the giant claw land in the center of the clearing. He did feel the tremor, however, and worked all that much harder to concentrate, praying he didn't know what it was.

The blue calm filled him and emanated through his skin, letting the glow shine through. Everything seemed to be up to him and the stress of that fact nearly rattled him.

Gwen's cackling halted at another tremor.

The chittering that followed broke even Swithin's concentration, and he opened his eyes to notice the bus-sized claw directly next to him. He could feel the tiny hairs of the claw against him and stepped aside.

"Mandy," he said in a conversational tone, "I'm up for suggestions."

His family and even Gwen winced, while looking up at the creature. Swithin dared to tilt his head to the sky only to be met with a barrel worth's volume of reddish drool. He shook it off and spit it out, but a look of satisfaction came over him as he licked it from his lips. "Tastes like waffles. Of course."

Gwen's mouth had fallen open in awe at the creature. "She's beautiful."

The creature in question quickly became agitated with confusion and ire about being here. Swithin, the haglets, Gwen and even the giant demon ducked for cover as the mammoth arachnid bucked about. Gwen's spell upon the Hooks was released upon her loss of concentration, and they hurried to their feet, scrambling to get somewhere safe. A giant leg swept through Heildonia's house, leveling it. Heildonia's containment spell held, so the big girl could not leave the confines of the swamp, but being trapped in a small space with a rampaging behemoth was no picnic.

Because Gwen had to seek cover, her spell to keep the weavers out lapsed, and they were on her in a moment's time. She shook them off again, but this time, they were more persistent.

Swithin found the gargantuan's leg and pressed his blue glowing hand to it, but it was too big and too foreign for him to effectively calm it.

"Mands!" he called.

Mandy still laid in the spot where Gwen had forced her down again, too pained to move, but Swithin's call gave her strength, and she pushed herself up yet again, crying from pain. Gwen had nearly eradicated all of the weavers from her person again and was building up another wad of energy to use.

"I can't calm her!" Swithin exclaimed.

"If you can't," Mandy told him, "we're in trouble."

Peter screamed from somewhere in the yard, and Helen squealed. The giant legs moving this way and that obscured any visual, but Mandy and Swithin scanned anyway, still unable to tell what had happened. Mandy suddenly realized that Swithin was holding her hand and, as usual, she had no idea when he'd done it. She looked at him, and he was gazing into her, obviously ready to kiss her.

"This is no time for your baby-making antics!" she yelled, fruitlessly trying to pull away.

He pulled her close. "Just trust me."

And he kissed her. It was the excitement of their first kiss meshed with the passion of all the others. Mandy let herself melt amidst the chaos, blocking it all out. Swithin had been right. She did regret all the time she'd wasted apart from him, but he'd finally caved into her harsh demand for immortality and now she had forever to make it up. The idea filled her with so much hope and happiness that she even let her thoughts drift to the possibility of maybe having a baby. Someday.

As if Swithin had felt her thoughts, his hand slid down her back and cupped her bottom tight with intent. Mandy's eyes shot open. "I told you no babies!"

"I am really sick of apologizing for being under a spell."

But Mandy hadn't paid attention to his retort. She felt wonderful and realized that she was glowing a faint blue.

"Holy shit," she smiled. "This is better than Thomas's Tonga stash."

"And it's the only thing keeping me from assaulting you right now."

Mandy rolled her eyes, but knew he was serious. They had to get Heildonia to lift that particular baby-making caveat out of the contract, but first things first. Still holding Swithin's hand, Mandy calmly waited for one of the giant legs to come near and then gently reached out and touched it.

"I need you girl," Mandy told the behemoth. "I'm sorry I brought you here, but I need you."

The thrashing stopped and the monster stood still at last. Gwen, who had shaken the small mites from her, gave out a gasp in alarm.

"The only weakness Swithin and I have is when we're apart," Mandy admitted to Gwen and the onlookers. "And you are never going to break us again."

The mother weaver simply tapped the ground, sending everyone to their feet, save for Swithin and Mandy. Gwen's self-containing spell broke, and she fell from her foot off the ground where she'd been safe from the weavers. And she laughed.

"I win, Amanda. You pulled that monster from the abyss, and it's only the first step. You will crave the power. You will need it one day, and it will be waiting." The weavers were upon her now, filling her skin and her clothes. "I made you, Amanda! You will always be mine, and I will live forever in your legacy!"

"Are you sure I can't go into the abyss and just erase her from history?" Mandy asked Swithin.

"Yes."

Gwen laughed and then gurgled as the tiny gods filled her mouth and lungs.

Helen could now be heard crying out for help, and Swithin and Mandy rushed to her side. Peter was out, lying in his mother's arms, bleeding from several places. No one knew what to do as his breaths became shallower.

Mandy was tempted again to reach to the abyss for help, but Swithin squeezed her hand as if he knew what she was thinking. Wendy pressed herbs and whispered spells over her brother's limp body, but he did not stir.

A hand came from seemingly nowhere and brushed over the eldest Hook child's head. They all looked to see a bruised and battered Heildonia before hearing Peter gasp to life.

"He'll still need mending, but he'll live," Heildonia assured.

Gwen had stopped moving at this point; still alive, but barely, as the weavers picked her apart to dig out the tiny bits of web that had embedded in her skin and the pieces that she had inhaled and swallowed in her greed.

Swithin and Mandy's glow had died, but Mandy looked up at the gigantress. "We need to get her back."

"How?" Swithin asked. "I'm good, we all know it. But I'm not sensing unadulterated joy, and this monster's proven a bit out of my league."

"No, she's not. She's a..." Mandy was cut off by the breeze and motion of a gigantic purple tongue lashing up the remains of Gwen and the tiny weavers which were attached to her.

Swithin took in a sharp breath and grabbed Mandy's hand. "Everyone, I'm going to need your support on this." His family all gathered round as the gargantuan became restless. His family all connected hands.

"Everyone!" Swithin ordered.

Heildonia sidled up next to Patrick, who was the last in the line, and they reluctantly locked palms. Gwen's remaining three witches linked together with Heildonia, glad to be out from under Gwen's rule.

Swithin channeled the energy from those around. His blue glow brightened around him as he reached out and put a hand on the giant claw. Wincing at her throbbing migraine, Mandy nodded and closed her eyes to draw them inward, back to the abyss and back to the edge of the universe.

Once Swithin and Mandy had clearly left the building, so-to-speak, and the behemoth had faded with them in a black twinkling, tensions rose quickly. Heildonia and Patrick yanked their hands from one another, and the Hooks raised weapons against the remaining witches.

Heildonia put a calm hand out, and Gwen's three covenettes took it, kissing it and purring. "This is the thanks I get for saving your brat?" she said of Peter. "Gwen is gone," Heildonia went on, "But the Agency will live on. She was not the only faction. It will not, however, live here. These girls were mine once and under my protection, they will be reformed into nice, normal witches with earthbound evil goals."

"I'm not leaving here without my son's soul," Patrick told her of Swithin.

She took out the parchment and held it high. "We have a deal, then, Patrick Hook? We are done with this feud?"

"Yes," Helen answered immediately for her husband before he had a chance to say anything which could be regarded as stupid.

Meanwhile, Mandy and Swithin had deposited the weavers back where they belonged, and they busied themselves fixing the mess. It could take seconds or eons. Time mattered not here. Eager not to overstay, Swithin pulled Mandy back toward the opening, but she resisted.

"Come on, Mands."

"We could stay," she offered.

"Love, don't start this again. Come on."

"You said you'd chase immortality with me. And here, we can have it. And no one will care."

He gripped her hand tighter. While he held her, the negative effects of the abyss did not affect him. "We will find immortality on Earth. Not wherever the hell this is. And The Clash is about to release a lost song album. Don't make me miss that."

Mandy longingly looked over her shoulder at the clear. "If I could just stay and figure it out," she pondered aloud. "I could go back and make sure I never broke your heart. I could keep you from ever being poisoned. I could..."

"What, Mandy? Keep Gwen from designing you in the first place? And as to the other things, it was our journey. Our choices. We might not make the same mistakes if we had a do over, but I want to move forward with you. Not back."

When she was home, on Earth, messing with the abyss seemed like the worst idea ever, but when she was in it, possibilities were tempting and endless.

Swithin pulled her into him and kissed her hard. "I'm going back," he said, tired of fighting and just plain tired. "Come with me or not, but I'm not staying here where we don't belong."

"Don't we? You and I could create Eden again."

"I don't want to parent the human race and neither do you. Now, come on."

He took a gamble, let go of her hand and exited the strange and quiet place to return to the land of the familiarity.

Swithin popped back into reality a second later and shook off the trip. If he never saw the inside of Mandy's head again, it would be too soon. He looked to Mandy, but she hadn't come back with him. "God Damnit," he cursed.

Patrick bristled. "I am not tired enough to slap you silly, boy!"

"What?" Swithin asked in earnest. "Oh. Right. Sorry."

"Don't apologize to me!" Patrick yelled.

"Oh, right. Um," he looked up to the sky. "Sorry."

Patrick grumbled, while Helen covered her mouth to hide the smile. Not that she thought Swithin's God would not forgive him, but she did like seeing her husband riled.

Swithin then noticed Heildonia holding up the parchment. "What are you going to do with that?" he asked.

"Your father wants it," she answered.

Swithin shook his head. "No. You keep it."

His family balked, but he held up his hand to silence any dispute. "She took my faith, not my honor. I signed a contract, and I will hold up my end of the deal."

"Swith," Mary put her hand on his arm. "If she has that, she can make you do anything she wants."

"I knew that when I signed it," he said. "And nothing has changed. Except the bit about giving you a baby," he emphasized to the witch. "I'm not giving you a baby. Take that out. Now."

Heildonia rolled her eyes and waved her hand over the parchment. "Who wants one anyway? Whiny brats. Fine, I'll hold onto this," Heildonia said of the contract. "I'll have no use for it, unless someone breaches it anyway."

Mandy still hadn't returned several minutes later, and Swithin began to worry. Heildonia and her daughters had mustered up a few spells to put order back into her little bubble, including fixing her house and replenishing her garden. Wendy and Helen tended wounds with some aid from Heildonia's medicine cabinet. Swithin just stared at Mandy's blank face.

"She'll come back," Thomas appeared suddenly next to Swithin who started.

"You're back!"

"I'm bound to her, remember?" he nodded to Mandy. "Besides, Gwennie wasn't concentrating hard enough to send me anywhere I couldn't wriggle out of easily."

"How can you be so sure she'll come back? That place does something to her."

Thomas nudged him. "Because I haven't lost my faith. What little there was to begin with."

Mandy finally gasped to life and Swithin's arms were around her. "Oh, ye of little faith," she jested.

"This whole religious thing is going to get real old, real fast, isn't it?"

Then, she noticed Thomas and broke free of Swithin's embrace to angrily shove her ghostly mentor to the ground in a fit of passionate relief. "Die one more time! I dare you! I'll see you never come back myself, you ass!"

Thomas only laughed.

Before they adjourned, Mandy could not help but remember Gwen's comments about handpicking her parents. Gwen was gone, but three of her sisters remained.

"Your mother is dead," unnaturally thin Agathon answered.

Mandy refrained from punching the creature's face off her head. Swithin was next to her and tried to remain as calm as possible for her sake. "Who was she? Where is her body?"

The sisters nervously looked to one another.

"Tell me!" Mandy insisted.

"Who do you think, dearlie?" Heildonia appeared on scene to keep the tenuous peace. She was holding the heart of her fallen daughter, which Wendy had mercifully buried in the flower pot. "Who has had a vested interest in you since you were born?"

Mandy's mind staggered. "No fucking way."

Heildonia shrugged. "If it helps any, Gwen used to be a Light witch. A long time ago. Perhaps that bit came through in your genetics."

"Your father is still alive," the short witch daughter Nharlthop rejoined, while both Mandy and Swithin were trying to absorb that last bit.

"Kind of," the third, bedraggled sister Jalajae smirked as she looked over Mandy's shoulder toward Thomas. Mandy squeezed Swithin's hand tightly, slowly realizing what the hags were telling her.

"Gwen picked the strongest genes from thousands of worthy candidates. Gods did the rest, I suppose." Agathon said, and then the women melted away into the mist surrounding them.

Mandy and Swithin turned to see Thomas prattling on to Helen about something or another.

"There is so much about you that makes sense now," Swithin offered.

"Not a word to him. I don't want anything to change between us."

Swithin sighed. "God works in mysterious ways."

Mandy let him have his beliefs and began to rally everyone together to go home for a much deserved nap.

CHARACTER INDEX:

Amanda Heart, b 1988
Raised by The Agency, Mandy has studied all subjects and has a pension for golden oldies and archery. Though she excels at fighting evil, her own demons are her truest obstacle.

Patrick Hook, b 1945
Swithin Hook's father, a devout Catholic and eldest active hunter. He is the hunting community's unofficial leader for his experience. He and Thomas have a sordid past.

Helen Hook, b 1945
The Hook clan mother to her eight living children, a pagan, a baker, a cook and adept monsterer herself. She still pays tributes to gods of old, much to her husband's chagrin.

Wendy Hook, b 1961
The eldest Hook child. She gave up a life of hunting to marry an American and work in social services.

Peter Hook, b 1963
The eldest male Hook child. He is a lawyer who specializes in helping out hunters who are in trouble with the law.

John Hook, b 1968
Specializes in protecting rare species including the small herd of unicorns left in the Hook family's care. Lives close to the Hook estate with his wife and three great danes.

Michael and George and James Matthew Hook, b 1966
Exemplary hunters of all beasties, triplets.
James Matthew specializes in ancient deities and monsters. Though he did not choose to be a priest due to his marriage, he accompanies them on many hunts.
Michael specializes in potions and lives with his partner, Jim, also a hunter. They also own a small home near the Hook Estate.

George goes where he is needed and knows something about almost everything. He enjoys reading comics in his spare time and likes to draw.

Tinkerbell 'Bell' Hook, b 1970- d 1980

An aspiring actress, Bell died when she was ten, trying to run away from a life of hunting.

Mary Hook, b 1978

Ten years older than Swithin, Mary resents him for stealing their father's attention. She is a fierce fighter and will attend any hunt.

Swithin Hook, b 1988

A monsterer by trade, Swithin is adept at swordplay and has a natural calming energy, which endears everyone to him. He is the only Hook with blonde hair and his birth is shrouded in controversy.

Florence

The aged cheery Hook head of house who knows everything and keeps the estate in order. No one can even remember how long she's been around.

Condel

The aged protector of the Hook estate. His family has been guarding it for many, many generations and he is often consulted by other hunters in regards to security.

Thomas Regal, b 1963

A successful, egotistical hunter, which most attribute to luck, and Mandy's mentor. He was originally mentored by Patrick Hook, but left his charge for unknown reasons.

Eleanor Fer

A werewolf, and the most powerful psychic living. She has helped with countless cases, but reserves her energy for the most perplexing or troublesome.

Dwayne Fer, b 1981
Eleanor's son. A happy go lucky young man excited for life and everyone and everything in it.

Dodson Fer
Eleanor's husband, also a werewolf, and a hunter. He leads a pack of wolves up in Alaska.

Erickson
The hunting community's go to scholar and researcher; a secretive man.

Marta 'Missy' Breathnach
Swithin Hook's childhood friend and aspiring deitist. An only child, she rebels constantly against her strict parents.

Headmistress Gwen
An elusive sorceress, responsible for Mandy's upbringing.

Heildonia
A powerful, reclusive witch wanted by the Hook family tree for several generations.

Bryson Pierce
An orphan and young, brash hunter with eyes for Mandy.

Henry Canon
Orphaned alongside Bryson, though they are not blood siblings. A book smart boy who becomes an apprentice for Erickson.

Doctor Husna Patil
An ex hunter who chose a medical degree over hunting, but she still makes herself available to hunters and victims of supernatural incidents.

Lama Dorje
A legendary hunter who has come out of retirement to tutor Swithin in a remote Nepali monastery.

Áine- (AW-neh)
Originally worshipped as a Sun Goddess. Like so many goddesses and gods, Aine has assumed many other roles over the years, being seen as a Moon Goddess, a Goddess of Love, a Fertility Goddess, a Healing Goddess, and a Sovereignty Goddess. Aine is also known as a Faery Queen. Her name means "brightness, glow, joy, radiance; splendor glory, fame", and she is associated with the abundance of summer. Taking the form of Lair Derg, a red mare that no one could outrun, she walked among her people, offering aide where needed. As a Moon Goddess and a Fertility Goddess she ruled over and protected both crops and animals. Above all else, Aine was the people's Goddess, who gave much to them and received their love and worship in return.
http://feminismandreligion.com/2013/07/31/aine-summer-goddess-of-love-light-and-fertility-by-judith-shaw/

Glooscap
Glooscap is the benevolent culture hero of the Wabanaki tribes of northeast New England. Glooscap is always portrayed as a virtuous hero and a good caretaker and teacher of the Wabanaki people. Sometimes he plays the role of a transformer, changing monsters into harmless animals and adapting the landscape to be more favorable to the people. Glooscap sometimes also plays the role of a trickster, but only in the mischievous/humorous sense, never the antagonistic/culturally inappropriate sense. Glooscap does not commit crimes or chase women (in fact, he is a confirmed bachelor in **most** legends.) In many traditions, Glooscap leaves the land of the Wabanakis at the end of the mythic age, promising to return one day if they have need of him.
http://www.native-languages.org/glooskap.htm

Catori
A victim of a nasty spirit and Swithin and Mandy's new charge. She is excited to roam the world in search of adventure.

Sister Tammy
A nun of indeterminable age who runs the Brainstead orphanage. Something good hums around the woman.

Cyndi
A Light Witch, and rarity, whose sole purpose is to create positive energies to release into the world. Light Witches are sought after by dark forces so must move a lot and are difficult to locate. Cyndi is an old friend of Thomas.

Thank you for reading! Hope you enjoyed it. Please visit me on facebook at The Goddess Particle to leave a review or please leave a review at your retailer! And check out my good friends for some great music to help support indie artists:

http://vernianprocess.com/
http://victorsierra.bandcamp.com/

Also, please consider donating to your local animal rescuers today! Money, used or new blankets/towels, cleaning supplies, and pet food are all appreciated!

You can see my book trailer for The Goddess Particle and other creative works at Day304.com

www.ingramcontent.com/pod-product-compliance
Lightning Source LLC
Chambersburg PA
CBHW030408180626
46812CB00005B/1978